time
won't
let me

ALSO BY BILL SCHEFT

The Ringer

time
won't
let me

·· **yet another novel by**

BILL SCHEFT

HarperCollins*Publishers*

FIC
Scheft

HarperCollins books may be purchased for educational, business, or sales promotional use. For information, please write: Special Markets Department, HarperCollins Publishers, 10 East 53rd Street, New York, NY 10022.

FIRST EDITION

Designed by Laura Kaeppel

Printed on acid-free paper

Library of Congress Cataloging-in-Publication Data is available upon request.

ISBN-10: 0-06-079708-8
ISBN-13: 978-0-06-079708-9

05 06 07 08 09 ❖/RRD   10 9 8 7 6 5 4 3 2 1

To Adrianne, always and all ways.

From now on in, I rag nobody.

—HENRY WIGGEN

**time
won't
let me**

chapter one

IF YOU REALLY WANT TO KNOW THE TRUTH, the roots were not rock and roll, folk, or skiffle. The roots of the band known as the Truants came from detention. In the little known "Fire Extinguisher Wars" of October 1964, at Chase Academy in South Chase, New Hampshire, only ten sophomores were captured. They were sentenced to four Sundays, nine to twelve, in the Music Room, located in the dankest dankness of the Pershing Memorial Auditorium basement. Why the Music Room when there were plenty of free classrooms for the g-pop miscreants? Detention duties went to the most recent faculty hiree at Chase. And by two days, the job fell to Briggs Wentworth, who had left the nearby Nashua public school system suddenly for what he felt was the noblest of reasons: too many squares.

Briggs Wentworth was mohair jacket/clove cigarette weird enough that when he asked to hold Sunday detention in the Music Room, the dean of faculty just walked away quickly. Six of the ten sophomores served their time in a clock-watching stupor that thawed only in the last two minutes when they loaded themselves into a telepathic starting gate spring-loaded for 11:59.9. That was their only activity in detention: the end of detention.

The other four lingered. Their eyes wandered during the three hours, but purposefully. The charts on the walls. The hiatused instruments. The thicket of akimboed music stands. Independently and at once, the four came to the same conclusion: This was not a place to escape. This was a place to escape to.

Wentworth remained seated while the other six rushed to the door, continuing to write lesson plans, glee-club arrangements, or thumb through *Downbeat*. He was available for any questions, but the four who stayed around had none. Three of them owned guitars but were afraid to play for anyone. The other had his eye on the four-piece, randomly pummeled black-pearl Rogers drum kit in the corner. After two Sundays of lingering, they agreed to stay an additional hour the next week and try to play the one song the three guitarists knew: "Michael (Row the Boat Ashore)."

Richie Lyman, John Thiel, Tim Schlesinger, and Jerry Fyne were hardly friends. They had fought on opposite sides during the Fire Extinguisher Wars for their respective dorms, Mulvihill (Richie and John) and Grays (Tim and Jerry). Richie and Jerry had shared one intimate prep school moment the previous spring as freshmen when half a dozen juniors dunked their heads in an unflushed toilet for the unpardonable sin of being Jewish.

Tim Schlesinger had been excused from the Freshman Yid Roundup. Medical reasons. The post-knee-surgery cast on his leg made it impossible to kneel commodeward. It was his second operation since football season, when a bad foot plant on worse turf ripped his knee in two directions and his four-year, three-sport career was finished, a destination he had never anticipated. By February, he was begging his parents to humanely yank him out of Chase and let him hobble at North High, where he would be merely a guy on crutches rather than the Jew cripple. An outsider only needs one distinguishing feature. Anything more borders on showy.

Tim's parents told him to finish the year, and he did. On the sidelines. Over the summer, the cast came off and a physical therapist suggested swimming three times a week. Chase had an indoor pool. North High did not. So, he was back the following fall, crutchless and more than fit enough to clean and jerk a fire extinguisher.

The physical therapist also said the restrengthening process might be sped along by—and this was only if Tim was interested—working the pedal on a bass drum a few minutes a day. This suggestion had slipped Tim's mind, but was lassoed the first Sunday he walked into detention.

It helped that they were equally bad. A four-way photo finish of ineptitude. And when one would poke his head in front—when Thiel picked clean the opening eight for "House of the Rising Sun," or when Jerry ditched his Guild for some cardboard bass that was much easier to play, or when Richie discovered if he screamed himself hoarse at the football game Saturday afternoon he sounded like an Isley brother Sunday morning, or when Tim didn't chase the beat like a bus into town—the others would aspire to that new touchstone, or risk the consequences: getting shit from the rest. Three months later, they still weren't exactly friends. If they had been, they might still be working on "Michael (Row the Boat Ashore)."

The hour on Sunday quickly became two, then backed up to include two hours Saturday morning and forty minutes Wednesday at noon, when the Chase class schedule was rejiggered to accommodate traveling athletic teams and no attendance was taken at lunch. Jerry Fyne would show up last to the Music Room with a gym bag of bread and peanut butter and half-pints of Hood milk. Nobody complained. Not even when Jerry laced his milk with a sweat-sock-sheathed half-pint of Old Crow. He said it made him play better. One of the few times he wasn't lying.

Once a month, on Saturday night, a hundred or fewer teenage girls were bused into the Chase Academy gym like kilted and cardiganed migrant workers. They came from places with names like Miss Porter's, Miss Hall's, Dana Hall, and—really, you can check; go ahead—Beaver Country Day. They came hoping to dance with someone who didn't look like another girl in their dorm or biology class. Preferably someone taller. They called such gatherings "mixers," a term that aspired to euphemism. Mixers. Like club soda or quinine water. Slight difference. Those kind of mixers, uh, worked.

Everyone got one dance, thanks to a "line up against the wall and pair off" boy-girl assembly-line ritual handed down from some ancient Sado-Victorian civilization wiped out after everybody danced once and no one procreated. Following that first dance/run-through, actual participants dropped by two-thirds, as The Not Enough rimmed the gym floor to watch The Selected, those whose adolescence came equipped with that factory-installed component: social ease. Better to stare at them with vicarious eyes than witness the lowering of their own self-esteem. They didn't need to see that. They could hear it.

The only thing that lifted a Chase Academy mixer out of its caste-party inertia was a live band made up of Chase students. That way, there was the needed distraction of a performance and the desperately needed distraction of a performance by cool guys you could pretend you knew. So, two performances. One from the live band, and the one you gave the Miss Porter's girl you'd placed yourself next to about the lead singer being your friend. Gilt by association.

Not just any five guys with amps and attitudes got the dance gigs. You had to be able to play for an hour. And you had to be good enough to stay up for an hour. Because, whoo, man, if Miss Porter's got bored with your pretend buddies, she could turn on you like a half-pint of Hood milk atop a radiator.

All of this was never a problem for the Protégés. In the fall of 1962, without the kismet of detention, five Chase freshmen would gather regularly in the space next to the Music Room and try to be

Buddy Holly and the Crickets. Two problems. The real Crickets never had a piano player and two saxophones, and the real Buddy Holly sounded like Buddy Holly, not a fourteen-year-old doing a sixteen-year-old's impression of Buddy Holly. None of this mattered to the Fire Ants, as they kind of called themselves, until one of the sax players brought his roommate to rehearsal, a hunched-over suburban Philly Jew named Mike Herman. After he heard the Fire Ants lurch through "Oh Boy!" as if they were playing the third string onstage at a pep rally, Mike Herman picked up his head and asked, "You guys know James Brown?" He leaned on the piano and banged out the relentless rhythm line of "Please, Please, Please" until the other guys knew enough to take over. The sax players followed diligently and the one guitar soon after. The drummer sort of got it, which was good enough. And then Mike Herman went from hunched over to doubled over and well, if he didn't sound exactly like James Brown, he sure as hell didn't sound like some kid whose closest brush with the blues was the day his housekeeper done got up and walked out dat do'.

The Fire Ants lined up behind this gangly visionary, who promised if they listened to the right records, his records, and followed along, they'd be playing dances sophomore year. And it happened exactly that way. And the most impressive part about it happening that way was that sophomore year fell smack in the middle of 1964, when the prep school dancing world preferred to gyrate to "She Loves You" and "All My Loving," not "Nadine."

Tough shit. The Fire Ants, who had picked up a better guitar player and become the Protégés, paid titular homage to the Beatles with "Twist and Shout" and "Hippy Hippy Shake" (both covers from the Isleys and the Swinging Blue Jeans), but that was not their business. Driving, grinding soul. Endless blues. Sound track from places these coddled coat-and-tied overachievers would never find themselves. "Night Train." "St. James Infirmary." "In the Midnight Hour." And the anthem of rock naughtiness, "Louie, Louie."

Because the Protégés were a year ahead of them, Richie, Tim, Thiel, and Jerry figured they had zero chance to be gigging at a dance until senior year. So, they kept their distance, dawdling just beyond the Music Room to eavesdrop on their rehearsals and far enough away in the darkness at mixers not to look too puppy doggish. One time, Tim was late for fourth-period Spanish, cut a corridor corner too tight, and juked in time to miss Mike Herman and his drummer, Kyle Sunderland. "That's a switch," Kyle said, "his nose is usually up my ass."

But three things happened shortly after Memorial Day 1965. Briggs Wentworth hung around as the four sophomores showed up for their Wednesday rehearsal and greeted them by saying, "Ah, the truants." Never more in time, Richie, Tim, Thiel, and Jerry said, "Can we have that, Mr. Wentworth?" Wentworth smiled. "Yeah, man," he said, "you can have it after you get yourselves a piano player." Two days later, the type of classmate they barely knew, an A student, filled in on the organ when Wentworth was too hung over to show up for final chapel. He played the first eight bars of "God of Our Fathers," the rockingest little number in the Chase Academy hymnal, and that was it. They rushed up after chapel and asked him to join their group. It was the first time Brian Brock had been asked to join anything.

Two days after that, while Mike Herman was cheating undetected on his physics final, his dorm master found a half ounce of marijuana in his room. In a plea bargain whose component was semantics rather than sentencing, Chase agreed not to expel Mike Herman, just not ask him to come back next fall. In return, the heart, soul, and progenitor of the Protégés had to give up the name of his pot source. Briggs Wentworth offered a fierce denial, then agreed not to come back next fall. Right after he was shitcanned.

So, four things happened.

The Truants did return in the fall of 1965. They let what was left of the Protégés fuck up exactly one mixer before they stepped over the disarray and onto the Chase Academy gym stage with a group confidence that was one part hubris, eight parts abject terror. Don't underestimate that terror thing. It works, especially when it releases that rare strain of adrenaline that actually makes one rise to the occasion.

If they hadn't loved the name Truants so much, they might have called themselves the Underdogs, because that's what they were. Nobody goes to the Daytona 500 to watch cars not crash, and the Chase student body buzzed around the Truants's maiden gig, the October grope-and-hope with Miss Hall's, with the adolescent glee of witnessing five classmates get into a short-sheeted bed.

It was a bomb that never detonated. Many reasons. They had all practiced over the summer. Practiced like sixteen-year-olds aren't supposed to. Indoors on sunny days because they wanted to practice. They showed up at school two days early, before classes started. While the new students were hatched into orientation, wandering around Chase, wondering around Chase what the hell their hormones had gotten into, the Truants sweltered in the Music Room. They had nine songs that didn't suck. They needed at least ten for a dance set.

That's when Michael showed up to stay.

"Michael (Row the Boat Ashore)" had been a number-one hit for the Highwaymen in 1961, then within two years had Pat Booned its way to "You like *that*?!?" punch-line status. There was no way, no way, a self-anointed hip teen band could trot that out in front of a bunch of guys they had to otherwise pass in the hall on the way to English lit. That's a long walk before short peers.

"Unless," said Richie Lyman, with rarified insight, "we announce it as a slow dance and play it for ten minutes. Then we're heroes."

Heroes indeed. Halfway through the first voyage of "Michael," most of the dance floor had already grinded their Miss Hall's charges by the stage and given Richie and his enablers a testosterone-fueled thumbs-up. Barely into the Truants's second gig, the seniors were yelling "Michael!" five minutes after everyone had been paired off, as if they were paging this grand ruse everyone but the chaperones were in on. Think about it. This feathery spiritual lullaby had become, just by relentless refrain, some kind of carnal anthem at Chase. The chance to lunge legally for ten minutes, pressed tight against a stranger in what was normally a decidedly non-contact sport, vigorously refereed. And all because the Truants couldn't work up a tenth tune. Although it would be a few short weeks before their playlist hit its second dozen, "Michael" never left. And no one would ever think of that song the same way again. No Chase student would ever hear *The river is deep and the river is wide, Hallelujah/ Milk and honey on the other side, Hallelu-jah . . ."* and not smirk at its lyric journey from folk song to fuck song.

The rest of the standard set ranged from savvy to sweaty, from inspired to aspiring. "Let's not forget," John Thiel would say over and over amidst fuzz-toned licks on his lead guitar, "no matter what we want to be, we're just a bullshit little dance band." By midwinter, 1966, the Truants's mixer menu had the comforting consistency of a campaign stump speech. "Route 66" (get it?) to "Twist and Shout" to "Midnight Hour" (their Protégés tribute medley, complete with dedication to "the late Mike Herman") to "Dirty Water" (the odd punk homage to Boston by the Los Angeles–based Standells) to "Johnny B. Goode" to "Don't Look Back" (by Boston-based rock legends the Remains) to "Baby Please Don't Go" to "Good Lovin'" to "Bright Lit Blue Skies" (by the Rockin' Ramrods, another local Boston band). Then, and only then, "Michael. . . ." Followed by "Gloria" (not the insane Van Morrison/Them original, but the more accessible Shadows of Knight cover) to "Hang On Sloopy" to "We Gotta Get Out of This Place."

They fought mightily over the order of the first twelve songs. But nobody argued about what the closer would be. "We Gotta Get Out of This Place" or "Outta," as it would forever appear on the run-down, only made sense last. It was the ultimate destination of any-one stuck in an all-boys prep school in 1966. Anywhere else. Outta this place. Jerry was the genius behind the post-"Michael" trium-virate ("Gloria," "Sloopy," "Outta . . ."). "They're all sing-alongs," he pointed out. "Nobody will remember how bad we were."

By then, nobody had to remember. Funny thing. The Truants weren't bad. Not even close. And they had pocketed some show-manship along the way. Tim learned how to twirl the stick in his right hand, a move nobody had ever seen attempted outside of a sequined majorette during a football halftime. Brian Brock, whose only other extracurricular activity was president, founder, and sole member of the Chase Classical Lit Society, turned into a musical centaur: Above the neck, he was glee-club chaste, below, he rav-aged his Vox (had to be a Latin root) Continental electric organ with heathen mischief.

Jerry would have his back to the audience, occasionally turning around to let them see how shit-faced he was, which never failed to get howls. Richie had sneaked underage into a club in down-town Boston and saw Barry Tashian, the leader of the Remains, jump around onstage as if he had been plugged into an amp. Richie figured during song breaks when he wasn't singing that was the best way to distract from his barely serviceable rhythm guitar. Right again.

Thiel, meanwhile, had developed into such an accomplished guitarist that he needed to hone no stage shtick, although once a set, as only a strapping jock can, he would run at Richie to get him to stop jumping. Which, come to think of it, if done more than twice, *is* shtick.

So, whether by derivation, confidence, or the exponential growth of the balls that got them up there in the first place, they were no longer just onstage playing. They were PLAYING. It was joyously undisciplined, and yet, to the chagrin of any 1966 ad-ministration, Chase Academy or LBJ, undisciplinable. Nothing would stop the Truants, short of Commencement. And with the cockiness of small pond stars, nothing could beat the band's opening salutation to their Chase classmates, when Richie would grab the microphone and shout, "How you Hoodsies doing?"

"Hoodsie" was the name of the half-vanilla/half-chocolate ice-cream cup marketed by the fine folks at H. P. Hood and Sons, New England's number one dairy pusher since 1846. Sometime in the mid-1960s, and for God knows exactly how long, the term "Hoodsie" was reincarnated at Chase Academy. It emerged one day on the main common of the all-boys private school out of the clear, constant air of adolescent teasing. Two otherwise faceless students, one undeniably larger.

"Come on."

"Forget it."

"One bite."

"I just gave you a bite."

"One more."

"No way."

"Come on. Don't be a Hoodsie."

Unlike its ice-cream forefather, "Hoodsie" began as a rather broad concept and widened with its legend. The definitions were as varied as the inflections. It was both adjective and noun. As an epithet, "Don't be a Hoodsie" could mean "Don't be stingy/greedy/cowardly/righteous/lame/shy/embarrassing/stupid/uncool/conceited/gullible/unfriendly/disloyal/slow/resentful/dramatic/goofy/stubborn/inappropriate." As a noun, there was only one interpretation. Fag. Don't be a fag. More specifically, if there is a nonsexual connotation of fag, don't be that. And what better place to find the nonsexual connotation of homosexuality than an all-boys school?

The last recorded use of the term "Hoodsie" can be found in the 1969 *Vault*, the Chase yearbook, two years after the Truants had graduated. Someone named Blaine Magruder, who stayed a postgraduate year only to be rejected again by Dartmouth, was voted "Hoodsie Emeritus" by his classmates. And that was it. What had sprung from nothing, meant anything, and whose cruelty was never really determined, vanished as harmlessly and indiscriminately as it had arisen.

Rehearsal time for the band was harder to come by in the spring, thanks to "Johnno" Thiel and his jock proclivities. Brian would show up anyway, waiting for nobody else, forever scribbling eight-bar notions on the keys of the Music Room's number two piano or the pad that lay on top of it. The inside pocket of his corduroy jacket held a smaller, spiral notebook, its bottom-right corner branded in tiny letters: *B.B.—Verba.*

One day, on his way to the Music Room, Brian heard noises. Unmistakable. *Plinking.* The plinking of someone who knew notes, but not the piano.

"Hey."

"You scared the living shit out of me," said Richie.

"What's up?"

"I think I wrote something for us."

"A song?"

"No, Hoodsie, a recipe."

"Can we do stuff like that?"

"Like what?"

"Original songs?"

"Yeah, why the fuck not? Who's gonna tell us no?"

Then, both at the same time, *"Tell us no, no, no, nonono, no, no, no, nonono . . ."* Like Zombies.

The idea was that Brian Brock and Richie Lyman would become some Brooks Brothers version of Lennon/McCartney. That was the idea. But here's the difference. Yeah, okay, talent and charisma and all that shit, but here's the difference. John Lennon and Paul McCartney were friends. And even if they weren't friends, they got along. And even when they didn't feel like getting along, they got along. The only way for Brian and Richie to get along was for Brian to act like he was there on a grant from the Richie Lyman Foundation. And he did that for a while. He did that for exactly the length of time it took them to compose the group's first song, "Get Psyched."

Like many songs of the time, "Get Psyched" was written to immortalize some catchphrase that may not necessarily be a phrase or catching. Unlike any song of the time, it was inspired by the catchphrase uttered before a baseball game with Exeter by Chase Academy's star junior, Johnno Thiel. Although it borrowed heavily from the Kinks's "You Really Got Me (Now)," deft key changes and an organ bridge camouflaged it more than enough. "Get Psyched" rolled in unassuming from the start and then settled into a relentless perch. It was, at the end of the songwriting day, an original.

Well, get psyched,
Get psyched
I know you want
To get psyched.
The way you walk, into a place,
I know you wishin', to see a face,
To find the reason you came around,
To find some action, to hear that sound—
To get psyched
Get psyched
I know you looking to get psyched.

So, get psyched
Get psyched.
I know you itchin'
To get psyched
You may be sleeping, in the night,
You may keeping, it in tight,
And there's that somethin' you can't explain,

It wakes you up now, and calls your name—
To get psyched
Get psyched.
Hey, Jerry!
Get psyched.
I know you hear me—
Get psyched.
Get psyched!!

It took Brian and Richie about forty minutes to write "Get Psyched," and ten minutes of that was deciding what name Richie would yell out at the end. The next hour, as Brian worked up the organ break, they spent asking each other, "Are you sure no one has written this song already?"

It took less time for this beginning to end. In the euphoria of completing "Get Psyched," Brian made the mistake of showing Richie a few pages from *B.B.—Verba* and offering up the nascent bars of a ballad.

"What's with these words?"

"What?"

Richie laughed. "'Yearning'? 'Cherish'? 'Ache'? 'Confusion'?"

"What's the problem?"

"Good luck rhyming them."

"I thought you might want to help."

"Nah. This is much too Hoodsie-ish."

"Hey, Richie. We did good here. But everything can't be 'Get Psyched.'"

"Why not?"

"Because then," Brian said, "we're just jerking off."

"Well, if that's how you feel, you write your shit and I'll write mine."

"Fine."

So endeth the complete Lyman-Brock discography.

Too bad. The ease with which Brian and Richie had written "Get Psyched" would never be duplicated by them individually. Their respective heads got in the way. Richie could never quite get "Get Psyched" out of his, Brian could never think of a lyric without projecting onto it Richie's inevitable disdain.

So, the unspoken competition was on. And nothing feeds productivity like competition. Between March 1966 and April 1967, Richie and Brian each wrote at least a dozen songs. And those were just the songs they brought to rehearsal.

Richie's offerings tended to be half formed, although the sales job before the song, like Richie himself, was fully polished, its bravado pitch-perfect. Brian and Johnno could tell immediately if there was something there, and would start tinkering, which is all Richie ever wanted, other people working for him. Meanwhile, Tim and Jerry would race to see who could say, "'Get Psyched'—take number eight!" faster.

They weren't wrong. The recording studio in Richie's mind was equipped with one track. So, for a while, just the titles told everyone his direction was maddeningly the same. "Psyche Me Down." "Get Wrecked." "Are You Up for It?" Even Jerry, state-of-the-art lazy, would complain. "Richie," he'd spurt, "can I play another fucking bass line before I'm twenty?"

But over the summer before senior year, Richie somehow rewired his "Get Psyched" psyche and batted out a couple of uptempo, folky efforts, entendre-ly titled "Came Too Easy" and "Line Forms on the Right." They quickly found themselves in the mixer rotation, now so corpulent the Truants could play for two hours without repetition. Even "Michael" now only played the first half.

Just after they came back from Christmas break, as the calendar skidded into 1967, Richie surprised himself and the others with his most fully formed composition yet. A thoughtful ballad, completely out of character. Even the way he presented it to the others was different.

"I got something," he said. "I have no idea what it is."

"Have you been to the infirmary?" said Tim.

"Oooh, how original," dinged Thiel. "What's it called?"

Richie fumpherred. "Uh, I don't know. 'What Now?'"

So, it became "What Now?"

My world had all the answers,
Today it has none.
I had all the angles figured,
All but one.
What happened to my strength?
Did you take that too?
What's this thing where my heart was?
Guess it always belonged to you.
Yeah, I guess it's all a performance,
Because ain't nothing that's real.
So I put on the costume,
Grab my cards off this deal.
And I'll look like I'm knowing
What the hell I should do.
But you're gone and I'm left
No reason, no rhyme—
What now?

Nobody would know for years that Richie had written "What Now?" over the break, when he returned home on the third night of Hanukkah and learned his father, the one-time Harvard hockey goalie, had pulled himself, just skated off, leaving his mother with the big house in Cambridge, the small house in Wellfleet, all the money she and her son would ever need, and nothing resembling an explanation. In kind, Richie never offered an explanation for "What Now?" He didn't have to. Nobody ever asked. And, as it turned out, he never wrote another original song. And nobody asked why. Brian thought about it, but what was the point? "What Now?" was the first time his undercurrent of all-purpose jealousy toward Richie was broken by the metallic-tasting quaff of specific, artistic envy.

By contrast, Brian's work was only brought into rehearsal when completed to his satisfaction, and was so self-contained it required little more than two play-throughs and a vote. The other guys helped. Actually, the odd number of other guys helped. (Looking to start a band? For the love of Christ, make sure you have an odd number of guys. If you put things to as many votes as you're going to have to, it's like buying no-tie insurance.) The Truants wavered between meritocracy and benevolent dictatorship. The best original songs did make it through and onto the dance playlist. And the fact that on some nights more of them were written by Brian ("You Lost Me," "F-F-F-Faster," and "Bad Neighborhood," to name three) didn't matter because they were still all going to be sung by Richie. Brian never had a problem with Richie singing his songs. He kind of liked it. It took the performance weight off of him, and, in the back of his karmic mind, he could construe it as Richie working for him.

The best thing about Richie Lyman's voice was that it sounded like him. Frankly, people can only take impressions, even good ones, for so long. Stevie Winwood got even more successful after he stopped doing Ray Charles. This is not an accurate comparison, but it sounds close enough. Which is how Richie sounded. Close enough. Actually, the best voice in the band belonged to Jerry, but he would be so drunk midway through the first set, he was best left back to the crowd, playing bass and singing slightly too-loud harmony. But good slightly too-loud harmony.

In April 1967, less than two months before graduation, and a week after he found out he wasn't accepted at Yale, Brian wrote a song that only he could sing. It was called "Furious."

When I first saw you,
My eyes went numb
You caught my spirit
And struck me dumb.
You made me helpless
But that was fine
Cause in your words, confusion ahead—confusion behind
Confusion behind
Furious, Furious
How can I be so, furious?
Help, furious.
So, I get out and I ignore it,
But it comes back,
I must explore it.
You made me shiver,
and I ain't cold.
I'm just here searching, this is so new—this is so old
It's getting so old
Furious, Furious
Why did you get me just, furious?
Don't you dare leave me, furious.
Guess I'll just go where I'm wanted,
But Furious. Just Furious.

The silence from the others after the first time he played it let him know how good, how something, "Furious" was. Thiel told him to double the tempo "or Richie might not get through it," but that was a few minutes after the silence, and that was it. The Truants lead singer interrupted. "Don't worry about Richie," said Richie. "Brian, that one is all yours."

Brian was finally a featured vocalist at the second-to-last mixer the Truants played in May. It would have been their last dance, but the boys scored an actual paying gig (their first) post-Commencement on the Chase campus when they made $50 apiece working three hours at the fifth reunion rave-up for the Class of 1962. They felt like big shots playing in front of 90 percent strangers, as if their notoriety hung like a sachet in the closeted prep community. And the money came in handy the next week, when they had to pay for an additional two hours of recording-studio time at Fantasia Studios in nearby Andover, Mass.

As their last few live performances were coolly gigged, like aced final exams, Richie began to introduce every song with the sardonic credit, "This next tune is from our upcoming debut album." The truth was, everyone, including the other Truants, was in on the joke but him. Richie had seriously wanted the group to record since April, when a friend from Andover had given him a two-year-old copy of *The Apostles: On Crusade*, by the former top in-house band at Phillips Academy. It was good, what the Protégés should have been, but music aside, the album's greatest inspiration was the sense of entitlement it embedded in Richie Lyman.

The Apostles: On Crusade and the thousands of records like it, one pressing of five hundred copies distributed among family and friends like consolation prizes, were called "vanity albums," a brutally frank classification that did not just imply, but screamed suburban self-satisfaction. Even the term was soldered onto the Beatles-spawned genre of music in America: "Garage bands." Come on, can you get any more suburban than that?

There was no garage at Chase Academy, and despite Richie's obsession with recording, one cannot fund a vanity album on vanity alone. Within a few weeks of relentless listenings to *On Crusade*, the overwhelming emotion among the sobered Truants was sadness, real and pragmatic. They knew they could do better, much better, just on the novel strength of including some original songs alone. But what was the point of such knowledge? What had held them together, the band, the only practical/interpersonal skills they had really learned in the last three years, was ending. They might wind up in other bands in college, but there would be no legacy of whatever this had been. In April 1967, that kind of a legacy cost $1,500.

By the first of May, Harvard acceptance waving in front of him, Richie was able to almost convince his mom that the still sore-to-the-touch grief over losing her husband might be softened by a check for, oh, say, $1,500, for the dream of her fatherless son about to attend Harvard, like his father, wherever the hell he was now that he had left them. Almost. Becky Lyman's choked-back sobs were briefly replaced by a coughed-up thousand dollars. Richie came back and told the others he had scored a major graduation present from his dad. Which, technically, was not a lie when you consider he had told no one the truth.

So, they were five hundred short of vinyl. Thiel got $200 and a lecture from his father, a navy pilot stationed in Norfolk and awaiting orders to head back to active duty in Southeast Asia. Tim's parents responded in unison, "I thought that set of drums was your graduation present." So, zero. Brian didn't even bother asking. Scholarship students who don't get into Yale don't tap their minister fathers for such laic tribute.

That left $300, and that left Jerry, who picked up the gauntlet faster than any textbook. In less than two weeks, he had the money (and more, but that's nobody's business) by using a three-pronged approach that should have been worth college credit for its hucksterism. He sold fifty-five fake draft cards at $2 apiece and cleared the first hundred. He booked $100 in Kentucky Derby bets and told the one kid who won on Proud Clarion that he'd been "shut out at the window."

The final hundred dollars he made in three minutes. Correction, two minutes, forty-seven seconds. Jerry bet Connor Searle, the richest guy in the junior class, that he could drink a bottle of Wish-Bone salad dressing in under three minutes. Connor Searle, of *those* Searles, was rich for a reason. He didn't give it away. A bottle of

Wish-Bone in under three minutes was good for only $50. But . . . a bottle of Wish-Bone, chased with a bottle of A-1 and three strips of raw bacon . . . well, that got you a date with Ben Franklin.

It was anticlimactic, as these things never are. Hell, Jerry Fyne had ingested much worse waiting for a bartender to refill the pretzel bowls. And for free. This? This was taking candy from a trust-fund baby. Sixty boys crowded around, but it was over before anyone got settled or satisfied, like Clay-Liston II in Lewiston, Maine. Although a victorious backslap from Thiel had almost tripped his launch codes, Jerry didn't get sick until long after Connor Searle had paid him and he had turned over the winnings to Richie. Around 2:00 A.M., he snuck out of his room in Donnelly Hall, chugged a half-pint of unlaced Hood milk, and tossed his admirable guts twenty yards windward of the headmaster's bedroom window. Jerry Fyne: Hero. Had a nice ring. Almost as nice as Truants: Recording Artists.

Everything is on the clock in a record studio. So, those extra two hours at Fantasia Studios were needed when what would have been the final two hours was spent in a decidedly off-key refrain of screaming, scuffling, hollow appeasement with a two-door-slam coda.

Small wonder, the two days before that, and the eleven tracks laid down, were the giddy nectar of disbelief. Out of school, and forty-eight hours to act like this is what they did. Rock and rollers. They stayed at Richie's empty house in Cambridge and drank like they knew what they were doing. And other than Jerry, they didn't. Then they jelly-legged in on maybe three hours' sleep and made an album like they were musicians who knew what they were doing. And other than Jerry, they did.

Jerry, for all his "fuck-it" joie de vivre, kept them all together on this hangovered foray. His well-miked laugh signaled the end of each take. And he put his own vocal stamp on "Respectable" during the midsong talk-over when he asked Richie, "Uh, did you squeeze her?" by imitating Brando in *Streetcar*. The vote to leave it in: 5–0.

That was the last of the unanimous tallies. This is how it looked as the Truants headed into the sixth and last cut on Side B.

SIDE A:
Don't Look Back
Get Psyched
Michael
F-F-F-Faster
Bright Lit Blue Skies
What Is the Reason?

SIDE B:
What Now?
Diddy-Wah Diddy
Mr. Wind
Line Forms on the Right
Respectable

"Respectable," their impressive cover of the underrated flip side to the Outsiders' giant hit, "Time Won't Let Me," continued the Truants's album-long theme of foisting their original songs on the hipless prep civilization while educating it to a deep, dark world below the Top 40. They adored the Rascals, but why do "Good Lovin'" when they could nail "What Is the Reason?" The Remains, who had inexplicably broken up a year before and whose legacy could be grokked only by the most devout, were well represented by their regional hits ("Don't Look Back" and the Bo Diddley geode "Diddy-Wah Diddy"), as were the Rockin' Ramrods ("Bright Lit Blue Skies," "Mr. Wind"), mercifully still the house band at The Surf in Nantasket Beach. "Michael" was included, a slow-eyed wink to the Truants and anyone else who got it, to remind them from whence they had come.

That left room for five originals. The plan, what there was of it, was to close the album with a second Brian song. ("Outta" had been dismissed as too commercial. Besides, they *were* outta this place.) "F-F-F-Faster" had soared on Side A, its naughtiness a tug-of-war between Richie's exaggerated stutter and Brian's wild solo on the Hammond B-3 organ. After its last track was laid down, Marty, the Fantasia Studios engineer and the only one in the room getting paid, gave them his most deft praise. "Boys," he said, "you'll want your moms out of the room on that one, man."

Brian was dying to do "Furious." It was his best work, his only vocal, and the most palpable evidence of where the Truants might go if they weren't all headed in different directions. But, as with everything, it would be put to a vote. Brian and Tim voted for "Furious," Johnno and Jerry for "You Lost Me," a deceptively haunting ballad. Richie chose "Bad Neighborhood," an early Brian piece that sounded a lot, though no rock court in the world would convict, like Richie's later offering, "Line Forms on the Right," which was already Side B's track 4.

The two-day session, which had moved with the urgency of a rescue mission, now stopped for the worst kind of conversation. Tired conversation. Every time "Furious" was brought up, Richie talked about "Bad Neighborhood." And every time "You Lost Me" was suggested, Richie said they had too many ballads, then reoffered, "What about 'Bad Neighborhood'?"

Brian tried to stay diplomatic. He said he agreed that they didn't need another ballad. He suggested another vote.

4–1, "Furious."

Hour Two began with no one wanting to answer Richie when he kept asking, "What about 'Bad Neighborhood'?" Then shuffling. Then mumbling. Then Jerry took a nice hard draw on a bottle of Seagram's 7 and said, "We don't fucking wanna do it, Richie. It sounds too much like 'Line.'"

"It sounds too much like 'Line Forms on the Right'?" said Richie. "No way."

They all nodded.

"What are you saying? That you won't do them both on the album because 'Bad Neighborhood' sounds too much like 'Line Forms on the Right'?"

Tim, Thiel, and Jerry nodded.

"No," said someone who sounded like Brian, only much stronger, "because 'Line Forms on the Right' sounds too much like 'Bad Neighborhood.'"

"Waiter!" yelled Jerry to himself as he belted back the bottle. Richie stared.

"I apologize," said the regular Brian. "Look, Richie, we voted. It's four to one for 'Furious.' We're running out of time. Here's the way I think we should work it—"

Richie smiled. "I am not doing a fag song on my album," he said.

"What?"

He grabbed his microphone, his official lead-singer microphone, still hot. The microphone too. "I said," he said, "I AIN'T DOING NO FAGGOT SONG ON MY ALBUM!"

Thiel jumped in between them, thinking for a second they were athletes. Tim started to, but kicked over his hi-hat. Jerry laughed, but that didn't stop this take.

Richie kept smiling. "I saw what you wrote. And I know why you wrote it." He stopped, and then, as if it had just come to him, "And now, I realize why you ain't going to Yale. They just didn't have room for one more fag."

"Richie, you've got about five seconds to apologize," Thiel said.

"Sure, I'll apologize. But first, ask Tinkerbell here how to spell 'Furious.'"

Brian stormed out and slammed the door. He was back less than twenty seconds later. "You're a cruel, selfish prick, Richie. Maybe something will happen to you and you'll grow out of it. I hope so. But you don't get it. You don't get this. You never got it. And that, that you can't change. Because you don't get it."

Second door slam.

Three months later, Brian received his Truants dowry. A hundred copies of the Hoodsie Records LP *The Truants: Out of Site* arrived via Railway Express and were neatly stacked outside the door of his freshman room at Trinity College, thirty-two miles of paved disappointment north of the Old Campus at Yale. He looked at the back of the cover just long enough to see his writing credit on "F-F-F-Faster," and to *not* see his cowriting credit on "Get Psyched." Departure tax. The last cut on Side B turned out to be Richie's "Came Too Easy," which, *came too* think of it, may have sounded better without a keyboard. That is, assuming he was ever going to fucking listen to it.

Brian went back into his room briefly and emerged with a piece of shirt cardboard on which he had written "FREE ALBUMS." The following Monday morning, it had been replaced by a new sign: "TRASH PLEASE." The superintendent put one copy under his arm for his thirteen-year-old daughter and carted the remaining ninety-three to the corner. Took about three and a half minutes. Or the length of a good song.

chapter two

"I FEEL LIKE I'M TAHKIN' TO RINGO'S SISTAH."

If nothing else happened, that would be enough. That would be the conversation stopper to last the rest of her life. She'd be working her shift at Gavin's, then some regular would bring in a regular-to-be and around the third round, he'd yell, "Hey, Lizzie, tell Sully the 'Ringo's sistah' story!" And he would have blown it by leading with the capper, but she'd tell it anyway. And everyone would be impressed, again. And there would be another five or ten or twenty in tips because of it. And when she woke up the next day on five hours' sleep to make her first lab, this bleary-eyed life of someone who should be much younger would make enough sense to continue for another day.

Of course, Lizzie Schlesinger had no way of knowing any of this, because the whole thing had just happened three phone calls ago.

Thursday was the one afternoon when she ate lunch like people who do that sort of thing. She made it to T. Anthony's, the popular Commonwealth Avenue pizza-sub shop, around 2:00, when it was almost humane after the lunch rush, and was about to enjoy her meatball parmigiana sub, small salad, and diet root beer garnished with the latest issue of the *New York Review of Books*. Initially, there had been two problems. Some wise guy had unscrewed the cap on the shake-on hot peppers and she would have some scraping to do. And there was no *Review* in her knapsack.

"Shit. Tommy, you got a *Globe*?"

"No, Lizzie. That dicklick Mitchell took it."

"Shit."

"Take a *Phoenix*. They're free, in the box outside."

Lizzie hadn't read the *Phoenix* since they'd stopped trying to charge for it. Which came around the same time she felt she had read enough articles with titles like "Capitalism: The New Marxism?" "My Six Months as a Black Lesbian in Finland," "Dylan: Visionary, Weirdo, or Both?" or "Six Great New Recipes for Ganja." Or a week before she started subscribing to the *Review*.

She turned to the music section, as if she had never stopped reading this tragically erstwhile hip tabloid. Maybe they'd solved the Dylan Visionary/Weirdo conundrum. No such luck. Instead, she found this:

Where Are the Truants, and What Are They Doing That's Worth $10G?

BY SETH BANNISH

Yeah, yeah, yeah. Your mom threw out your baseball cards, otherwise you'd be breaking bread and swapping lies with Bill Gates and Jeff Bezos and those other nouveau-Rockefellers. But quick, go to the attic, the basement, the garage. Look through the albums. Not the ones you still play. The ones not good enough for a yard sale. If you have a copy of *The Truants: Out of Site*, you won the lottery, amigo.

In 30 years, since its virtually silent release on the one-time vanity label Hoodsie Records, *Out of Site* has become the most coveted album of the under-appreciated rock genre, New England Prep School Garage Bands of the 60s.

Go ahead and laugh. Last month, a collector in Germany paid $10,000 for a once-played copy of *Out of Site*. So, start looking. It doesn't mean every copy is worth ten Gs, but start looking anyway.

The Truants—Richie Lyman, John Thiel, Brian Brock, Jerry Fyne, and Tim Schlesinger—were five classmates at toney Chase (NH) Academy who, just prior to graduation in 1967, raised $1,500 (I'll guess five $300 donations from their parents) and recorded *Out of Site* in two days at Fantasia Studios in Andover.

Now, there are literally thousands of these albums around. Every upper-middle-class kid who was forever changed by the Beatles on *Ed Sullivan* considered it his birthright to be part of a band. Even a bad one. Usually a bad one. But some of the bands were good enough, facile, with the requisite amount of cover tunes, to play school mixers. A few were self-reverential enough to record vanity albums. A couple (the Apostles, the HaPennys) actually didn't suck.

And one made a record that is worth ten grand.

I found it. Tracked down a copy in Arlington, in the formidable cache of record archivist ("Collector sounds too scummy.") and garage-band connoisseur Dino Paradise. Dino himself played the album for me because he would not let me handle it, let alone leave his sight. Wouldn't let me even look at the sleeve longer than it took to jot down the members of the group (not that you'd know any of them). And it still cost me fifty bucks.

It's not that the Truants are that much more skilled than the other bands of the era. It's that their tone is always consistent, even by accident. And, more important, that they had either the foresight, conviction, or grandiosity to put five original songs on the album. Five. Or four more than any of their contemporaries dared.

Even the cover choices are inspired. Two each from New England garage gurus the Remains and the Rockin' Ramrods. The others are a cover of the Outsiders' cover of the Isley Brothers' "Respectable," the Rascals' "What Is the Reason?" and (my ears actually double-taked) "Michael (Row Your Boat Ashore)."

But guess what? It was worth it. The fifty bucks, that is. I might have even paid $75. I don't know about ten grand. You'll have to ask the guy in Germany. If he ever plays his copy a second time.

Lizzie got change for a dollar and left her meatball parmigiana sub the length of a bathysphere. She called information to get the number of the *Phoenix*. Called the *Phoenix* and somehow got Seth Bannish visiting the newsroom for the first time in nine months.

"How did you know I was here?"

"I didn't," said Lizzie.

"Did you talk to my wife?"

"No. Look, my older brother is Tim Schlesinger. The drummer for the Truants."

"The what? Oh, the ten-thousand-dollar guys. Great. Cool. Look, I gotta go to court."

"Do you have Dino Paradise's number?"

"Arlington. He's listed."

"Do you think—" *(click)*

Dino Paradise picked up on the seventh ring.

"Hit me."

"Mr. Paradise?"

"If you want my fahthah. I'm Dino."

"Hello, Dino, my name is Lizzie Schlesinger. I—"

"As in Tim Schlesinger? The drummer for the Truants?"

"Yes."

"Holy shit. Fuck me."

"What?"

"I feel like I'm tahkin' to Ringo's sistah."

RICHIE LYMAN UNROLLED THE SLEEVES of his cream-colored shirt and put his cuff links back in. Normally, he would not have gussied up so for a former classmate. But the guy was a client.

"You get a studio apartment," he began. "You live there for a year. You're never seen in public with anyone you're not related to. You behave. You stay calm. You refer everything to me. This is over in a year. I know it seems like a long time. But it's finite. Three hundred and sixty-five days. And here's the beauty part. Tomorrow, it will be three hundred and sixty-four."

"I get a studio apartment?" said John Thiel.

"That's right."

"Why?"

"Because you need a place to live."

"But what about a one-bedroom?"

"What do you need a one-bedroom for?"

"Well, I, you know, the space."

"What, are you planning on entertaining?"

"No."

"Because as your attorney, I would strongly advise against entertaining."

Thiel exhaled. "I just think a one-bedroom would be more, ah, civilized."

"And more expensive."

"Well, yeah."

"Look, if you want to spend more money, I'd be happy to up my fee."

"No thanks, Richie."

"Okay then. So we won't be entertaining and we won't be throwing money around on things like another room."

"But I would like to be comfortable. I mean, I am the one who graciously agreed to move out."

"Yeah, that was damn gracious, Johnno," Richie said. "I don't know how to tell you this, Mr., ah, Dr. Thiel, but it's not about your comfort at this stage. You want to go nuts and get yourself a queen-size mattress, for your *studio apartment*, I'll look the other way. But that's as comfortable as you're gonna get."

Richie Lyman saw his client's lips seal like an unshucked oyster. "Johnno"—he reprised Thiel's old prep school nickname—"how do you feel? Like you're being punished?"

Thiel's oyster lips were now joined by his "What are you, a fucking mind reader?" eyes. "You're goddamn right I feel like I'm being punished."

Richie's second link was in. He cleared his throat. "Johnno, I'm going to say something brilliant to you right now. It will be the last brilliant thing I say. Because after this, it's going to get very boring, because I'm just going to keep repeating this."

"Which is?"

"It's not how you're feeling, it's what you're doing."

"Richie, what the fuck does that mean?"

"It means," said Richie, "you do the right thing, take the right action, and give that more weight than however it makes you feel."

"I don't get it."

"You don't have to get it."

"Great."

"Just get the studio."

"Okay."

Thiel stood up. He looked good. Had he always been that tall? Richie wondered. What had he gained in the three decades since they had gone off to college, two pounds? Well, at least Richie's hair was still brown, and in more frequent need of a trim. Call it a push.

They shook hands. "Now, get out of here before I dawdle into the second billed hour," Richie cracked.

"You would overbill me, you Hoodsie."

"Jesus, I haven't heard that expression in twenty-five years."

"Thirty," corrected Thiel.

Richie Lyman, divorce lawyer, walked John Thiel, divorcing dermatologist, out of his office and into the reception area. He reached up to put his arm on his client's shoulder. "Johnno, just remember one thing."

"What?"

"'The truth is the light.'"

Thiel smiled. He knew the song. "'The truth is the light'?" he backed up.

"'And the light is the way.'"

"'The light is the way?'"

"'The less folks know.'"

"'The less they know?'"

"'The more they have to say—'"

They both came in together, on key, "'Yeah, yeah. . . .'" "Don't Look Back." Barry and the Remains. 1965.

"Now that," Thiel said, "I definitely haven't heard in thirty years."

"Yeah, but when was the last time you thought about it?"

"Last month." He was right. It was last month. Thiel and his wife, Gail, had shown up late to a black-tie dinner after he had opened the wrong garment bag in his closet and found his old tuxedo-black Les Paul Gibson and spent twenty minutes tuning it. Okay, five tuning, twenty playing.

Back went Richie's hand on his shoulder. "I'll be in touch. Until then, this is very important."

"What?"

He popped a cuff link out. "Can you look at this bump on my arm?"

"It's nothing. A dried cyst."

"Okay, one more."

"Richie, for Christ sake. Come to my office. Madison and Sixty-fifth."

"Jesus, now who's being a Hoodsie?"

They laughed and drew the appropriate stares from Richie's secretary and the impatient-looking blonde sitting to her right.

Thiel left and Richie turned his attention to the blonde.

"Did we have an appointment, Mrs. Brennan?"

"No," interrupted the secretary.

"She's right. But I was nearby and I wanted to make sure you got these papers."

"I told her she could leave them with me."

"Yes, she did," Mrs. Brennan smiled, "but I'm silly."

"You're a Hoodsie," he said.

"What?"

"A Hood—forget it. I'm silly." Richie Lyman Esq. laughed. He did it easily, as forty-eight-year-old single men who look thirty-nine and act twenty-nine do. And he smiled at the impatient-looking blonde, so easily it made the laugh seem like an opening act. "I'll take that. But in the future, Mrs. Brennan, there's no need to wait if you don't have an appointment. You can leave anything specifically marked for me with Ms. Lazarony. She'll never open anything that's personally dropped off."

"Okay."

Mrs. Brennan, Mrs. Wallace Brennan, handed over the envelope and tried hard not to linger. She did pretty well.

Richie ducked back inside his office and opened the envelope. Just what he was expecting. Four sheets of paper, each with a letter or number in the bottom-right corner, wrapped around a plastic hotel key card.

CHERYL NUDGED HER HUSBAND.

"You exhausted?"

"Yes," said Tim.

"So, getting laid is out?"

"I didn't say that."

"No, I did."

"You're exhausted too?"

"Yeah. How can that be? All we did was go out for dinner with the Hennesseys. We weren't even gone two hours. And they drank, not us."

"Cheryl, I told you how come."

"Please. Not the introvert-extrovert thing."

"Introverts get their energy from within, not from others. They can be very social. Introverted doesn't mean shy."

"Can it mean bitchy?"

"Why?"

"Shut up, please," she said.

"Well, why do you think you're tired?"

"I don't know . . . Doc."

"Seriously."

She sat up in the bed. "Oh, seriously? Maybe it's working ten hours with the old ladies, organizing a going-away party for Grace, grocery shopping, forty-five minutes on the bike, and then two hours with people who used to be fun but now seem to only want to talk about some bullshit stock or something fabulous a fucking ten-year-old said."

"So, not bitchy."

"You were a big help, Tim. You told the coffee-cart story and the 'Get him a headset!' story, then you got sleepy."

"Well, those take a lot out of me. And I told them well."

"That's true. We got nothing from them. I gotta go two hours like this." Cheryl Schlesinger did the frozen, slightly open-mouth

"Kill me now" smile of someone whose leg was caught fast in the trap of mundane conversation. Tim loved that look. He knew it was for him and not because of him. As smoothly as a guy married fifteen years and lugging fifteen more pounds, so not at all, he propped himself up on his elbow and pulled her toward him.

"Oh no," she said.

"Hey, maybe getting laid isn't out of the question."

"I thought you were exhausted."

"That has never stopped me."

"That," she said, "has always stopped you."

He kissed her much more hello than good night. "I'm trying to change."

"We'll see." She straightened up and wouldn't let him see her surprised. Not that he would see it. But she was. Instead, Cheryl cross-armed her T-shirt above her head and they began to make love for the first time in a good couple of months.

It would be 8:00 the next morning before Tim noticed the light blinking on the answering machine.

LIZZIE TOLD HER BROTHER EVERYTHING that Dino Paradise had coughed out between "Fuck me"s. He wanted to get the original Truants back together, rerelease *Out of Site* on CD with half a dozen bonus tracks from a couple of promotional live gigs, all leading up to the official reunion at their Chase 30th reunion in June. Dino would act as their producer, the difference being that rather than put up all the money himself, he would have coinvestors. Namely, the original Truants. The worst that could happen was everyone would break even in two, three years. The best-case scenario was numerous reorders of the CD and another record deal. "'I've seen it happen, Lizzie,'"—she imitated Dino—"'I've seen it happen with garahge bands who shit the fuckin' bed.'"

Tim heard little after the phrase "live gigs." That's right. Live gigs. An hour's drive, if you were lucky. An hour and a half setting up and sound-checking, if anyone cared. Five hours playing. Half an hour to break it all down. Half a stale sandwich and all the warm beer you could keep down. An hour's drive back. Two twenties in your pocket if you weren't the "gas man" that night. The whole goddamn scene so much closer to community service than a career. So much closer to Willie Loman than Mitch Ryder.

It had been all of that thirty years ago. And it was the last, last time Tim Schlesinger had gotten his energy from others rather than himself. Little wonder why he heard anything his sister said after "live gigs."

He called the office and told them he'd be an hour late. Dead battery. He knew it would be closer to two. He changed into a T-shirt and crawled into the attic with the shitty clock radio and three dish towels under his arm—like Donald Pleasence in *The Great Escape*—and he had everything ready in less than twenty minutes. Cartons bulldozed aside, camouflage unsheathed, tom-tom attached, bass pedal tightened, hi-hat primed and pumped. No less than Tim, already breathing hard and ready to sweat as no treadmill could yield. He was about to lay the dish towels over the snare, tom-tom, and floor tom, but you know what? Screw it. Screw that shit. Cheryl was gone and the nearest neighbor was a Van Halen kit away. He turned on the shitty clock radio and twirled his Pro-Mark 5Bs for the first time in eight years, waiting for the 9:00 news break to end, praying for something he could deal with when it did.

"*Now back to more of your favorite oldies on WGZR— Geezer 98. . . .*"

"Jesus," said Tim. "I hope so."

The guitar came in, and he knew it on Note Two. Johnny Rivers. "Secret Agent Man." 1965. Plenty good enough to start with.

There's a man who leads a life of danger.
To everyone he meets, he stays a stranger.

With every move he makes, another chance he takes.
Odds are he won't live to see tomorrow . . .
(Rrrrrrolll—Quick twirl!)
Secret Agent Man.
Secret Agent Man.
They've given you a number, and taken away your name . . .
(Long, long twirl!)

Just like riding a bike you were supposed to get rid of, like you promised.

Beware of pretty faces that you find.
A pretty face can hide an evil mind.
Aw, be careful what you say,
Less you give yourself away.
Odds are you won't live to see to-morrow . . .
(Rrrrrrollll—Quick twirl!)
Secret Agent Man.
Secret Agent Man.
They've given you a number, and taken away your name . . .

Long, long twirl with the feet-syncopated bass/hi-hat *crash-boom-crash-boomboom-crash-boom-crash boomboom.* No, you never lose it. You're a drummer. You never lose it, and you can't get rid of it. Even though you promised. Even though the two of you agreed. He played through the bridge like he'd built it.

Swinging on the Riviera one day,
Then laying in a Bombay alley next day.
Aw, don't you let the wrong word slip,
While kissing persuasive lips,
Odds are you won't live to see tomorrow.

He bagged the *rrrollllll/quick twirl* and attacked the whole glorious apparatus—the thirty-one-and-a-half-year-old electric red Slingerland kit with the three thirty-one-year-old Zildjian cymbals—with the simultaneous glee and fury that befitted a great drumming song ending too soon. Or at all. *Another chance he takes.* Another chance to wail. You're a drummer. You never lose it. You may lose chances, but that's all. Eight years since he had last played. Might as well have been eight minutes with the deftness lost. Eight years since the last conversation. Eight years since he loaded up the Civic and came back with $500 (good for a spontaneous Cheryl "Spouse Appreciation Day" blow job right there in the kitchen with the cash on the counter). Eight years minus a day, when he returned the $500 to his sister Lizzie and brought everything back from her apartment and erected the camouflage in the attic. Even though he had promised. Even though they'd both agreed that forty was too fucking old for a man to be spending hour after hour in a window-less hunchspace, shaking the foundations of the unspoken rickety-ness of house and vows—for what? To play along with a radio? To get better? To get better at what? Being distant? Like some zombie?

"*GZR-98!!! Here's a Geezer double play. From 1969. The Zombies . . .*"

It's the time of the season, when the love runs high . . .

MRS. BRENNAN FIGURED SHE'D WAIT until Richie rolled off her before asking, "Were you ever married?"

"Technically? Technically, yes."

"Christ. Typical lawyer response. Just like my idiot husband."

Richie, undaunted, as only the post-climax afterglowing can be, continued on his righteous tightrope. "See, by 'technically,' I mean I look at it now not so much as a marriage, more as a research project," he parsed. "You know, like a doctorate."

"Man, are you in the right profession."

"Ow."

She paused. "Doesn't what we're doing seem a little—"

He had to interrupt. "Do you know the difference between a lawyer and a rooster?"

"No."

"A rooster clucks defiance . . ."

"Oh."

". . . and a lawyer . . ."

"Something with cock?"

"*Ehhumph-hah!* Yes, that's right, Fran."

"Hey, Mr. Lyman, counselor. Get the name right."

"Your name isn't Fran?"

"No. It's Mrs. Brennan."

Here's the deal. It wasn't even his idea. Meeting up with Fran Brennan in the middle of the afternoon at the Drake and assailing her Equinox-detailed body, okay, that was his idea. But the concept of sex with the stranger who'd hired him to get her out of a marriage for as small a fee and as big a settlement as passive-aggressively as possible, this was much too intricate, too well thought out for Richie Lyman. Too original. Like everything else that worked in his life, he'd copped it from somewhere else. Divorce? That was his ex-wife's brainstorm. Leaving corporate law for family practice? That was the obscenity-bookended suggestion of the second attorney in his divorce. Having affairs with his female clients? *Cosmopolitan*, March 1984.

". . . and a lawyer fucks de clients."

"What?" she said.

"Nothing."

He hadn't even come up with the hotel-key-in-the-manila-envelope-at-his-office move. That belonged to Helen Klein, his third voyage into the Gulf of Conflict Interest. Until then, he'd been a blow job/go-down-on-her-on-the-desk kind of guy. You know, classy. "Eatin' ain't cheatin'" and all those other fidelity loopholes just large enough to drive a euphemism through. But Mrs. Klein wouldn't have any of it. "Look, mouthpiece," she'd said. "I'm not gonna bag my panty hose, then hop up on that table and have you wrinkle Donna Karan. Can we be just a little discreet? If we're going to do this, let's do it right. I'll be at the Roosevelt, under the name Mrs. Roosevelt."

Richie Lyman Esq. had his rules, his ethics. He did not date two clients at once. Okay, he did not date two clients in the same week. He was up front with them about what this was. How it was as much part of the transition process for them as anything else. He actually might lead up to that, get lost for words, and let the woman supply the phrase "transition process," like some Special Adultery Edition of Mad Libs. He liked the phrase "transition process." He also liked the term "self-limiting." That was a big one. "This is a self-limiting situation. We both came into it knowing that," he would say. "Otherwise, we wouldn't have hooked up." "Hooked up," that was another term he liked.

"Oh," Mrs. Brennan said. "I get it."

"What?"

"Fucks de clients."

"Yeah. Silly."

"Is what we're doing going to cost me any money?"

"Hey, I know I'm good, but I never considered . . ."

"No, jerk-off. In the settlement."

"I don't see why it would."

She pulled her bra off the lamp by the phone. "I know why I'm doing this, but what about you?"

"I like to get laid," Richie said. He had his ethics. Be honest at all times, except when to do so would injure others, or himself.

It might mean something if the story of Richie Lyman was one of unfulfilled promise, but that just wasn't the case. He was a B-minus student at Chase Academy with no extracurricular activities except the rock band he started sophomore year with three other B-minus students. He got into Harvard only because his father, Don Lyman, had had the good taste to be an All-American hockey goalie and then a ridiculously successful builder of shopping centers. Richie, despite his jockish hair and chin, was relentlessly unathletic. He made it through four years at Harvard by taking all the easy courses and always being the guy with beer money. And good timing. "Everybody hated Nixon, but I loved the guy," he would say whenever the thirty-seventh president's name came up. "He bombed Cambodia my junior year, we started marching, and I got out of four papers and three finals."

Everything after that which worked out, which was just about everything else, was something he copped from somewhere else. So, no unfulfilled promise. Outside of a cologne margin error of plus/minus 10 percent, he was right where he should be. Divorced divorce lawyer, specializing in self-limiting transition periods.

Richie had come up with one original idea in the last five years: the karaoke bar second date. Just when the latest Mrs. Estrangedlove would feel squirrelly about this decidedly non-litigious detour (ten minutes after she got back home), Richie Lyman Esq. would suggest they go over some papers some night the next week in the very public lounge at the Sheraton on Fifty-second and Seventh. Around the second drink, the karaoke machine would start up and the businessmen and tourists would become hilariously brave. Richie would wait an hour, for the first lull, rise up, show a little cuff link and have the deejay cue up "In the Midnight Hour," "We Gotta Get Out of This Place," or "Route 66" and for the next three minutes look like booked entertainment. Just slightly more on key than the rest of them, but with the cocky presence no shower or driver-seat soloist could ever plumb in front of a house. What had Nicholas Cage said in *Peggy Sue Got Married* in that fucked-up deviated septumed voice of his? *"You don't understand. I'm the lead singer."* The businessmen and tourists would always pound their glasses for a second song. And Richie, jacket now doffed and hung on the mike stand, would always give them one. He'd get back to the table and his client would cross a leg over his lap and purr, "You've done this before." And he'd always twinkle and say, "Not since I was the lead singer for the Truants in nineteen sixty-seven." And there'd always be a third date.

"Let me ask you something," Fran Brennan said.

"Uh-oh. I mean, go ahead."

"What are you going to do when someone wants more than some flippy-flop while waiting for an appointment with an arbitrator?"

"Mrs. Brennan, are you falling for me?"

She laughed big. Crazy-woman big. "Shit no. Look, you got a nice voice and a nice cock. You think I'd ever want to wind up living with *another* lawyer? What are you, out of your fucking mind? Ever get into an argument with a lawyer?"

"Couple times," said Richie. "What, Gary was like that?"

"What do you think? Sixteen years of *'This isn't an argument, Fran. This is a discussion.'* And we'd argue over that. *'Well, what is your definition of an argument, Fran?'* Oh gee, Gar, I'd have to say anything that involves a salad plate whizzing by your head and smashing against the CD rack."

"So, no to lawyers. Present company excluded."

Fran Brennan threw her bra back on the lamp. "You just lie there, get hard and shut up, and we'll be fine."

"Will do."

"What I meant was, what happens when *you* become part of the settlement?"

Shit. He had missed that issue of *Cosmo*.

chapter three

●●

OCTOBER

"COME ON. GIVE IT TO ME. You gottah fuckin' love it. And you gottah fuckin' respect it."

Tim Schlesinger turned to his sister. "Hegel," he said.

Dino Paradise had just finished walking them through his vision for a Truants reunion that June. Tim and Lizzie sat with knees sternum high on a sofa that would play absolute havoc with their lower backs should they try and get up, drinking Tab *(Tab!)*, and not eating whatever snack-food detritus was in the bowl from at least two nights before. Dino hitched up his jeans for the thirty-eighth time. He silently thumbed through a shelf of 45s.

"Ah."

He whisked the record out and held it to his chest so his guests couldn't identify the label.

"I want you to have this. Are you ready? Do you have any idea what I have here? Ah, screw it. It's—you gotta fuckin' love it— Mistah Sunshine."

"Mr., uh, Sunshine," said Tim.

"Mr. fuckin' Sunshine."

Tim shook his head. "Don't know it."

"Chirco."

"Chirco?"

Dino tried not to be deflated. "Barry," he said.

"The Remains Barry? Barry Tashian? Was he in Chirco?"

"No, but he wrote 'Mr. Sunshine.' Timmy, come on. He fuckin' gave it to them. 1972. He was there. He was playing when they recorded this."

"He's on this record?"

"Fuck yeah."

"How do you know that?"

Dino flicked his ear. "I think I remember him telling me."

"Can we see it?" said Lizzie.

"See it—I want you to fuckin' have it! It's worth three bills, it's the only copy I have, but I want you to have it. That's how much I want to be in the Truants business."

Lizzie took half a look at the 45. "Wait a minute. This doesn't say Chirco or Mr. Sunshine."

"What?"

"This is 'It's Cold Outside' by the Choir."

Dino grabbed the record back. "Fuck me. I switched them."

"Good song," said Tim. "Lizzie, you remember this."

"Vaguely."

But her brother was already into the refrain. "'. . . *and now it's cold outside . . .*' It came out the fall after we got out of Chase. '. . . *and the rain is pouring down, and the leaves are turning brown, can't you see . . .*' I think these guys became the Raspberries."

"Fuck yeah," refrained Dino. "You gotta respect this guy." Back outstretched went the 45. "Keep it."

"How much is this worth?" asked Lizzie.

"Six."

"Six bills?"

"No," said Dino Paradise. "Six. Six dollars."

"Oh."

"Fifteen, if you can find some dink who thinks Eric Cah-men is singing lead."

Tim and Dino shared a laugh. He nudged his sister, who looked at the twenty-nine-year-old hardly chart-busting single and the illogic of it all. Lizzie nudged Tim back and he knew what she wanted him to ask.

"Dino," he said, "I know the Choir, but nobody knows me. How can this be worth six dollars, and our silly album be worth ten thousand?"

Dino Paradise rehiked his pants, popped the top on another Tab, and tried to start. "Look, if I told you it's a combination of things, is that enough? Rarity for one. Timmy, how many *Out of Site* you press, five hundred?"

"Yeah, exactly."

"I know that seemed like a fuckload in nineteen sixty-seven, but believe me, five hundred is not a lot. I get a thousand sheets on a roll of Scottie fuckin' tissues, and that's gone in a week. How many copies do you think are still out there?"

"I don't know. A hun—"

"Playable fuckin' copies."

"Oh."

"But that's only the staht. A rare album, a good one, that'll get you five hundred. Nice. A lot of five-hundred-dollar bills built all this—Chez Dino." He gestured like a real estate agent who didn't want to spill his diet soda. "And then there's all the other shit. Little shit. Bigger than little shit. What's the word I'm looking for?"

"Subtle?" said Tim.

"Nuances?" said Lizzie.

Dino put down his Tab and squeezed his head. "Bingo! Subtle fuckin' nuances!" He dropped to his knees, gingerly pulled twenty albums off the bottom shelf, straightened the stack on the only open space on the floor, and dug his head in the space he had created in the shelf. The unmistakable sound of a safe being opened, a deep exhale, and then Dino emerged with a mint copy of *Out of Site*. He handed it to Tim and stayed on the floor.

"Timmy, do me a favor. Count the numbah of original songs."

"I already know," said Tim. "Five."

"Do me a favor. Count them in front of me."

"Do you two want to be left alone?" Lizzie giggled.

Tim exhaled. "One . . . two . . . three . . . four . . . five."

"Nuance," said Dino. "Now, Lizzie, what would you call the two photos on the cover?"

Lizzie peered. "I don't know. A double exposure?"

Dino nodded. "Nuance. Okay, now both of you, read the last line of the back-cover blurb."

Dino mouthed as they read, *"'For best results, we recommend playing this record on the best possible equipment and at the highest possible volume.'"*

"Giant fuckin' nuance! Come on! Who puts that on the back of an album in nineteen sixty-seven but ass-out-the-window visionaries?" He snapped his fingers for them to return the album. He grabbed a nearby chamois and gave a loving once-over to the original cellophane. Back into the safe. Back went the other albums into the space.

Lizzie waited until his head reemerged. "So, all that gets us to ten grand?"

"There's more. A shitload more. But isn't that enough for now?" Dino struggled to his feet. He was good and winded. This, the world of the record collector, was a speech he rarely had to give for two reasons. Reason One: A noncollector never understood it. The noncollector would just politely wait for him to finish, then pick up the nearest item and say, "What can you get for this?" or "So, all that gets us to ten grand." That's why Dino Paradise only talked with other collectors. That was Reason Two why he rarely had to give the speech. Collectors know why they're collectors. Some guy in Germany hears *Out of Site* once and pays $10,000 for the album. That is not a case of what the market will bear. Some guy in Germany has to have that album, and the next thing he says is, "Okay, ten thousand." What the market will bear is insanity. Ultimately, that's why it is healthy. There is no explanation. A guy in Germany *had to have it*. That's all it took. That's the other thing the market will bear. No explanations.

But, his wind now back, Dino Paradise had to explain. "I have every record I want. I could give you my only copy of 'Mr. Sunshine,' and I would've, you saw me, and I would still have every fuckin' record I want. Until your sistah called me last week, I was done collecting. Had been for a while. Six years too late for the ex-wife, but that's another fuckin' story. That guy in Germany paid ten Gs for my favorite band—That's right, I wasn't dry-humpin' you with the 'Ringo' shit. You guys are the nuts. The complete sack—and I was done. What's the fuckin' point? Now your dick is bigger, Hans? I looked around and asked myself what's left for Dino and his shit-the-bed flea-market life here in Ahhlington?"

"Buying a vacuum?" said Lizzie.

"Good one. She's fuckin' smaht, like you, Timmy. Why don't you two look alike?" Neither of them knew how to answer that. Lizzie was from wherever the fairer, more petite side of Eastern Europe lay. Her brother, dark and now bordering on cuddly, had, at various times, been mistaken for her accountant, super, or weird downstairs neighbor. Never her brother. "Fuckin' smaht," Dino went on. "So, she calls me and diddy-wah diddy, it came to me. What's left for Dino is to *create something*. Fuckin' create something."

Tim was shaking his head, as if he had an invisible pair of headphones on and was still grooving to "It's Cold Outside." Tim wanted nothing better than to join Dino Paradise on this delusional journey as ill-fitting as his jeans. But he knew the personalities involved. There was a reason his wife, Cheryl, had dubbed him Most Acquiescent Man in Middlesex County. Here he was, nimbly at it again. Going along with Dino, while shaking his head, already hearing "NO!" from the others.

"Love to do it, Dino," he said, "but it'll never happen."

"I know everything about you guys. You're the one they listen to."

"Hardly."

"Well, you're the one who gets along with everyone."

"Gotcha," said Lizzie.

Tim didn't need to go through it again in his mind. The RSVPs would not change. Thiel—yes. In a second, yes. Jerry—yes. If there was money in it, yes. Brian—yes, on one condition. No Richie. Richie—absolutely no. Okay, yes on two conditions. Some girl to pay attention to him. And one other. What was it? Oh yeah, no Brian.

But it was fun thinking about it. The Truants drummer exhaled in 4/4 time. The carbon dioxide of the Most Acquiescent Man in Middlesex County.

"Dino," said Tim, "run it by me again."

And Dino ran it by them again. A week of rehearsal. Okay, three days. A half-hour set in Cambridge at the Inn Square Men's Bar, opening for one of the two hundred local bands that owed him a favor. Twenty minutes with Dicky Dunitz on WBCN playing tracks from *Out of Site*. Two sets Friday night as part of "GarageApalooza," a one-night '60s underground rock festival which was at the moment at least two other bands and a venue short of reality, and a concept that had not existed forty-five minutes before Tim and Lizzie had been enveloped by his couch.

"And we tape everything," Dino added, "but you know it's all a rub-fuck to get to June twelfth." June 12. The thirtieth reunion at Chase Academy. "That's when we load the van and the Truants return to the fuckin' homeland. I'm telling you, if I could still get it up, I'd ruin these dungarees."

"Uh, Dino?" said Tim.

"Wait. Here's the best part. Guess who's at the reunion?"

"Someone who can get it up?" Lizzie asked.

"Close . . . The German guy."

"The guy who bought the album for ten grand?"

"Shit yeah."

"Why would he be there?"

"Lizzie, he has to be there," said Dino. "He's a collectah."

Tim jumped in. "Speaking of collecting, what was this my sister was telling me about you needing money from us?"

"Look around you, Timmy. Look at this place. Look at me. Do I look like Whitey fuckin' Bulger, rolling guys with winning lotto tickets? Do I have a tan? Do you see any jewelry?"

"How much are we talking about? I work for the state."

"Like a grand."

"A grand?"

"From each of you."

"So," Tim said, "five grand."

"And I don't need it until May. What kind of a fuckin' con man could I be if I don't ask for the money up front? Let me set everything up first, then, when we get everyone together, you help defray some of the costs. That's all. Defraying, man. And for that bullshit risk, you're in for a bigger taste off the reissue CD with the bonus tracks."

"Uh-huh . . ."

"Which means that you get your money back in two years rather than three. Of course, if we bag the fuckin' German guy, we all make a little."

"Uh-huh . . ."

"Look, you know how I feel about the Truants. Me, and the fuckin' German guy. And a couple othah whack-job collectahs. But until we put this out there a little further, it's, you know what it's like, Timmy?"

"I know what it sounds like," he said. "It sounds like fantasy camp."

Dino yelped. "THAT'S WHAT I WAS JUST GOING TO FUCKIN' SAY! Come on. You're one of me. Admit it. Fuckin' embrace it."

"Descartes," muttered Lizzie.

The head shaking began again, but now all Tim could think about was, Forget getting the other guys together, how about seven months for him to get $1,500 together? Yeah, $1,500. At least. What's five grand split three ways? At least $1,500. Richie and Thiel had it. Jerry could come up with it, then borrow $700 back to get home. Brian would give you a thousand-dollar story. Tim hadn't seen some of them in twenty-five years, but he was already assessing the necessary surcharge. The Truants had never divided anything equally. Credit, blame, solos, practice, support, shit that was funny, shit that wasn't, beer, booze, pot, No-Doz, secrets. And certainly not expenses. Why start now? Because time had passed? Hah! Time. Another pizza with eight slices for five.

"How long do I have to get the other guys?"

"End of Mahch," said Dino. "And I'm being nice."

"So, five months."

"But you'll be cahling me Christmas telling me we're all in. In fact, I'm inviting you and Lizzie and your families to Christmas dinnah he-yah. And the rest of the Truants."

Lizzie softened. "You do something every year with your family?"

"Shit no. My wife bolted in ninety, my kid's a quee-ah. I figured we'd order some chinks and watch the Bluebonnet Bowl."

So, March.

IT TOOK LIZZIE AND TIM THREE DAYS to find the time to meet again. They talked every day in the meantime, sometimes twice, mostly trying to outdo each other with their Dino Paradise impressions. Lizzie's Dino was by far superior, the combination of being around guys who tahked like that for ye-ahs waitressing at Gavin's, not being married, and not being married to someone who every time you lapsed into Bostonese would say under her breath, "So common."

Cheryl Shaw Schlesinger and Lizzie should have gotten along. No, they shouldn't have. Not in a million years. The adoring sister and the close-cropped, full-lipped Barnard babe four years younger, who had begun digging an emotional moat around Tim the day after they returned from the honeymoon in 1981. For the last fifteen years, the two relentlessly self-possessed gals had *détented*, Lizzie respectfully observing boundaries and Cheryl summoning her in-law cordiality on no more than a quarterly basis. Fine, Lizzie thought. Her brother seemed happy, even if from her distance it appeared his life was being managed like a zero-risk bond fund. And really, who was she to judge? A forty-three-year-old unmarried third-year med student/barmaid? Wait. Forty-three, unmarried, med student, *and* a barmaid? Well then, she was more than qualified to judge.

But she didn't, and although she knew Cheryl was as formidable a foe as age and ego in getting the Truants reunited, that was her brother's problem, not hers. So, they yakked on the phone, and when Tim's raucous, decades-melting laughter whiplashed to phone whispering, she really knew it was his problem.

They met at Gavin's Thursday night around 5:00 and talked while Tim helped his sister set tables for the bar's surprisingly loyal dinner trade. Tim would get whatever contact information he could from the Chase Academy Alumni Affairs Department and go from there. He was sure the data on Richie Lyman and John Thiel would be updated by the quarter hour. That's why those two were successful. The idea of the network? They got that. Not him. Tim Schlesinger '67 had left Chase and lost the address. He remembered telling Cheryl on an early date that it had never occurred to him to use prep school or college friends when he had originally pursued a career in sales before realizing after ten years it involved way too much interpersonal contact. "I think that's sweet and honorable," she said, "but you gotta grow the fuck up." In fact, the Chase people probably didn't know he was married, unless Thiel had blabbed.

If Chase had nothing on Brian Brock, Tim could probably track him down via the Internet. He knew Brian wafted around in the ether of academia, so he would have left a reputable trail. Tim knew that like he knew he'd have to hire a private eye to locate Jerry Fyne, although he could try Jerry's brother, who had been class of '69, two years behind them. What was his name? Another question for the folks in alumni affairs.

He was not looking forward to that call. Tim would hang on too long, and the alumni geeks would end up asking the questions, at least half a dozen involving the phases "capital drive," "endowment fund," and "your continued support." But he had to make the phone call. He had to grow the fuck up.

Lizzie agreed with him that John Thiel was the first guy they needed to get onboard. Absolutely. You go where you're wanted.

"I think he's still practicing in Scarsdale. I'll get the number and call him."

"Maybe you should go down there," she said.

"We."

"We go down there?"

"Yeah."

"What do you need me for?"

"So I don't get talked out of this."

"Okay, but when?"

Tim folded another napkin. "When I can think of a lie."

Lizzie did not respond. His problem. "Isn't Richie Lyman in the city?"

"Yeah, so?"

"We might as well see him while we're there."

"No. I gotta get Johnno first. You don't know the whole story. I've thought about this, and I can't even begin to approach anyone else until I'm sure he's in. Then we'll go back to New York and talk to Richie."

"So," Lizzie screwed tact and restraint, "you'll have to think of two lies."

"At least," said Tim. He looked at his watch. 6:05. If he left now, he wouldn't be home in Bedford until at least ten-of. He had told his wife 6:30. Radiator overheating. In October? Come on. Dead battery. Dead battery because he left the parking lights on. That was good. Plausible. That was something.

Yeah. At least two lies. At least.

HE STOOD AT THE END OF THE HALL with hands on hips for effect. An effect that would go unnoticed.

"Fellas, what did we talk about?"

Three doors slammed, leaving one boy in the middle of the corridor, the fresh victim of a water-balloon attack.

"Dwight?"

"Come on, Mr. Brock. Tomorrow's Friday."

"Which makes tonight Thursday night. All right, everybody out in the corridor!"

Fifteen other seventeen-year-olds silently competed to see who could coolly shuffle out last. It was about a twelve-way tie. Brian Brock began to talk, but it was a withered repeat of the speech he had given the previous Thursday night. There are classes on Friday *blehblehbleh*. You must have work to do for those classes *blehblehbleh*. I know *I* have work to get done for tomorrow *blehblehbleh*. I know Mr. Fabiani was much cooler about Thursday nights but I can't just black out at eight o'clock like he used to *blehblehbleh*. Didn't we have an agreement about the music and the horseplay?

Were the ancient Greeks the only ones to whom a moral contract *blehblehbleh* . . .

Brian stopped himself and tried the buddy approach. Again. "Maybe I'll be less of a hardass when I finish my thesis. You give me two more hours of quiet tonight, till eleven, and next Thursday, *next Thursday*, maybe I can work in a McDonald's run."

The whistles and high-fives were broken up by some future litigator. "Are you willing to put that in writing?"

"Yeah, Fleming. Stop by after eleven. Or send your secretary. It's Prentiss, isn't it?"

Louder whistles, oooohs, and high-fives. How about that? The forty-seven-year-old unmarried doctoral student/marathoner/house sitter with a resting pulse of thirty-six had just buried a wise-ass prep school junior. Chase Academy's foremost expert on the Latin lyric poet Propertius wheeled on his Adidas flip-flops and headed back to his apartment at the end of the corridor. The hall cleared and he stood in front of his door for another two minutes until the room tone settled.

"Thanks, guys."

A cyber game firing up roared.

"That's a little loud with the computer," he half-pleaded.

A door slammed.

"Thank you."

Brian Brock had lost only ten minutes of desk time with the scene on the corridor. His corridor. Donnelly II. Donnelly Hall, second floor. He lost the next hour giving himself shit in the privacy of his own apartment. The corridor master's quarters.

The thesis. He had to bring up the thesis. What was that thing he'd said? *Maybe I'll be less of a hardass when I finish my thesis.* Good Christ. Like he just had to proofread the last chapter before sending it out to Kinko's. Who the fuck was he kidding, besides everyone?

Such self-examination for Brian was rare. Rare as the loss of his privacy. Rare as his new home address. It had all gone sideways in the last month. What had been the latest rent-free tryst in a torrid twenty-four-year affair with the academic calendar—house-sitting the well-stocked cottage of Chase Academy's sabbaticaled "poet-in-residence" in exchange for one forty-minute class in *The Aeneid* and two hours in the afternoon as the rabbit for the cross-country team—had turned like fall foliage.

The poet, some fop with the wince-optional name of V. V. Crispin, had hobbled back to his poeting residence to convalesce after rupturing his Achilles tendon chasing a pickpocket at the Brighton train station. It was almost an awkward situation, but Crispin returned to an empty cottage. Two days before, Fabiani had the good taste and timing to go into alcoholic shock during his fourth-period trigonometry class. Between detox, rehab, and administrative spin, he might be back at Chase in six weeks. And if all went v.v. well with V. V. Crispin's recovery, his Achilles would only sulk in its tent for another month or so.

Until then, Brian Brock, the only man on-site who could correctly inflect delirium tremens and knowingly laugh at the wicked irony of another man's reference to Achilles sulking in his tent, had new digs. Living in a dormitory for the first time since My Lai. Thirty-one years, and thirty-four feet from his old room, junior year at Chase Academy, Donnelly II-14.

Other than the otherwise foreign pangs of unexpected upheaval, the actual move, like the hundreds of moves before it, was nothing. All of Brian's worldly possessions could fit in the trunk of his 1994 Chevy Lumina. He was curiously proud of that fact. So much so that he would introduce it as soon as possible into his first exchange with anyone. *("How was your trip?"* / *"Fine. Just me and my 1994 Chevy Lumina and all my earthly possessions. . . ."* *"Do you think the economy can survive the Whitewater scandal?"* / *"Speaking as someone who can fit all his worldly possessions in the trunk of his 1994 Chevy Lumina, I'm hardly an authority. . . .")* It made great sense given the need to pursue free, tasteful, scholastic-based lodging unfettered. Upheaval, that was standard issue in the engine of any house sitter. But this, this unannounced eviction and administrative quarantine in a, ugh, dormitory, herding seventeen-year-olds no less, was not house-sitting. It was bivouacking. And it was beneath Brian Brock, B.A. Trinity '71, M.A. Northwestern '73, Yale Divinity '77, M.A. Iowa '81, Lumina '94. Almost as much as paying a monthly rate for a motel room.

"That's still a little loud!"

But he would be a good sport.

"Fellas! Loud! *(door slam!)* Thank you!"

The setup in Donnelly was temporary, and if there was one concept the house sitter had to embrace with religious adhesion, even a house sitter without paperwork from Yale Divinity, it was the notion of finite space over a finite time in an unending, infinite universe. The good-sport thing was essential as well, if one wanted to be eligible for the next finite space.

No one had to tell Brian to be a good sport even once. Nineteen ninety-six on the calendar and he was still New Frontier clean and Peace Corps polite. This was the guy you brought home to meet the folks. Especially if the folks had a summer place in the country. This was the guy who, by 10:00 P.M. the first Friday of the first weekend, had let the girlfriend's father beat him twice at pool and oxford shirt/chinos/no socks/loafered the mother into thinking he might run away with her. Especially if the mother could run away to a two-bedroom Cape with a deck overlooking the ocean. Either ocean. In or off-season. That's just how good a sport he was.

A dozen or so years ago, while teaching expository writing during summer school at Lake Forest College, Brian opened a class by reading Edwin Arlington Robinson's classic poem "Richard Cory," the seemingly perfect man who commits suicide. He was trying to show his students the concept of a succinct beginning, middle, and end. "Thoughts?" he asked, and a hand in the back went up.

"This guy Cory reminds me of you, Mr. Brock," the student said. "But without, you know, the bullet in the head." Brian never forgot it. Too good a story. And as the years rolled on and his worldly possessions were en-trunked and disen-trunked, Lake Forest became the University of Wisconsin, summer school expository writing became a graduate seminar in verse, and the "bullet in the head" line was now delivered *to* the student *by* him. Dynamite ice-breaker. Some guy who'd interviewed too many pseudo-pseudos for some third-rate grant would ask, "So, Mr. Brock, tell us a little about yourself," and Brian would have the Cory story loaded and cocked like he was doing panel on a talk show.

Another water balloon, another door slam. More laughter. More shushing. More laughing.

Brian pushed his chair back from whatever he hadn't been working on and changed into his Detroit Country Day gym shorts, Gazelle International T.C. sweatshirt, and privately financed running shoes. The shorts were old-school short, but everything else hung a little bit. Brian had always been thin. First, nerd thin, now runner thin. Although now, in his late forties, clean, single, living in an all-boys dorm, his fit leanness was the source of whispers rather than envy.

Brian checked the batteries on his FM Walkman. He didn't want to hear the boys weakly try to be quiet as he left.

The main road sloped down to the lower level of athletic fields. The quarter-mile cinder oval was lit better than well by the moon. The original *Lumina*. He did a light, easy stretch, cut short when the Oldies-111 jingle singers came in over his headphones:

"The hits we re-mem-ber, nineteen sixty-SIX . . ."

He was off and in stride by the eighth bar. He had to be. The song was "Time Won't Let Me" by the Outsiders.

I ca-an't wait for-ever
Even though you-ou want me to.
I ca-an't wait for-ever
To-oo know if you'll be-ee true . . .

For the next hour, or ten miles, or fourteen favorites from the '50s, '60s, and '70s, Brian Brock passed time and distance in the way he relished. Running and singing. Hard and loud. Perfect in pace and in pitch. He couldn't do this with the cross-country team or in the light of marathon-training day. So, at night, alone, belting all the parts but praying for Beach Boys or Smokey Robinson to flex his falsetto. Never at a loss for wind. Running and singing. The thing he did the best. Maybe the thing he did better than anybody else. But there was no way to check that. So, no one would know. Just like the songs he had written years ago. Why bring it up? Why confuse things? Why make a big deal of that part of his past when the deal might be too big to fit in the trunk of a '94 Lumina?

Time won't let me—no!
Time won't let me—whoa, no!
Time won't let me-eee-eee-eee
Ah-wait that long.

MAYBE.

Maybe, but Jesus, let's not get ahead of ourselves here and actually think it, things are going right this time. That would make it the first time in a while for Jerry. A while. Like since Super Bowl XX a while.

The plane was fifteen minutes early, and the weather was that February eighty-eight degrees and sunny Caribbean bullshit that will make the most negative guy feel like he conned the solar system. No check-in hassle at JFK. None foreseen here at Grand

Cayman Island. And was that his ride he saw as the plane taxied in? A fat guy in a Hawaiian shirt standing by a 1983 Skylark? Perhaps. Or maybe it was the fat guy in the Hawaiian shirt standing by the Skylark next to him.

Okay, the legs were a little stiff from the flight. And sweaty. Maybe his choice of clothing: sweatpants over four rolls of Elastoplast athletic tape. He had rehearsed with duct tape, but quickly realized that although it held the cash down, it had no give. Zero. Show up at the international terminal swaddled in that shit and the next thing he'd hear would be *"Frankenstein, pick up the white courtesy phone. Frankenstein, to the white . . ."*

The Elastoplast had the give of an Ace bandage. And it breathed a bit. And when you added the crutches and the pained look, suddenly everyone in Terminal 8 was pulling off to the side for the "guy coming through."

Sure, Elastoplast is a pricier item, but when you've got a million bucks taped to your legs, price should not be a concern. It could have been worse. He could have had to cough up another $40 for the crutches. But Jerry already had his own pair. Actually, he had two. Classic wood, and lightweight aluminum for one of those post-telethon, "Wait a minute. How can I *not* have this thing?" days. Standard issue for a hypochondriac. Like the pained look.

Jerry Fyne. Hypochondriac. Degenerate gambler. Equal addict. Wrong billing. It should be Degenerate gambler, Equal addict, Hypochondriac.

The million dollars taped to his legs represented neither winnings nor losings. It couldn't. It wasn't his money. It was an errand. An Internet gambling site (www.lockcity.com) in the Caymans needed a 5-foot, 11-inch balding Elastoplast wallet and guess who volunteered? Come on, guess.

It was a pretty good travel package. Round-trip air, two nights on somebody's floor near the beach, $35,000 wiped off a $40,000 tab, and no ass-kicking in exchange for the remote risk of some moderate jail time. A risk that was now being lifted as Jerry was waved through baggage claim and crutched himself into the light of almost getting straight with his bookie.

Wham. Sun. Migraine.

Unnoticed, his pained look glided from dramatic to real. He ducked back inside, into the men's room. The two light blue packets came out of his pocket. No cups. In one move, he tore the top off with his teeth and threw the crystals to the back of his throat. He took two good gulps of tepid water. How do people go four hours without this stuff?

Jerry Fyne liked to tell anyone that there were three things he'd never paid for in his life: Equal, Wite-Out, and pussy. That may have been his best joke. And the fact that it started out with an innocent premise and raced to an inappropriate end, well, cancel the biographer, we're done.

"Señor Feeb?"

"That's me," said Jerry, acknowledging his gambling nickname. Heeb Feeb. "Where we going?"

"What do you care?"

"You have a point."

"Get in the car."

"Is there someplace where I can get an iced tea?"

"In the car."

The fat guy in the Hawaiian shirt (not one of the two he saw taxiing in; completely different shirt) grabbed his knapsack and Samsonite roller and let Jerry crutch his way across the lot to the least filthy 1974 maroon Buick Regal.

Jerry tossed down another three packets of Equal on the way to wherever it was none of his business they were going. Normally, one packet fifteen minutes after the last one would have been enough. But he made the mistake of opening the floor to his favorite topic of small talk.

"You see this shit?" he said, holding the empty packet up to the fat guy. "I live on this shit. Can't stop. I know it's bad, but what am I gonna do, sugar?" Nothing. *"Como se dice* this here? *Egal? Igual? No mas asucar?"*

"Sweet'n Low," said the fat guy.

"No, pal. That's the pink stuff. I don't use that. Saccharine. Aftertaste. Bullshit. Feh!"

"That's all we got here, *amigo.*"

"Are you sure?"

"Hey, Señor Feeb, look at me. You think I don't know the difference, man?" He grabbed the empty packet. *"Igual.* Equal. Blue, right? *No azul.* No blue. On the whole island. *Solamente rosado aqui.* Only the pink shit here."

Headache. That's when Jerry threw back the other two. There was no way he had brought enough to last two days. The second-to-last thing he had wanted to do on the flight down was get busted for grabbing spare packets from the drinks cart. Normally, he loved the *"Excuse me, sir. We're going to need those for the flight back. You can have two." / "How about ten?" / "Okay, but sit down and I'll bring them to you later"* banter with the flight attendant. It was almost like dating a stewardess. So, he faked a nap during beverage service. That was one reason why he hadn't had anything to drink. No score. The other was to avoid having to get up and go to the bathroom and do the Elastoplast lavatory lambada.

"What about Diet Coke?"

"We're here."

"Where is it?!?"

"No, Señor Feeb. We're here." Chico's Car Wash.

"Can I stay in the car? I love going through car washes. Especially if they do the hot wax. I guess you don't have that down here—"

"Get the fuck out."

Jerry had for the moment forgotten why he was where he was.

He did that a lot. Which meant people said, "Get the fuck out!" to him a lot.

The fat guy, whose Regal could have embraced the full services of Chico's Car Wash, led him into the manager's office. Another fat guy, another Hawaiian shirt.

"Good flight?"

"Yeah, great." Again, Jerry did that thing where he forgot why he was where he was. "Hey, pal, can I ask you something? What's the deal with no Equal on this island?"

"Pull your fucking pants down!"

The two fat guys each took a leg

"I'm a little sensitive," said Jerry. "This won't hurt that much, huh?"

"Nah. Not if you shaved."

"Uh, shaved?"

Jerry only screamed for a second or two. Fainting helped. The fat guys worked quickly. They had to. They had to pull the tape and the cash off before the blood hit the bills. There was just enough time in that window of hair yanked from skin and the clear red surge moving into the spot like angry new neighbors.

And there was a lot of blood. After the fat guys stowed the cash, the cologne and newspaper they used to weakly try and stop the flow did little except revive Jerry.

"Señor Feeb, we gotta take you to the hospital. Can you walk?"

"Ahhhhh! Shit no!"

"Get his crutches."

There are those who'll insist that there's nothing a hypochondriac enjoys more than when something is actually wrong with him. But it would probably be something other than both legs ripped raw, covered with newspaper, and smelling like an explosion at the Paco Rabanne plant.

The original fat guy set Jerry's Samsonite roller, then backpack, then Jerry, on the curb just before the entrance to the hospital. He stuffed a hundred-dollar bill in the pocket of his clot-riddled sweatpants and said, "Coral reef, *amigo*."

"Huh?"

"That's what you say if they ask how this happened. Coral reef."

"Are you leaving?"

"*Sí.*"

"So, no chance of running in and getting me a Diet Coke?"

"*Que?*"

"Diet Coke."

"What the fuck is wrong with you?"

That was usually a long answer for Jerry. He didn't have time right now. He didn't even have the time to say what he really wanted to say, which was, "I think I saw a machine inside. Come on, you're up." But the filthy Regal was gone.

THE REALTOR SCRAPED SOME PAINT off the doorknob with her fingernail while his back was to her.

"So, this is it. Cute. Perfect pied-à-terre for a man wearing a nice suit, like yourself. The only bad thing, the only bad thing, is you're next to the fire stairs. So, a little foot traffic from time to time."

"Like when there's a fire."

"Hah!" she said. "You're a cutie."

John Thiel smirked. "Don't try to soften me up, Mrs. Mallinson. It's still eleven-fifty, right?"

"Yeahyeah, eleven-fifty."

"Fine, then. Let's do it."

"You sure you don't want to see the one on twelve? Twelve M? It's a much better setup. Opposite end of the hall. Higher floor. Higher ceiling for a tall man like yourself. Dishwasher, alcove, and it's only thirteen twenty-five."

"Studio?"

"Are you ready?" The realtor paused. "One-bedroom!"

"Can't," said Thiel.

"Can't today?"

"Can't."

As she fumbled with the lock, they heard a set of quick feet up the stairs. The fire door opened and a man, same suit, ten years younger, fifteen years more disheveled, puffed at Thiel and then looked at his real estate agent.

"Misty?" the man said.

"Misty?" said Mrs. Mallinson. "Do I look like a fucking Misty?"

"HERE'S ALL YOU NEED TO KNOW about God. It ain't you."

Two decades sprung from divinity school, that was the entire contents of Brian Brock's spiritual stockroom. Nothing else remained, and inventory was still taken on a regular basis. *"Here's all you need to know about God. It ain't you."* September 1975. The Red Sox a month away from the World Series. New Haven. Day Two at Yale Div. The Reverend Daniel Toms. A year older than him with hair that worked in mysterious ways. That was this guy's opening line. And twenty-one years later, that line was all the evidence of a higher being Brian still had on him.

Did Brian Brock believe he was being taken care of? Is the pope fond of big hats? Does a house sitter shit in a dormitory?

And say, speaking of shit, what was this shit now? An hour ago, Brian had been hunched over the open trunk of the Lumina, looking for a new battery for his Walkman, about to escape, again, the male harpies who were killing another night on Donnelly-II. Ten o'clock and Academy Lane empty as a junkie's promise. Who walks by? That prick Widmare. Pardon. Assistant Headmaster Widmare. *"Shouldn't you be on your corridor, Mr. Brock?"* / *"Just grabbing my concordance."* / *"Little cool for running shorts."* / *"That's how I work."*

Then Widmare sees the keyboard. The goddamn motherless Yamaha piece of crap Brian hadn't touched since he lost the adapter in Lansing five years ago. Still worked. But you pay $10 for eight goddamn D batteries every month. *"Hey, nice keyboard. You play?"* / *"Uh, yeah."* / *"You know, we have a pretty nice organ in Pershing Auditorium."* / *"Sure. I know. I went here."* (Stop talking!) *"I used to play it during morning chapel."*

Then this is what happens when you don't look at bulletin boards in hallways. *"Hey! We were going to cancel morning chapel tomorrow and next Monday because Farnham is going to that glee club conference in St. Paul. Now we don't have to. Terrific. So, six forty-five then."*

Brian had tried to bring up the provisions of his deal at Chase, the good sport he was being about covering the dorm for Fabiani or how 6:45 A.M. hadn't existed for him since whenever was the last time he'd served a hitch at a church pancake breakfast. But that prick Widmare had said, "I'm keeping you from your charges," or some other prep prig conversation cork. He slammed the trunk of the Lumina as if that was the only way he could close it, walked back into Donnelly Hall, down the first-floor corridor, and out the fire exit in the rear.

That was an hour ago, the moment when Brian Brock decided that maybe he was no longer being taken care of by whoever it was that was not him.

The eight-mile run had shaken most of his fury, but not his will. He would not stay in Donnelly after the Thanksgiving break. He would not play the organ for anyone, let alone someone else's music, let alone "Lead On, O King Eternal." Or "Stand Up, Stand Up for Jesus." Or, what was that hymn that absolutely made his flesh crawl, even when he'd been an alleged believer? "I Sing a Song of the Saints of God." That was it. Great. Now that pious toe-tapper would be gyroscoping his consciousness for the next two days. He cranked up the Walkman, but "I'll Be

Doggone" in the headphones was no match for the catechismic noise in his head.

I sing a song of the saints of God,
Patient, brave and true.
Who toiled and fought and lived and died
For the Lord they loved and knew . . .

In the last hundred strides of his run, with Donnelly Hall in pain sight, some piece of the darkness swallowed his left leg and Brian collapsed mid-verse to what sounded like champagne being opened. The knee, again. Sprain? *Aw-fuck-yeeee!* No, really bad. Surgery bad.

And one was a doctor
And one was a priest
And one was slain by a fierce wild beast . . .

He lay there, briefly nurtured by the notion that he was justified in going ahead and feeling sorry for himself. And then it hit him: Sometime, sometime soon, I will be in a hospital bed. I will be out of the dorm. I will not be allowed to play the organ because of the cast on my leg. Maybe I will be on Demerol.

He sprang to his good foot and began the sixty-yard tear-studded hop back to Donnelly, where he would call an ambulance. Ideally, one with crowd-drawing lights. He couldn't request that. But the Demerol, that he could request.

Brian would have to be a fool not to know now. Know he was being taken care of. Suddenly, his hop was accompanied by the brave whistle of the song in his head.

And there's not any reason, no, not the least
Why I shouldn't be one too.

chapter four

JERRY STOPPED RUBBING SUNSCREEN on the top of his head and began coating his ear. "Do you know where I can find Pressure Chief?"

"Why," asked the kid, "are you looking for a waste of time?"

This was the third day Jerry had wandered the beach looking for this guy. Pressure Chief. The nurses had taken island pity on him and let him stay in the hospital for two weeks. Three days for the "coral reef" cuts to heal, and another eleven after he convinced them he had to detox from Equal. They had beds and he was funny. Funny, like they thought he was so fucked up he couldn't say "alcohol." He kept saying, "Equal." Every time.

Finally, the "alcohol/Equal" thing got old. But he was better. As better as Jerry Fyne got. Which was good, but broke. As opposed to good and broke.

"You should see my boyfriend, Pressure," said Delilah, the biggest, nicest, and potentially scariest of the nurses.

"Pressure?"

"Pressure Chief. He'll set you up."

"Where is he?"

"On the beach. He'll set you up."

Delilah gave him a full-color business card with her and an older, elegant-looking black man sitting in beach chairs with arms outstretched. No phone number. Only the words "Pressure Chief: I'll Set You Up."

It turns out Pressure Chief "set you up" by renting beach chairs, umbrellas, towels, rafts, masks, fins, snorkels, fishing poles, and, with twenty-four hours' notice, a twenty-four-foot catamaran. That is, when anyone could find him. It took Jerry three days of pacing the beach to find out "set you up" meant everything except what he thought it meant. Which was, "set you up" with work.

When he finally met the man, he realized why he had walked the beach so unsuccessfully. First, unlike the full-color photo on the business card, Pressure Chief was partially white. Second, Pressure Chief was partially white because of the flour.

"Delilah at the hospital told me you'd set me up."

"Who?" said Pressure Chief.

"Delilah. Your girlfriend."

"She not my girlfriend."

"What's she doing in this picture?" He showed Pressure the card.

"She gave me twenty dollars."

"*She* gave *you* twenty dollars to make up business cards?"

"Is that what she told you?"

"No."

"Because Pressure Chief don't have no girlfriend."

"I see."

"And Pressure Chief don't have no business card."

" 'kay."

"The oven is Pressure Chief's girlfriend."

"What?"

He turned to two local kids hanging out in front of Happy

Hooks Fish and Beer Shack. "*Como se dice* Pressure Chief's business card?"

"*Puto!*" the kids squealed. And every non-white and non-floured non-white squealed along with them.

Jerry Fyne had spent the largest portion of his life not being in on the joke, so this was familiar turf to him. Just sandier, with a bit of a tradewind.

"Delilah said you'd set me up."

"What do you want, mahn, a chair?"

"No, a job."

"You got twenty dollars?" Pressure asked.

"No. More like eight."

Pressure Chief laughed and beat some flour off his arms. "You really do want a job, mahn."

"Yeah. Come on," Jerry said, never above whining, "do it for Delilah."

"Who?"

"The woman in this picture."

"What did she say about me?"

Jerry, with more sunscreen than taste, went into a bad, bad Flip Wilson Geraldine impression. "'Talk to Pressure. He'll set you up.'"

"Nothing else?"

Jerry knew nothing else. But he did know a move to use when he knew nothing else. Picked it up from years of hanging around wise guys and near-wise guys. "You mean," he said, "the other thing?"

"Yeah. Did she mention my baking?" Pressure Chief had bit. "Or something else?"

The flour, thought Jerry. Go with baking. "No, the baking. That was the first thing she said. I forgot to, ah, mention that."

Pressure Chief smiled, turned toward the ocean, licked the flour off his fingers, then stuck them back in his mouth and whistled loud as a lesbian trucker. Two ten-year-old boys trying to surf on what looked like half a door reacted as if a shark horn had sounded and were back on the beach scurrying toward him in less than a minute. It took both of them to drag the piece of wood.

"Okay, you're hired," Pressure Chief told Jerry. "You're in charge of advertising."

The boys turned their surfboard over:

PRESSURE CHIEF						
Chairs	$10	Deluxe Chairs	$12	Umbrellas		$8
Rafts	$5	Mask & Fins	$11	Snorkels		$5
Fishing Rod	$10	Bait	$1	Fish Cleaning		3 fish
Kayak	$20	Sailboat		$50 (plus deposit)		
Cakes, pies, breads, pastries $2/piece						
Anything Else? Ask Pressure!!! (plus deposit)						

The saltwater had worn the lettering down to where the prices could only be read by someone standing six inches away and out of the sun. Which, Pressure Chief pointed out, made everything negotiable.

"You carry the sign around the beach. Hustle up business."

"Where's the stuff?"

"Oh, Pressure has the stuff."

Jerry realized he would have to break a promise over two decades old. No lifting for others. The only thing he would pick up of his own free will was a bass guitar and an amp. And, since he'd hocked his amp fifteen years ago to keep Con Ed off his ass, that left just the bass. That was it.

Until now. This gig with Pressure Chief looked like nothing but lifting, starting with this sign.

"What's a deluxe chair?"

"One with a cushion."

"How many do you have without cushions?"

"Right now?"

"Yeah."

"Zee-ro."

"So, when people ask for a regular chair, I'm supposed to say, 'We're out of regular chairs. But I'll give you a deluxe chair at the regular price.'"

"Pressure thinks you've done this before."

"Yeah," said Jerry. "Just now."

Everything was negotiable, except Pressure's terms. Jerry would get 25 percent of all the rentals, but not the cakes, pies, breads, and pastries. For that, his cut was zee-ro. But he would get all the cakes, pies, breads, and pastries he could eat. Plus a place to sleep, which turned out to be one of the deluxe beach chairs in Pressure Chief's storage shed, a mere three hundred meters from the beach.

"How far is three hundred meters?" Jerry asked.

"You know the hundred meters in the Olympics?"

"Yeah."

"Three of those."

Jerry figured if he hustled, really hustled, really busted his ass, actually suspended his hypochondria to where he could accept that the pain came from actual labor, he could have the money for a return flight to JFK in a month. Six weeks tops. Now . . . when was the last time he'd hustled? Thirty-three years ago. Brook Ridge C.C. Some asshole named Reverend Daly, who paid him three bucks for the round, slapped him on the back as they walked off the 18th green and said, "Shalom, boy."

"Okay, you got yourself a gofer. But I'll need some money up front. Just to have."

"You have eight dollars."

"I could use twenty."

Pressure Chief licked his fingers and whistled again. The two boys who had been surfing with the sign were busy throwing jellyfish at each other. They stopped, and he yelled some island idiom at them. They ran off.

"Give me ten minutes."

"Okay. I'll wait here."

"Why don't you try to make Pressure some money in the meantime?"

Like a guy who was used to doing what he was told, which would be just about anyone else, Jerry grabbed the edge of the sign and felt his lower back laugh. Pressure turned and disappeared into the back of Happy Hooks. Jerry flipped the sign end over end to the nearest shade. Maybe thirty meters. He leaned against a tree in his now-cut-off sweatpants, thinking first about who he could hire to do this, then thinking he could use a nap. Five minutes later, the two boys returned, dragging a woman clearly on vacation. Freckling, giggling, and drunk. They led her to the back of Happy Hooks. The bigger boy, by about three-quarters of an inch, knocked on the door, then they both ran away.

Pressure Chief emerged, freshly floured. The woman handed him what looked like a twenty. He stuffed it in his shirt pocket, beat the flour off his hands, and opened his bathing suit. The woman stopped giggling, screamed, stopped screaming, looked again, screamed again, and ran screaming and giggling back to the freckling alcohol-drenched land from whence she had come. The regulars at Happy Hooks did not look up from their beers or fried fish, although a couple gave polite golf-type applause as Pressure pulled the drawstring on his suit and headed for Jerry's tree.

Jerry was no longer thinking about a nap. "What the hell you got in there?"

Pressure Chief handed him the twenty. "Business card," he said.

"MRS. THIEL ON LINE TWO."

"Mrs. Thiel? Okay, thanks, Laz." Richie half-cleared his throat.

"Hello, Mrs. Thiel? Richie Lyman, Johnno's attorney. I went to prep school with your husband."

"This is amazing."

"What?"

"I was predisposed not to like you, and in your first ten words to me you've managed to piss me off an additional four times."

"Don't tell me, let me guess. Calling myself 'Richie,' calling your husband 'Johnno,' and invoking the phrase 'prep school.' Help me. I can't come up with the fourth."

"Johnno's *attorney*."

"I thought that was part of the predisposition not to like me."

"It was."

"Well, it shouldn't count twice."

"So, fucking sue me."

Richie chuckled. "Maybe when things slow up after the holidays."

Gail Thiel might have laughed in a previous marriage. "Look, dipshit, my Palm Pilot died and I'm running out of anytime minutes. Can you just give me my husband's new phone number?"

"Sure. I've got it right here. Hey, what do you say we dump Johnno and I represent you in this case? I forgot what a drag the guy is. He was like that in the band—"

"HEY!"

"JL five-eight-seven-two-two. You know I'm kidding . . . hello?" Richie laughed. Divorce lawyers never hang up first. Check that. Divorce lawyers never *get* to hang up first. The good ones, anyway.

Richie looked at his desk. All clear, except for the Wednesday envelope from Fran Brennan.

BY NOON, ALL FOUR OF TIM'S COWORKERS had come up to him and said either "Is everything all right?" or "Are we all right?"

That's what happens when people are used to walking by your office and seeing you in a staring contest with your computer. They are not used to seeing you on the phone, energized and animated, like, like some, like some *salesman*. Not here. Not here at the Central Repository for State Government Publications. The Mass. *Ah*chives. A two-thousand-square-foot dilettante hatchery that would make a Christian Science Reading Room look like Bourbon Street.

Every time anybody wrote a document, pamphlet, guide, or book that would be used by a government agency in Massachusetts, five copies had to be sent to the central repository, where they were catalogued and stored wherever they stored all that shit. Tim didn't really know. He could tell you when you called if they had your document and when they got it and that all five copies were safe, but everyone couldn't get in a van and ride over to see it, like some antique watch in a safe-deposit box. Not that any of that was ever a problem. Nobody called. The central repository was a protocol nuisance. You dropped your five copies off wordlessly. Which was what made this place, the *Ah*chives, so inviting for Tim and the five people under him. Like working at the morgue without all the formaldehyde.

Quiet. Bureaucratic quiet. The gurgle of small talk, the pitchless hum of fluorescent lights, the occasional techno yelp of a misstruck keyboard. All raising their hands to interrupt the real room tone: That silent ticking of the meter running on a sweet state pension. The unspoken brandy snifter atop every civil servant's piano. *Benefits*. The glue that held your feet fast and your eyes front. *"What do you do?"* / *"I work for the state."* / *"Oh . . ."* "Oh. . . ." Might as well be, "What are you in for?"

It is unfair to say Tim Schlesinger had been hiding here for nineteen years. It's not hiding if more than four people know where to find you. So, don't call it hiding. It's unfair, and it's uncivil. And one should never be uncivil to a civil servant.

And not to be uncivil, but who the fuck was this guy on the phone? Laughing and cajoling and being excited? And a lot of "That would be great, man."

And lying. Phone lying. Saying, "Hey, I just got off the phone with Johnno," when he hadn't talked to Johnno on the phone since Lennon was shot. Which isn't bad, considering he hadn't spoken with Brian since they went 302 and 305 out of 366 in the 1970 draft lottery.

Hadn't until now, that is. The weirdest thing. Tim made his first call, the easier one, the mildly confrontational one, to the Chase Academy Alumni Office. Within a painless few seconds, he had phone numbers and addresses for Richie Lyman Esq., Park Avenue, Manhattan, and Dr. John Thiel, Scarsdale or Madison Avenue, Manhattan. Jerry Fyne's last known address came up Social Director, Plifkah Bungalow, Catskill Mountains. However, his little brother Howard, class of '69, was a board of trustees wet dream with a capital capital drive. Howie Fyne was the model class agent, a loyal pest who biannually hectored his former classmates for donations and every three months sent the alumni newsletter, a manifesto of aggressively trivial notes from the class of '69 *(Bart Mattoon and Pud Dunbar ran into each other on the same lift line at Mount Mansfield last President's Day!)* from his home/office just across the border in Methuen, Massachusetts. Forty-five minutes north of the Central Repository for State Government Publications.

"Is that it?" the lady in the alumni office asked Tim.

"Just one more from my class. Brian Brock."

"Hah! Hold on." She put the phone down, which was odd. For the other numbers, it had been "Hold on" and then the clattering of computer keys to which only a fellow clatterer like himself could tune out. This time, Tim heard footsteps.

"Hello?"

"Hello?"

"This is Brian Brock."

"Holy shit, it is!"

"Who's this?"

"Tim Schlesinger."

"Holy shit. It is!"

How could this be? "What the fuck are you doing there?"

"I just came from the infirmary."

"What do you have, a twenty-nine-year case of bronchitis?"

"You could tell if I had bronchitis," said Brian.

"How?"

"I'd sound like you trying to sing."

That was the first time the coworkers at the Mass. *Ah*chives heard Tim say "Fuck you . . . No, *fuuuuuck yooouuuu* . . ." That phrase they recognized. Not from him, but they recognized it. It was the other word that kept coming up during his subsequent phone play. *Hoodsie.* That, like this guy talking on the phone, was new.

At first, Brian tried to handle the call as if Tim was some dean interviewing him for a grant next semester. His standard rap. The elusive chase of his doctoral dissertation. The false starts with Tibullus and Cassius Dio before settling on "elegy's brilliant step-child," Sextus Propertius. The worldly possessions. The Lumina. The marathons. The resting pulse. The Richard Cory story. And it would have gone on if Tim hadn't said, "Brian, I think if Propertius were here today, he'd say, 'Fuck you.'"

"No, fuck you."

"No, *fuuuuuck yooouuuu* . . ."

He still had to get Brian's attention. As the hiatused house sitter revved himself up for Chapter 2 of his curriculum vitae ad nauseam, The Fold-Out Couch Years, Tim falsely segued, "Speaking of writing, you still banging out songs on the piano?"

Brian jammed his brakes. "Who wants to know?"

Then Tim tried without panting to lay out the German collector/$10,000/Dino Paradise/Truants reunion saga scenario. He got as far as, "So, this guy wants us to get ba—" And that's when the phone lying had to begin.

"Tim, I have to talk to Thiel. Have you spoken with him?"

"Uh, I just got off the phone with Johnno."

"What did he say?"

"Brian, don't be a Hoodsie."

"Is that what he said?"

"No," said Tim, "that's what I said."

"But what did Johnno say? What was his tone like? Does he know I desperately have to speak with him?"

Tim laughed. "How old are you?" he asked. But it was too late. Brian was already back there.

"Hey, Timmy, you know what lunch was yesterday?"

"What?"

"Libby's canned peaches."

"Huh?"

Brian said it slowly. "LLLLLLibbbbbbbeeeeeees cannnnnnnned-duh peachezzzzzzz!"

"Yeah?"

"Remember?"

And Tim did remember. He remembered Brian Brock was nuts.

TIM HAD HUNG UP BEFORE BRIAN COULD get Thiel's phone number. Thiel would call him. Isn't that what Tim had said? But when? And at what number? Here at the alumni office? At the infirmary? Donnelly Hall? Shit, no. Not Donnelly. Maybe he should call Tim back right now.

"Brock, how's that knee?" He didn't even have to turn around. Assistant Headmaster Widmare.

"I'll never be able to play the organ again. Or at least until Farnham gets back from the glee-club conference, whichever comes first."

"Are you getting around okay?"

"I'm not sure. This is the first day I've been out of bed since I had the thing scoped."

"Well, I'll tell you what let's try," Widmare said. "Why don't you try to stretch it out by walking with your crutches over to the main school building and taking Hohner's third-period sophomore English class. It's only two doors down from your fourth-period Vergil. And after lunch you can rest up, back in your room at Donnelly."

The fucking dorm. But first things first.

"Sir, I know nothing about American literature."

"Nothing? Surely you must have studied the early writers— Emerson, Thoreau—while you were a sophomore here."

"As a matter of fact, that was the last time. Thirty-three years ago."

"Then this should be a real challenge. Actually, it shouldn't be for a literature scholar such as yourself."

"This is not my field."

"Well, Latin isn't my field, but I managed to muddle through Troy with your ragged bunch the last two days in your stead."

"With all due respect," Brian sighed, "this is not part of my agreement here at Chase."

"You do like to point that out."

"Well, it is—"

"You know," smiled Widmare, "you have an astonishingly clear and rigid sense of what you're supposed to do and not supposed to do. It's admirable. And yet, twenty-four years later, how far are we along on that doctoral dissertation?"

"Sir—"

"—You have twenty-five minutes until third period. That's not twenty-four years, but it is enough time to get yourself prepared. I mean, I was able to prepare for your Vergil class in twenty minutes, and I only have one master's."

Widmare turned away before his smile could get any bigger and walked out of the alumni office. Brian Brock threw down his crutches like an evangelist's shill and propped himself up to look at the computer screen. He would not have to figure out the code. The name was already there:

Thiel, Dr. John ('67)
326 Madison Avenue
New York, New York
(212) 555-3334

He chanted "326 Madison" under his breath as he tried to bend down and pick up the crutches. *Ow.* It took three squats. The orthopedist in Nashua who'd done the scope said most people would have pain for three weeks, but because he was "a bit of an athlete," he'd be 80 percent after ten days. Three weeks, ten days. He had neither. *Time won't let me-eeeeeee-eeeeeeee, ah-wait that long.*

He stopped back next door at the infirmary to act like he was getting his overnight bag. Which he was, but the main purpose of his visit was to check the corner of his prescription bottle to make sure under "Demerol" it said "Refills: 2." It didn't. "Refills: 1." Like his options.

"Going back to the dormitory, Mr. Brock?" asked the nurse.

"Yes, Miss Coates."

"You could leave your medication here and come by when you need it."

"Nah. They kill my stomach."

"Then leave them here."

Brian deftly redid his tie while leaning on the crutches, and ladled his best lacquer of grad-student charm. "Miss Coates, you wouldn't deprive a Chase alum and career straight arrow the chance to flush some pills down his own toilet, would you?"

"Of course not."

"This has been a wonderful three days, but I hope it's the last time we see each other professionally." That, he meant. "Oh my, it's ten of. I don't want to be unprepared for Hohner's sophomores."

Brian wheeled on his crutches, and Miss Coates went from nursing back to her medicine: The prose of Jackie Collins. If she had listened, she might have heard the belch of the water cooler in the hallway. And twenty minutes after that, a car engine muttering much too anxiously for this time of the morning.

JOHN THIEL DECORATED HIS NEW STUDIO apartment with a bed, a lamp, a chair, and a cardboard dresser from Ikea. And two signs he made himself. One was affixed to the back of the front door. It read: "STOP TELLING PEOPLE WHAT YOU DO!" The other was taped to the cord of his phone, where it hung like a UL warning label. It read: "DO NOT THROW PHONE THROUGH OR OUT WINDOW!"

In two decades as a physician, Thiel knew, but had yet to learn. What he knew was whenever you tell someone, anyone, you're a doctor, their next question is "What kind of doctor?" And whenever you tell someone, anyone, "Dermatologist," they don't have a next question right away. They're too busy rolling up sleeves, pulling down collars, or dropping their pants. That's right, middle of a cocktail party, the *bipbipbipbipbipbip* of small talk, "dermatologist" is uttered, down go the trou. Then comes the next question. *"What is this?"*

Oh yeah. And the pants dropper? It's always a guy. And always the last or second-to-last guy in the room you want with his pants down. And you can't go anywhere, because you're holding his drink. Always.

STOP TELLING PEOPLE WHAT YOU DO!

No scion of Hippocrates has it worse than a dermatologist. The outside world is nothing but one continuous oral pop quiz in your chosen field. What Thiel wanted to do, just once, okay, every time someone showed him some skin infraction, was jump back, turn his head away, suck in saliva, and yell, "Run for your lives, it's Reptillicus!" But he wasn't that kind of guy. Thiel was the kind of guy who might be able to say, "*What kind of doctor? I'm a doctor who refers people to other doctors.*" If only he could remember the line. He knew, but he had to learn.

The sign on the door was five years old. It was the only thing he'd taken from the Scarsdale house besides his clothes and his black Les Paul ax. The phone sign was brand new. In eleven years of marriage, he had only thrown two phones out the window. Unfortunately, it happened twelve days apart. He had taken enough math to know that might be considered a trend.

John Thiel, with his sandy-haired wits and subtle swagger, had succeeded at almost everything in his life, except getting angry. He used to tell his wife, back when Gail was still sympathetic, "I lose my temper once every two years, and it's always at some guy who was just in a car accident." And Gail would say, "Oh come on. I've seen you get angry," in her best this-conversation-bores-me voice.

Six weeks ago, she saw him get angry. It was the two dozenth discussion about separating. He wouldn't. The dozenth about seeing a marriage counselor. She wouldn't. What about individually? *Why?* What if you just called and made an appointment? *Why?* Because it's important. *To you.* Well then, do it for me. *Right now, you're the last person I'd do it for.* Here's the number, just make the call. *You dial it.* Okay . . . here. *You're fucking pathetic. (CRASH) Good, John. Now you can work on your vacuuming.*

Thiel had a good arm. Still. Varsity baseball sophomore and junior year at Chase before he was lured by his hockey teammates to his true athletic calling—lacrosse. His one season as a rangy midfielder was eye-opening enough to get traditional college lacrosse factories Johns Hopkins, Cornell, and Virginia fighting for his services. He ended up at Hopkins, figuring he could save some money four years later just moving his couch across the street to the med school. Which was the way he planned it, and the way it went.

Two concussions sophomore year, both unplanned, ended the collegiate career he wanted and the military career he dreaded (which is another story, but when you look like the son of a decorated navy pilot and don't become a decorated navy pilot, well, that may explain why you only allow yourself to get angry once every two years). It also turned Thiel into a coach before his time. For the next twenty years, he helped out with high school teams in Maryland, New Jersey, and Long Island. That ended when he moved his practice to Manhattan. But he still kept his sticks, both of them, in the office. Part memorabilia, part hopeful prop. Maybe some fifteen-year-old private schooler would come in and instead of pointing to some violation on his face would point instead to the sticks and say, "Wanna catch?"

Ten years now. Nothing. No kid had piped up. The last time he used one of the sticks was six weeks minus twelve days ago. A call from Gail. *No more dithering. Get a lawyer. Get a place.* Some other shit, but Thiel was too busy scooping the phone into the mesh webbing of his STX aluminum-shafted attack stick, cradling it maybe two to three times, then firing the entire apparatus through an opening in the window no bigger than a phone and a half. It landed on the roof of the parking garage twenty stories below. His nurse-receptionist, the too-competent Zeneda, bought him a replacement during her lunch break, but only after she failed to convince the manager of the parking garage that possession really wasn't nine-tenths of the law. It was just an expression. Like sending a phone on a twenty-story plunge.

He still hadn't bought an answering machine for the apartment. Big problem. It meant he couldn't just sit there on the Ikea bed and run through playful non-amped riffs on the Les Paul while he screened callers. I'll tell Zeneda to pick me up a machine tomorrow, Thiel thought, as he had thought for days. But until then, whenever the phone rang in the new studio and he was there, so began the tape in his head that every self-tortured people pleaser has on an endless loop: *It may be important. You must answer it. Pick it up. PICK IT UP!!!!*

Today had been a pretty good day so far. No, better than that. Gail had called to remind him of their daughter Zoe's soccer game tomorrow, and to commend him on "selecting the greasiest divorce attorney in Manhattan," which made him laugh. Why were they splitting up? Oh yeah, her idea.

Richie called to tell him Gail was going to call and added, "I forgot what a trip she is. I don't know why you two are splitting up . . . oh yeah, her idea."

Zeneda called and said she'd given this number to *"your drummer?"* Tim Schlesinger and she'd drop off an answering machine tomorrow afternoon.

Thiel was on the phone for forty-five minutes with Tim and his giddiness over the possibility of a Truants reunion and his best friend from prep school coming to Manhattan to hash it out was interrupted three times. Once by the realization that he, Thiel, would have to reach out to Brian and try to smooth things over. Twice by guys knocking at his front door asking if "Misty" was there. No, fellas, that's 11D. Not 11B. D. D, like "degenerate."

He hung up after talking with Tim and assaulted the Les Paul like a man with thirty years of rust removal on his mind.

The phone rang once more.

"Dr. Thiel, sorry, it's Zeneda. I've got a friend of yours here—"

The phone on the other end was snatched from her. "Johnno, Brian Brock. I'm here in the city, I'm broke and I need a place to stay."

Thiel looked at the sign hanging from the phone cord. It worked.

• • •

SO, I'LL FAIL MY FIRST MIDTERM. What kind of an idiot thinks she can become a doctor at forty-six anyway?

Lizzie had to say those kinds of things to herself all the time to get through med school. And to allow herself to do those things that most people trying to get through med school don't do. Like drive to New York and kill a Sunday.

And go alone. She had shown up at her brother's house at 9:00 A.M., and that was the last time things had gone as projected. Tim was waiting outside.

"Cheryl found my drums."

"Shit, Timmy. I thought they were hidden behind boxes."

"She needed a box."

"What does this mean?"

"I can't go," he said.

"I thought Cheryl knew about us going. I thought she was all right with it."

"She was all right with it because she thought I was going with you to look at hospitals for your internship. Or residency. Something."

"What?"

"Then she found the drums. Me lying to her for the last eight years about selling them. That, she's having a problem with."

"Shit. So, did you call Thiel and Richie and tell them you can't come today?"

"No." Tim looked at the ground. "I figured you'd go alone."

"What?"

"Look, I'm dead for weeks here off this thing with my drums, and we don't have that kind of time for Dino. So, you go down there and see where they are. See how interested they are. Get Johnno to talk to Richie."

"About Jerry?"

"No. Forget Jerry for now."

"About what, then?'

"He'll know."

"But I don't."

"What do you care? You get to see Johnno . . ."

"Cut it out."

"Johnnnnnnnnnooooooo," Tim singsonged, in the sharp key of provocation only an older brother knows.

"Shut up. I was thirteen."

"Twelve," Tim corrected. "But you'll go."

"Timmy, this is stupid."

"Joh—"

"All right, shut up. Jesus. Can you at least call him and tell him it's just going to be me?"

"I did. There was no answer, but I'll keep trying. Go ahead. For me."

For me. Long before *So, I'll fail my first midterm,* that was the phrase that carried Lizzie through. Her older brother never asked for much other than to get him a Coke and, as far as she was concerned, he never asked enough. In return, she got to hang around where twelve- and thirteen-year-olds girls were usually shooed— with seventeen- and eighteen-year-old boys.

He had to say it. He had to say, *For me.* The clarion call. So, she went.

Just after Hartford, Lizzie was able to pick up 101.1 FM on the radio in her Skylark. CBS-FM. The Rosetta Stone of rock oldies. They were counting down the top twenty songs from that week. In 1967. Four months after *Out of Site* had come and become its title. And the Truants, five Chase boys held together by prep school mixers and mutual teasing, careened into five colleges like a trick pool shot. Her brother too far away to Colgate. Richie Lyman hugging coattails to Harvard. Brian Brock to Trinity, Hartford's Yale and now a few exits in Lizzie's rearview-mirrored past. Jerry Fyne to . . . to . . . ah, right—Rollins College in Florida. Tough school.

No tuition, but a stiff cover charge. What was that old joke? They could never have had the birth of Christ at Rollins College because it would have taken three wise men and a virgin. Somehow, Jerry had flunked out, then hopped the 1969 local to Canada. That was the story. Shit. Good luck finding that guy.

John Thiel took his tall dreaminess to Hopkins. The next time she saw him was ten, maybe twelve years later, when he was the same guy, only nicer. There might have been a dinner invitation in there, but she was late to meet her dealer and, well, you know how those guys are about promptness. The next time was eight years after that. She was clean, ready. Johnno had stopped by to see Tim on his way to the twentieth reunion at Chase. With a woman who was everything Lizzie wasn't. Confident, with tits. Gail Something. Right, Gail Thiel. For that Lizzie was clean, but not ready. She excused herself after fifteen minutes and tried to call her dealer from a pay phone at the Shell station. Disconnected. No new listing. Well, you know how those guys are about permanence. That was as close as she had come to picking up.

She was outside Thiel's apartment building by 1:00 and got a Sunday parking space. The doorman was looking at a much younger girl and she was in the elevator without being announced. As she walked down the long corridor toward 11B, she could hear the sound of a football game. Loud. Single-guy loud. That got her excited. Lizzie stopped to gather herself. Her hair had been long the last time they had seen each other, and not as professionally colored. Would he recognize her? Just then, the fire door opened and a guy in shorts and loafers, dragging a chocolate Lab, appeared. Both of them were panting. He looked at Lizzie.

"Misty?"

"No."

"Right." He turned and banged on 11B.

Steps shuffled. "I didn't order it, but this better be a fucking pizza." Thiel yanked open the door. Shirtless, sockless, sweatpants in between.

"Mis—"

"—ELEVEN FUCKING D! D! D, like 'dog.' Like your fucking dog, who knows where to go by now. Ask him."

Shorts and loafers and Lab turned just as a door two letters down the hall opened. Thiel looked up, waiting to see the pinned-up back of a blond head and one arm of a silk robe. Instead, his line of sight was interrupted.

"Lizzie, is that you?"

"Yeah."

"What the fuck are you doing here?"

Not exactly *Wow, you look great! How was your trip? Come on in.* "Didn't Tim talk to you?"

"Not today. My phone is, ah, uh, broken. I thought I was going to see him."

"Change of plans. He sent me."

"Well, you gotta go."

So, she said it. "Wow, you look great! How was your trip? Come on in!"

"Lizzie, you can't come in now. I'm getting a divorce and if I'm seen with another woman outside the office, my lawyer will kill me."

"Who's your lawyer, Richie?"

"How'd you know? Shit, I just thought of something. Did you sign in downstairs?"

"No."

Thiel sighed. "Thank Christ."

She tried again. "Wow, you look great!"

"I'm sorry," said Thiel. "Do you have somewhere to go?"

"I was going to see Richie and then drive back to Boston."

"If you stay over, I can see you at my office tomorrow."

So I'll fail my first midterm. "I don't know. Maybe. Look, if

I don't see you, when I go back, what should I tell my brother?"

Thiel gave a resigned wave. "Tell him, 'Same shit. "Furious."'"

"What the fuck does that mean?"

"He'll know. You gotta get out of here, Lizzie. You can't let anybody see you." Thiel closed the door. Lizzie turned, then turned again when it opened. "You do look great," he said. The door closed again, for good. She started to walk down the hall, but she heard the elevator door open and saw a guy heading toward her. She broke coolly for the fire stairs. She stopped halfway between the tenth and ninth floors, when she could have sworn she heard pounding above and a voice yell, "Come on, Thiel, cut the shit. I forgot my key. Open the door, Johnno!"

Nah.

Twenty minutes later, Lizzie was in the lobby of Richie Lyman's apartment building in the West Seventies, doing the Sunday *Times* crossword and eating a buffalo burger she'd bought at some place called Big Nick's. If he didn't show by the time she finished the puzzle, she was gone. She'd buy another buffalo burger at Big Nick's for the trip back. It was that good.

With eleven blank squares left, a guy who had no business wearing a beret ran into the lobby and hit the doorman up for cab fare.

"Edgar, all I got is C-notes, man."

"Why not you ask your friend, Mr. Lyman?"

"Do I know you?"

"Lizzie."

"Uh-huh." Richie gave her a quick scan. Pretty in a familiar way, but that rack skirt and jeans jacket was too low end for a client.

"Schlesinger."

"Ah." He calmed down. "Timmy's little sister. Where's Ringo, taking a shit?"

"He might be. But I'm the only one here."

"Wife didn't let him out to play?"

"You know her?" said Lizzie.

"Only by example. Come on upstairs. Edgar, *tengo compania?*"

"No sir."

"Dynamite." A taxi's horn yelped. "Lizzie, you got a ten?"

She had caught Richie on the right Sunday. The guest room, which looked a lot like a thirteen-year-old boy's room, was free. And the bottom bunk was surprisingly comfortable, even though the candy under the pillow was stale. Lizzie had hoped to study maybe a little for the next midterm she might fail, but come on. She was the guest of Richie Lyman, which, after the free dinner delivered from Big Nick's, came dangerously close to resembling a hostage situation. All regular programming was suspended, and in its place, an eight-hour musk-scented infomercial: The Lies and Times of Richie Lyman.

Somewhere around ten, Lizzie had her first big laugh. Richie said, "So, what are you doing here again?" She told him about Dino Paradise and the German guy and the Truants reunion and the visit to Thiel's apartment and the door closing.

"I love when clients follow my advice," said Richie. "It's so rare. Like an eclipse. Too bad this was the one time he didn't have to do it."

"He told me he can't be seen outside the office with a woman."

"Yeah, but you don't count."

Lizzie thought about being insulted, but good Christ, consider the *tengo compania?* source. "So, what about the reunion? You in, Mr. Lead Singer?"

Richie hand-raked his hair, hair Nicholas Cage wished he had, for the eighth time. "Depends," he said.

"On what?"

"If you get everybody. . . ."

"We're going to try," said Lizzie. "Jerry's tough to track down. You could get off your ass and help."

Richie finished, ". . . because if you get everybody, you don't get Richie Lyman."

"What?"

"You heard me."

"Why?

"You know why."

Lizzie mumbled, "Same shit. 'Furious.'"

"YES! FUCKIN'-A RIGHT 'FURIOUS'!!" Richie screeched. "I knew you knew."

Now she was tired. In the morning, she'd fess up and say she didn't know why, that she was just repeating what Thiel had said. But Monday came and the breakfast-sausage patties at Big Nick's made the buffalo burgers look like a student film, and by the time she had given Richie a lift to 425 Park Avenue, she knew she didn't want to hear whatever his version was.

She got out and thought about coming up to see his office, but then realized that's not the kind of thing you do with your car after 9:00 A.M. on Park Avenue. So, she leaned against the passenger side and heard another five minutes of his beret-capped bullshit. Maybe she'd get the truth behind this riddle when she got home. If there was any truth left.

"So, what do I tell my brother?"

Richie looked past her, as if he may have spotted a mirror. "Hey, people got to make choices. You want to do *Star Trek* without Kirk, go ahead."

"Jesus."

"Just kidding," said Richie. "I get more ass than Kirk."

"How come I always feel like smacking you?"

"Hey, it's not how you're feeling, it's what you're doing."

"Richie, what the fuck does that mean?"

"I have no idea. Give us a hug, little sistah."

They locked in a long, rocking embrace that could only be interpreted by Park Avenue onlookers as playful. Unless you were onlooking diagonally across the street, just coming out of the Drake Hotel, with that afternoon's room key. Which Fran Brennan was.

At that moment two women who had never met had the same thought: "Okay, Richie, that's enough." Although Fran Brennan would add the out-loud postscript, "You piece of shit."

chapter five

RICHIE HAD BEEN A LITTLE ABRUPT on the phone with Thiel. He may even have hung up first. Nah. No divorce lawyer ever gets to hang up first. He was in a hurry to meet Fran Brennan at the Drake and did not want to be late. Fran had been testy the last meeting, maybe even a little curt. And that's not something to be encouraged, especially since he was close to a settlement in her case and even closer to dismissing her as an afternoon hump. What had Michael Douglas said to Charlie Sheen in *Wall Street* about Darryl Hannah's availability while talking on that enormous Go-Go '80s cordless phone? "Exit visas are imminent?" Well, that's where he was. Although what Richie Lyman was doing mixing himself up with Michael Douglas, Charlie Sheen, or that movie—hell, he shouldn't be allowed to rent *Wall Street*—was, in its own solipsistic Osterizer, appropriate.

Thiel had been annoying. Fourth grade teacher mak-ing sure-ure he un-der-stood annoying. Needlessly stretching out the conversation like *he* was being paid by the hour.

Could he have a male roommate? *Sure, sure.* How does it look?

Who the fuck cares, but fine. Responsible, thrifty, but who the fuck cares? How would it look? *What did I just say? Go ahead.* It's someone he's known a long time. *Yeah, yeah. What else?* Is that okay? *What did I just say? Do you want to know? Dying to know, Johnno. Can you tell me later?* Are you sure? *What did I just say?* Because I don't want to do anything that looks bad. And you said—*Yeah, yeah. I know what I said.* So, you're okay with it? *What did I just fucking say?* You probably should know. *I gotta go.* So, you're signing off on this? *No, I'm signing off on you. Jesus, go pop a kid's back and fucking relax. . . .*

Now, would that be considered curt?

Richie bolted from his office so quickly, he took the paper with the room-number code, but not the plastic key. His heart was pounding as he crossed Park Avenue. Something about this part of the process excited him. The end of the hunt. He wondered for a second why Fran had canceled the week before—not even a snippy phone call. Ah well, poor kid. They all have to fight the tendency to get too attached. A nice quick preliminary settlement usually helps.

He whisked the revolving door and did the half wave in the Drake lobby to no one in particular, like Dustin Hoffman on his way through the Taft to Anne Bancroft's leopard-print bra. Hoffman, what a putz. No moves. He danced out of the elevator and knocked on the door.

"Turn-down service?" he said in his worst drag voice.

"I'm checking out. Come back in an hour."

Checking out? Hmm. "It's your attorney."

Richie Lyman never saw the point of a Jimmy Choo "Hi, heel" bury itself in his scrotum. Never saw the housekeeping cart he fell back into and knocked over. Never heard Fran Brennan say, "So long, scumbag," though that's what she probably said. The next thing he remembered was English slightly less broken than him.

"Turn down now?" the maid said.

"No. Already turned down," said Richie.

IT MUST HAVE TAKEN HER AT LEAST AN HOUR. Down the stairs of the attic, one piece at a time, then walking it out to the curb, then setting it up just like on the back of the album. Okay, maybe the floor tom was a little wide. (And forget about reattaching that goddamn bass pedal.) Then covering the entire electric red Slingerland kit with a white sheet, like she was waiting for the boys from forensics to show up. Instead, it was just her husband, home early with flowers.

"These are for you."

Cheryl tossed them on top of the sheet, as if Tim's drum set had come out for a curtain call.

"Thanks." It was the first thing she'd said to him in thirty-six hours, since she'd found the drums in the attic.

"What's up?"

"What you should be asking," said Cheryl, "is 'Any messages?'"

"Okay . . . Any messages?"

She exhaled and began. "Brian Brock is staying with John Thiel. You have that number. He wants to know when your wife will let you come to New York. Richie Lyman needs to know what kind of money we're in for, and, hah-hah, when your wife will let you come to New York. Somebody named Howie wants a $500 donation to Chase, $200 if you let him play bass. And there were five different calls from Dino Fuckin' Paradise. That's not me being angry. That's what he called himself—DINO FUCKIN' PARADISE!"

"Uh-huh," said Tim. "Well, as long as you're not angry."

Tim began to walk toward the kit. Slowly. Like they tell you. Don't show fear.

"Unless you're planning to move that shit into the middle of the street, I'd stop right now," his wife said.

"Would you like to hear my explanation?"

"For lying to me the last nine years?"

"Eight."

"Oh, that's an excellent start."

"Okay, the band I was in at Chase—"

"The Deviants?"

"No, the Truants, but I think I like the Deviants better. Where were you when we were naming ourselves?"

"Teething," she growled.

"Okay, well we made this silly little album, which now turns out to be worth ten thousand dollars to collectors, collectors like Dino Fuckin' Paradise, and he wants us to get back together so he can reissue it and make us all a little money. That's why Richie and Johnno called. We've been trying to get everybody together."

"We?"

"Lizzie and I."

Cheryl arched an eyebrow. "Lizzie and I?"

"Lizzie and me? No, I think I was right. It's 'Lizzie and I.'"

"And when were you going to tell me about all this?"

"When I had some concrete information."

"Or when I'd—hah, hah—let you go to New York."

Tim felt the ground open beneath him. No, that's wrong. He would have loved the ground to open beneath him. "That's just prep school ball busting. Guys giving me shit because Lizzie went to New York Sunday to find out who's interested. You know she's got a big crush on Thiel."

"Chico?"

"Johnno."

"Right."

"All right," said Cheryl, "that explains everything. Except this. Why did you lie to me for eight years about selling your fucking drum set?"

Despite the "Lizzie and me?" crack, Tim was not usually a wise guy. Not anymore. "Okay, until last week, I hadn't played those drums in eight years. Since I told you I sold them. Not once. But I just couldn't get rid of them, and I knew I couldn't make you understand why I didn't get rid of them."

It was starting to get chillier. The weather, too.

"So," he went on. "I hid them in the attic. For that I deeply apologize, Cheryl. Really. It was childish. Absolutely childish. Like something a sixteen-year-old would do. Of course, I wasn't that clever when I was sixteen. I was a B-minus student who wasn't permitted to play contact sports and wasn't going to get into an Ivy League school and would probably stay in the first job I got out of college. The only time I would ever come out of what I was destined to be was with these other four guys. We didn't like each other all that much, but we knew how to play dances. We got good at it, and we liked being good at it. And we never admitted to each other how important that was. We didn't have to, but maybe we should have. So, I hung on to that, like I hung on to my drums, which was sad, I know it, until about two weeks ago. Now, it's exciting. And I can't remember the last time I was this excited."

"This is all very flattering."

"Again, I'm sorry. But I thought, I thought you might be happy for me."

"When?" crossed Cheryl. "When I found the drums you 'sold' eight years ago or when you got around to telling me the 'exciting' news you've known about for two fucking weeks?"

They had never argued like this. Okay, maybe three times in fifteen years. But the layoff hadn't hurt. The depth of his wife's rage had registered and stuck, and Tim, who had just tried honesty with vague results, now went with one of the two ill-advised neutralizing tools he had left. Exaggeration.

"You're acting like I cheated on you."

"I would almost have preferred that. At least it would have been something an adult does."

Then he went with the other. Giggling.

"Would it, would it help," he blurted out, "if you had caught, caught . . . me humping the bass pedal?"

"You think this is funny?" she said.

"No," Tim said. "I think it's sad. But funny too. Jesus, come on. I'll never lie to you about hiding drums in the attic again. We're talking about one long weekend seven months away."

"Is that all we're talking about?"

"YES! This is something I do well, and I'm proud of. Don't you want to see that?"

"No."

"No?"

"No. So, figure out what you're going to do with those drums."

"Are you serious?"

Cheryl continued, "My choice would be to leave everything right here for tomorrow's trash pickup. But I know you. I know you'll load them up and take them over to Lizzie's."

"I hadn't thought about it."

"Well, think about it. And if that's where you're headed, make sure your sister has enough room in her place for the drums, and you."

Cheryl walked back into the house. Tim stood there and thought of a couple things to yell out. *"Can we talk about this later?" "Is this the problem, or is it something else?" "Am I supposed to stay somewhere else tonight?" "What about the night after that?"* He dismissed all of them because he didn't want to know the answers. There were really only two answers he wanted. *"What can I do to make everything go away, except the drums?" "Can I come in and get Dino Paradise's phone number?"*

"Cheryl." His wife stopped. "What can I do to make—" She interrupted him with silent open-mouthed horror. "This is nuts."

"Well," she said, "at least we agree on something." The door slammed. Tim looked at his Hyundai. He'd have to make two trips.

• • •

RICHIE CALLED AT 7:00 A.M.

"Johnno?"

"I'll get him," said Brian.

"How can I tell if I've had a concussion?" Richie asked before Thiel could begin.

"What's the flip side of 'Expressway to Your Heart?'"

"'Hey Gyp?'"

"You don't have a goddamn concussion."

"Great," said Richie, "I can go into work. Who was that who answered the phone?"

"Brian."

"Brian . . . Truants Brian?"

"Yeah, look, before you go, I think I may have a slight problem with this building." Thiel gave a faithful, dispassionate account of the latest events. Around three that morning, the 136th john looking for Misty, the call girl in 11D, had mistakenly rung his doorbell, 11B. Brian, in his underwear, politely showed the trick to the correct door, but in the process locked himself out. Not wanting to pound on the door and risk waking Thiel, he sent Misty down to get the spare key from the doorman. By the time she came back, everyone was in the hallway—Thiel (also in u-trou), Brian, the john, and two detectives. Fortunately, everything was smoothed over when Brian told one of the detectives Thiel was a dermatologist and he wrote the cop a script on the spot for venereal warts and gave him a standing free appointment. Other than that, things were quiet. So, he may have a slight problem with the building.

Thiel then hung on for about five minutes of *Uh-huhs*. All Brian could hear, standing on the other side of the studio apartment, was what sounded like highly agitated static.

Thiel hung up.

"What did Richie say?"

"I need to move out of this building."

"I guess that makes sense," Brian said. "With the divorce pending and hookers living down the hall, I guess that could be misconstrued." Brian paused. "Did Richie say anything about me?"

"Yeah," said Johnno. "He said you need to find yourself another roommate—"

"Really?"

"—and," he finished, "another band."

SHE WAS THREE DAYS PAST THE DEADLINE to get reimbursed. If she was smart, the financial-aid officer explained, she should hang in there until December 15, finish the semester, have the grades count, and then take a leave of absence for up to a year. That way, nobody gets hurt. This way, it looked like Lizzie Schlesinger was quitting med school in her last year. Just quitting. And they weren't too forgiving about that. It was medical school, not Midas. You couldn't just give up and ask for your money back and maybe come back later for your muffler, when you were in a better place emotionally.

"Take a day and think about it," the nice woman said.

"I already took a day," said Lizzie.

"Take another."

"How old are you?" Lizzie asked the nice lady.

"Thirty-six."

"Well, I'm forty-three."

"You don't look it." And Lizzie didn't. And it wasn't just the jeans jacket, T-shirt, $5 earrings combo. It was the clear-eyed, smooth-skinned template of the perpetual kid sister.

"Well, I am."

"Take another day."

Another day? Sure. There couldn't possibly be any more room on her plate for any more shit than had been served up the last two days. Or the last five. Ever since she returned from New York. Ever since she failed her first midterm. Ever since she didn't think it was going to bother her, but it did.

Who am I kidding? Lizzie thought for the half-millionth time. A doctor? I can't even diagnose my own fucked up-ness. And I sure as hell can't treat it. Can't treat it like I want to treat it.

For someone whose only connection to the Truants had been genetic, Lizzie had become everyone's lynchpin. Not unwittingly. It's great to be wanted. And not wanted in the way she was wanted at Gavin's—*Hey, gorgeous, get me another Bud and why won't you blow me?* wanted. The pull was different, and familiar. Toward Tim and Johnno and Dino Fuckin' Paradise. To be forty-three and thirteen at the same time. Sure, it was confusing. It was confusing without med school. And it was differential calculus when coupled with the laughing disbelief in her head—"*You? Med school? A junkie/doctor/barmaid? Hah! Good one!*"

For a while, it was manageable. Furtive plans with Tim and Dino and hot dreams of John Thiel amid the sleepwalk obligations of med school and shifts at Gavin's. A while. A month. Then it got too packed. Everywhere. And the only place there was still room was Lizzie's head. Room for more noise. That month ended Monday, when she returned from New York City and found three messages on her answering machine. The latest was from her prissy clinical psych section leader, who told her she had indeed failed the midterm and threw in this gem, "Unless you have a good excuse for not showing up, and menopause is not a good excuse, this grade will stick."

The other two messages were from her sister-in-law. "Lizzie, Cheryl," the first began. "Nice going. Really. You should be very proud of yourself." Four hours later, all her machine could haul in was five seconds of dead air, a whispered "Fuck it," and a two-bounce hang-up.

Tim pulled into her driveway Monday night, the first of two trips in the Hyundai. The second carried his floor tom, cymbals, and a suitcase.

Lizzie had always been better off not being reminded of her loneliness. Med school and Gavin's and collapsing at the end of the day helped. Suddenly, wordlessly, her large one-bedroom in Watertown was crowded. No, full. Her brother was here, back, and that was the last of the wordlessness. They yakked through salad with Ken's Dressing and three identically nondescript Lean Cuisine entrées. They rushed to each other's defense and then raced back to the past to see who could get there first, but letting the other win. Tim's wife, Cheryl, was just being selfish and threatened and bereft of compassion, though not as much as the fucker who wouldn't let Lizzie retake her midterm.

She knew he would have to go back the next day. She couldn't be the Neutron Sister: Kills in-laws, leaves the nuclear family standing. And she knew the laughter, the pulmonary havoc another story about their father skiing or their mother playing cards would have on her, was as gloriously relentless as it was finite. But . . . to finally drop off to sleep and wake to the crash of an ill-placed Zildjian medium ride on the way to the john, wake up startled and not think, "Oh no, who is this loser I let stay over?" was home-made-chocolate-pudding comfortable.

Lizzie sent Tim on his way Tuesday. She had just returned from her meeting with the nice lady in financial aid who told her to take another day and she didn't look forty-three, and he had left work early to come by and practice for a couple of hours. Tim harangued his drums like he was trying to beat his present into submission and revive his future. Lizzie agreed to house the kit indefinitely, but her brother had to try and go home. So, her large one-bedroom was still crowded, though no longer full. She had three beers on an empty stomach, maybe the first three beers she'd had since high school, but you don't forget the first thing that knocked you out. She never even made it to the end of *NYPD Blue*, and it was an all-new one. Shit.

Fourteen hours later, Lizzie finally talked herself out of bed. It took fifty-five minutes for her to shower, brush her thankful teeth, make coffee, and put on enough makeup to get herself to that place where she could look in the mirror and say, "Nice going. Nice going. What are you going to do now?" And she knew. Knew exactly what she was going to do. Except her buzzer rang.

"Timmy?"

"Brian."

"Brian?"

"Brian Brock."

"Oh. Truants Brian?"

"Yeah. Can I come up?"

"How did you get my address?"

"I called—"

"Cheryl?" Lizzie interrupted.

"Yeah. Lizzie, please."

"Come on up. Three A."

"God bless—"

Now, it had been a long time, and although her dated memory of him was shy, Aryan, and weird, Brian had been the Truant the thirteen-year-old Lizzie paid the least attention to. And she couldn't trust the eight-track technology of her building's intercom, but it sounded like the guy had been crying. She plastered on her barmaid *"What'll it be?"* smile, and as she opened her door heard brave sniffles.

"Long time—"

"Lizzie, I'm lost."

"Well, you found me okay."

Brian laughed much too hard, the kind of laughter that can only become tears. He waited until they were hugging before he started to cry. "When did you get so beautiful?" he choked out. And really, that was enough. She pulled Brian in, skirting the snare/hi-hat combo and began to kiss him. It was the only thing that would keep her from sobbing.

They were smart enough not to talk. It would ruin whatever nourishment this was. Lizzie couldn't remember the last time a man had been inside her at this hour (key word: "man"), or when she'd had this kind of ravenous energy or when there was no condom involved. Early '80s? It would have made for great conversation when they were through, when she would emerge from the bathroom wiping off her chest with a lukewarm towel. Would have been great. Except that Brian continued to writhe on the bed, alone.

"My back!"

"What happened?"

"I tried to pull myself up by the headboard with one hand. I reached back wrong. Good God, shit. It's like I've been stabbed."

Lizzie scurried behind Brian on the bed and wedged herself between him and the wall. She was going to try and push his legs off the mattress and onto the floor. That, and she wanted to be out of his sight if she started laughing. If. There was no way she was going to start laughing. Unless, of course, Brian started crying. On the third try, she got his legs onto the floor. Now, the pain of his scar-tissuing, repaired knee joined his back.

"I'm so ashamed."

Snort. She missed covering her mouth.

"What was that?"

"The bed," gritted Lizzie. "Now try and sit up on the edge of the bed. I'll help you. And take your time getting dressed. I'd get you some Advil, but that ain't gonna work."

"You don't have any Demerol laying around, do you?"

"No," said Lizzie, "but I've been meaning to pick some up for the last twelve years."

She gathered up his clothes and put them on the bed, then went by Tim's drum kit to throw hers on.

"Nice going, Brian. Real butch," he mumbled. Just not quietly enough.

"I heard that."

"What? The bed?"

"No," said Lizzie. "'Real butch.' Don't worry. Your secret's safe with me."

"What secret?"

"Honey, you wouldn't be the first gay guy I've slept with."

"How do you know I'm gay?"

Lizzie was matter-of-fact. "Only guys who do coke call it 'blow.' Only gay guys say 'butch.'"

"How did you know?"

Lizzie jumped into her jeans. "I didn't until just now." And then, as she zipped up, "I guess I'm a little off. Usually, I'm right on it. It's innate. Like having a photographic memory. To be honest, I'd rather have the photographic memory. I can't tell you how many men I've seen over the years, at the bar, in class, on the T, in detox, and I've seen something, that extra piece of baggage, and thought, 'God, do I have to break it to this guy that he's gay?' Of course, I never say anything."

Brian tried to be glib through his grimace. "Until now." Lizzie came over and helped tie his running shoes. His incredulity helped dull the pain. "So, you know this for certain?"

"Yeah."

He thought about standing up, "Well, Lizzie, you're a couple steps ahead of me . . . AH!!!!!"

He Frankensteined down the hall and the front steps to Lizzie's car on his own, but it took Dr. Sapas and his kid to pull him out of the Skylark. Ernest Sapas and Son. Chiropractic. Serving the Greater Belmont area since 1960.

"How long's it been, Lizzie? Couple of years?"

"Yeah, Doc, I'm overdue for a visit. Soon. I promise."

"No. You're fine. Don't you remember? I saw you six months ago."

Right. She'd been by last April for her wrist. Carpal-tray

syndrome. Sapas meant it had been "a couple of years" since the last time she'd brought a guy around. An untied shoes, shirt misbuttoned, shirttail hanging, *My back!* guy around.

Lizzie waited however much time she thought it would take for Sapas and Son to get him on the table and have the old man start jumping on him. She left the motor running and ran in to give the kid $30 (It was always $30. Crack n' Go n' No Insurance.) and leave a twenty and her house keys for Brian. Back in the Skylark, she counted the cash she had left. Forty dollars. Enough. Plenty.

It had been twelve years, but her disease knew the way. It took hold of the wheel and pointed due east. When they weren't recounting ski stories, Lizzie and Tim used to laugh about their father, whose idea of encouragement was saying, "You won't be happy till you break it." Good old dad. Another drunk. Maybe he knew. Is that what she was trying to do? Break shit and be happy? Promises? Plans? Other people's marriages? Other guys' backs? And this one—he's gay and Lizzie Schlesinger couldn't tell immediately? Was that broken too?

She pulled into a Mobil station just before the Southeast Expressway and bought a pack of Kool kings. Might as well get it all going again. What was with the shiny *Millennium's a comin'!* packaging? Had it been that long since she'd smoked? She fished out a pair of quarters and made two calls. One to her answering machine, telling Brian to make himself at home, she didn't know when she'd be back. The other message she left with the nice lady in financial aid. "Well, it's another day," she began. "I'm gone."

The first big drag hurt in the best possible way. She was halfway through the pack when it started to get dark and she found the right nowhere street in the right wrong neighborhood. Might have been Dorchester. She stopped the car and waited for nothing. She had plenty of time to think. Nothing but time. And she remembered. It had been six. Six guys she'd had to cart over to Sapas. She laughed and asked herself what else was wrong.

You know what? Nothing. Nothing was wrong. There was no crisis. Things were okay. She was relieved about med school, really. It was enough. For the first time in six-plus years, since she had gone back to college, Lizzie did not feel fraudulent. Finally, she could look into any mirror, in this case the rearview, say, "Who are you kidding?," and answer, "Nobody, anymore."

And the Truants? Sure, she was hopeful, but it was somebody else's dream. Somebody else's expectation. Somebody else's ultimate fraud. Not hers. Not hers anymore.

She went to start the car and she remembered something another addict had told her when she was coming up on a year clean. "You wonder what you're gonna do when something really bad happens. When someone dies or you get your ass fired or you get a thing or your old man leaves you," the woman said. "But you won't pick up because of that shit. You won't go back out over that. You'll pick up because it's fuckin' Wednesday."

A tall, thin man with more rings than teeth knocked on her window. It was still Wednesday.

HE WAS THE OLDEST GUY IN THE PLACE. Okay, maybe not. The bouncer said Bill Wyman had just left, ducking into a limo with three girls young enough to be his ex-wife. But he was definitely the fattest guy there. That was no contest. It was never any contest. Maybe if he went to DisneyWorld he'd have some competition, but that wasn't going to happen. Dino Paradise never went anywhere that didn't exist prior to 1970.

The Rathskellar in Kenmore Square more than qualified. Hell, the Rat hadn't seen a can of Lysol since 1964, when they'd remodeled the Frog and started booking oompah bands. Four guys were making noise onstage. A Tuesday-night act working Thursday.

Fine. Go nuts. Knock yourselves out, boys. Dino wasn't interested. He hadn't been interested since the accountants and lawyers had strip-mined the New England music scene and paved it over on the way to the Jersey shore.

"Dino Paradise, ladies and gentlemen!"

"Is he hee-ah?" Dino asked.

"Would I have called you if he wasn't?" the kid said.

"Point fuckin' taken."

"When was the last time you were here?"

"To see the Cars."

"1976?"

"Something like that."

"They did okay," said the kid. "Ric Ocasek and them."

"Yeah, I heard that. Little too fuckin' *boing boing boing* for me, though."

"Hah! You're exactly like my dad said. When was the last time you saw him?"

"Probably the last time you shampooed the cah-pet here. Jesus, it smells like Les McCann fahted." Dino started coughing, at first in delight over his reference, because Les McCann had probably stopped by the Rat after his set at Lucifer's in 1976, but it got away from him quickly in the club's fog-strewn air. His face wiped red and his normally docile eyes bugged out the way they did when a country song came on a jukebox unannounced. He hacked and wheezed and held his hands up as the owner/owner's son, Jay Sweeney Jr., ran to get him a glass of water. The band onstage, whatever that noise was, played forty feet behind his back. Nobody turned around. Nobody gave a shit. A Rat's-ass.

"You okay?" Jay Sweeney Jr. asked after Dino's face had throttled back to hot pink.

"Yeah. Sorry your old man couldn't make it."

"He told me to be sure and take care of Dino Paradise. I know he would have loved to see you."

"Screw seeing him. I just don't like being the oldest fuckin' guy here."

"Nah," said the kid, "Wolf's older."

"Who taught you how to kiss ass?"

"My father."

"And you know who taught yah fahtha?" Dino jerked a thumb in the direction of his cheek, now the color of raspberry yoghurt.

Peter Wolf was not that much younger than Dino, but he could make up the difference when one figured in twenty-five years of the rock life and a marriage to Faye Dunaway. The former or current front man for the J. Geils Band (depending on *their* reunion status) was a crucial link to Dino's plan for the "GarageApalooza" festival in June. Come on. Dino was kissing his own ass. Peter Wolf was THE crucial link to "GarageApalooza." Without him, there was no legitimacy, no attached name, no promotional vehicle, no sponsors, and most important, no up-front money from no sponsors. Without his euphemistic old friend, "GarageApalooza" was Dino Paradise singing along with the Standells into a hairbrush, which was pretty much every weekend in his living room since the wife had walked in 1990.

"What's he drinking?"

The kid banged a bottle of Dom Perignon on the bar. "C-note."

"Give me two."

"Okay, looks like a deuce." Dino put his beefy hand on Jay Sweeney Jr.'s shoulder. He gave him a look that said, very clearly, "I don't think 'Looks like a deuce' is what your dad had in mind when he said to take care of Dino Paradise." And which the kid read fluently as, ". . . a deuce is for the goobers who walk in off the street."

Dino waited for the noise to end its forty-five-minute set before heading to the back table, double-barreled in Dom. He'd been waiting almost a month for the call. Jay Sweeney Sr. had promised he'd let him know the next time Wolf was in the Rat. Wyman, his old coke customer, was the bait. His kid would call when it happened. Be ready.

He was stretched across two chairs and in between two blondes. There were two other guys at the table. One to keep people away from Peter Wolf. No matter how much time diluted the public consciousness, people, especially people in and around Boston, would always want to get near Peter Wolf. So, that guy would always have a job. You know how if you learn to shoot pool, shoot it well, you'll never go hungry? Same thing.

The other guy looked familiar. Combination childhood friend/fetcher/recording secretary. He looked like a guy who had taken great care to look like a guy who might look like a rock star. And then he blew it by sitting at the same table as a rock star.

"PETE-AH!" Peter Wolf turned around. "Good news. The Spinach fell out, I can get you and the Hallucinations into the Unicorn next fuckin' Saturday."

"I hate the fucking Unicorn."

"Okay, how about the Moondial?"

The guy who would never go hungry moved in between them. Peter Wolf smiled.

"Dino." He remembered. "Dino Shangri-la." He really remembered.

"I used that name for two weeks in nineteen sixty-eight, you prick." Dino put the two bottles of Dom on the table, a gesture that winded him. Peter Wolf kicked a chair his way. The childhood friend/fetcher went to get another chair. The blondes were sucked into the Rat's idea of a ladies' room.

Dino knew he had whatever time it would take Peter Wolf to open the first bottle of Dom and let it breathe to make his pitch. Minute and a half.

"I know, I know," he began. "I'm a little heavy. I'm anorexic, but I fight it." Good opener, even if he'd stolen it from some fat comic. Peter Wolf laughed. "Look, I'm putting together something that you're gonna fuckin' love. Early June. Weekend after Mem Day, the kids will still be he-yah. One night sixties to seventies garage-band festival. Are you ready? GarageApalooza. A thousand to fifteen-hundred venue. Figure five, six bands. Maybe more. I'm flexible. Anybody you or Geils want to throw a hump to, fine, they're in. We headline with fuckin' Barry. Filling it out won't be a problem. I got guys ready to suck my dick who don't do that sort of thing. All I need from you is to show up at the top—'How the fuck are yah? Babybabybabybaby . . .' That sort of shit. And one day a month before. Radio, a fag taking pictures, done. Couple hours. That's it. You're the only guy I thought of who I'd want to be out in front of this. Otherwise, you and I know it's just a rub-fuck."

"You got the Remains? You got Barry?"

"No," said Dino. "But that's not tough. Barry's in Memphis."

"Nashville," Wolf corrected.

"What the fuck. I call your old roommate, I say, 'Barry, Pete-ah says can the clip-clop shit for two days and get your boys together.'"

"Who do you have, Dino?"

"Besides you?"

"Dino."

"I got the Truants."

"Who?"

"Come on, don't rim-job me, Pete-ah. The Truants. The guys from prep school. They made one album, *Out of Site*, thirty years ago, the thing's worth ten grand."

Dino pulled a small bag off his shoulder that had been obscured by his physical plant. A still-shrink-wrapped copy of *Out of Site* slid out.

"This yours?"

"No, Pete-ah, it's yours. Call it an advance."

"Ten grand?"

"Shit yeah."

"Some asshole collector in Italy, right?"

"Nah. Not Italy. You're way the fuck off."

"So, Germany."

"Heh."

"Ten thousand. How much if I open it?"

"Five thousand."

"How much if I listen to it?"

"If you listen to it? The great Pete-ah Wolf? Back up to ten."

"Cut the shit." He kicked out the replacement chair, took a long draw on Dom Gift Bottle No. 1, and glanced at the back of the cover. "Hah! The Rockin' Ramrods."

"Yeah, two cuts." Peter Wolf gave Dino the "I can read" look. The rock star turned to the fetcher. "Slats," he said, "give him Donnie's number. Call this guy in the spring, but only, fucking only, if you get the Remains."

"Dynamite."

"And when you call, make sure you leave the name Dino Shangri-la."

"You prick."

That, and to be honest, the men's room, brought Peter Wolf to his feet. On his way up, he decided to hug as much as he could of Dino Paradise. A million years ago, he had been there, fat even then, but one of the few guys who was slaked by the music and stepped aside to let the slick boys gorge. And now here he was, hand just a bit out, but stepping aside again. This time so Peter Wolf could get to the men's room.

"Gotta go. Take care of yourself, Dino."

Dino anachronistically nimbled through the late-arriving crowd into the luxurious gape of Kenmore Square. On the street, breathing Rat-less air, his shoulder bag empty, his pocket full of nothing resembling a "Fuck, no!" from Peter Wolf. Victo-fuckin'-ry.

He yelped and clapped his hands, and got to enjoy it all for about fifteen seconds before someone put a lit match to his chest.

Well, that's what it felt like. Fuckin' heartburn. Like the fourth time in the last month or so. Well shit, he *was* excited. Had been excited for the last month. And that's what it must feel like. Anyway, he'd be home in fifteen minutes, where he had a big jar of Rolaids. They were in the living room, right next to the hairbrush.

chapter six

PRESSURE CHIEF HIP-CHECKED the oven door closed.

"I don't get you. Is it that you don't think island people will kick your ass, or that you know they will and you miss it?"

"I'm doing this for us, Pressure."

"Stealing?"

"No," said Jerry, "getting us a poke so we can go to the States."

"We have enough. And Pressure has some money saved."

"Well, I need a little more. I have expenses."

"So, you steal."

"Look, just give me the wet suit and loosen your drawstring. We've got customers."

The wet suit had been in the storage locker, unrented for years, until a week ago. That morning, Pressure Chief had found out how Jerry had been spending his time after sunsets. He had put his arm around some gangly teenager who would pay him $25 for the wet suit, snorkel, mask, and flashlight ensemble, who would then troll the water hazards at Grand Cayman's two legitimate golf courses, the Brittania and Safehaven Links, gathering the horrific shots of duffer tourists. The next evening, Jerry would sell the balls to the new nine-hole course at the Sunrise Family Golf Center. On a good night, the kid might find fifty balls, which looked like fifty bucks, minus the rental and Jerry's $10 broker fee. Five nights now and Jerry had cleared almost $150. Why hadn't he thought of this before?

Simple. Because somebody else had. Jerry hadn't invented this gig, he had merely poached it from local people who needed the money to feed their families, not get straight with a Thirty-sixth Street bookie.

"If they come around," said Pressure, "and they will, Pressure can't protect you. Not like here on the beach."

"What? Should I be afraid?"

"You? Yes."

"Okay, tonight's the last night. I swear."

Pressure Chief threw the wet suit on top of an unopened sack of sugar. "Aren't we making enough now?"

"Maybe you," Jerry said.

"Yeah, since I got mixed up with you."

In the last five fiscal weeks, Pressure Chief had grossed $10,726. Here's the breakdown:

10	Chairs rented	$100
10	Umbrellas rented	$80
413	Muffins, cakes, pies sold	$826
486	"Tickets" sold	$9,720

Jerry Fyne had lugged the wooden sign for three days, really hustled, and hey, you see the results. Ten chairs, ten umbrellas. $180. His take: $45. It was just enough money to get him on his feet and passed out, thanks to eight shots of rum at Happy Hooks. That cost him $25. The other twenty he gave to his boss, for a look. By Day Four, the ten-year-old kids on the beach had their surfboard, the sign, back. By then, Jerry had seen his deliverance. Couldn't miss it. It was cradled in Pressure Chief's pants.

There is no reason to go into some pavilion of comparison or detail—anatomical, mathematical, trigonometrical, historical, hysterical, pornographic, paragraphic, or hyperbolic. Very simply, you saw Pressure Chief's penis and you wanted to conference-call Guinness, Ripley's, and anyone with the last name Freud. It was best left to no one's imagination. Although, to be fair, Jerry's imagination came close. Somewhere around Rum Shot No. 5, Day Three, an hour after he had paid to see it, an hour before he would fall face-first next to his "deluxe" beach-chair bed in the storage shed, Jerry Fyne had this thought:

"I bet he could get a dozen doughnuts on that thing."

Of course, that's not nearly what he said to Pressure the next day. It had been so long since he'd been drunk—Jesus, like two months—he had forgotten how much better he functioned with a hangover. It was as if the pain fit. The one pain his hypochondria hadn't coughed up. And the desperation to be out of pain forced him to matriculate from star-crossed small-timer to, are you ready, the kind of guy people got mixed up with.

His head pounded until its beat made sense. *Good baker, big dick. Good baker, big dick. Good baker, big dick. Good baker, big dick . . .*

"Hey," he said to Pressure on Day Four, "have you ever heard of the Erotic Bakery?"

"Where's dat?"

"New York City."

"You lie about everyting, but dat I believe."

"So?"

"So?"

"How'd you like to be a big-time baker in New York City?"

"Pressure would."

"We're going to need five thousand."

"Who we?"

"You're right. We're going to need ten thousand."

Pressure Chief laughed and beat the flour off his arms. "I'm going back to my work. Maybe you'll figure it out hustling business."

"I've already figured it out."

"How?"

"Hustling business."

Their deal remained the same in principal. Jerry's cut was still 25 percent of everything except baked goods sold. Slight change in his title. Jerry was no longer in charge of advertising. He was in charge of promotion. The big change was in, uh, inventory. Huge. Jerry was no longer renting beach shit. Oh, he could still "set you up," send one of the ten-year-olds to the storage shed for an umbrella or a deluxe chair if anyone asked. But nobody asked after Day Four. Jerry was too busy. Too busy promoting his inventory: One item with a shelf life that seemed limitless. Pressure Chief's shlong.

For a man normally so easygoing, Pressure was conflicted. He did not want to be bothered, almost as much as he wanted to go to the States. He had none of the hang-ups about his anatomy that characterized the rest of the nonalcoholic, non-French male world, and yet he let himself long for the day when he would be known as just a gifted baker rather than a giant dick/oh here, try a muffin. He would never let the smell of his lemon-poppy cake become sullied with the whiff of someone trying to work him, although once in an unrestrained while, the chance to con a con, shit a shitter, was too pungent. Too rich.

"Too rich" were Jerry's words, not his. "If we do this, it will make you too rich," he said. "That's if you stay here. But I know you. That's not what you want. That's not being a big-time baker in New York."

"Okay," sighed Pressure. "Let's see what the white boy who owes everyone money can do."

Pressure gave Jerry six weeks to change both their lives. He knew the Caymans and he knew it would take two months before the police would come around and shut everything down. That's if they were being discreet. If they weren't, the cops show up five days earlier. It was now the beginning of Week Six, and, well, loosen my drawstring if Jerry didn't have a smooth, self-contained operation that did not interfere with the beach ecosystem or Pressure's regular baking schedule.

Here's the thing about Jerry: He was not greedy. He even let Pressure hold all the money, including his cut. Such is the small-time mind. When you find a stocked fishing hole, you don't want to catch all the fish in one day. You want to keep coming back. You want the illusion of demand. You want action. Such is the small-time mind. Why make one $1,000 bet you're pretty sure of when you can make 100 $10 bets you're just a little cloudy about?

The goal was ten to twenty paying customers a day. No more than three showings a day. 10:00 A.M., 2:00 P.M., 5:30 P.M. About a half hour before, ahem, curtain, Jerry would walk a half mile in either director, barking about the next Pressure Chief "Bake-Off."

"A one-of-a-kind island tradition. Space is limited, folks. I only have room for three more people this morning. Let me know. All you can see, twenty dollars."

He would wait for someone to come up and either correct him ("Don't you mean 'all you can eat'?") or say, "Twenty bucks? That's a little steep." Then he made his pitch. And, and who does this on a tropical island, give his money-back guarantee. If you can look Jerry in the eye after it's over and say, "That's not the biggest dick I've ever seen," you get your $20 back. Once you scream, though, the offer is void. You weren't allowed to say, "Holy shit, it's alive! Run! Save yourselves! And I'll catch up after I get my refund. . . ."

He made sure each audience was themed and relatively the same age. 2:00 was traditionally the drunk single girlfriends show. 10:00 was either teenage boys who'd been on the beach since dawn, or old couples who thought it was part of a tour they'd missed. The 5:30 was drunk marrieds waiting to get a table next door at Happy

Hooks. The fact that people always got turned away created enough spillover buzz to the next morning's eye-opener.

There was not a lot of repeat business. But the word of mouth? Gigantic. And *avec* or *sans entendre*, that's really all Jerry needed.

In perhaps the most literal use of the word "show" in the history of live entertainment, the entire Pressure Chief experience lasted maybe two minutes. The audience was led to the screen door of Pressure's kitchen, which was a twelve-by-ten afterthought attached to the side of Happy Hooks. An AM radio may have bleated news, sports, Gloria Estefan, or Kenny G. Pressure, lost in torte, was shuttling in the three-foot aisle between oven, stove, and counter. Completely oblivious to the six to ten folks who had gathered at the door. Or so it appeared. In a move a close-up magician might have missed, he somehow catches the drawstring of his roomy white cotton pants under a rolling pin. That was the bite on the line. He would make a few feints back to the stove, just until the hook was in fast. And then, fast, he turned. The drawstring caught like he was trying to start a mower. The pants dropped like sails. And Pressure Chief, proud baker, did his best Coppertone girl "Oops!", then took his cinnamon-bun sweet time pulling up. A good minute.

The 2:00 P.M. women would scream and run, then run back and scream again before staggering away laughing.

During their second smash week, Jerry gave himself a line: "Ladies, let me apologize for Pressure Chief. I am so sorry. Please, don't tell anybody what you witnessed today."

It was hardly a bargain at $20. But really, "bargain" is such a relative term. The image stayed with you. You saw it Monday and still knew what it looked like Friday. So, that works out to like four dollars a day. Shit. You couldn't rent an umbrella for four dollars a day.

Jerry discouraged repeat business because it brushed up against a seediness that was for the moment beyond him and Pressure.

Okay, beyond Pressure. Right now, the whole deal was still on the harmless, partly shady side of Benny Hill.

"How many customers dis time?" Pressure asked after they had ended the wet suit discussion.

"Seven."

"Seven?"

"Three twos and a guy who was here yesterday."

"Fat man with hat?" asked Pressure. "He saw Pressure Monday too. Ten A.M.."

"Right. Well, this is it. I'll talk to him."

"Okay. No more."

Six minutes later: *Ladies, and gentlemen, let me apologize for Pressure Chief. I am so sorry. Please do not tell anyone what you witnessed here today. . . . Please, have a slice of banana bread on us.*

The "banana bread" line was new. And the $14 for seven slices would come out of Jerry's pocket. A peace offering to Pressure for the return trip of Fat Man with Hat.

"You ever thought about putting Baker Boy here in some porn?" asked Fat Man with Hat between bites.

"Jesus, no," said Jerry. "Are you a producer?"

"No, just a fan of the genre."

"He's a baker."

"Hey, pal, I can see banana bread whenever I want. This guy makes that *Boogie Nights* kid look like an appetizer."

Jerry kind of thanked him and asked that he not come around anymore. Fat Man with Hat said he was leaving tomorrow anyway. Getting out before the families came down for Christmas vacation.

Shit. Christmas vacation. Families. Now they'd have to shut it down. At least until the wholesome left and the airfares returned south. So, that's what Jerry would do. Shut it down. Take a little time off. After all, he'd been busting his promotional ass for almost six weeks.

"We should close next week," said Pressure as he scoured a pot.

"I agree."

"Too many tourists."

"You got that right, amigo. We'll start up again after the holidays. Finish the poke off."

"The poke is finished," Pressure said. "Let's go next week."

"Where?"

"New York. I'll stay with you in the Queens Village."

"You don't have a passport."

"Came today."

"We can't. The airfare is too much."

"We'll fly stand-by."

"Pressure, bad time of year."

"Not for a baker," he said. "Not for a good baker. Somebody wants a baker. Maybe your erotic friends."

Busted again . . . until the next morning, when Jerry was hung over enough to be thinking clearly.

"You know what?" he told Pressure, just before the 10:00, "you're right. We'll leave next week. I think I can line up some parties for you."

"MASS. ARCHIVES, TIM SCHLESINGER."

"What are you, Timmy, stuck up?"

"Who is this?"

"This is Howie."

"Howie?"

"Howie Fyne. Jerry Fyne's younger brother. Chase '69."

"Right. Sorry, I've been busy."

"How busy? I've called a dozen times. Finally, you pick up."

"Yeah, what a break that I was here at seven-fifteen in the morning." Tim stuffed the blanket and pillow under his desk and looked for his pants as Howie Fyne yammered.

"I have no idea where my brother is. The only place I know he's not is jail, otherwise I would have gotten a call for bail. Timmy, I'm not telling you anything you don't know. My brother is a scumbag. And not even an accomplished scumbag."

"Look, I'm sorry I bothered you. It's just—"

"I know why you're calling. They're reuniting the Truants. I know. That's why I'm calling. You don't need Jerry, you got me. I was always the better bass player, and, Timmy, I'VE NEVER STOPPED playing bass. The last twenty-five years, I've been doing weddings every other month at least. Ask anyone in the Lowell-Lawrence metroplex, they know the Post-its. Well, we've only been the Post-its for five years. Before that, we were Win-Win Situation and then out of college we were the Receptions."

"Yeah, the Post-its. You did a Christmas party three years ago at the assisted-living center where my wife works."

"Well, we can't all have a fucking twenty-thousand-dollar album."

"Ten thousand."

"I heard twenty."

"Howie, I know you can play bass. Believe me, it would be easier because I know where you are. But there's no Truants reunion without the Truants, the guys from Chase."

"This doesn't make any sense. I'm a better bass player, and I'M FROM CHASE! Jerry's done nothing for the school since he left. It's like he was never there."

"Hey, Howie, what can I tell you?"

The forty-six-year-old adult man was ready. "And I talked to Dino Paradise and he said I could play bass."

Tim found his toothbrush next to some paper clips in the top drawer. He straightened his back. After twenty-some nights on the floor, it didn't take that long.

"Hey, Howie, all the stuff I just said?"

"Yeah?"

"I was being nice. I was being diplomatic. Dino ain't the band. The band is us. And none of us wants you. If you hear from your brother, either let him know or don't."

"Those are my options?"

"Or you can eat me."

Tim heard a sharp intake of air on the other end of the phone. "Nice. Nice school spirit, man," was all Howie Fyne could muster. But it was plenty. It was the first big laugh Tim had had in twenty-some days.

RICHIE'S INTERCOM BUZZED.

"I have Gail Thiel on line two."

"Thanks, Laz. . . . Mrs. Thiel, it's me. Counselor Dipshit."

She had to giggle. "Pretty good, Richie."

"Look, I'm calling on behalf of Johnno, uh, John."

"Yeah?"

"He's too embarrassed to ask. So, this was my idea to call. You hate the idea, hate me."

"I'll try."

"He told me you both agreed the kids miss him and you need a break. He also has run into some housing problems in the city and doesn't want to waste any more of your mutual assets than he has to living in a hotel. So, I suggested, my suggestion, and he said to ask you—"

"He wants to stay in the converted room downstairs until we work out the settlement or he gets something permanent out here or in the city?"

"Uh, yeah, right. How did you know?"

"That's what I suggested three months ago."

"Really."

"Look," said Gail, "I know you must think I'm a stone bitch after our last conversation, but I was a little ambushed here. John never wanted to separate and I never wanted to go to counseling. Total impasse. Nothing happened. No talking. Well, that part didn't surprise me. Then one day I call, fed up, I say get a lawyer, he does. The next day. Not just any lawyer, some lizard he was in a band with."

"And I surprised you?"

"Your sleaziness, no. I worked on Wall Street for twelve years. I can catch guys like you bare-handed. But who knew he was ever in a band?"

"He never told you about the band?"

"No."

"Did he ever play the guitar for you?"

"Once. He played 'Michael, Row the Boat Ashore.'"

"That was one of our hits!"

Gail Thiel burst out laughing. "Sorry."

"I'm going to bet that was your reaction when he played 'Michael.'" She was still laughing. "Look, why don't the four of us meet here Wednesday to hammer this out."

"Four?"

"Your attorney."

"I fired my lawyer."

Richie straightened up and swiveled his chair. "Okay, then how about Wednesday night, seven o'clock, for drinks in the lobby of the Sheraton on Fifty-second and Seventh?"

Gail paused. "Isn't that a karaoke bar?"

"Uh, a karaoke bar? I don't know. Maybe. I don't know, that's where John is staying. Why did you fire your lawyer?"

"Asshole tried to hit on me."

"Oh."

IN THE FORMIDABLE HOUSE-SITTING CAREER of Brian Brock, now in its third decade, there was a story for every abode. A story, as in one, differing only in whether his lodging was the result of opportunity, persistence, pity, or a gumbo therein. And although decor, square footage, and climate may have varied, they all ended identically. The owner/tenant returned. And around an hour later, the Lumina drove off to its next set of copied keys.

That said, the setup with Lizzie was a room and board *hapaxlegomenon*. A *hapaxlegomenon* is a word that occurs once in literature. Just once. There's no chance this situation would ever occur again. It was as original as the set of Lizzie's house keys Brian was still using.

Two days ago, Lizzie had knocked on her own door and been let in by the guy whose vertebrae she had left without explanation ten days before that. They had spoken twice in the interim. The first time she sounded sleepy. "Stay in my place. Don't worry. I took a vacation," was the extent of the first call. "I'm paying for my vacation. We'll work something out when I get back," was the second. So, he would not be leaving when the tenant returned. *Hapaxlegomenon.*

"Vacation" was a three-day relapse on junk, living out of her car or worse. "Paying for the vacation" was the week she spent in detox at some hospital, maybe New England Baptist, if they still called it that. That's as close as Lizzie would get to specifics after she reclaimed her apartment. More would be revealed, just not right now. For that, Brian was relieved. As for right now, she told him he could stay as long as he wanted, all he really had to do was drive her to and from Gavin's, and wait for her in the parking lot when she went to NA meetings or her outpatient program. For that, he was beyond relieved.

"We'll look out for each other," she said.

"You think I need to be looked out for?"

"Maybe not you, but the guy who was here ten days ago, the guy who cried, then fucked me, then thought he threw his back out because he was gay? That guy might be better off not alone."

That was the other condition of Brian's stay with Lizzie. He had to come clean on his ambiguous exile from the Truants. He had been as evasive as his host during those first two days, mostly running around making meals and playing her to sleep on his keyboard. And, man, she slept a lot. Went down and stayed down. Lizzie was due back at Gavin's tomorrow for the lunch shift. Denny Gavin had bought the vacation story from Brian, who lied with the ease of a man who had spent twenty-some years calling in sick to the nonacademic world.

"So," said Lizzie, "when am I gonna hear it?"

"What?"

"The big story."

"I'm getting to it."

"Well, in the meantime, I'm broke. Can you lend me a hundred until I can get some tips going tomorrow?"

"A hundred?"

"Yeah. Or forty. And while I was, uh, gone, you didn't happen to take some good ol' prep school initiative and bust out December rent?"

"Ah, no."

Lizzie yawned. "We may be screwed." She yawned again. "Well, we're not screwed tonight, although it does feel like he's already turned off the heat."

"Feels okay to me."

"Really? Then it's probably me. Junkie chills."

"Or the quart of Brigham's peppermint stick we just split."

"Hah!" Another yawn. "Didn't I just wake up?"

"Not really."

"Let's do the big story later."

"Fine."

When Lizzie finally shook herself to sleep on the couch under three blankets, Brian ran out to the Lumina and opened the trunk just to make sure. There, under the cartons of literary criticism, the dead running shoes, a toaster oven, and reams of doctoral false starts, cocooned in those quilted throws movers use, lay the entire ancestral fortune of Brian Brock. Two industrially laminated, unopened copies of *Out of Site.*

Dino Paradise was listed in the Arlington phone book, and the fifteen-minute trip from Watertown took a half hour with three stops for directions. It would have taken longer, but at the last stop, he just asked the cashier at the White Hen Pantry, "Where's Dino Paradise's place?" The guy, a local guy, had a good line: "Take your second right, then your first left, and keep going until you hear Freddie 'Boom Boom' Cannon."

It wasn't Freddie he heard, but Paul Revere and the Raiders. Pretty damn close, Brian thought. Not the guy who sang the theme to *Where the Action Is*, Dick Clark's short-lived weekday outdoor version of *American Bandstand*, but the show's house band.

Dino answered the door and greeted the phrase, "Hi, I'm Brian Brock," with brief but scary hyperventilation. Lizzie had said he was fat, but Brian was never prepared to be met by so much.

Dino knew the look. "I'm anorexic, but I fight it," he said, again. Nothing. "Brian Brock, you bag of shit. Come in! Just when I think it's gonna be another night of Dino pullin' pud to the Raiders, one of the Truants shows up like I'm some dying kid in that Lou Gehrig film."

"Pride of the Yankees."

"Those cocksuckers," coughed Dino. "You remember Tony Conigliaro? Tony C.? He made two forty-fives when he was with the Sox. I had 'em both. He died in like 1985, and believe me, I cried like a fuckin' baby. Coma thing. Fuckin' shame. Well, the next day some guy offers me two grand for 'Little Red Scooter.' What am I gonna do? I'm a businessman. My wife is all over me to get my stomach stapled. Even if I had insurance, it doesn't cover that shit. It's fuckin' elective. So, I take the two grand. Then the staple guy I was gonna see loses his license. Résumé thing. Never got it done. Well, you can fuckin' see that. No regrets. But I wish I had that goddamn forty-five back. *'She'll go around the town, and bring you down, the little putt-putt. . . .'* Women. What does Zevon say? 'You can't start 'em like a car, you can't stop 'em with a gun'?"

"I think he said that about love."

"Right. What can I get you, Professor?"

Brian declined a beverage. His hurry to get back to Lizzie before she woke had metastasized during Dino's paean to Tony Conigliaro. But at least that had been a story about buying and selling. He motioned Dino to walk with him out to the trunk of the Lumina and delicately peeled back the quilted movers' throw.

"Good fuckin' Christ," said Dino. "Unopened?"

"I've never even heard it."

"Jesus, Larry, and Curly."

"Look, I don't have much time," Brian began. "I need some money if I'm going to be able to hang around awhile, let alone until the reunion, let alone if there is a reunion—"

"Let alone if they let you in the reunion."

"Touché."

"Soup du jour."

"The point is, I'm not a businessman. All my worldly possessions fit in this trunk here, but somebody thinks this is worth ten grand. Which means"—he reached under the quilted throw again—"two of these are worth twenty grand."

Dino had ignored the first frigid spurt of cold sweat on the back of his neck, but not the second, third, and fourth. "Shit," he muttered. He knew he had maybe a minute.

"But I'll gladly take ten grand for the two. I mean, that's fair."

The fire started just below his left shoulder. "Brian, I can write you a check for five hundred right now, but you have to wait until Tuesday, no, Wednesday, to put it in."

"Five hundred. You mean to start?"

"No. That's it. That's today's offer."

Brian, who had used up the worldly possessions line, did Pacino in *Scarface*. "Ho-kay, dees ees business talk," he said. "What about two grand and I'll hang on to one. Come on, two grand. Like 'Little Red Scooter.'"

"Professor, it doesn't go that way. I'm working for you guys. Look, it's another five months until we get going. Then it'll get back up to where the fuckin' German guy came in." Dino went on, the oven timer in his chest ticking as he cautioned Brian that he did not want to screw him out of the inevitable windfall that would come his laminated way come spring.

"Dino, I'm broke."

Dino fished a twenty out of his jeans and closed Brian's free hand around it as he began to back up. "All I can give you is gas money. Speaking of which, I gotta take a wicked shit. Keep it. And keep these LPs. You got fuckin' plutonium here."

"Dino . . ."

A man can tell when another man really has to get to the bathroom and is not just ending a conversation. No, wait. A woman can tell that. Men can't tell shit. So, the best Brian could do was assume that it was a little of both. Dump, then dump. What he had no right to be able to project, to scenario-ize, was that Dino's destination was not just his bathroom, but his medicine cabinet, and the small bottle of clear pills on the bottom shelf. No one could have guessed that. Not even a woman.

SHE HUNG UP THE PHONE AND TOLD HERSELF she had done the right thing. And she went back to her whistling, which she had been doing all morning. Which Gail Thiel never did. Ask her daughters, who asked her during breakfast, "Mom, why are you whistling? You never whistle."

"Sure I whistle."

"Is it 'cause Daddy's home?"

"I just whistle when you two pests aren't here."

Books have been written about the insight of kids, but the girls were flat wrong here. Johnno, on his first morning in the basement after the karaoke-bar summit with Gail and Richie, had left for the train around 6:30. He had made himself coffee and found his old commuter cup ("I'm one of those assholes now," he had said after he sprang for the thing at Dunkin' Donuts two years ago) and, are you ready, *wiped every surface down and rinsed out the sponge!* So, the two months alone in the city hadn't been a complete waste.

Impressive, but let the record show Gail's whistling had started in the shower, twenty minutes after her husband was out of the house. It was tough at first. Combination of the water running on her upturned face, and the fact that she had kind of forgotten how to do it.

The call came just after ten. A gulp-crying woman who had to reintroduce herself. Cheryl Schlesinger.

Schlesinger . . . Schlesinger . . . right, they had met twelve-something years ago. The wife of some Chase classmate of John's. Tim. Right, Cheryl. Younger than him. Pretty. Easily thin with ready-to-go hair. Younger than *her*. It all came back. She hadn't liked her. But that was long before the crying and gulping, which sounded much older and not pretty.

Tell me if I'm being silly. That was Cheryl's premise. She had no one else to call. There were no other active wives in the Truants. She went through it all. Tim promises to get rid of drums. Tim lies. She finds drums. Drums go on street. Tim tells her about reunion. Tim joins drums on street. Drums find an apartment. Tim doesn't.

There was more. With refrains, it went on for another ten minutes. *Tell me if I'm being silly. . . . How can I trust him? . . . How can I take him back, even if I want to? . . . What else don't I know about? . . . I can't believe he lied to me for eight fucking years. . . . This sucks. . . .* Gail waited until Cheryl was finished, with a patience that normally lay in a time zone beyond her. There was great familiarity to Cheryl's tone. Who did Gail know who talked with that kind of stridency, surrounded on all sides with three-inch-thick justified anger? Oh, right. Her.

It was much too uncomfortably familiar to listen to while sitting down. Gail walked upstairs with the cordless phone and lost contact only when she pulled her sweatshirt over her head (probably during an *I can't believe he lied to me for eight fucking years. . . .*). She paced around the bedroom in her well-conceived bra and panties, listening and wincing. Occasionally, okay, six times, she saw herself walk by the mirror on her closet door. Pretty fucking great for forty-seven. The girls she ran ragged on the courts at the club would never admit it. They'd say, "I hope I play as good as you when I'm your age, Gail." And what they meant was, "I can't play like you now. And where'd you get that ass?"

But that was momentary. This was all too compelling. To be on the other end of the line, listening to what sounded way too much like the out-of-town previews of somebody's one-woman show about Gail Thiel. That is, Gail Thiel until last night, when everything changed. When she was pretty sure she may have gone home with the wrong guy.

At the last *Tell me if I'm being silly . . .* , Gail sat down on the edge of her bed. The first thing she did was thank Cheryl for calling her. And mean it. And be stunned that she meant it. She said she understood and related to everything Cheryl had gulped up and felt uniquely qualified to respond. That was all she could remember verbatim now, just after she had hung up. The rest of it was a coherent, positive, momentum-fueled hum. She had said something like *Look-he-never-cheated-on-you, he-never-hit-you, you-must-have-feelings-for-him. You-have-to-let-him-have-this. It's-a-weekend. It's-his-past. You-don't-have-to-enjoy-it, but-let-him-have-that. They're-passionate-about-that. You-might-want-to-see-what-that-looks-like. I-think-I-do. And-so-what-if-I-don't? He'll-be-passionate-about-you. It's-exciting. What, you-never-lied-*

to-him? Take-him-back. What-do-you-think-you're-going-to-find-out-there?

What indeed. Gail meant what she had said to Cheryl. Every word she could barely recall. She had taken her husband back . . . correction, had agreed to take her husband back . . . correction, back in . . . clarification, back in but living in the basement. She had agreed to do that, for expediency only, and in the process, amidst all the amicability and civility, amidst all that late 1990s Respect My Boundaries twaddle, Gail Thiel had glimpsed the urgency of the past and found it understandable, unstoppable, and relentlessly sexy. All in the most inane of places. A karaoke bar. Housed in the unlikeliest of vessels. The forty-two-short Armanied smile from which coursed "We Gotta Get Out of This Place." Gotta indeed.

Tell me if I'm being silly. Gail picked up the phone, resumed whistling as she dialed Richie's office, and told herself she was doing the right thing.

"I'M GOING TO TRY AND TELL THIS chronologically, but I may have to double back. I haven't even thought about this shit in twenty years."

Brian was lying, of course. He had thought about it a great deal. Maybe every other day. It was just that somewhere around twenty years ago, as he was unpacking whatever car trunk was then containing his worldly possessions at whatever stop this was (Bowdoin? Colby? Michigan State?), he'd finally gotten tired of dictating this unresolved story in his head. Like some book on tape that gets eaten by the cassette deck in your car around page 150.

Maybe he just hadn't told it out loud. Ever. Well, that made sense. Nobody had ever asked. Until now. There was Lizzie, fed, blanketed, her weary yet eager face propped up by the back of her right hand. The best audience he could hope for. Brian took a deep breath and told himself to try and steer clear of self-pity.

I came to Chase as an outsider, he began. He walked onto the campus that first day, a scholarshipped sophomore from Cincinnati, son of a minister and a music teacher, and saw nothing but wealthy, confident B student/A athletes from New England and New York. Waves of them. It was then he understood what people meant when they talked of "exclusive" boarding schools. Exclusive of him.

And so, he grinded. That's what they called studying back then. Grinding. Nourished by books and words and key points hurriedly scratched on a blackboard. Everything came easily, except science, where he opted for a rare Chase gut course, a non-lab biology class. Rec bio, they called it. It was filled with sophomore jocks, including Johnno Thiel. Brian chuckled and corrected himself. *Dr. Johnno Thiel.*

Distancing himself from his contemporaries was nothing new. But where Brian Brock began to lap the field was in Latin. He had taken so much Latin in junior high that when he arrived at Chase, he was placed in Latin IV, an advanced Vergil class with five seniors and two juniors.

Chase Academy had three faculty members teaching Latin. Lonlan and Hoyle (who learns any teacher's first name?) taught first and second year. Mr. Fordyce taught everything else.

Paul Fordyce was ten years out of Yale, nine years at Chase. *He was so funny. Funny like a guy who wasn't a Latin teacher. But that's all he wanted to be. He'd been at Chase nine years and would probably still be there. . . .* Brian blew his nose and put his head down. He kept it down as he continued.

The Vergil class was wonderful, but the next year, his junior year, Fordyce introduced Brian and the other two Latin IV survivors to Latin V: Roman Elegy and Lyric. They spent the year studying the great Latin poets. Catullus, Horace, Tibullus, and Propertius, to whom Brian would devote his quixotic, quarter-century thesis. Thirty-one years and 562 classes later, it was still the best course he'd ever taken. It taught him the value of the word, the endless currency of wordplay and, at seventeen, locked him in on a college major and a life's pursuit. That's all. Nothing much else.

Brian might have gone all three years at Chase not speaking to anyone but Fordyce, except that every once in a while he would poke his head up from his scholar's gated isolation and play the organ in chapel. At first, all that did was give his outsider status a sound track. But just before the end of sophomore year, Thiel, Richie, Tim, and Jerry cornered him after a particularly playful rendering of "God of Our Fathers."

I was grateful they found me. But I was always treated like the A-student, son of a preacher man. I mean, we were all outsiders— we used to get pissed the Outsiders had stolen our rightful name— except Thiel. You know, jock. Your brother was always nice, quiet, funny. Jerry would call me "Ray" when I would ask him not to bring a bottle into the Music Room. Ray. For Ray Righteous. That I didn't mind. And Richie was always Richie. None of us were really close. Maybe Tim and Johnno, and not that close. And I was never as good at giving shit as they were, although one time I called Richie Frank Sin-not. Pretty good. We just knew the five of us had the only chance of being what we were there. And then. Whatever that was. Whenever it was.

The Truants were Brian's only distraction, although he never strayed too far. When he began to write songs junior year and the summer thereafter, it was his attempt to brush up against lyric poetry. Fordyce actually encouraged it. "You'll want to keep doing it senior year, when you and I get into the dry stuff," he said.

The band came back to Chase a week early senior year to rehearse, and Brian went looking for Fordyce. He would have no classics peers this year. It was going to be a nine-month tutorial on the historians Tacitus and Sallust. Just him and Fordyce. One-man class. Latin VI. A graduate school-level quiver from which Brian could endlessly draw when he left for Yale (where else?) the following fall. That was the plan.

One problem. At first, one problem. Fordyce was not there and another teacher was staying in his room in Scaife Hall. Brian went to the dean of faculty, Miller Russell, who told him Fordyce had left on a half sabbatical to finish his last ABD (all but dissertation) courses. He would return after Christmas.

It sounded like bullshit, but Brian wasn't as distrustful then. Ray Righteous. He spent the fall term, the last one that counted for college, taking introductory Homeric Greek with Hoyle and sitting in on the Cicero class with the juniors, which was as good as being held back. He finished with a ninety-three average, good for third in his class. *I wasn't working nearly as hard. My grades went up on rep alone.* He was still industrious, just not driven. Any grinding was now devoted to the musical elegies he wrote for the Truants.

By then, we were like celebrities. We even went on the road to do dances. Thiel may have actually gotten laid. But he would have been the only one. If Richie had scored, we never would have heard the end of it. I wrote a lot of songs then. Mostly sappy. But it was the closest I ever got to lyric poetry. And I had something to look forward to. Mr. Fordyce coming back for my last five months. And getting into Yale.

Brian made Lizzie laugh for the only time when he talked about how he never knew how many gay teachers they had at Chase. *I'm not good at that. Hell, I still can't tell in my own house.* There were a couple of no-brainers, fussy types who would wear dark glasses when they walked by the showers, but they seemed there to fill some sort of quota. Usually harmless.

Usually. In the spring of Brian's junior year, two teachers, shower/sunglasses guys, had been fired for going into nearby South Chase and bringing back local elementary school boys for a, ahem, tour of the academy. The police had been trailing them for months and were deferential enough to wait until the students were all in the gym taking finals to arrest them. South Chase was, still is, whatever can fit inside of a small town, so the scandal never seeped farther than a mile in any direction. And Chase Academy made the whole thing go away faster than the two teachers by donating a pool for the elementary school. The only evidence that anything had happened would surface transparently in the elitist air, in the smart-ass taunts of those who came back the following fall.

When Brian returned from Christmas vacation, he found a letter waiting for him from Fordyce. He explained why he would not be coming back. The day the two gay teachers had been arrested, the last day, one of them had borrowed Paul Fordyce's Mustang to go into town. The teachers stood up and cleared Fordyce with the cops, the town, everyone. And the school understood that while he hadn't been involved, it might be better for him to stay away until Christmas. By November, Chase and its board of trustees, maybe just after signing the first check for the pool, decided to extend Fordyce's exile for the rest of the year. In the pariah conversion chart, that works out to forever. He closed his letter to Brian with no return address, only the last line of Catullus poem #101: *"Atque in perpetuum, frater, ave atque vale."* ("And into eternity, brother, hail and farewell.")

I couldn't tell anybody. Then, two months later, Yale turns me down. Incomplete application. No written recommendation from Fordyce. The healthiest thing I could do was write this fucking song. "Furious." After I wrote it, I changed the spelling to Furius. Furius was a young boy Catullus seduced after his affair with Lesbia ended. I looked at it and it made me laugh. Two devastating letters and I had created this deep inside joke with myself. The irony is that I've never been able to re-create that kind of wordplay since. I've never come close to the artist I was that day. So, no thesis, no home, no examples, no registered sexuality.

Richie must have seen it written in Brian's notebook. After all this time, that was the only explanation he had. Saw it in his note-book. Saw the way it was written.

"F-U-R-I-U-S." Put it all together it was over some guy. Of course, by then the story of the fired teachers was ensconced as school saga, but rewritten with Fordyce squarely in the mix. Richie must have waited, as guys like that do when they have a fifth ace in their shoe, and played that card in the studio that last day they were recording the album. Brian walked out and never stopped looking back.

He was about to offer to use up the last bit of battery juice in his Yamaha keyboard and play the song for Lizzie. Play "(Furious)," the most courageous thing to ever emerge from Brian Brock, the only thing he ever felt like he finished. But he looked up for the first time in ten minutes and decided against it. Why wake her?

chapter seven

SHE TRIED CALLING HIM TIMMY. That usually worked.

"Timmy, just do it one more time."

"Cheryl, come on."

"Once more. I swear, that'll be the last."

"You just said that. I was here. I heard it."

"This time I mean it. And then no more. Come on. You know you love doing it."

"But it hurts."

She laughed, and he was right behind her. Laughed like she knew it wasn't the last time, and laughed like neither of them knew when it would no longer be entertaining. Just punitive.

She pushed her husband behind the door. "Assume the position," she said, and closed the door. "Now, I'm coming to see you at your office for the first time in three weeks." She was now playing two roles, "'Is Tim in his office?' / 'Yeah, Mrs. S., but you bettah knawck first.' / 'I've never knocked in my life.'" She opened the door. *Crack.*

"Ahhh! Shit!" Now wider, and there was her husband, on all

fours, scrambling toward an open book on the floor. "Ahhh! Sh—here it is!" He looked up, and even though it was another reenactment in the Bedford house weeks later, Tim could still manage to raise the same surprise, embarrassment, and joy when the Mass. *Ah*-chive colleague he thought had barged in without knocking turned out to be his wife. He could also still manage to raise the same angry welt on his head.

They collapsed in silent, pained hysterics until it sounded like someone's tea was ready. "Train whistle," said Cheryl, pointing to herself. A bout with childhood asthma had left her with an occasional high-pitched rail, brought on by helpless laughter. Tim responded as he always did, miming a conductor pulling on an emergency cord. And he stopped the train whistle with a move he had developed just recently: bear-hugging his wife from behind and resting his chin on the top of her head. Once the whistle passed, she got spun around and kissed like he was home on a forty-eight-hour furlough.

Never underestimate the end of a fight between two people only good at avoiding confrontation. It is awash in gratitude. When Cheryl had showed up at the Mass. *Ah*-chives unannounced (and unknowingly landing the bout's only blow), she surrendered *and* won. And nobody understood that better, quicker, than Tim, clothes wrinkled slightly less than his will. Beneath the mutual chant of *Sorry,no,I'msorry,no,I'msorry,no,I'msorry* they agreed on the other thing they had to agree on. The drums would go back into the attic, unpacked and in plain sight, and could be played whenever and as long as Tim was alone in the house. And if he was able to clear more space, he could rig up the bedroom CD player they never used and play along to that instead of waiting for the FM cut of Hendrix's "All Along the Watchtower" that never came.

He'd been back living in the house over a month now, and still Tim would be at his office at the Mass. *Ah*-chives and find something—a white shirt button or glob of toothpaste on the carpet, ranch dressing on a chair leg—that would remind him of his twenty-some days on the floor. His Gandhi-like price of non-acquiescence. Of course, the idea had been to make his point to Cheryl, but by Day Three, when everything smells like your ass on a seat cushion and you've perfected nothing except how to shower in a men's-room sink, you become choir and preacher. And that's as it should be. Because the only person Tim Schlesinger needed to convince about the sanctity of his musical hard wiring was himself. And even though it was January and nobody in the band had heard anything or if they had they weren't talking even more than they'd not been talking before. Even though Dino Paradise sometimes sounded too broke to buy his own bullshit. Even though it was almost impossible to call Lizzie's apartment and not have to ask her or Brian, "Have you been crying?" Even though he had a welt the size of a small concession, there lay in Tim's grasp the greatest gift a too-long-hiatused drummer could imagine—the POSSIBILITY of a gig.

This he had to explain to himself before he could explain it to Cheryl. And she didn't need to get it. She had gotten most of what she needed to get from Gail Thiel's speech on the phone. The rest she copped from something she'd been told by a former classmate who was working in the White House. Apparently, the President, the President of the United States, had been hiding some twenty-two-year-old intern under his Oval Office desk, enjoying the occasional hummer while he was on the phone with the, ahem, joint chiefs. Meanwhile, her husband was curled *next to* his desk, alone, and willing to stay there as long as it made sense to him.

Cheryl would muse about exactly when (a year? six months?) this surreal soft-core porn trailer might begin to play out in the media—*This just in: President's dick in heavy-set girl's mouth. No film at eleven . . .*—and yet it still took a couple of weeks before she let herself get to the conclusion that there, now there, there was a bad marriage. There was a guy who really lied. Not here. There.

And as much as Gail Thiel's words had helped, Bill Clinton's alleged actions had flung the gates guarding her righteousness off their hinges. Cheryl Schlesinger was probably the only registered Democrat in the country grateful that Clinton wasn't able to keep his legacy in his pants. Okay, maybe her and Bill Bradley. And you could add her husband, if she ever told him.

She kissed the bump on Tim's head gently enough to tingle her.

"Ow?" she asked.

"Ow."

Those were the last two words exchanged for the next twenty minutes. Key word: words.

They exchanged everything else—on the floor, in the bed, in the wing chair next to the bed—with passion summoned by sweet care rather than urgency. Tim and Cheryl had always been affectionate with each other. But suddenly, *"Act now, and we'll throw in absolutely free!"* suddenly, there was a lot of sex. A lot. Thanks again, Mr. President. It did wonders for Cheryl's self-esteem. She had even asked Tim to invite Lizzie and Brian over for dinner. Dinner she would prepare. Tim said sure, even though he was usually physically vanquished by guests, socializing, and anything that smacked of a light evening. But who knew a regular, really regular, sack dance with his wife would give him energy—the energy of an extrovert?

"Roll over," he said twenty-one minutes later.

"Well, well."

"I thought we'd add a little music."

"Tim."

"Come on. I did the door for you."

"Tim."

"Come on. You love this."

"No, *you* love this."

"Oh yeah, well who said, just the other night, 'You know, I love when you drum on my ass?'"

"You did."

"That doesn't sound like me."

"That's because you said, 'You know, I love *to* drum on your ass.'"

"That sounds like me."

She was laughing, and when he tried to nudge her top shoulder over, she shook and snorted. "How old are you?"

"One song."

"Jesus. All right."

She lay on her stomach facing away from him. He threw down the covers.

"It is a great ass."

"Thanks. It's a Remo."

Tim shrieked. "How did you know that?!"

She swung around and propped herself up on her left elbow. "When you're carrying drums out to the curb, you have a lot of time to read." The fact that Cheryl had not only remembered the make of the skins on his kit, but had somehow reformed this knowledge into monogrammed entertainment for her husband, well, those were the steps he'd seen daily from her the last month. Steps toward him.

Cheryl flipped back over. "You know what," Tim said, kissing that gorgeous behind, "let's forget it."

"No. Go ahead. One song."

"Okay, but if you guess this, you earn a lifetime exemption from ass-drumming."

Tim began the light, staccato syncopation:

> *Bahd-a-bip*
> *boom-boom . . . bip-bi-boom-boom*
> *bip-boom-boom bip-bi-bid-ah-boom-bip*

"No idea."

*Bahd-a-bip boom-boom bip-bi-boom-boom bip-
boom-boom bip-bi-bid-ah-boom-bip*

"Hint?"

"Okay."

"The Turtles."

"'Hey, Hey, We're the Turtles'?"

"No. That was the Monkees."

"Well, that's my guess. I'm wrong. No exemption. Let the ass-drumming continue."

"'You Baby.'"

"What?"

"That's the name of the song."

"Never heard it."

Tim sang, like a drummer, and drummed. *"'Every time I go to sleep till the morning comes I dream about you baby . . .'"*

"Never heard it."

"Come on. A classic."

"When did it come out?"

"Nineteen sixty-seven."

"I was three. Did you guys play that song?"

"Nah. We didn't have the vocals. As you can hear."

"Shouldn't you be practicing something you might actually play?"

"All right. How about this?"

"How about ever getting laid again?"

"How about me making dinner?"

Tim hopped out of bed and Cheryl flipped back over and, in one move, smacked his rear end.

"What was that?" he said.

"Gary Numan. 'Here in My Car.'"

They sang lyric-lessly:

Here in my car,
I dah dah, dahdahdah,
I dah dah, dahdahdah
And dah dah, dahdahdah
In my car, dah dah (SMACK!) dah dah, dah dah. . . .

But together.

RICHIE'S HANDS STILL SMELLED. Forget that nonsense about lemon juice. It may have worked on Susan Sarandon in *Atlantic City*, but then again, that was a film and we had to take her word for it.

He'd get used to it. He had to. For the last two Wednesdays, Richie had left his office at 10:30 and walked the five blocks south to St. Bartholemew's Church, into the side entrance on Fifty-first Street, rolled up his Egyptian broadclothed sleeves, and made two hundred tuna sandwiches before noon. The homeless, the ones Giuliani hadn't exported, would start lining up around 11:30. He did not wait around to serve. He couldn't. He wanted to, but he felt that job was better handled by people who deserved the gratitude of others. Richie's reward for ninety minutes of service was beyond appropriate. Almost custom-made: stanky hands.

"Laz, can you order some lunch?"

"I thought you'd eaten already," she intercommed back. "It smells like the Bumble Bee plant."

"Good one. I liked it almost as much as when you said it an hour ago."

"Regular order?" said Ms. Lazarony.

"Yeah. Make sure no whipped cream on the Jell-O."

"Okay. Chicken soup, a million saltines, and Jell-O, no whipped cream."

The bland diet was not symbolic. It was all Richie Lyman could successfully digest. So, ah, it was symbolic. Since his release from

New York Hospital/Cornell Medical Center, the Hyatt Hernia, he had decided he could only change his life by first seeing if he was capable of doing one decent thing a week. Hence, the two hundred tuna sandwiches.

Fran Brennan's aim could not have been more lethal if she'd had a telescopic sight on the point of her shoe. Before the incident, Richie's least favorite word in the English language had been, going away, "rectum." Now you had to flip another sixty-five or so pages in the dictionary, still under *r*, to find it.

Rupture.

A testicular rupture, a tear in the *tunica albuginea*, the connective tissue that surrounds the—well, you get the idea, must be surgically repaired within seventy-two hours. Which makes sense, because it takes the average guy about seventy hours to realize his zipper ain't down and he didn't cut himself shaving. Richie could have called Thiel and asked him to recommend a urologist, but that would have been like handing his former classmate a gift certificate for a lifetime supply of ridicule. Which also explains why, when the bill came to Richie's office from the hospital, he told Laz he'd gone in for an ingrown toenail. He just didn't say whose toe.

He spent the holidays with his balls on ice and concluded that God was trying to get his attention. Well, mission accomplished. Even though he had no idea what the hell had come over Fran Brennan or why it had happened, that wasn't the, uh, point. Whether or not fucking one's clients while you're handling their divorce was in fact a victimless crime was never an issue. But now, suddenly, just like that, it made no sense. He could not sit there, however uncomfortably, and justify it. Maybe for other lawyers, but not for himself. The enemy had been subdued.

And, five, maybe ten minutes after Richie had achieved this epididymal epiphany, came a voice over his message machine. The first phone call from Gail Thiel.

She called twice more over the next ten days, less innocently each time (*"Do you have any advice for getting an old Animals song out of your head . . ." "Are your New Year's Eve plans as nonexistent as mine?"*). Hey, he may have been irrevocably altered, but he knew that voice. He called her back January 2 and, unplanned, found himself telling her exactly what had happened. Exactly. All of it. He knew she wouldn't tell Johnno, because he knew that voice. Instead, he made an appointment for her at the office the following Thursday.

Say what? Irrevocably altered, our ass!

Calm down. By then, Richie Lyman had made his first two hundred tuna sandwiches. And, other than the complete inefficacy of lemon juice, it had gone quite well. Seeing Gail Thiel in his office, in fabulous broad daylight, would be the second decent thing he would find himself capable of doing. He was not worried.

"Counselor Lyman?"

Counselor? "Very funny, Laz."

"Your food is here."

"Fine." He thought he heard giggling, but it might have been his stomach.

His office door opened and a somewhat serious-looking older black man, a bit of a stretch from the traditional delivery *chicos* of the Palace coffee shop on Fifty-seventh, entered holding the cardboard take-out tray in front of him.

"Didn't my secretary pay you?"

"No."

"How much is it? All I got is a twenty."

"Twenty is fine."

Richie turned to fish out his wallet. "That's a little large."

"That's what they tell me," the delivery man said.

He turned back and where his lunch was supposed to be he saw what looked like a giant penis, only gianter.

"Yeah," repeated Pressure Chief, "that's what they tell me."

That's when Jerry Fyne came staggering into the room. So, it was giggling he'd heard. Jerry threw a pair of pants at Pressure.

"You should see the look on your face," said Jerry. "Priceless."

"No," said Richie, "twenty dollars."

"This is Pressure Chief. I met him in the Caymans and brought him back to New York."

"Nice to meet you. Where the fuck is my lunch?"

"I've got it!" yelled Laz.

"STAY OUT THERE!" Richie yelled back, even though Pressure was fully sheathed. He took a cellophane-wrapped brick out of the cardboard tray. "What is this?"

"Banana-apricot cake," said Pressure.

"Where'd you get it?"

"I made it."

"He's a good baker," Jerry said.

"I'm a great baker."

"Look, is it Pressure? I'm kind of on a bland diet."

"Perfect for bland diet," Pressure said.

"I'd love to take your word for it, just on your résumé alone. Jerry, I haven't seen you in fifteen years, since you sold me those counterfeit Knick tickets. Why are you here? I guess you heard about the album."

Jerry walked around the desk and gave Richie the tightest of fake hugs. "You've seen it. You know people," he whispered. "How can I get this guy into the porn business?"

"Get the fuck out of here."

"No, I'm serious."

"So am I. Get the fuck out of here."

"Nice meeting you," said Pressure. "Try the cake. I'm looking for work."

"I told him," said Jerry.

"Go away," said Richie.

Jerry didn't. "What album?" he asked.

"Go away."

"What, our album?"

"Laz!"

Ms. Lazarony dropped Richie's real lunch on his desk and hustled Jerry and Pressure out all in the same move. That was the first invaluable thing she did. The second was five minutes later, when she ran back into Richie's office and demanded he take a bite of the banana-apricot cake. "If you don't think this is the most amazing thing you've ever eaten, I will quit, walk out of here, track that guy down, and go door-to-door selling this friggin' stuff for him."

"Okay, it's great." He took another bite. "It's uniquely great." Laz began to take it back and Richie grabbed her hand. "Where you going with my lunch?"

Richie had two briefs to finish and an arbitration on Monday he hadn't even begun to prepare for, but it all vanished like the last morsel of what had moments ago been before him. You know, he reasoned, not like a lawyer, but rather a member of Odysseus's crew, I would be fine just eating this cake for the rest of my life. He would try to get this Pressure Pack, Pressure King, whatever he called himself to the ungawking world, a job. A legitimate job. Next week. That would be the decent thing he'd do next week.

"Laz."

She walked back in. "You ate it all? I hate you."

"Did Jerry leave his number?"

"Yeah." She handed him a business card with at least four previous phone numbers scratched out. "He said to use this one, and if it's disconnected—"

"Try Charley O's on Seventh Avenue?"

"How'd you know?"

"That's where I picked up the bogus Knick tickets fifteen years ago."

Laz was on her way out and had begun to close the door before pivoting back in.

"You know I never say this."

"What?"

"There's an absolute babe out here to see you."

"Is it Thursday?"

"No, Wednesday."

Richard found a stray banana-apricot crumb, too large to ignore, on his blotter. As he popped it in his mouth, he smelled the tuna on his fingers and recoiled in his chair just enough to fling a dart of postoperative pain to his refurbished ballroom.

"Tell her I'll see her tomorrow. Thursday."

"'PIANO MAN!'"

"Look, I promised myself when I was lucky enough to get this gig last month that the customers were always right—"

"'Piano Man!'"

"And I would try to never disappoint you folks. Give you people what you want—"

"'Piano Man!'"

"But it's been three weeks, and we've got forty people here where we used to have twenty, and I made myself one promise—"

"'Piano Man!'"

"That no matter what happened, no matter how drunk you got, how drunk I got, how many threats you made—"

"Fuckin' 'PIANO MAN'!"

"I was NOT going to play 'Piano Man.' Come on. It's 1997, for Christ sake. I can play anything. The more obscure, the better. Rock, blues, folk songs, Duke and the Drivers . . ."

"Duke!"

"He ain't here. My point is. I think we can do better. I think we, all of us at Gavin's, should aspire to a higher level. Honestly, haven't we really had enough of 'Piano Man'?"

"Brian?"

"Yes, Mr. Gavin."

"You're fuckin' fired."

"It's a pretty good night for a Saturday."

"It's Wednesday."

"Eat me . . . *The regular crowd shuffles in . . .*"

Never failed. He needed Gavin out from behind, in the kitchen, and a shill or two at the back tables, but they loved the "'Piano Man!'" bit. Like all things that worked, it had occurred spontaneously his third night, and Brian was luckily not taking himself seriously enough at that moment to realize it would always work.

The idea of Brian playing cocktail piano at an Irish bar was likewise stumbled upon, as all things that work are. He would come in and help Lizzie set up, then stick around until closing. Gavin was comfortable with this two-beers-in-ten-hours arrangement for about one day. That's when he asked Lizzie, "Does it do anything else besides watch his fuckin' Bud Dry evaporate under the lights?"

"He'll play the piano for a hundred a night."

"Tips."

"Fifty and tips."

"Thirty, two beers, dinnah and tips."

"Fine."

"And no 'New York, New York.'"

"No problem."

"And no fag stuff."

"No show tunes?"

"No," said Gavin. "I mean no, you know, no 'New York, New York.'"

Brian could have easily said no, and somewhere, he probably swears he did say no. But this was not Widmare micromanaging him to play the organ in chapel. This was Lizzie, her raised eyebrows saying, "We're broke and we should keep an eye on each other." It was a logic that had not existed in the rent- and dissertation-free world previously.

"Can I think about it?" he had asked.

"Like 'What songs should I play?'" said Lizzie. "Yeah, I would give that a great deal of thought."

You know the great thing about working in a bar? There's always plenty of ice. And when you go from banging on some Jap plastic a couple times a month to six hours a night on the genuine article, ice helps. Helps a lot. There's also a lot of lemon and hot water, which also helps when you're no longer singing in the dark to yourself while running. There's other stuff. Dollar bills. Attention. And whatever they call that numbing momentum that makes you forget how tired you are for as long as you're there. What the hell is that? Oh yeah, work.

There should be a point in everyone's life where they realize not only that they don't know anything, but that they don't have to even pretend to act like they do. And it should be around age twenty-two. But why quibble over numbers? Here, at forty-eight, at Gavin's, was the opportunity Brian had not been training his entire life for. Sure, he had been a teacher off and on for the last twenty-five years, and sure, teaching is the ultimate service position. But you really can't compare the satisfaction of imparting to a roomful of earnest would-be scholars the reckless depth of choral odes in *Antigone*, and the yelping joy you get from one drunk who, thanks to your handout, finally, finally knows all the lyrics to "Honky Tonk Woman."

Having history on your side helps a bit. Gavin's had been a traditional, "Hey, put the fuckin' game on!" Boston sports bar, but the winter of 1996–97 yielded a steady below-zero windchill of local interest. The Bruins were uncharacteristically staggering and in danger of missing the playoffs for the first time since the Truants had been alive and playing dances. Three months into the season, the Celtics had managed seven wins and gone into the tank like there was mob money riding on the first draft choice. Originally, Brian's gig was supposed to be light tinkling until ten, then, after the Bs or Cs had coughed up another losing effort, the request line opened up and the search for a comfortable key commenced until closing. But by Week Two, Brian had scored an unexpected triumph when a Celtics-Cavs showdown was muted at halftime.

Brian could play anything, with or without music, and in a joint that careened from rock to show tune to Irish folk to standard to substandard ("You're So Ugly," the dirty version of the *Beverly Hillbillies* theme), this was a skill whose muscles were flexed on the half hour. The ease with which he could re-create the actual song some footman from Boston Gas had in mind when he leaned in and Miller-breathed a couple *dahdah di dah dah, baby, sugars* on him came as a monster surprise to Brian. But only Brian. Everyone else at Gavin's assumed he could do it, and it spawned a demand that bordered on entitlement. Hell, it didn't border on entitlement. It ran through the center of Entitlementville, a gated community Brian Brock knew well. Might even have done some house-sitting there.

And it was all fine. Better than fine. And don't ask him how he could be forty-eight, gay, no savings, no prospects, in a land where his academic passport was not accepted—and feel safe.

And did we mention gay?

Too many social historians have written too many words about the enigmatic provincialism of Boston. Basically, it boils down to this: If you're different, be different. But, and this is key, be different on your own time. Be black, be Jewish, be the Irish even the Irish don't like, be Asian. But be it on your time. When you're with us, we're all from Boston and everybody else sucks.

And by all means, be gay. But, as the least subtle joke ever goes, don't shove it down our throats.

Gay men and women came into Gavin's all the time. And they all had virtually the same experience: Nobody gave a shit. This is what Brian observed almost immediately from behind the piano. Nobody gives a shit. It was a distinctly different vantage point than he had enjoyed over the last quarter century. Behind the piano, sitting in the middle of it all, as opposed to on the outside looking in. Or worse even, house-sitting on the outside looking in, where his perspective was always addressed in care of someone else.

But—and here's where Brian had to pay attention, here's where he had to understand that he was no longer an avid spectator of his life from bad free seats, but a participant—within the gaping freedom of nobody giving a shit about who or what is gay, anybody who began to show up at Gavin's after 10:00, ready to belt down and belt out, gave a shit about being there. And their musical helmsman, their Jason, could not be reluctant, because they gave a shit about him. It was a nice change. It was not part of any plan, but it was the first thing since Yale Div. that worked.

And speaking of divinity school, that guy who'd said, *"Here's all you need to know about God. It ain't you"*? Brian remembered something else the Reverend Daniel Toms had told him as he walked into Gavin's with Lizzie the other night. *Stop trying to figure things out. Answers are never figured out. Answers are revealed.* . . . He had never told Lizzie about his visit to Dino or the collector's odd behavior, which he couldn't figure out. Nothing was being revealed, either, because despite more than a few calls from Lizzie, Dino had yet to show up at Gavin's to hear him play. Too bad, because as of last week, Brian had been tossing in one song nobody knew. Around 1:30, when the goodwill was high and the men's/ladies' room lines long, Brian would tap the side of his glass of club soda and say, "Here's one I wrote thirty years ago. I'm okay now, but I might have been a little angry then. See if you can tell." And the rest room line-ees would laugh the first time he hit the word "Furious." After that, they just liked the song, and after that, they'd join in and yell, "Furious!" On queue.

Brian never would have thought to do "Furious" and deprive the patrons of one less chance to butcher "Woolly Bully," but Lizzie talked him into it.

"You promised you'd play it for me."

"No, I didn't."

"Right. Play it anyway."

That was typical of their exchanges. Light, quick, pointed. Support so implied, yet so new it still had the smell from the showroom. Many nights, they could go an entire shift without a word between them. Other times, it was a ten-hour conversation yelled in shorthand from twenty feet away. Same thing. And somehow, their jobs, this nightly maelstrom of taking orders and requests, never interfered with what Brian and Lizzie did, which was be on call for each other.

As new as this situation was for Brian, this blossoming without baggage in plain view of the off-duty world, the footing was just as unfamiliar for Lizzie, despite the turf. For years, she had been used to breezing around the tables at Gavin's in a brassy bravado of self-assurance wrapped in the puff pastry of endless, easy flirtation. And she could still do it. You never lose other people's image of you. It's like riding somebody else's bike. But ever since she'd come back after slipping on junk and junking med school, Lizzie Schlesinger was, at long last, on to herself. She had to admit that anyone, including her, who tried to run that Sam Malone crap about a bar being like a family had not spent enough conscious, unmedicated time in either.

Nobody was paying attention. Nobody gave a shit. Except the piano man.

"Can I ask you a question?" Brian asked one night early into his new gig when she dropped off a fresh club soda after working the room.

"No."

"How many marriage proposals have you gotten here over the years?"

"Ninety-three."

"Wow. Ninety-three different guys."

"No. Ninety-three proposals. Big difference." He seamlessly played the refrain from "Brandy (You're a Fine Girl)" *(. . . what a gooood wife you would be . . .)* and it took her six bars before she said, "Good one, Mary." Lizzie had started to walk away, then turned back. "Wait. You meant proposals from guys?"

"Yeah."

"Eighty-three."

Exchange over. They smiled and went back to their jobs.

Yes, they're sharing a drink they call loneliness,
But it's better than drinking alone . . .

"Jesus, who wrote this crap?" Brian yelled.

"Keep fuckin' playing!"

"Yes, Mr. Gavin. . . ." *Oh, la, la-la, diddy dah . . .*

Big laugh from the regulars. Never failed.

IT WAS 4:00 IN THE AFTERNOON when Jerry woke up, and 4:10 when he realized he hadn't woken up, he had come to. He played his answering machine. Five different messages from twelve hours ago. From five different escort services. Well, the escort services were different. Not the messages. They were the same. Pissed-off women, in various street accents, saying, "Motherfucker, you just called me. I told you I'd call you back in fifteen minutes. Is this some motherfucking joke?" None of them sounded familiar, which seemed to be a bit of a theme. Nothing was familiar. His apartment looked like someone else was living in it. Someone who could probably remember how and when he had gotten there.

And who was burning licorice?

He shuffled into the bathroom. The world's fattest cockroach stared at his foot, next to the bowl. What a shock. A cockroach in Queens. But not moving. Not trying to get out of Queens. He readjusted his focus. Wait. That was no cockroach. It was a coffee bean.

Wait again. Maybe he knew who was burning licorice.

He went back into the living room and lifted his leather jacket off the radiator. He inhaled too deeply. Sambuca.

He went through his pockets, usually an exercise in humility. The left held a dozen packets of Equal. He was back. The right pocket held his keys and usually, always, nothing else. Now, like the end of somebody's stage act, there were two very new hundred-dollar bills tucked inside. Hundred-dollar bills existed for Jerry only in transit. Never the next morning. Or afternoon.

He caught another whiff of the sautéed Sambuca and his temples screamed. He grabbed the Equal and left the money and went back into the bathroom. It had been a while since he'd done this, which almost guaranteed it would work. He ran the water and tossed four blue packets and four Alka-Seltzer into an eight-ounce glass. He filled it cold and stirred with the nonbusiness end of his toothbrush. He drank the sweet fizz down in five monstrous gulps. It took a couple of minutes, but he could feel a few bricks loosening up there. His invention: *Head-Ade*. If he did the proper paperwork, all of it, was there any money coming his way? Head-Ade. He laughed.

That's the last thing he remembered. Laughing. Wise guys laughing.

Jerry and Pressure Chief had arrived at Bravissima on Eleventh and First just after 10:00. At the back table, just off the kitchen and just before their salad plates were cleared, sat five men. Jerry only recognized one. His bookie, Lou Gray, who had arranged his trip to the Caymans. The others were Frank DiCaesare, the paper owner of Bravissima, a clean, older man who was introduced as Lou Brown, and two younger, eager, twitchy greaseballs who kept raising their glasses and saying, "To a full acquittal."

"So, Feeb." Lou Gray addressed Jerry by his gambling nom de phone, Heeb Feeb, "Where is he? We're all waiting."

"Who?"

"The guy with the joint."

Jerry pointed to Pressure. Lou Gray jumped up and walked Jerry toward the front. "The shveem?" his bookie asked.

"Yeah."

"What are you," he lowered his voice, "what are you, fucking soft? You asked me to set up a business—business, Feeb—meeting with my boss because you have, and I fucking quote, 'A porno gold mine,' and you walk in here with some sixty-year-old stove who I swear I bought a dime bag of catnip from in nineteen eighty-fucking-one?"

"Just look at it."

Now Lou Gray felt like raising his voice, so he put his arm around Jerry and led him to the bar in the front of Bravissima. He also felt like a drink, which meant everybody with him felt like a drink. Sambuca.

They heard laughter from the other room and Lou Gray decided to wait until they were summoned. The laughter must have been when Lou Brown asked Pressure Chief, "You the movie star?" and he answered, "No. I'm the baker." Must have been, but they weren't there.

"Frankie," Lou Brown coughed to the owner, "go watch this guy make me dessert."

Pressure smiled and reached into his jacket pocket. The two wise guys clumsily leaped out of their chairs, racing for the right to frisk him first. But they were hopelessly late before he pulled a small Saran-wrapped square out of his pocket.

"Banana-apricot cake," Pressure announced.

"Fine. But I'm looking for something with almonds," said Lou Brown before he turned to Frank DiCaesare, "that's not your almond-torte-fucking surprise."

More laughter from everyone, which kept Jerry and Lou Gray in the bar.

"Teddy, two more. Doubles. Feeb, are you listening, you fuck?"

"Thank you," he probably said way too early. Who could recall? He never saw Pressure Chief or the back room or anything except his bookie's mouth working and the stare of three coffee beans at the bottom of a transparently bad idea.

The Alka-Equal serum was in its midrace stride. Jerry looked in his refrigerator for a beer. Eggs, sugar, cream, raisins, unsweetened chocolate, marzipan paste, kiwi. What was all this shit?

He owed $7,500. The $5,000 still on his tab after he left for the Caymans hadn't been wiped out and had swelled another $2,500 since he'd returned. One bad play after another. Who bets the Nuggets on the road? Jesus, Etan Patz had more success away from home than the Nuggets. Let it go. Bad play. And hey, it wasn't $7,500, it was $7,300, if you counted the two yards in his pocket. And if you counted it, you'd be as big a fool as Jerry. Etan Putz. No, he'd have to go back to work for Lou Gray in "the office," wherever that was now. Or maybe he could make another run for them. This time he'd do it right. An open-ended round-trip ticket. Masking tape. Plenty, plenty of Equal. Come back ten grand to the good. Maybe the boys would advance him a little so he could stay in a real joint. God knows, he could use a break. And a vacation.

He heard the key in the door. Shit. Had he told Lou Gray he had $1,000 to give him? Was that the $200? Was that what he was going to give him or what he got back to walk around with or something else? What was his figure? Shit, he always knew his figure. Here he was searching for a number. A number? How about an inkling of what, when, or why he'd made it home? Now there was a project.

The project was shelved while Jerry crouched unconvincingly behind a folding chair as the door opened. Pressure Chief walked in. He was wearing white cotton pants that were much too short and too thin for January, Jerry's old pea coat, and one of those stupid white paper/mesh hats. He was carrying a six-pack of Red Stripe and a gloriously exhausted smile.

"How'd I get here?" Jerry asked.

"I don't know. I took the N to Thirty-fifth Street, like you'd told me."

"What?"

"I was working. I'm a baker."

"What?"

"The Italians hired me. I slept in the kitchen, then worked five to three."

"What?" That, and the two hundreds, was all Jerry had.

"Heh, heh. The broke white-boy gambler got Pressure Chief a job. I'm a baker in New York City."

"Did you show them your dick?"

"No, mahn. They're paying me to bake."

"Get the fuck out of here."

"Really, I didn't need to."

"No. Get the fuck out of here."

Jerry was never the source of drama, just the target. That switched in a second. He cleared the contents of his refrigerator onto the floor and shoved Pressure Chief toward the door, artfully, too artfully for him, grabbing a beer off the plastic ring in the process. Pressure asked for five minutes to grab his nonperishables. He put the spare set of keys in the pea jacket and laid it on the radiator. You could see the full-white kitchen worker's uniform and the cloud of flour that came off it. He pushed the stupid white hat through four layers of shirts and gathered up whatever else he'd brought north and stuffed it into one of those shiny purple parachute nylon bags nobody had anymore. He picked up a bottle of Jamaican allspice off the floor, secured its wooden top, and found room in his pocket. Jerry pretended to look out the window, amazed that this guy was leaving so quietly and in less time than his headache. Oh, and his headache? It wasn't a headache anymore. It was a brain tumor.

"I still owe you," said Pressure in lieu of good-bye. As Jerry tried to think of a figure to stick him with, Pressure zipped the parachute bag with a telepathic flourish. "I know I gave you two hundred while you were at the bar last night"—Jerry turned around—"but that was just thank you. I still owe you." He shouldered his bag.

"Where you going?"

"You kick me out."

"What? You thought I kicked you out? Come on, give me a little credit. That's what everybody else does." Never smoother, Jerry reached down to the floor and grabbed the box of raisins and popped a couple in his mouth. "I have been looking for these all day." The bag came off Pressure's shoulder. "You've got to get tougher if you're going to make it in New York."

Pressure smiled. "I've made it in New York."

Jerry threw his bag on the couch, took a giant gulp of the Red Stripe, warm, then threw up in the kitchen sink. A raisin was the last thing to ride out of him down the drain.

Wait. Not a raisin. A coffee bean.

Ow. It was definitely a brain tumor.

RICHIE GAVE A SHARP OUTTAKE OF AIR and tried to get comfortable in his chair for the eight hundredth time.

"When I was five, I came home from kindergarten. I walked into our living room in Porter Square and my mother was sitting there, crying. I said, 'Mom, what's wrong?' And she said, 'Oh, Richie, it's your father. I know he's cheating on me. I know he's with another woman. I know he's going to leave us!' And I said, and I'm five, 'No, Ma. He's at work. He's at the shopping center. He'll be home for supper. He told me.' And she blew her nose and stopped crying, just like that.

"Well, this went on for the next twelve years. I'd come home, she's crying. 'He's cheating on me, Richie! I know he's running around!' I'd say, 'No, Ma. He's at work. He's at the office. He's at the new mall. He'll be home for dinner,' and she'd calm down. On and on and on. Never missed a month.

"So now, I come down for Thanksgiving from Chase. Just turned eighteen. I walk in and my draft notice is sitting there on the hall table. One-A. I'm gone. This is nineteen sixty-six. I walk into the living room, there she is, crying. I think she's crying because of the draft notice. Nineteen sixty-six. One-A. Good-bye. Guess what? Same shit. 'Richie, Richie, I know he's running around!' So, I get fed up. I say, 'You know what, Mom? You're probably right. I bet he IS cheating on you. Not only that, I bet he's got a couple of women on the side. At least.' This time, no nose. She stops crying, laughs, shoos me away with her hand and says, 'Nah. He's down at the shopping center. He'll be home for dinner. . . .'

"Three weeks later, I went home for Christmas vacation. He'd left two days before. And that's how I got out of the service."

"So your mom was right."

"No, Gail, she wasn't. Not close."

"What do you mean?"

Richie stood up and walked toward her chair. "I think that's all I want to talk about today."

"This is some date. Cold coffee in your office talking about your mother." She checked her watch. "And not even an hour. I have to figure out what to charge."

"This isn't a date."

"And whose fault is that?" She rose and her jewelry jingled to announce her presence. If *Richie Lyman, Divorce Lawyer* had been a movie, they would have canceled the audition for the part of the cuckolded estranger when Gail Thiel jingled in. She was, in all her perfumed athletic single-mindedness, bigger than life. Bigger than his life. Finally, a woman, a babe, walks in who wants to do all the work. We mean, *all* the work, and he is going out of business. Richie started giggling. Who wouldn't?

Gail wouldn't. "What?" she hissed.

Richie rubbed his eye. "I've always wanted to ask somebody this. Somebody who wasn't a client. How come when the husband kills the wife, it's horrific, but when the wife kills the husband, it's hilarious?"

"Hilarious?"

"Yeah," Richie coughed. "Hilarious."

Gail started to laugh. And not the, *"Hah hah, is this going to help me get laid?"* guffaw / guffawn. Rather, the *"Goddamn you, now I have to think about this and you know, it is funny"* unwanted titter.

"I guess," she offered, "you just assume, no, you know, that for the wife to kill the husband, it was probably over something like, 'Babe, these eggs are a little cold.'"

Richie was trying to come up with something to top the cold eggs, but everything came into his head in a voice that sounded like David Brenner. He couldn't do any better. How could he expect to come up with a more believable motive for hubby-cide than a divorcing wife? So, he just kept laughing.

"Was that what it was with Johnno? Cold eggs?"

Gail straightened the red cocktail dress that needed zero straightening. "I think that's all I want to talk about today." She stopped jingling. "This ain't gonna happen, is it?"

Richie looked away. "You're a little late."

"How late?"

"Fifteen years. Or a month." Gail, Mrs. Thiel, tried to get formal, extending a hand through the cashmere coat gathered on her arm. Richie grabbed the coat and helped her on with it. "You can call me anytime, Gail."

"You know, I thought he might have a girl."

"Johnno?"

"Last Monday, he stayed over in the city. He called me the next morning, just when I was about to get good and bitchy, and made up some bullshit story about going to see Paul Lester, some big guitar player—"

"Les Paul?"

"Yeah, something like that, and staying for the late show. Look, I know a little bit about show business. My father was a big-shot publicist and I worked for him for a few summers. I know nobody works on Monday, let alone does two fucking shows. I had him. I really had him. One problem. As John is going on and on, apologizing and raving about the guy, I look down. There's the *New Yorker*, laying under my coffee, open to page eleven, and there's the fucker's name in bold, working at Iridium on the West Side. Every Monday night. Two shows."

"For like the last ten years."

"All right, I get it. Meanwhile, he's been back there the last two weeks."

"Sounds like Johnno's getting serious."

"Unlike us."

"Gail—"

She finished for him in a smoldering whisper, "You know you can call me anytime."

Richie patted her now-coated shoulders.

Gail Thiel returned to her regular voice. "Okay," she said, "cold coffee, your mother, and then the pat on the shoulders after I come on to you for the third time. I admire the loyalty to my husband, but you're getting dangerously close to me telling people you're a fag."

Telling people you're a fag. Richie felt pain everywhere except his balls. He jumped back. "Shit!" He looked up. "Okay . . ."

Gail's coolness was momentarily shaken. "Are you all right? Come on. I was kidding. Mostly."

"Yeah, I know," said Richie. "You just reminded me of something I have to take care of."

"Given that reaction, I don't want to guess what it is."

"Nothing. Just something with the band." He brightened again. "Hey, maybe you'll come to rehearsal. See what all this is about."

"Rehearsal? John hasn't mentioned anything about that. Just the reunion in June."

"Yeah, well, right now everything is a bit chaotic. The other guys were waiting to hear from me."

Chaotic indeed. Thwarted, confused, and yet knowing she'd somehow been spared, Gail was uncharacteristically uncomfortable, and not just because her great red cocktail dress was now covered. Nonetheless, she tried for last leverage. "Waiting to hear from you? You're that important?"

Another twinge hit Richie, "No. I just think I am. And they let me."

"So, Karaoke Boy, when's the big rehearsal?"

"Johnno and Tim were talking about March."

"Tim? What the fuck is Tim?"

"Tim Schlesinger. Our drummer."

"Oh, right. I met his wife." Gail smiled to herself, back in charge. "March, huh? I'll try to keep the eggs warm until then."

"Uh, okay."

It took almost ten minutes until after she'd left for Richie to figure out the "eggs warm" line. Ten minutes. Not bad, for a fucking man.

He composed an e-memo for Laz and was about to click on SEND, but decided to save it as a draft instead. There would be no need to revise it. Nothing more need be said other than, *"Effective February 1, 1997, Richard Lyman Esq. will only be handling male clients."*

Wait. *Handling?* Bad choice. *Performing services* for male clients? Yeesh. No. *Servicing male clients exclusively?* Whoa.

He'd work on it tomorrow. Friday. Send it Monday. Next week's good deed already in the bank.

chapter eight

DINO PARADISE HAD LITTLE USE for computers until 1994, when a collector friend casually mentioned to him that he had bought three catalogs from Jack's Drum Shop in Boston (1962, 1965, 1967) for five bucks on eBay. That was it. His kid came over with a glacial-speed laptop and showed him how to get around the keyboard, and the days that had been filled trolling thrift shops and garage sales and other collectors' basements were now spent combing sites like www.waxphilosophical.com, vinylexit.com, yeahyeahyeah.com, and other less-inspired domains. But it gave Dino some quality time with the boy, then nineteen and in Dinospeak, "some kind of tech quee-ah," until he no longer needed his help. And, perhaps more important, if you walked in and saw him hunched up against a screen rather than trying to carefully eat a fudgesicle over some liner notes, he looked like a guy at work.

Dino now had a computer that was only a couple years behind everybody else, and it enabled him to blast-e-mail the vintage-record world. He was even thinking about having the "tech quee-ah" come back and help him design a Web site. That is, thinking about it until Dino's twenty-twenty paranoid foresight had the IRS dot coming through his front door.

Dino made himself the same tuna fish sandwich he'd been eating every day at noon since his wife left in 1990. He cracked the seal on a new two-liter Diet Pepsi and went to check his e-mail, collectah@yahoo.com. Same old shit. Lot of replies and replied replies from buyers, sellers, and traders with fetishingly urgent subject titles ("C'mere, quick!" "Got it, got it!" "Thank you for playing Score-O!"). Dino dashed off his favorite counter-offer: "Stop rimming me!" to a few colleagues, then settled in with a four hundred-word discourse on the evolution of the 45 rpm label for Roulette Records to some memorabiliac with the cyber handle Numberoneoneone680.

When he finished the Roulette treatise to Numberoneoneone, he went back to his in-box. One new message from Tashianmusic, which he read as one word, which he still did, so he had no idea who it could be. In the subject box were the words "Sorry so late . . ." Okay, someone apologizing. A good start. He opened.

Dino—

Sorry so late getting back to you. Doing some studio stuff for Emmylou (Harris). Sure, I remember you.

Well, I don't remember you, chief, Dino thought.

Do you have dates for this garage thing? If the money's right, I can get Chip, Vern and Briggs.

Fuck me.

We're doing a Remains gig in Spain next year (we're huge there). It would be our first in twenty-six years. Our first, that is, unless you can put something together.

Fuck me.

Keep in touch. If it doesn't go, I'll understand. These things come up from time to time and rarely pan out.

Well, you don't know who you're dealing with.

It would be great to see Peter and work with the Lost and the

Barbarians. Never heard of the Truants, but if you get us our price, maybe I'll be able to afford their album.

All right, I fuckin' get it, Barry.

Look forward to hearing from you.

Barry Tashian

Dino got up too quickly and had to grab the underside of the desk. He looked at the screen again, to make sure the author was who he already knew it was, and saw more writing underneath the name.

P.S. Dropped something in the mail a couple of days ago to the address in Arlington. Figured you'd get a kick out of it.

Dino turned around in the direction where he heard heavy breathing. It was him. He reached for the jug of Diet Pepsi, but the imbalance pulled him back into the desk chair.

"Dino, cahm down," he coached himself. "It's just a fucking e-mail. Nothing's happened yet. Keep it in your pants. Easy, big guy." He typed a quick and shockingly cool reply: *Dates to come. What's your figure?* and saved it as a draft so he could send it in a couple of hours, as any too busy, too successful live-event promoter would. Maybe set up a bogus e-mail address for his bogus assistant. Janie. No, Heather. No, more Boston sounding. Donna. donnacollectah@yahoo.com. Beautiful.

He got up gingerly and went out front to check his mail. Final notices, junk, one decent catalog from Sam Ash. And a Nashville-postmarked Jiffy bag. Return address: Tashian Music.

"Fuckin' Barry."

It was an oversize paperback. *Ticket to Ride: On Tour with the Beatles.*

"Holy shit." Dino threw the other mail to the side and lurched onto his couch the same way a sixteen-year-old pulls into traffic on his road test.

The day after Christmas 1965, Barry and the Remains were plucked out of national obscurity and local-legend adulation when the Boston-based hard-rock band appeared on *Ed Sullivan*. Six months later, just after the four BU dropouts had performed their regional hit, "Diddy Wah Diddy," on *Hullabaloo*, the Remains (as they were now known) got what insiders might call a good gig. They were booked as one of the opening acts for the Beatles' final live tour. Fourteen cities, eighteen days, nineteen shows. That was August. By September, shortly before the release of their first album for Epic Records, the Remains had disbanded. "In the weeks following the tour, I became very discouraged. I knew we were never going to be as great as the Beatles," explained their leader, twenty-one-year-old Barry Tashian. So really, what was the point? The album, and a later-released demo audition for Capitol, survived like the tail of a comet. Thirty-one cuts that defined and executed the British Invasion–influenced garage-punk sound of the States and spawned only derivation. But really, what was the fucking point?

Barry's father, sensing history, told his son to keep a journal on the tour. Thirty years later, reconciling with history, Barry had done enough cutting and pasting with ticket stubs, local articles, reviews (*Sixteen* Magazine called the Remains "showstoppers"), and photos to bring it all to commercially viable life. More scrapbook than scrapped book, more sights than insights. But he'd been there, and we hadn't, so bring it on. Bring it back.

Lost in the book's provincial padding was the pivotal role the Remains played on the tour besides performing their own six-song set and backing two of the bill's other warm-up acts, the Ronettes and Bobby ("Sunny") Hebb. The group had built its reputation throughout New England on its dynamic live shows, which were cauterized by raucous energy detonated at a volume that bordered on sonic testing. The Remains spared no expense to achieve this ear-splitting glee, and their state-of-the-art sound system was laughingly superior to anything the ballparks, racetracks, or hockey rinks could provide the Beatles over their postwar PAs. Hours before the first show at Chicago's International Amphitheater, after reviewing his audio options, Beatles manager Brian Epstein hired the Remains sound man, Bill Hanley, and used *their* equipment. Who knew?

Great stuff. Dino Paradise never got to it. He opened the limited first edition, and on page one saw the red rubber stamp: "'66 Beatles Tour / 30th Anniversary," and, underneath it, Barry Tashian's signature.

And his heart exploded.

THIEL'S EYES WERE THREE-QUARTERS bugged out.

"Want to grab some coffee?"

"It's quarter of one. Don't you have to work tomorrow morning?"

"I started scheduling my first patient on Tuesday at ten-thirty," he said. "It takes me a while to get to sleep anyway. Another beer?"

"I'm done, but I'll be happy to sit with you," resigned Richie. "Where do you want to go?"

"We'll stay here."

"Johnno, I think they're closing. We can go upstairs."

"But then we'd miss him."

"Who?"

Thiel sniffed, "Who."

"Les Paul?"

"Yes!"

Richie worked his hand through his hair. "But we just saw him for two hours. We didn't miss anything."

"I forgot to ask him something."

"Johnno, you were just up at the front of the stage, having a private conversation with the guy for like ten minutes. He's a million years old. Let him go home and lie down."

"No, he's fine. He's like this every week."

"Then let me go home and lie down."

"Spoken like a true Hoodsie. Okay, we'll get out of here."

Thiel raced up Iridium's two flights and out onto Broadway's version of early morning February. That woke him up even more. He shadow-boxed and tried to remember the new, dickered-with, first five bars of "Short Circuit." He had enough time to get it down before Richie wheezed through the door and joined him.

"Johnno, did you leave a tip?"

"No. Wait, yes. No, no. Wasn't he unbelievable?"

"Yeah. How old is he?"

"Eighty-one. Remember what he said at the end? 'You wouldn't be standing if I was sixty-one.'"

"Right. Now I get it."

"Unbelievable. The guy's got one working arm."

"And one good testicle." Richie referenced the guitar icon's mention of his recent surgery. (He had actually called his two side-men the "Less Ball Trio.") They began to walk south. Thiel was staying at the Mayflower.

"And he's still kicking everybody's ass. Did you hear the change on 'Moon'?"

"No," said Richie. "I ain't here every week."

"Did you see the treble knob was missing?"

"No."

Thiel started walking backward. His voice was raised. "You know what that means?"

"No."

"He's still fucking around! He's still tinkering with the thing. He's not done."

Richie had never seen Thiel so animated. And this wasn't four beers excited. This was *"How long until next Monday?"* excited.

"Was that opening line new?"

Thiel's eyes rebugged. "The Fender line? Nah. He starts the show like that every week." The Iridium stage was dark, except for the silhouette of three figures. The next thing you heard was an old man say, "What is this, a Fender?" Big laugh. *Boom!* Lights up, and with them the banjo-y reverbed strains of "How High the Moon." Les Paul, who put Gibson on the electric-guitar map in thirty-six-point bold all caps and multitracked his shit all over the recording industry, was breaking your ice and his chops.

"But you laughed like you'd never heard it before."

"But it's him," said Thiel. "One arm. One ball . . ."

"Speaking of which, you know he's fucking nuts." They turned left on Sixty-fourth and headed toward the park. "But you don't care."

"I'm getting a lesson every Monday night. I'll go practice in my room until four, get five hours, cup of coffee, then people start rolling up sleeves and dropping trou." Thiel went into a poor East Side whine: *"Is this ennything, Dr. Thielman?"*

"I guess five hours of sleep may be the best way to deal with that."

"Or not."

"What?"

"Nothing," said Thiel. "I'm just glad Gail hasn't been difficult about this." Richie snapped to and reached inside his jacket. "In fact, she's been pretty great."

They stopped for a light and Richie handed Thiel an envelope. "I'm glad you mentioned that. I've been meaning to give you this all night."

Thiel gave him the fake tough-guy look with the eyebrows as he opened the envelope. A check for $6,236. He figured it out instantly. "This is awfully generous, Richie, but my birthday's not for another three months."

"That's what's left on your retainer. You know, I'm pretty sure giving it back to you is grounds for disbarment. Especially since you're actually owed this money."

"What's this about?"

"I'm not going to represent you anymore."

"Richie, this is silly. Look, we're right here. Let's go upstairs to my room and talk about it."

Richie smiled. "Nah. I've got to get home. And you've got to practice."

"Can you at least tell me why?"

"You know me. I'm a selfish prick. I'd rather be your friend than your attorney. I don't want to have anything to do with this divorce."

Thiel was suddenly too cold to pursue things. "Jeez, I feel like shit all of a sudden."

"Johnno, what did I tell you? It's not how you're feeling, it's what you're doing."

"I never fucking got that shit."

"Johnno, you're going upstairs to play your Gibson Les Paul for three hours. And your wife, who's still your wife, is fine with that. I'd say you're doing great."

Thiel found himself nodding.

"It doesn't mean," Richie added, "you still don't have choices."

Thiel squeezed the check in his hand and threw his arms around Richie, who screamed, "Watch the balls!"

"Hey, when was the last time you played?"

"Guitar? Jesus. My kid's first Christmas. Eighty-three."

"How were you?"

"You know. Shitty crowd."

"Bad sound guy?"

"Yeah. That too." They both laughed. "I'm still playing the same four friggin' chords I was playing in nineteen sixty-seven."

Thiel blew on his hands. "Speaking of nineteen sixty-seven . . ."

"Save it, Johnno."

"No, you save it. Gail said you mentioned something about us rehearsing."

"Yeah, well . . ."

"All of us?"

"Yeah, well . . ."

Thiel poked Richie with the retainer envelope. "Richie, if you could have a change of heart about my divorce, then you can have a change of heart about Brian."

"Yeah, well . . ."

Thiel laughed. "And it's that kind of skilled articulation I'll miss from my attorney. Jesus, I'm glad I got my money back." He pocketed the envelope, then cocked his head. "Or . . . are you doing all this—me, Gail, Brian—because you see a bigger investment paying off, like with the album?"

"Johnno, you have to believe me. I could give a shit about the money."

"Me, neither. You know what that makes us?"

"What?"

"Musicians."

Richie laughed. He had never been called a musician. "Nah. You, Brian, Tim. You were the musicians."

Thiel squeezed Richie's neck, jock style. "Nice to hear you mention Brian. Look, it turns out we, all of us *musicians*, did something thirty years ago that turned out to be valuable. Valuable to people other than us. Come on. We have a chance to do something with that."

"Yeah, well . . ."

"Even change how it all ended."

"Don't push it," said Richie.

"You mean, 'Forget it'?"

"No, I mean taxi."

"What?"

Richie waved. "Taxi!"

The cab stopped and he gave Thiel a shove to get a running start across the street.

The wind came up and Thiel took the hint. He ran inside the

Mayflower. Maybe he'd play till five. It wasn't like he still didn't have choices.

THEY STARED AT EACH OTHER across the table. This was going on three hours now. The only random punctuation was either both of them opening their mouths in silent screams, or finishing the other one's sentence. Always the same sentence. Always, "Can you believe this?"

The pattern was broken once, around Hour Two, when Cheryl said, "I thought you had, you know, a problem."

"I guess the operative word here," said Tim, "is 'had.'"

They had given up on the prospect of starting a family a dozen years ago. Although, "given up" may be the wrong choice of words. "Surrender" is better. Surrender, as in drop your arms and come over to the winners. Not that the childless are winners, but what would you call a couple who accepted science and *didn't* pay some fertility/infertility rumrunner $50,000 to recommend boxer shorts and sitting on top of the refrigerator an hour a day? Losers?

"We have our hands full trying to raise each other," Cheryl would say whenever people asked. People hadn't asked in years, but she had the line loaded up just in case. Now she had a little over six months to come up with a new line.

Cheryl was thirty-eight years old, but thanks to spending most of her non-treadmill days standing next to either her husband or the addled old ladies at Holyoke Hills Nursing Home, she always looked just north of coed. And Tim still pursued her with the same zero-countdown ardor as when she had met him at twenty-two, when she had actually been just north of coed. Of course, the pursuit is always easier and more accessible if there is never the possibility of tripping over a Tonka truck or Title IX Barbie.

Since Tim had returned home, the frequency of sex had returned to the levels of the mid-eighties. The Go-Go eighties. And slightly more creative. Three weeks of sleeping on your office floor will do that. So, maybe it was that, maybe it was the bump on his head, maybe it was El Niño. But whatever it was, this was no drill.

Tim snorted.

"What?"

"Remember what you used to say years ago, when people would ask us how come we still lived in an apartment?"

"Sure," said Cheryl. "I said we ate our first house."

She wasn't being flip. Maybe, on Christmas night, one of them might have gone nuts and scrambled a couple of expired eggs . . . on toast! But that was it. Eventually, the nightly eat-out, three-movies-a-week, four-vacations-a-year pace was throttled back enough to pounce on a real estate lull in Bedford ten years ago. A no-fixer-upper, perfect for the professional couple who had no plans of adding on. They even used the stove a couple times a month for a while, until they realized that was best left to others. Now Tim and Cheryl's lifestyle, what the guys who cover the NBA call "the two-man game," was about to go over the wall and leave no forwarding address.

"Okay, so we're doing this."

"Of course we are," said Tim.

"Having a kid."

"Oh, I thought you meant putting more shelves in the bedroom."

"Tim!"

"You know, I think we can do both."

He stood up and threw out the six-pack that had been in the refrigerator since they'd had some people over to watch the Oscars— the 1995 Oscars—making a big grandstand gesture of hustling the demon ale to the trash can at the bottom of the back steps. It had been snowing for over two hours, but they'd both just noticed it. Cheryl joined him ("*When did it start snowing? How preoccupied are we?*") and they walked to the end of the driveway.

"Do you think we stored up enough sleep for this?" asked Tim.

"First of all, you can't store up sleep." Cheryl smiled. "And second, no."

She looked to her right at the sidewalk, just off the curb. Tim bear-hugged her from behind and proofread his wife's mind.

"Don't worry. When we need the space, I'll do something about the drums."

Cheryl turned back to face him, snow-dappled joy, and they resumed their open-mouthed silent screaming and *"Can you believe this shit?"* until the flakes were cold and wet and no longer cute. Straight into adolescence.

Halfway up the driveway, they heard the phone ringing. Tim started to break, then mumbled, "Machine."

"But we have news!"

"What?" he said. "OH!" He skidded off, up the steps, and grabbed the phone just after the beep. Lizzie.

"Lizzie."

"You gotta change your message. We don't need to hear both of you. We get it."

"Yeah, okay. Lizzie—"

His sister interrupted. "Listen, I have some news."

"No wait. You listen. Guess what?"

She squirmed on the other end. "What?"

"You'll never guess. In a million years."

"I don't want to guess."

"In a million years."

Deep exhale from Lizzie. "Cheryl's pregnant."

"How did you know?"

"I was fucking kidding!!"

"Can you believe it?"

"No."

"Is that Lizzie?" said Cheryl. "Tell her I love her."

"Did you hear that?" said Tim.

"Is she drunk?"

"No. You can't drink when you're pregnant. A doctor should know that."

"Yeah," said Lizzie, "a doctor should."

Cheryl was taking her shoes off in the kitchen. "Ask her when she's coming over."

"Did you hear that?"

"Yeah. She's drunk. Look, Timmy. I'm really thrilled for you guys. Really. I know I don't sound like it, but I am."

"What's your news?"

"It's about Dino."

Tim pumped his fist. The "Do good things come in twos or threes?" fist. "I knew it," he said.

"You free this Thursday at ten?"

"I can be. Meeting with Dino?"

She went back to squirming. "No. Funeral with Dino. He dropped dead two days ago. Heart attack."

Come on, Lizzie, Tim's mind pleaded, say, *"I was fucking kidding!"* again.

Instead, Lizzie said, "And then there's something over at his house. You want Brian and me to pick you up?"

"You're not kidding, are you, Lizzie?"

"No . . . Dad."

They giggled. "I'll try to make it. Say hi to Brian."

Tim hung up and felt Cheryl's hands on his shoulders. She was jumping up and down like she wanted him saddled. "What are you going to try and make?"

"Dino's funeral."

"The collector guy? He died?"

"Yeah."

She rubbed his arm. "I'm sorry, sweetie . . . but he is just one collector, and the album is still the album. It doesn't have to end with him, does it?"

That's it, Tim thought. She's drunk.

• • •

BRIAN AND LIZZIE DECIDED TO DISTRACT themselves from the news of Dino's death by driving in the rain into Central Square Cambridge and eating Szechuan food at eleven in the morning. Brian was driving, even though it was Lizzie's Skylark and he had no idea where he was. He had to drive. "Look, maybe one day I'll be comfortable enough to be the nelly in the passenger seat," he pleaded, quite nellyish, "but you have to give me this for now."

"Shit," she said. "I have to go to the bathroom."

"I'm sure the Chinese restaurant has a ladies' room. Aren't we almost there?"

"Wok On?" Lizzie huffed. "Please. I'd rather go at a gas station. There's a Mobil up on the left."

But it was too late. Brian pulled over, five yards past the entrance to the Mobil station and as close to the curb as the banked snow would allow. He stopped, then thought about backing up. A minivan was stopped in the road ten feet behind him. He rolled down his window and waved for the car to pass them, with more than enough room on the left.

Now, he sighed. "Jesus, what is this guy's problem? He's just sitting there." Brian beeped. The minivan didn't move. The light changed. Brian looked at Lizzie for a second, and when he looked back in the mirror, a man with bad teeth from ten feet away was walking quickly toward the Skylark.

"Stay right there, pal," the minivan driver said. "You just caused a major accident."

Before Brian could say, "Huh?" the passenger door of the minivan opened and an older woman started to climb out. The guy with the bad teeth wheeled and screamed, "Stay in the car!" The woman wasn't listening.

"Stay in the car, Mom!" Ahh. That's why she wasn't listening. The minivan driver, the guy with the bad teeth, left Brian and ran toward her as if he had no choice. And when Lizzie and Brian heard his next line, they realized why he had no choice.

"Ma, stay in the car. This is going to be money."

Other cars were soon rubbernecking easily on the left. The rain had begun to let up, unlike the guy with the teeth. He ran in between the two cars, screaming, "Don't move!" for however long it took him to figure out he better start grabbing his neck.

"This is nonsense," said Lizzie. "But I might as well take advantage of it." She got out of the Skylark and saw another car, a Pontiac, limp its damaged front end into the Mobil station. So, there *had* been an accident. Well, what do you know?

"Where are you going?" the guy with the bad teeth freaked.

"To take a piss."

"Call an ambulance!"

Lizzie grandly waved him off. "I think I'll make it."

On her way back, Lizzie walked up to the driver of the Pontiac, some otherwise solid citizen who looked like he was on his way to pick up some dry cleaning. She told him the *"This is gonna be money"* remark.

"Thanks," he said, "but I hit him. Look at his car. Not a scratch. But he's going to screw me. He's going to screw all of us."

"But nothing happened to him!"

"That," the Pontiac driver said, slowing his shaking head, "that's all gonna change."

"Wha—" Lizzie was interrupted by sirens, then lights. Two radio cars heading up Memorial Drive. An ambulance surely on the way. Lizzie looked back, and the guy with the bad teeth was waving traffic by with the hand not on his neck.

"Let me get this straight, sir," one of the cops would say to Brian. "You were stopped. You didn't hit anyone, you weren't hit, you didn't see anything, you didn't hear anything. Pahdon my French, but what the fuck you still doing he-ah?"

"The guy told me to stay."

"Uh-huh."

"And my friend had to pee."

The cop looked at Lizzie, now glaring at the minivan. "Go with that," he said.

The ambulance showed up in less time than it took to respond to a stabbing. Lizzie had returned to the Skylark. "I gave the lunatic my insurance information," she said. "He's been through this before. I know what he's thinking. He figures, two years and maybe I can clear fifty thousand. Nice racket."

"Ready to go?" Brian asked.

"Are you kidding?" spat Lizzie. "And miss Act Three of Scamboree 1997?"

"This is a scam?"

"Just watch, Dorothy."

It took another twenty minutes. It might have taken less time, but the guy with the bad teeth was meticulous in instructing the EMTs in just how to put on the neck immobilizer and load him properly onto the collapsible stretcher, then into the ambulance. Even though the paramedics were stifling giggles. Lizzie knew these last few moves had jacked up the price to $75,000. Maybe $100,000. She had worked in an insurance office one summer when she'd been straight and this was the only thing she knew about business. Out of nothing, create demand.

She waited until they closed the back doors of the ambulance before opening hers.

"Excuse me," she told Brian, "I'm going to chat with Ma."

Ma had scooted over to the driver side of the minivan. The side with the undeployed airbag. Lizzie rechecked the back end of the car—zee-ro. She somehow managed a smile as she knocked on the passenger-side window.

"Your son has my insurance information. I gave it to him as a courtesy, seeing as how I was not hit, didn't hit anyone, and didn't see or hear anything. So, I don't expect to be hearing from anyone."

The ambulance pulled into the street. Mild, sporadic lights, like the last days of disco.

"I think I hurt my neck," said Ma.

Lizzie hissed, "Yeah, I'm sure. But somebody's gotta drive this thing to the hospital." She leaned her head into the minivan. "I'm telling my insurance company not to settle, to the point where I am willing to assume all liability. If your son wants to take this to trial, that's fine. But there's at least three of us who heard him say, 'Stay in the car. This is gonna be money.' And I ain't counting you."

"Well, I didn't hear him say that."

"Then my lawyer won't call you to the stand."

"Look, miss."

"Lizzie Schlesinger. You'll recognize the name under 'Plaintiff' when I countersue for filing a frivolous lawsuit." She looked at the watch she wasn't wearing. "Hey, you've got to run along. Your son should be released in a few minutes."

Lizzie made a big point of shaking hands with the cute cop on her way back to the Skylark. Brian handed her a Gavin's sweatshirt from the backseat to dry her hair.

"How'd it go?" he asked.

"Let's eat," she said. Brian pulled safely into traffic and didn't bother asking where. Anything would do. Two blocks down, a deli appeared without drama.

Lizzie covered her head, then face, with the sweatshirt. "Out of nothing, create demand!" she screamed clearly, though muffled. "Brian, I'm screwed. Where am I going to come up with the money for a lawyer? They're going to see that guy's teeth when he gets to the ER and think he hit them on the steering wheel."

Brian laughed until he cried. Two seconds.

She pulled the sweatshirt off her head. "I hope," said Lizzie, "you're crying because you're hungry."

Brian stared nowhere. "No. I'm crying about this whole thing with Dino. Sweet guy."

"How do you know? You never met him."

Brian thought about correcting her. "You're right. I'm hungry."

IF THAT DEFCOM 1 CORONARY HADN'T killed Dino Paradise, the scene at his house the afternoon of his burial would have. In the middle of the wake, a flea market kept trying to break out. Record collectors from eight states filed in four at a time to pay their respects to his ex-wife and son, or anyone who looked like they might be his ex-wife and son, and keep their saliva in check long enough to try and backhand a business card with an embarrassing lowball offer on the back.

> "Can I take that Swamp Rats cover of 'Psycho' off your hands for $450?"
>
> "I spoke with Dino last week. He was holding Dirty Wurds 'Why' for me. Did my check for $975 clear? If not, I'll write another on my girlfriend's account. . . ."
>
> "I know this is a bad time, but I need anything you have on Justice Label. Watch out for these other guys. Major bags of sleaze. . . ."

It was reasonably civil until two dealers got into a shoving match over who was responsible for dropping a silver-dollar-size glop of deviled egg onto a full-color 45 sleeve of Michael and the Messengers doing their cover of the Reflections "(Just Like) Romeo and Juliet." Dino's son, DJ, the "tech quee-ah," cleared the place by announcing that prices would go up 5 percent for every five minutes the vinyl vultures hung around appraising. The collectors filed out adroitly, now dropping their business cards in a mildly chipped tiki bowl, stolen from the Aku-Aku Lounge on Route 2 around 1977, and worth a bid in the near future.

DJ and his mom, the former Rita Desantis (and never Rita Paradise), had anticipated this day since the mid-80s, when Dino downed six Whalers with cheese and got stuck in his first Burger King booth. But not *this* day. They were not prepared for the fact that a memorial service would provide them with background information on the husband and father they had been able to reach on only the most obligatory level. The hundred-plus who had shown up were 80 percent strangers, as if the funeral home had hired seat fillers. But they were real people, erstwhile club owners, musicians, hangers-on, sleazebags of varying size, disc jockeys, and record-store owners, sprung from that compartment of Dino's life that had all but closed just before the moon landing. When the air was free. When local radio stations were not soundproof to the notion that there were choices other than those listed on the Orwellian menu of the major record labels. When a guy with nothing at stake except the need to hear during the day what he was hearing by night at the Rathskellar, the Surf, or Where It's At would pop by your studio during his lunch hour with a couple of 45s and a note: *"They'll go nuts for this. Have I lied to you yet? Dino."*

Rita had not expected education to be delivered in eulogy, or that it would taste so salty in her tear-flavored laughter at the stories. They had met at an engagement party in 1974. She was thirty, slim, with nurse's hair and a biker mouth and her dukes permanently up from relatives asking her why she was still single. But somebody had told Rita that the fat ones don't cheat. And he was sweet enough to ask her to the wedding, and sweeter still to ask her to theirs the week after Christmas. DJ (Dino Jr.) popped by a year later.

Although terminally distracted, Dino never failed to show up for his wife or son. He was as unfailingly available to them as he was unreachable about this passion. This thing that they, and the rest of the unschooled, called a hobby. Yeah, it was a hobby. Like breathing. By the time he had settled down, Dino's obsession with that corner of rock and roll—1963–68 Garage/Punk Bands—was a privately held trust. It was not discussed, unless you were of like mind. It was not explained. It was not allowed to be judged. It was not supposed to be understood. Dino Paradise sat and listened and cranked the volume when no one was around. And when people who didn't get it were around, he left and went out hunting for more. The goal was three copies of everything: one mint condition, never been played, covered in brown acid-free paper and slipped inside a heavier green cardboard sleeve; one good-to-excellent condition trade version, which he played for potential transactors, those of like mind; and one good condition, the "whack wax," the one he played for himself, with himself.

"What am I supposed to tell people when they ask, 'What does your husband do?'"

"Tell them I'm an entrepreneur."

"What is that?"

"Fuck if I know."

"Jesus, Dino."

"Tell 'em I'm in sales."

"Well, that narrows it down."

"Tell 'em I'm a nutritionist."

"But you weigh three hundred pounds."

"Okay, so I'm not a great nutritionist."

Bills got paid just ahead of the more traditional collectors, thanks to Rita and her sympathetic bosses at Bay State X-Ray and Diagnostic Center, and nobody went without for too long. If you don't count space, nobody went without. Eventually, the stacks of yet-to-be-cataloged albums and 45s that NO ONE COULD FRIGGIN' TOUCH mud-slid into every available and unavailable square foot of the house. Rita and DJ good-naturedly slithered and sidestepped around the warehome until there was no room for them. Dino secured them an apartment in Medford and promised to have things "straightened up" in six months. That was 1990. It took him sixteen months, but by then his wife and son had been convinced. The best way to be together was in isolation.

And now, even after the special-order extra-wide coffin and the unexpected additional costs from the unexpected turnout, came the bottom-line stunner. The husband and father who never took care of himself had amassed enough with his all-consuming hobby— "hobby" like fucking breathing—to take care of them. In perpetuity, and whatever came after that. Employee parking, perhaps. The yield from Dino Paradise's vinyl vineyards was almost nothing but very good years. Who knew, other than the handful of guys who made it their business to know?

The tech quee-ah was already broadly scratching it out in his head *(Thirty-two dealers so far . . . average offer $500 per piece . . . ten pieces per foot . . . eight twenty-foot-long shelves per wall . . . four walls . . . 64,000 pieces left IN THIS ROOM . . .)* It helps to keep one's mind distracted at a time like this. Remember: You can't spell *memorabilia* without "m-e-m-o-r-i-a-l." With a couple weekends of geeklike research, DJ could begin to slowly—nothing but time, nothing but timeless—auction off the Dino Paradise Foundation piece by piece, on eBay, or just stick a cash register next to the Aku-Aku tiki bowl and have people bid by lot number, and money would never be an issue in their lives again. And the guy lying in the special-order extra-wide coffin wouldn't mind. You either made the music, or were made by the music. You were either a collectah, or you weren't, chief. Everything else was just a rub-fuck.

"Mrs. Para-ah . . ."

"Rita. Dino's wife."

"Hi. I'm Tim Schlesinger. I'm so sorry."

"Thank you." She moved to shake Brian's hand, and looked back. "Tim Schlesinger, from the Truants?"

"Yes!" Lizzie leaned in.

"You're the sister?"

"Yes!"

"I know all about you. This is the only conversation I've had with Dino in the last year."

Brian hip-checked Lizzie. "I was also in the Truants," he puffed.

Rita got excited. "Richie, right?"

"No, Brian."

She kind of recovered. "Well, he said 'bossy.'"

"So," said Tim, "you know about us."

"Well, not him"—pointing needlessly to Brian—"but I know about the album. All about it. Dino never talked to me about any of this shit. Never shared anything. Even when we were living together. He knew I wasn't interested, or as interested as you had to be for him. I couldn't tell you one group in that mess. Okay, maybe the Four Seasons or the Beach Boys or Bobby Vee or crap that a normal person should know. But the Truants? You remember when you ask the guy you're going to marry his favorite band and he says, 'You've nev-ah heard of them and you won't remembah.' It was one of the few albums he played for me more than once. Good. I mean good. He loved you guys. Thought you were unappreciated and overlooked. And I never forgot. You don't forget your first end table. But nobody ever gave a shit, except him. And then, six months ago, out of nowhere, he calls me, first time since ninety-one, and says, 'I'm gonna finally get to make the Truants big-time balls-in-the-sack stahhs.' That's when I heard about you guys coming over here." And then to Brian, "Not you."

"I was here," said Brian.

"Well, he never mentioned it."

"When?" said Lizzie.

"I'll tell you later."

"Anyway," Rita continued, "anyway, that's when he told me the thing about planting the story in the paper about some high roller in Europe." She snorted. "I told him, 'Dino, make it from some weird country they can't check.' You know, if he'd been that smart years ago, I might have stayed in this house. I know we would have had more room here."

Rita, still 1970s slim, got out of the chair and smiled. "So, how many do you want? My son told me not to sell anything today, because we don't have a handle on the price and, you know, the funeral, but he was talking about the other stuff. You guys should have them."

"How many what?"

"Albums."

She unplugged the lamp, lifted it off the small square table, and laid it on the floor.

"Give me a hand, boys."

They each took a corner of the deep-green-draped table covering that looked like it had been crudely cut from the corner of the infield rain tarp at Fenway Park. Heavy. Galvanized rubber heavy. They peeled it back. The shrink-wrap blurred but did not obscure what was there. Forty, maybe fifty, copies of *Out of Site*.

Tim spoke first. "Is that all—"

"Yeah," said Rita, "that's all we have. Four dozen. Dino used to play two of them all the time. You don't want those. And I should keep a minty. So, forty-five."

"I meant," he finished, "is that all *us*?"

"Shit yeah. You don't forget your first end table."

Ah, end table . . .

Rita saw relatives beginning to hover, and DJ, smelling unauthorized commerce, not far behind.

"Ma!"

"DJ, look, it's two of the Truants! How's about a break for Dino's pets?"

The kid referred to a printout. "Truants, Truants . . . *Out of Site* . . . 1967 . . . Hoodsie Records . . . mint, three hundred ten." He walked away.

"Forty-five times three-ten is like ninety times one fifty-five . . . Look," she side-mouthed, "I have no use for this stuff. Just give me eleven thou and take the whole friggin' stack."

Open-mouthed silence. Out of nothing, create demand.

"So," Tim finally coughed. "He made the whole thing up?"

"Of course," said the Widow Paradise. "I thought you guys were in on this. Son of a bitch. Well, maybe you can keep the scam going. Me and DJ won't tell."

"I knew it," Brian mumbled.

Back to silence.

Rita Dizzy Gillespied her cheeks and then blew out hard. "Okay, nine grand. Shit. Here comes my kid again. We'll talk later. Now, screw."

chapter nine

WHO IN THEIR RIGHT MIND LOVES Tuesday nights? Maybe, maybe during the last three months of 1993, when David Caruso was doing his sotto voce bare ass/badass cop shtick during the first season of *NYPD Blue.* But that's it. And that was over three years ago.

And it wouldn't explain the behavior of Gail Thiel, who didn't know David Caruso from David Carradine, and frankly, hadn't let herself make the connection between her happiness and Tuesdays until tonight. Tuesday night. However, as she put a candle in the middle of the napery-strewn kitchen table, *and lit it,* she saw her reflection in the window overlooking the driveway. "You look," she said to herself, "like a girl who knows she's gonna get laid." So honestly, who in their right mind wouldn't love Tuesday nights?

It had as much to do with Monday nights as anything else. When John Thiel would carry himself back to Scarsdale after an evening/early morning in Manhattan split by Les Paul's ax and then his own, he walked up the flagstones, just to the right of the kitchen window, and into the house panting like the first dog to discover squirrel chasing. He made sure he got to Gail before his daughters ran down the stairs to extort him. He grabbed her by the shoulders, which was all he thought he was allowed to do, and kissed her forehead. "Thank you so much for letting me go," he would say every time. And then, "Let me grab something to eat. If you feel like talking, I want to hear everything." He would say that every time as well.

For the first couple of Tuesdays, Gail didn't buy it. Come on. What man wants to hear everything? Are there *any* stats to back up this claim? Forget that. What man wants to risk saying he wants to hear everything on the oft chance a woman may want to take him up on his conspicuously out-of-gender offer?

But here's the thing: Johnno meant it. He meant it on Tuesday nights. By Week Three, Gail took him up on it. And from then on, from eight to eleven, and sometimes up to and through late local sports on Channel 2, Dr. and Mrs. John Thiel yammered across the kitchen table about all the things they had stopped talking about since who knows when? Five years ago? Ten years ago? The month after they became Dr. and Mrs. John Thiel? It would end with him pouring the rest of his second beer down the sink, kissing his wife on the head, and both of them retiring to their neutral corners.

But here's the thing: Johnno only meant it on Tuesday nights. By Wednesday, there was the commute and work and more strangers rolling up sleeves and dropping pants outside the office. And whatever Les Paul sheen remained on his mood was completely tracked over by Thursday.

Gail was okay with all of it. The guy who was showing up Tuesday left a cleansing mist of hope and change that lingered until the weekend. Weekends had never been the problem. Weekends were fine. Chauffeuring the girls and running errands and napping and the smallest of talk and takeout and "Welcome to the final round of the Buick Open" fine. So, by the time Gail started actually missing that guy, it was already Monday. Yesterday.

She turned back from the window and saw herself in the door of the microwave. She looked good. She looked like she had taken off her heels and undone a couple of buttons on her blue silk blouse and then forgotten about changing. Which is exactly what she wanted you to think. She put her hair in a ponytail to keep it out of her eyes while she finished with dinner. Which was complete bullshit. She put her hair in a ponytail because if John wasn't going to get the chance to undo the second and third buttons on her blouse, she knew he'd damn well want to take her hair down.

The car in the driveway. The man carrying himself up the flagstones. The Tuesday-night guy.

He had barely grabbed her shoulders and told her, "Thanks for letting me go," when she kissed him hard enough to tell herself she may have wasted her time making dinner and lighting the candle on the kitchen table.

May have.

Their foreheads leaned against each other. "Gail," Thiel whispered, "as much as I'd like to carry you off to the bed of your choice right this second, we should probably talk first."

"Can it wait?"

"Probably not."

"Is there a chance I won't want to have you inside me after we talk?"

"I don't know."

"You don't know." She took her own hair down. "In that case, it can wait."

If you don't count blowing out the candle and turning off the stove, there was no foreplay. They went downstairs—to his place. Even in rumpus-room light, the Thiels were still great looking and great to look at. As one might expect with two people weaned on athleticism, John and Gail's lovemaking had always teetered between competition and ticket-worthy exhibition. Yet tonight, somewhere amidst the drought-ending passion coursed a different type of adrenaline. Its normally bitter flavor was replaced by the sweet ease of a safe landing. Familiarity-bred content.

They were focused, and undistracted by the impending conversation, so the whole conjugal repast didn't take very long (it never really does, and if anyone tells you otherwise, they're either lying or between takes on the set of a porno film). "Okay," said Gail, as her husband dutifully kissed her back, "what couldn't wait, but did?"

Thiel turned his wife toward him so she would not misinterpret his tone with the expression on his face.

"The guys are rehearsing this Sunday in the city."

"Really? Everybody?"

"So Richie says."

"That's great! So you'll be staying over two nights?"

"No. I thought I'd come back."

"You don't have to."

"Maybe I do."

"Just as long as you get here by Tuesday," said Gail, as she squeezed his thigh.

Thiel sighed, "You're making this very hard"—Gail gave a fake wicked laugh and stayed on his thigh—"I mean, you're making this very difficult."

"What? You're gonna leave me?"

"For a little while." And then Thiel explained. He liked what he had become Monday and Tuesday. It was the rest of the week that rendered him at best inert, at worst fraudulent. His career in medicine, that unquestioning trudge to titular triumph (Dr. Madison Avenue!), felt as devoted to the principles of healing as a scratch-off lottery ticket is devoted to long-term financial planning. Their marriage, the robust signs of carnal life notwithstanding, had almost caved in under the catatonic weight of mile-wide civility and inch-deep compassion.

Last night, as he was leaving Iridium, Les Paul had asked Thiel if he was happy. And Thiel knew, Monday and Tuesday notwithstanding, that it takes someone else asking "Are you happy?" to realize how unhappy you are.

His voice caught. "I'm going to try and get through this without using the phrase 'midlife crisis.'"

"You're doing fine," Gail said. And she meant it. He had never been more eloquent. Or courageous.

Thiel forthcame some more. He had spent the day between patients running the numbers. All of them. He could do this. This could be done. And then he called Chase Academy to offer his services. They were thrilled. So . . . two weeks from Sunday, he planned to pack up the Saab and spend April and May back at his old prep school as an unpaid assistant varsity lacrosse coach and dorm master. The rest of his waking moments you could find him playing his Gibson.

Big strong John Thiel looked away, as if he had just noticed his eyes watering. "At any rate, that's the plan," he said. "You know I wouldn't go unless you were okay with it, but I feel like this is my only shot to have more than one day a week when I don't feel like a failure. And my best chance of getting all the good people back."

He felt his back being kissed. "Forget me," Gail said. "I'll be fine. Just make sure Les Paul signs off on this." And she dragged him back down. Rather easily. Either she was surprisingly strong or he was surprisingly light.

Both. It was still Tuesday night.

JERRY CAREFULLY POURED TWO PACKETS of Equal into the liter bottle of Diet Pepsi. He put it next to two other similarly doctored liter bottles of Diet Pepsi. That would be enough to take him through work. Two hours taking bets over the phone for Lou Gray at an office on Thirty-sixth and Fifth. The job, fifty bucks a weeknight for the two hours, a hundred a night on the weekend for six hours, had been gasoline on the debtor's fire. Jerry now owed his bookie $8,965. But forget the $8,965. Unforgivable was the forty dollars he had wasted that afternoon at a medical-supply store. The plan was to put a cast on his arm and show up to work with dummied outrage over a beating from a shylock he had turned down for being too seedy. A great plan. Great. One problem. On the way back, he remembered he had already done the fake-cast move on Lou Gray. 1993. So, there went forty fucking dollars. He could have gotten his figure down to $8,925. And if that isn't a show of faith, you're just attending a different church.

That was the bad part about being off booze and back on the artificial sweetener. He remembered everything. All local blackout restrictions were lifted. So, when Jerry tried to wise-guy himself, asking, "What happened in the last twenty-three hours?" he came up way short. Which was nothing unusual, coming up short. He knew what had happened. It all came back to him. From *"Hey, bad news . . ."* to *"Sorry, mahn . . ."* to *"Well, fuck you . . ."* to *"Hey, scumbag . . ."* to *"I have a giant idea . . ."* Came back easily, as if it had never left. Which was the problem. It never had left.

Jerry looked at his phone with the contempt of a man exclusively on the receiving end of either shit or shit that broke bad. "Why," he besought, "do I bother to plug you in?"

A week ago, the figure was $4,200-something. But who cared? Pressure Chief was paying the rent, and Richie had finally gotten through after six weeks of dialing and told him about the album and *blahblahblah* ten grand and *blahblahblah* rehearsal in a couple weeks and *blahblahblah* promoter *blahblah* Barry and the Remains (*Blahblahblah* indicating the tricky midtransition from Absolut to aspartame). He hung up, popped an Equal, called his brother Howie, and edgily gave him the address in Queens to send his copy of *Out of Site*.

That was a week ago. The phone had stayed on the hook without the answering machine and without incident until just before 6:00 last night. Twenty-three hours ago. It started when Jerry called into the office, told another clerk to cover for him because he was running late preparing the Diet Pepsis, then made four thousand-dollar bets, *four dime plays*, to try and get even. That was the last call he had made.

With one arm through his coat, the phone had rung. *Why do I bother to plug you in?* Jerry figured it was the office calling back to confirm his plays. No. It was Richie. Good news, bad news. Gave the good news first, which any moron knows you're not supposed to do.

"Richie, I'm out the door."

"Okay, quickly. We're rehearsing this Sunday, the fifteenth. Tim and Brian are coming down. Johnno's here already, as you know. That's the only day we all had free. I'll let you know when we hammer down a time and space."

Okay, Jerry thought, now give me the good news. Instead, he said, "Brian?"

"Yeah, well, I figured it's time. I do shit like this now."

"Since when?"

"Couple months. I tried calling you to get that friend of yours, Pressure Pack, a baking job."

"He, uh, I took care of that. What else?"

"Nothing. Oh yeah. *Hey, bad news.* Our album isn't worth ten grand, it's worth three hundred. The promoter dropped dead, and there's no gig with the Remains."

"What?"

"Hey, didn't you say you had to leave?"

"Yeah."

He thought about calling into the office and canceling the four dime plays. Instead, he reached down to unplug the phone. He was distracted by the door opening. Pressure.

"You're here early," said Jerry.

"No, mahn. You're late." Pressure looked weird, but Jerry didn't have time to ask. Even if he'd had time, he wouldn't have asked. But give him credit for noticing the guy looked weird.

Jerry ended up staying longer than usual at Fifth and Thirty-sixth. No point in leaving. There were no bars in his immediate Equal-laden future. And he wanted to baby-sit his four bets at least until halftime. The Celtics (plus 11 points) looked good. The Knicks (minus 7) were doing that Knick sweat-out thing. Cleveland (vs. Denver, over 165 total points) was headed for 90 for the first time since, well, since '90. Seattle (minus 1 ½) didn't tip off with the Lakers till 10:30. On the way out, he had tried a good-sport wave to Lou Gray, who put his hand over the receiver and said, "I'm rooting for you tonight, you wacko degenerate loser!"

And Jerry would have made it all the way out, but he realized there was a third of a laced Diet Pepsi on his desk, which he needed for the N train home. Lou Gray had his back to him now and he overheard him say, "Nah. I hate shaves. Although, a rescheduled, nonconfy Friday nighter is as lockdown as they come."

Jerry couldn't help himself. "Where?"

"You still fuckin' here? Go home and pray. Better yet, go down to the Garden and watch Ewing miss free throws."

He had made it home by quarter of eleven, forty-five minutes after Ewing had missed his last free throw. Knicks 89, Bucks 84. A dime loser, just like the Celtics and the Cavaliers. Minus $3,300. That had been eighteen hours ago. He heard the TV. Pressure Chief was up, watching *ER* for the first time ever.

"What are you doing? You gotta be up in three hours."

"I quit."

"You what?"

"I quit."

"Why?"

"I miss Cayman."

"What are you, eleven?"

"And I'm tired of being cold."

"You're a baker! Your office is an oven!"

Pressure laughed. "I know how cold it is outside."

"Are they going to let you?"

"Who?"

"The boys."

"Boys are fine. As long as Pressure don't go nowhere else. Except Cayman."

"But why?"

"Because I wanted to do it, I did it, and now it's done. That simple. *Sorry, mahn.*"

Pressure Chief had said most of the same things to Jerry for the next hour, getting happier instead of more exasperated with each round of explanation. And then he closed his eyes and fell asleep. A dreamless sleep, no doubt. Jerry had two Diet Dr Peppers and stared alternately at his soon-to-be former roommate and the ESPN2 ticker. He nodded off before he saw the final. Lakers 110, Sonics 83. Another loser. 0-for-4.

Richie's 10:00 A.M. call this morning had been his alarm. *Why do I bother to plug you in?* Rehearsal was all set. Sunday, the fifteenth, two to six P.M., at some place on Avenue A Jerry wouldn't bother to write down.

"We scheduled it for two because we figured you'd be just getting up around then," said Richie.

"Which is why you called me at ten this morning."

"Hey, relax, Hoodsie."

Jerry was surprisingly pithy on no wake-up Equal and less than nine hours sleep. "Unless you're awarding need-based scholarships, I will be unable to attend your prep band fantasy camp."

"What, you need cab fare from Queens?"

"Fuck you." Well, maybe not pithy.

"I don't get it."

"Richie, that's the first thing you've said that I agree with."

"Come on. We have to rehearse. The Remains thing is dead, but we're going to try and play at the thirtieth reunion in June. At the very least, we'll all be together and have some laughs. Okay, so we got a little hustled with the album. No harm. Hey, I'm grateful. It got us all talking about getting back. This is what's important."

Jerry, now in his fourth decade of handling his finances a little less responsibly than Popeye, finished washing down two blue packets with a dead Diet Dr Pepper and belched, as if to punctuate the beginning of his remarks. "You know this 'little hustle' shit you referred to? Like it was a break for you from your life? That *is* my life. I'm not going to chase down someone else's idea of the good old days. Especially guys I haven't heard from in thirty years. You know what the best part of being in the band was? Getting to drink during the dances. Filling a couple bottles of Coke with Early Times and just having it sitting there on top of my amp. I've come a long way from those days. I've grown. I'm now lacing cans with shit that might give me MS."

Richie didn't ask for clarification. Instead, "You never think about us?"

"Not until I heard ten grand for the album. And then that turned out to be bullshit. Some other guy's hustle. Some other guy's life. So, no, I don't think about us."

"Okay, maybe I called at a bad time."

"Yeah," said Jerry, "nineteen sixty-seven to the present."

"Look, I'm sorry you're so sure everybody got the cash and prizes but you. Fine. Don't play the reunion. But do this. Jesus, it's one day. Four hours. Maybe we'll all get a meal."

"Gee, a meal?" Jerry cracked. "Is that another part of your *I'm a recovering asshole* restitution to Brian? Because if it is, I think you're way, way light on that payment."

Richie paused. "Okay, you busted me. I want to make it up to him. What happened at the studio."

"You mean when we were recording our ten grand, I mean, worthless album?"

"Yeah, that's right. Except it isn't worthless. Like Thiel says, 'Who knew we did something that was valuable to someone other than us?' Jerry, come on. This has now become about more than some jerk-off collector, more than the ten thousand."

Jerry laughed. "Richie Lyman, unoriginal to the end. Quoting Johnno Thiel. Another philosopher who stepped in shit. How come the guys who talk about *value* and *worth* are never the guys who need the fucking dough?"

"Right again," said Richie. "Look, I want to get right with this. With Brian. But it doesn't work unless everyone is there. I need everyone there."

He heard what sounded like someone blowing out a match on the other end of the phone. "Jesus, Jerry, don't you have anyone in your life you want to get right with?"

"No."

"No one?"

"No. I got no one," Jerry said. "I missed out on all the cash and prizes, remember?"

Richie tried a soft toss. "One day. What's the big deal? Would it kill you?"

"Counselor," Jerry sighed, "when you put it that way, well, *well, fuck you.* And now, if you'll excuse me, I have to go buy a fake cast and pretend like I got the shit kicked out of me."

Jerry had thought the ringing came from slamming the phone down so hard. No. It was the phone. Again.

"Hey, Richie, what part of that message don't you understand?"

"*Hey, scumbag,* who's Richie? Some other guy you're into for eight dimes?"

"Lou, I was just going to call you."

"Bullshit."

Well, Jerry thought, if it's bullshit you want. "I have an appointment with a gentleman at noon. To arrange financing."

"Call me when you get back, fucko. At the office. And I better see you tonight. On time. With something. And on time. Thursday. Lot of college baskets."

Jerry had gotten back from the medical-supply store a little after 1:00. Sometime around 1:10, just as the first layer of plaster was drying, he remembered he had done this in 1993. He'd been washing the caked crap off when Pressure came back. Pressure had a little flour on him.

"Did you change your mind about leaving?"

"No, mahn. I went to pick up my check and they kept me waiting, so I put in a couple of hours. Pressure's going-away present."

"What about my going-away present?"

Pressure pulled an envelope out of Jerry's too-small peacoat and handed it to his uncasted hand. Next month's rent. $1,100. Now, how to keep that away from the assholes . . .

The phone rang. *Why do I bother?* Before Jerry could say "Don't answer it!" Pressure was on.

"'Allo?"

"Don't give me that 'Come to Jamaica, mahn,' shit, it's Lou."

"For you," Pressure said, running through Jerry's frantic waving.

"Lou, just gonna call you. That scumbag shy didn't show."

Lou Gray's voice got soft. Really soft. Scary *"Now you've done it"* soft. "Where," he mused, "does a guy like you come up with five grand to stay alive?"

Jerry began to hang his head, and on the way down noticed Pressure reaching into the other pocket of the pea coat and pulling out another envelope. Plane tickets. "When?" he mouthed. "Tomorrow morning," said Pressure.

"Lou, *I have a giant idea.* How much is another money run to the Caymans worth?"

"Plenty, but you can't go. What the fuck is wrong with you? They hate you down there. They had to run you to the hospital, and then you hung around and pissed off the locals. Besides, they've tightened everything up at the airport."

"Not me. Pressure Chief. He quit the restaurant and he's going home tomorrow morning. One-way ticket."

"DiCaesare okay with him quitting his place?"

"Sure, DiCaesare is okay. He taught the other guys all his moves," Jerry said loud enough to prompt Pressure, "and the old man, too." Pressure nodded, and then arched his eyebrows when he heard Jerry say, "Come on. You can strap a half mil to his dick alone."

"My mother-in-law's ass," said Lou, the ultimate accolade. "Feeb, you may have gotten a call from the fuckin' governor."

In the hour before his bookie called back, Jerry was able to convince Pressure that for the price of a slightly uncomfortable trip home he could get his ticket paid for and a bit more. Everybody's going-away present.

Lou Gray called back. Everything checked out. If Pressure got back to the restaurant before 5:30, there would be people there to apply the cash. Professional people. Not like Jerry Fyne and his all-Elastoplast orchestra. Pressure would get four grand plus his one-way ticket. Jerry would have $4,000 deducted from the Heeb Feeb account. Four grand. And Lou Gray took great pains to add that this was him being nice.

Jerry was enraged enough at the decidedly less-than buyout to finally unplug the phone. So, that's what had happened in the last twenty-three hours.

He threw the three Equal-ly doctored bottles into a plastic shopping bag and grabbed a soft brick of Pressure's lime-poppy cake out of the refrigerator. He put $100 cash of Pressure's rent money in his pocket and stuffed the other grand inside a hollowed-out "Mr. Met" head. As he began the nightly rummage for his keys, there was a knock at the door. What? Had Pressure forgotten his keys?

No.

Some kid, maybe nineteen, thrust a reasonably clean copy of *Out of Site* at him.

"Hey, Dad."

Jerry dropped the album, which hit the hallway floor and was immediately downgraded to slightly worn.

"How did you find me?"

"Uncle Howie."

"How'd you get here?"

"I drove."

Jerry actually said what he couldn't stop thinking, "You pissed off?"

"A little."

He saw the resemblance and smiled. Then he smiled again. "You busy?"

"No."

"How'd you like to take a drive to Virginia?"

"Okay."

Jerry reached inside his door and grabbed Mr. Met's head.

OF ALL THE SPIRITUAL EQUIPMENT Lizzie had been outfitted with during this last round of cleanliness and sobriety, the notion of acceptance was the item she had the most trouble fastening. At the end of every NA meeting, when everyone held hands and recited the serenity prayer *(God, grant me the serenity to accept the things I cannot change, the courage to change the things I can, and the wisdom to know the difference . . .)*, Lizzie would mumble to herself, "One for three."

When this all started, when the *Phoenix* article fell into her lunch that day five months ago, Lizzie did not see it as the augur of change. So, there was no need for serenity, courage, or wisdom. Okay, maybe wisdom. She envisioned herself making a few phone calls, then standing back when the Truants came hurtling back together. Taking no credit, but luxuriating in the self-knowledge that comes with being a wellspring.

Anything else but this scenario was unacceptable. And anything else had happened. Other people made calls without her knowledge or blessing. Suddenly, there was a rehearsal date. The fifteenth. The irreparable cleft between Richie and Brian was now, she had heard, through the efforts of no one, reduced to "They'll talk at rehearsal." Her brother Tim was playing an *uncovered* drum set in his *own* house and his wife was no longer a landmine-in-law. Where was her cc on that memo? Thiel was ducking into a midtown hotel with his Gibson and fret-ting Monday nights away, leaving no room for the romance she could have sworn she smelled wafting. (And honestly, is there any more sound basis for torrid ardor than seeing someone in a hallway of a building he no longer lives in five months ago and being told, "You look great. Get out of here"?)

And we ain't even talking about Dino being dead and Jerry a ghost and *Out of Site* turning out to be Solid Fool's Gold. What do you call it when even the hype is a hoax? Piltdown Mania?

Lizzie had nothing to do with any of what had happened. The only reunion she could take credit for was the three-day gig between her and dope last December. And yet, the Truants, what was rising out of the *Phoenix*, were coming together. And she was standing back. And she couldn't stand it.

"You'll never guess what I found at the Star Market," said Brian.

"Mint-flavored butt plugs?" Oh, one other thing. Lately, Lizzie had been a little short with Brian. No reason, just everything.

"What?"

"I'm sorry. What did you find at Star Market? Not 'the Star Market.' Star Market. STAR MARKET! Tell us. An anxious nation awaits."

With a flourish, Brian unearthed four small red-and-white cups. "Hoodsies!!!!" he squealed. "I guess they're making them again."

"Maybe Hood heard about you guys all getting back together," Lizzie sniffed.

Brian, excited and good-natured enough these days to merit a warning: *May Induce Vomiting*, kept the fantasy going. "Maybe they want a piece of all that big album money. You know, Hoodsie Records."

"Yeah, that's right. They're going to file a lawsuit. The case should come up right after . . ."

Both at the same time, ". . . the guy with the hand on his neck!" Lizzie laughed for the first time in almost three weeks, since the night some idiot stood on the bar at Gavin's and stuffed an entire apple in his mouth.

Their laughter was almost interrupted by the phone.

"And there he is," giggled Lizzie. "That must be the lawyer from Hood." She picked up the receiver and accosted, "How'd you get this number?"

"Uh, I looked it up," said the voice. Vaguely familiar. "Lizzie, this is Seth Bannish from the *Phoenix*. I'm doing a follow-up story on Dino Paradise."

Whereupon Lizzie, with mouth-agape Brian as her witness and God busy watching *Sportscenter*, summoned all of the *courage to change the things* she could and launched into a tale with so much spin it kept bouncing back to her for another hit.

Masterful. She spared no prevaricated details as she explained what had happened. Massive coronary, my ass. The man had died of a broken heart. Just when Dino was on the verge of seeing his dream of a Truants reunion, attorneys from H. P. Hood and Sons (probably one of the sons) had stepped in and threatened to sue over the unauthorized use of the term "Hoodsie" on the Hoodsie Records–labeled LP, *Out of Site*. While, of course, this made the $10,000 album THAT MUCH MORE VALUABLE, the legal sabre-rattling threatened its rerelease and may have all but killed "Garage-Apalooza," if it hadn't killed Dino first. Fortunately, galvanized by circumstance and thirty years overdue, the Truants had begun to rehearse and were trying to get enough rust off for a fitting memorial for the last man standing with them.

Lizzie even gave Bannish a headline ("PARADISE LOST?") before saying good-bye. She put the phone down and gleefully shivered.

"You know what's really scary?" said Brian, mouth now capable of closing. "I believed you."

Lizzie laughed for the second time since the idiot tried to eat the apple in one bite. "That's the idea." Then serious, "Why should we have to bury the scam with Dino?"

"Huh?"

She was ablaze. "The fake lawsuit! Out of nothing, create demand!"

"Lizzie, again," asked Brian, "huh?"

"Now we work on the settlement."

"What settlement?"

"To the fake lawsuit! Let's go. You've got maybe two weeks to write a Hoodsie jingle."

JERRY'S SON, WHOSE NAME TURNED OUT to be Jason and not Justin (*"Are you sure? Where did I get Justin?"* he said every seventy-some miles on I-95 South), had turned out quite well. Even Jerry, who as a rule kept track of nothing other than changes on a tote board, couldn't help but notice. Nineteen, in college, driving a car with a working muffler and a clean ashtray.

Polite too. Somewhere around Delaware, Jerry decided to stop trying to finish the kid's sentences and let Jason ask or tell whatever he needed to ask or tell. What was the worst that could happen? He'd ask for money? Hey, take a number. He'd tell him he was hurt and disappointed? Take another number.

Jerry hadn't seen the kid since he was two, when his ex-girlfriend had strollered past his table during a street fair on Third Avenue. The exchange was quick. *"Hey, Paula. Congratulations. Who's the lucky guy?"* / *"You, shithead."* It cost him six pairs of jeans to get her to keep moving, but he could have sworn before she left he heard her call the stroller "Justin."

"And that's the only time you've seen me?"

"Yeah. Isn't that what your mom told you?"

"She said to ask you."

Jerry half-coughed, half-sighed. Suddenly, the nineteen-year-old driving the car was the only person in the world he felt he owed the truth. "Look, after I saw you, I knew you'd find me someday. And when you did, I'd either get a beating or a conversation. And I ended up getting a ride."

"Where are we going again?"

"Virginia."

"But where?"

"The University of Virginia."

"Charlottesville."

"No, big shot. Lynchburg."

"Uh, Lynchburg is Virginia Tech," said Jason, and then, like he had no choice, "Dad . . ."

"Shit. Get off at the next exit."

Both Virginia and Virginia Tech were playing at home the following night, and both were favorites in nonconference makeup games, but the Tech spread (against fellow near-Atlantic hoop titan Towson State) was the much more shaveworthy eleven points 7:30 P.M. tip-off. In Lynchburg. Halfway there, and he had just found out where the game was. Nice going, Dad.

Now, the bet.

Obviously, he couldn't make his play at the office. $8,900 in the hole and not in for work. No. What he needed was a guy. Or better yet, a guy who knew a guy.

He borrowed the kid's phone card and called Mickey Mantle's restaurant in New York.

"Mantle's."

"Can I speak to Eric?"

"Please hold . . . Mantle's, this is Eric."

"Can I speak to Mickey?"

"Asshole."

"Come on, Eric. It's Jerry."

"Jerry the scumbag?"

"No, Jerry. From Queens. Used to run for Lou Gray. Jerry. With the Equal."

"Oh, *that* Jerry the scumbag," logged Eric. "Jerry Blue Packets." Damn. Why hadn't he thought of that nickname? Jerry Blue Packets. So much better than Heeb Feeb.

"Right. Hey, who was that guy you told me about who liked fixed games?"

"My manager? Cary?"

"Yeah, something like that."

"Hey, Jerry Blue Packets, this better be good information. Cary is decidedly up my ass for letting some broad do a table dance during brunch."

He must have just learned the word "decidedly," Jerry thought. "Eric," he answered, "this is giant. I want to go for ten dimes, and tell your manager I'll give him a grand just for making the play. So, no risk."

"So, if you lose, you owe him twelve."

"Something like that."

"How much do I get for bringing him to you?"

"A hundred."

"Why only a hundred?"

"I figured that's what you got for the table dance."

Jerry was on hold, agonizing over how much time was left on the phone card. Cary finally came to the line and needed almost zero persuading. Guys like that never do. They hear the words "fix" or "shave," and they are in. Decidedly in. And the free grand for making the call clinched it. Cary almost hung up before Jerry could give him the game. Towson State against Virginia Tech. At Lynchburg. Take Towson and the eleven points. He'd call tomorrow at 6:15.

"Let me ask you something," said Cary. "Why can't you make your own play?"

Jerry had spent most of his adult life unsuccessfully trying to come up with just the right lie for that kind of question. But with this nineteen-year-old he had just met waiting in the southbound car, he was already pointed in the direction of rectitude. Decidedly so.

"You know who I work for? I found out about the game from him. Except he doesn't know I found out. That's why."

"Oh."

Jerry kept going with the honesty thang. "Look, I don't want to burn up my son's phone card. I'll call tomorrow."

He walked back to the car and the kid was reading some textbook by the map light. Jesus, even his map light worked.

"Thanks, Justin. You wanna eat?"

"Jason. And yeah, I could eat."

"There's got to be something around here."

"Fine. Now, why are we going to Virginia Tech again?"

Jerry's truth tank was low. "Do you like college basketball?"

"Not really. I went to some games freshman year because I knew some guys in the band."

"Band fags."

"No, music majors. Like me."

"Sorry, Jus, ah Jason." Okay, Jerry thought, I might as well grow gills and start flapping on the dashboard.

"Don't worry. They call themselves band fags."

Who raised this kid to be so forgiving? So easygoing? A good question for later. But right now, right now, while they were still in Delaware, and there was still time for this impressive stranger with all the noble nutrients of Jerry's blood to dump him and head back to wherever he came from. That place where youth takes responsibility for turning out okay, where victimization goes to die. Maybe if he just leveled with the kid, and told him, *"Look, whatever your name is, your old man is a degenerate gambler. We're going to a fixed game that I've bet on with somebody else's money to get even. Which makes you not just my son, but my wheel man."* Maybe that would send him on his way.

But instead, Jerry said, "Hey, there's a Denny's! You like Denny's?"

"I like it more than college basketball."

"Dynamite."

"Great," said the kid. "We'll eat, and you can tell me about your band."

"Jason," finally getting it right, "I'll tell you everything I can remember."

THERE IS NOT A LOT OF SHTICK you can do in the modern semiprivate hospital room. If you start playing with the curtain, you piss off the other semiprivate patient. Some guy whose HMO only allowed for doctors to take his spleen out on layaway. And you can only stand in front of the monitors and do the "Can I get a price check on depilatories?" so many times. Okay, ten.

And the worst part is, the door is way too heavy to do the napping-head-*crack* "Oh, I'm sorry, I didn't see you . . ."/ "I was looking for something . . ." routine. And too far away. Even if Tim had risked it, Cheryl never would have seen the full impact. The view from her bed was blocked by the monitors, the curtain, the other guy.

Fortunately, the need to lighten the mood had long since become obsolete. Mother and unborn child were 99 percent fine. The abdominal wind shear of late Thursday night, this morning, and this afternoon and the emotional napalm it dropped had calmed to the light twitch of staring and exhaling and silently asking each other how they could have ever had the right to even think about what it might be like if this ever passed.

Dr. Newell had just left. Seventy years old and looking like every obstetrician captured on screen from 1940 to 1971. But he was the only real one still around, the last Checker cab. James Newell. Soft-spoken and reassuring as ice cream, now on his third generation of deliveries in the Greater Boston area. Remembered every one too, like a golfer's mind backswinging a thousand approaches to the pin. Especially the Schlesinger kids, Tim and Lizzie.

Pain gone. The untold shoals of first-trimester spasms stilled. Cheryl would stay the rest of the night. ("Hell, you've paid for the room," said Newell.) Then she could go home like nothing had happened, other than everything. There was one minor, minor test, blood work to check on whether antibodies were hovering around the umbilical cord, that Newell wouldn't have the results from until Monday. But even a positive reading just meant a week of something ending in -cillin. In fact, "ninety-nine percent fine" had been his phrase.

"Have a great weekend. No horseback riding," was the last thing Newell said.

Tim kicked off his shoes, put his feet on five square inches of Cheryl's bed, and began to slide his butt recline-ward in the chair, eyes closed because he already knew the way.

Cheryl wouldn't have it. "Tim, I'm okay. You can't sleep in that chair two nights in a row. You'll be a pretzel by the time you have to leave on Sunday for New York."

His eyes stayed closed.

"Tim?"

"   "

"Tim?"

"   "

She might have called him a couple more times, until she saw his body shiver and the first tear or two make a break for it down the side of his cheek.

"Please," he whispered, eyes still closed, "don't ask me to leave anymore."

NORMALLY, JERRY FYNE WAS ALL BUSINESS when he watched a game he had action on. The action varied, from ten bucks all the way to the land of "ten dimes," but the business was the same. Every sentence began, "Okay, in a perfect world, this is what I need to happen . . ." And he needed no one else present to have that conversation. That was normally. And normally, no matter how many times Jerry said it, the world he lived in wound up at least a point, a goal, a run, a nose, or three seconds from perfect.

That said, who the hell was this guy sitting courtside at Cassell Coliseum on the campus of Virginia Tech, in animated conversation with his son, back kitty-corner to the game?

"How much did you pay for these seats?"

"Four hundred," said Jerry, in yet another blaze of truth.

"But you have no money."

"I figured you've never sat courtside. Fuck knows, I haven't."

"Cool. Thanks."

That was the first and last exchange between father and son that brushed up against basketball. Although Jerry's eyes never wandered too far from the scoreboard, the Virginia Tech-Towson

State rescheduled showdown had the disinterested, perfunctory hum of an off-season scrimmage. The crowd behaved as if waiting for attendance to be taken. And so did the players, which made the game anything but urgent. You could have fed the whole thing into a white-noise machine. Polite. Nice. And nice and close. Towson actually led at the half, 37–34.

Jason did most of the talking during the game. Jerry had dominated the highway chatter from Delaware to Virginia with the saga of the Truants, and the four bands he was in during the ten years after the release and disappearance of *Out of Site*. The last group, Old Yellin', was a Lynyrd Skynyrd cover band. "That was my cue to leave," he had told his son. "When people would scream 'Freebird'! and we had just finished playing the fuckin' thing—for the second time!"

The kid loved that, so much he yelled out "Freebird!" after a couple Virginia Tech three-pointers. This Jason—Jason was it? Right, Jason—was something. A good-looking version of Jerry, a little more defined build, but a close-enough-looking version it must have regularly driven Paula the ex-girlfriend nuts. A rare win for Jerry Fyne.

"Freebird!" Another trey for the Hokies: 56–53 with 4:00 to go.

Forget the resemblance for a second, because Jason operated with an engine that was scarily high performance. Music major, math minor. He played five instruments ("and I can hop on the drums if needed, but I suck"). Was equally comfortable and appreciative of classical, jazz, metal, band fag, or "that folk-punk-psychedelic-Commitments stuff you used to play." To Jason, they weren't different genres or tastes, just different processes. That's where the math came in.

Jerry mostly stared. It was easy. *Good Christ, he looks like me!* easy. The only thing he said which may have added to the discourse was, "I understand about ten percent of what you're saying, but I love the sound of all of it. All I know is that it's thirty years, and the one thing I never hocked was my Fender Mustang bass. Of course, I haven't had an amp since nineteen-eighty, but that's not the point."

The little point guard from Towson sliced through the lane. Fouled on the way in, but the layup was good. Missed the free throw: 67–62, Tech. 1:38 left.

"I wish I'd seen you guys play," said Jason.

"They're rehearsing Sunday in the city."

"No shit? You going?"

"I wasn't gonna."

"Why?"

"Just not up for the recaptured adolescence crap," yawned Jerry. Then, remembering who he was with, he coughed up the truth, "I can't remember ever playing when I wasn't loaded. I'm not anxious to see what that's like. And I don't have an amp."

"Pop, you can rent an amp . . . Freebird!" 70–64. 0:41.

Jerry didn't look at the board. "Pop, huh? All right, maybe we'll go. Maybe."

"Freebird!"

"You love that story."

Jason was early. The crowd exploded. Jerry looked up: 73–64. 0:19.

The kid didn't look up. Too excited. "Great. Call the guys and tell them you're coming. Maybe I'll jump in. Could you use a sax?"

Steal by Virginia Tech. Whistle. Foul. 73–64. 0:06.

"Excuse me."

Jerry raced fifty feet and launched himself to the free-throw line just after the Tech player released his first shot. What was left of the crowd paid little attention to the ball clanging off the front rim. They were too busy admiring a textbook flying tackle of the foul shooter, too distracted by the pretackle squeal of "Freebird!"

The one man not in a basketball uniform or referee jersey kicked and yelled long enough under the pile to ignite three other fights. By the time six security guards had straightened their wind-breakers and made it onto the court, the referees had called the game with six seconds left. The final: Virginia Tech 73, Towson 64.

Tech fans milled onto the court. The band fags stayed in their seats and played the CBS NCAA tourney theme. Only two arrests were made. The flying-tackle guy, and some college kid who had unsuccessfully tried to pull him out of the pile. Even the cops re-marked on how they kind of looked alike.

chapter ten

MARCH 15

YOU CAN GET ANYTHING ANYTIME in New York City. Except a drum machine on a Sunday. And, if there was such a thing as a bass machine, if some music-industry Philistine who wanted to save even more money on session people had ever bothered to invent some contraption, some Bill Wyman-in-a-box prototype with a name like BASS-Ixx 2000, you wouldn't be able to get that on a Sunday either.

That only Richie, Thiel, and Brian made it to the Truants's first rehearsal in thirty years was not surprising. Tim had called Friday night and said he had to be with his recuperating wife. And Jerry was who the fuck knows where, his permanent address.

"You want to wait for Jerry?"

"Why?"

"You know, in case he shows up."

"He ain't showing up," said Richie.

"How do you know?"

"Two reasons. He knows the album isn't worth anything."

"How does he know that?"

"I told him."

"What's the second reason?"

All four answered at once: "Because he's fuckin' Jerry."

The fourth was Lizzie Schlesinger, who Brian had convinced to come along. Seven months ago, she wouldn't have missed this for the world. Now she felt her presence was required only to make everyone else in the room equally awkward. Not just Brian.

In that case, mission accomplished. They walked into JP Studios twenty minutes late, thanks to Brian's disbelief that there really was an Avenue A and Eleventh. Lizzie, leather jacketed and lean from envy, pushed the door open for Brian and his keyboard with the unexpected strength of being unexpected. Thiel blushed, and Richie said, "Hey, no dates." Then Brian said, very, very faggy, "Jealous?"

The line was not a tension breaker. There was, strangely, no tension to be broken. Awkward does not necessarily mean tense. Who knew?

"Start off with 'Get Psyched'?" suggested Richie.

"I was thinking of something easier, like 'Sloopy,'" Thiel said.

Richie fessed. "'Psyched' is as easy as it gets for me. It's also the end of my playlist."

"We need Jerry for the bass intro."

"No we don't," said Brian as he plugged in. "I'll fake it underneath over here." He played the seven quick notes, which they all noticed sounded way too much like the start of the Michael Jackson song "Billie Jean." Hey, screw him. They had beat the genius by sixteen years, or twenty-three plastic surgeries. *They* were the innovators.

"Get Psyched" sounded, well, great. One problem. Richie wasn't lying. They tried "Sloopy," then "Gloria," then "Twist and Shout," even "Line Forms on the Right," which he goddamn wrote, and it was as if Richie was playing his Strat into the phone on one of those talk-radio shows with a seven-second delay. He had barely practiced and years of pushing papers and finger-fucking clients had atrophied his once serviceable hands. Meanwhile, Thiel, eschewing a traditional guitar pick for one of Gail's Lee Press-on Nails, was a gleeful blur of clean sound. And right there with him, shuttling between his keyboard and the practice room's decidedly non-cocktail piano, was Brian.

Thiel and Brian were patient with Richie, and encouraging. And even though they would have sounded a thousand times better without him, they refused to let him sit out. That kind of generosity had not made its way into Richie Lyman's lap, like most everything else in his post-Chase life. Or if it had, he hadn't noticed it. Now, as vulnerable as he'd been when Fran Brennan swung her leg back, he couldn't help but notice.

Toward the end of the second hour, they almost made it through some basic "Red House/Hootchy-Kootchy Man"–type blues before Richie went flat and sharp at the same time. They all laughed, and Richie began to angrily pull the Strat over his head. "Wait a minute," said Brian. "I'm the only one who's allowed to storm out."

There was only that one moment of tease, one mild piece of shit. Everyone laughed. And everyone laughed. And when everyone stopped laughing, Richie had his guitar off. "Well, how about if we take a break while I look for an all-night Band-Aid store?"

Thiel was monkeying with the tape on his Lee Press-on. "See if you can find some Super Glue."

On his way out, Richie motioned to Brian. They walked out into the street like smokers.

"You guys sound great."

"We've been playing," said Brian. "And you're clearly getting more comfortable." He began to pull off his sweatpants.

"Hey!"

"Relax, Youngblood Hawke," he added, revealing a pair of long-enough nylon shorts underneath. "I just figured while we were breaking I'd go run around for ten minutes."

"On Avenue A? What are you, fucking soft?"

Brian smiled. "Hey, if anything happens, I got a doctor and a lawyer." Now, he was stretching his quads.

"And Lizzie."

"What about her?"

"Well, what about her?"

"Richie, you of all people shouldn't have to ask." Brian did a couple quick toe touches, then bounced in place, his engine turned over, awaiting the shift to drive. He might have even slipped in a jeté.

Richie walked over and put his unblistered hand on Brian's shoulder. The bouncing stopped.

He looked away and cleared his throat. "Look, Brian, maybe this isn't the best time. Maybe it's thirty years too late and shouldn't even fucking count. I apologize for all that bullshit at the studio with the album."

Brian ecumenically put his hand on Richie's shoulder. "I forgave you for that a long time ago. I had to, or they wouldn't have let me out of Div School."

"Yale Divinity, right?"

"That's right," said Brian.

"So, you finally made it to New Haven."

"Yeah," he said. "Apparently, they changed their admissions policy for fags. What a break, huh?"

Brian laughed enough at his self-effacement to let Richie know it was all okay. That made it easier for Richie to continue. For a second. And then it made it much harder. Since when did honesty have such ambiguity?

He cleared his throat again. "That's the other thing," Richie began. "I didn't say that shit to you years ago because I was an insensitive asshole. Well, it wasn't only because I was an insensitive asshole. When I went home for Christmas vacation senior year, my dad had already left. It wasn't a surprise. My mom used to run through this with me all the time—'Your father's cheating on me.

I know he's running around.'—and I would always have to calm her down. There's a whole story with this, but I'd just be stalling to tell you it. The point here is that he left—did I mention he left?—and my mom and I had no idea."

Brian was down to his undershirt. "That's when you wrote 'What Now?'"

"That's when I wrote 'What Now?'"

"Man, was I envious of that song."

"Really? Well, this should take care of that envy." Richie stared at the ground. "We don't hear from my dad for three months. Then I get a letter at school. March, I guess. Short letter. Really short. *'Richard: My choice was between a life and a lie. I did not leave you and your mother for another woman. I left for another man. Maybe one day you'll understand. It's taken me the last thirty years. I hope acceptance will come to you sooner. I love you and your mother. You'll never be without. Just without me.'* No return address. Still none."

"That explains a lot."

"Yeah, sure, now," said Richie. "Today. But until last month, when it dawned on me that you and I might get to see each other, I hadn't figured it out. That's the way it's been since January. Figuring out things. Or things being figured out for me. Before then, I was just arrogant and entitled and self-centered and two-faced. And that was just my dick. And thirty years ago, when it all exploded on paper in front of me, when the Faggot God had ruined my life, I was just—"

Brian had to interrupt. "Furious?"

"Yeah." The irony took half a syllable to hit Richie. He laughed. "Exactly."

Richie dropped his head and felt something hit him in the face. Brian's pants and sweatshirt, which he threw in lieu of a hug. "I'll be back in ten minutes," Brian said. "I'm off running. Not running off. Big difference."

Richie walked back inside and found Thiel and Lizzie sitting there looking equally embarrassed that they'd been left alone together for that long.

"I'm going to have a cigarette," she said.

"You smoke?" asked Thiel.

Lizzie gave an exaggerated couple of sniffs. "No, but I think the guy who runs this place does. He's my connection."

"Hey, Lizzie, while you're there, ask him if he can loan us some drum sticks."

"Who's gonna play drums?"

"You are."

"She is?" said Richie.

"Yeah, on my guitar case. Just keep the beat. I'll show you. Go. We only have until six o'clock." Lizzie left. Thiel turned to Richie, "This will help you."

"Great. I'm all for that. There's something else I'd like to try. Let me run it by you."

Thanks to another disbelieving turn on Avenue A, Brian ran fifteen minutes instead of ten. By the time he returned, the practice room had three new items. Sticks in Lizzie's hands, microphones in front of Richie and the keyboard, and sitting in the middle of the floor, a portable tape recorder.

"What's this?"

"Just in case this is it for us," said Richie, "I figure we'd tape the last two hours. I'm a lawyer. I need evidence."

They opened, again, with "Get Psyched," an attempt to buoy Richie to a place where he felt he might be able to not suck. The presence of a microphone helped. It proved both a point of focus and a distraction. Richie's vocals, while karaoke fresh, had a playfulness that can only come from not taking oneself seriously—and not trying to get laid. He even ad-libbed a line. Near the end, "Hey, Jerry!" became "Where's Jerry?" and got a nice punchy giggle from the others.

That was Richie's last true solo. Everyone joined in on "We Gotta Get Out of This Place," which muffled the sonorous buffet of three different keys with your choice of tempo. Lizzie was fine when keeping a simple, steady beat on Thiel's case. But stir in her voice and the sticks tended to, well, stick.

"Route 66" was a little better, thanks to Thiel's ten-minute tutorial of Richie on the relentless rhythm riff. Brian sang, and stunned himself with the ease with which he remembered the lyrics. When it was over, Lizzie and Thiel put dollars on the top of his keyboard, and Richie pretended like he was looking for his checkbook.

The Truants had never had this much fun at a rehearsal. Which gives you an idea of how badly they were playing. It looked like "Route 66" was going to be the last song they made it all the way through. Richie's challenges aside, no drums, no bass, and Thiel and Brian trying to earnestly compensate, began to turn each attempt— "Slow Down," "Why Do I Cry?" "House of the Rising Sun," "Like a Rolling Stone"—into something rivaling your aunt's first lesson on a standard transmission.

They thought about doing "Michael (Row the Boat Ashore)," but that was scotched when they realized it would mean nothing without a floor crawling with slow-dancing pubescents.

You know what nobody ever mentions about sucking? It's exhausting.

Now it was 5:30. Richie looked at Thiel. "Now?" he said. "Yeah, sure. Now," said Thiel. Brian thought they were shutting rehearsal down. He moved to turn off the keyboard.

"Why don't just you and Johnno play?" Richie told Brian. "I'll sing."

"Are you sure?"

"He's sure," said Lizzie. "His voice is the only thing without a blister."

"Fine," Brian said, "but what?"

Thiel was on cue. "Let's do 'Furious.'"

Brian's disbelief scrubbed what layer remained of his divinity-schooled patina. "Get the fuck out of here," he said.

Richie pulled a sheet of yellow legal paper out of his pocket. "Are these lyrics close?"

Brian scanned the paper. There were his words. And judging from the hasty, felt-tipped way it coursed down the page, they'd been written down recently. "Yeah. This is it. Except this one line. It's *'so I get out.'* Not, *'so I bust out.'"*

"Sorry."

"No, this is better. How did you remember?"

Richie shrugged. "You know when you can't get a song out of your head?"

They checked the tape in the cassette recorder. There was plenty left. Brian reacquainted Thiel with the chord changes and agreed to let Johnno "roam" for a while before they closed with a reprise of the second verse. And then they were off.

It was hardly equivalent to that moment in Memphis when a pickup truck from Crown Electronics delivered the tectonic plate shift in popular music to Sun Records. Hardly. But the eight minutes the three present Truants scratched out "Furious" had its weighty significance. And though drumless, a constant gleeful thud came through. All that ponderous middle-age baggage being tossed. Richie's redemptive vocals, Thiel's liberation-laced guitar licks, and Brian's clean, clear organ of self-acceptance. Which, if you count his heart, made two.

Lizzie watched and understood what all the fuss might have been about, had there ever been any real fuss. It made a nice story, a nice less-than-twenty-five-word pitch to some Rolex-wristed hot-shot sitting across a desk. Five guys get back together when they find out the album they made as kids thirty years ago is now worth $10,000. But the lesson was more compelling. Five privileged prep schoolers singing about confusion and anger and changing the world and freedom, whether they knew what they were playing or not, and who thirty years later, in that same changed world, could not all get free for one fucking Sunday.

She wouldn't have seen the irony if she hadn't been there. And not just been there, but been there paying attention. Something Thiel had said to her while Richie and Brian went outside and euphemistically kissed and made up. Lizzie would have loved the same from Thiel, but, you know, without the euphemism or the making up. She got none of that. Instead, he told her about heading to Chase for spring term and his wife being all for it. "I guess," he said, "she believes I have to find out why the things that drove me that I never questioned ended up stopping me without any answers."

"I'll take male menopause for one thousand dollars, Alex."

"Look," Thiel sighed. "If it's fear, fine. I think I can get to that. I'll know. But if I'm happier helping kids than squeezing their faces, if I'm supposed to be alone, not some distant married guy, I'd like to know that too."

Lizzie made what any court in the land would consider a move, inching closer to Thiel. "I don't find you distant."

Thiel smiled. "Lizzie, stop it. I'm trying to make things less complicated. Less distracted. So far, it's working. You might want to try it."

That's when Richie had come back in and Lizzie had excused herself to look for a cigarette. She returned with the drumsticks for the last half of the last Truants rehearsal and promised herself she was done with such—what had Johnno called them, she wasn't really paying attention—right, distractions.

And she might have made it, except five minutes after they had finished "Furious," Brian paused from breaking down his equipment to, well, break down. He began sniffling not so quietly, shook his head, and said to himself, "Look at me crying. What a Hoodsie." With that, Richie walked over, put an arm around him and sang, note perfect: *"Hoodsie-us . . . Hoodsie-us . . . How can you be such a Hoodsie-us?"*

They laughed, and Lizzie was distracted again. She quick-stepped over, under the guise of helping Brian take his shit out to the car, and whispered, "We just got handed our jingle."

chapter eleven

AFTER THREE NIGHTS IN THE LYNCHBURG, Virginia, county jail, they were all caught up. Nothing strengthens the father-son bond like a third guy with a key. Normally, they would have been out in twenty-four hours, but there was no night judge that weekend. And even if there was, they were Yankees with scalped tickets, and that was good for another thirty-six hours.

The public-disturbance fines, $250 apiece, were reasonable. They may have even been face value, or all-inclusive with a Saturday-night stay. Anyway, the $500 cleaned Jerry out. Luckily, Jason still had enough on him to get them back to Manhattan and Mickey Mantle's restaurant and payday. A good sport, *and* gas money? Whose kid was this?

A cop walked them out of the courthouse to the car. Jerry had been around the police enough times to know such parade duty was unheard of. But again, this was the South and they were Yankees.

"We're good, Officer. Thanks."

The cop leaned in, smiled. "No," he said, "thank YOU." He put his hand on Jerry's shoulder and mumbled, "I had Towson."

Jerry blinked and nodded. He should have known enough to say nothing, but he felt obliged to blurt out, "And thanks for those directions." The cop walked away, whistling the old Gillette theme.

Jason waited until they were ten miles out of town before saying to his father, "You know, I get it."

"What?"

"The Gillette theme? Shaving? Shaved points? Is that what this was?"

Okay, now they were all caught up.

MANHATTAN THE DAY BEFORE St. Patrick's Day is a giant guest bathroom, perfunctorily tidied up and waiting for the world to hang over the bowl. Any bar within a square half-mile of the parade route quadruples its prudent reserve of beer, whiskey, and whatever fad concoction the kids are throwing up these days. Walk inside and quaff the giddy scent of anticipation. Tomorrow's forecast, same as last year: A tsunami of cash amidst a light undertow of broken glass and vomit.

Jerry got the big-shot treatment when he walked into Mickey Mantle's. The "Hey, look who's here!" treatment. It was a nice, subtle change from the greeting he was accustomed to, which went "Hey, look who decided to finally show up!"

Eric the bartender gave Jerry a big handshake and said, "This isn't the package you're expecting, but I hope it will do while you're waiting," then reached under the bar and plopped a food services–size carton of Equal in front of him. Unopened. Jerry had rationed himself to three packets a day in jail, *aspartame* maintenance, so this score was Tony Montanan. He might have ripped open the top of the carton and buried his face in it, but Jason said, "Great, Dad. You're set for the rest of the week."

That brought Jerry back to the drive they had just completed up from jail, a six-hour conversation whose recurring theme was

"*So, what the fuck are you going to do when you grow up?*" Jerry had less than no answers for his son then, other than, "*Well, I'll try not to fuck up with you as much.*" And when Jason told him he hadn't fucked up, yet, Jerry figured that was as good a start as he could hope for.

"No thanks, Eric. Keep it," he told the bartender.

"I don't believe it. Come on. I'm talking to Jerry Blue Packets here."

"Just get me the envelope so I can get straight with the world."

"Sure," said Eric. "Cary is out putting it together. He told me if you showed up to feed you."

"Just the left side of the menu?" asked Jerry, remembering the last time he'd been offered free food at Mantle's.

"No," said Eric. "Anything. AN-NEE-THING. You know, except the lobster."

"Well," said Jason, "that doesn't suck."

The bartender just noticed the kid. "Oh, he's with you? Okay. Try not to go nuts." He grabbed a second menu.

Cary the manager, a coke-thin guy who hadn't been asked if he was a model since Skylab, walked in as Jerry and Jason were thinking about dessert. He mouthed to Jerry to give him five minutes, patted the inside of his jacket, then made his rounds of the downstairs dining area, back-slapping and neck-squeezing a light lunch crowd. Twice, he gave Eric the little abracadabra index finger twirl, restaurant mime for another round. He did it a third time as he approached Jerry, but that was just to get a Dewar's for himself.

Plop. The envelope hit the bar with all the subtlety of a Chris Farley line reading. "I believe you ordered the cake for dessert, sir?" Cary smirked. Jerry got the executive neck squeeze.

"Great. Did you take your grand?" Jerry said.

Cary may have even clicked his heels. "Done. Thanks, man. Now, if you just had something you liked at the Meadowlands tonight, we'd be in business."

"Heh."

"Man, you should have seen my guy Lou when I went over to collect. Was his ass red."

"Wait a minute," said Jerry. "Your bookie's name is Lou? Lou Gray?"

"I don't know his last name. That sounds right. Gray. Some bullshit legit name like that."

Jerry's hand tightened around the envelope. "His office on Thirty-sixth Street?"

"Yeah," said Cary. "I've never been down there because I never had a score this big."

"Shit."

"Shit, yeah," he went on. "Man, was this guy ballistic. He kept shaking his head and calling me a 'once-a-fucking-decade cowboy.' Then, he gives me the money and says, 'Hey, jerkoff, go ahead and puff that chest out like you knew something.' On my way, I hear him say to someone in the office, 'How about this guy? Plays the wrong game, still fucking wins.' What did he mean?"

Jerry took a sip of his Diet Coke to give himself time for his bullshit to carbonate. "'Wrong game,'" he said. "Yeah. That's what the wise guys call fixed games. Wrong." Then, in his best grease-ball lilt, "'Hey, Jackie Zipper, you have Wake-Cincy last week? Did I fucking tell you? Wrong game.'"

Cary the manager bought it, but he'd be the only one. Jerry had come back into town thinking he'd be a hero for preserving The Boys' monkeyness with the Virginia Tech-Towson State game. Three nights in jail and exposing his kid to all this underbelly would be worth it. Hell, Lou Gray should wipe out the $5,000 he still owed for that tackle alone.

But that was before he found out they were shaving in Charlottesville, not Lynchburg. Wrong gym. Wrong game.

He walked Jason to the parking garage, gave him a grand, hugged him. The kid took the money without a word, and he hugged him again. He knew Jason wanted to get back to school. There was some small talk about them going to a Red Sox game, and maybe a resurrected promise about him seeing the band at the reunion because they'd missed Sunday's rehearsal, but who remembers?

"Call me when you get in."

"Ah, I don't have your number," said Jason.

Jerry ripped off a corner of the envelope and wrote his number down. He looked at it, started to write "Dad" above the number, but thought better and stopped after the first line in "D."

"That's okay," Jason said. "You're the only 718 guy I know."

Jerry smiled. "Yeah, I guess so." He thought about asking the kid to stay over one more night, but what could he say, other than, "Well, this was something."

"Well, this was something."

"Dad, you didn't fuck up."

"How about how I had the wrong game?"

The attendant brought Jason's car around. Jerry handed him his last two singles. Jason climbed in and rolled down the window. He looked back at his father with fake blankness.

"What game?"

What a look. Such potential to be an aimless wiseass. Definitely his kid. "You sure you can't hang out a little?" Jerry asked.

"Nah. I gotta get back. Thanks for asking, though. I can give you a lift back to Queens. That's the best I can do."

"Nah," said Jerry. "I gotta pay my guy. Be responsible. That shit."

The attendant brought up another car behind them and gave a garage-acoustics-enhanced honk on the horn. One more hug.

Jerry went back to Mantle's and called Lou Gray from the pay phone by the men's room.

"I'm coming over to settle."

"You got guards with you?" said Lou Gray.

Jerry laughed, "Yeah."

"Keep laughing, scumbag, because the figure is now a million."

"What?"

"Your pal, the baker with the huge crank? Mr. Sara Lee shlong or Pressure Dick or whatever the fuck his name is? He's in the wind."

Jerry gently let the receiver dangle so his former boss would think he was still on the line. Anyone on their way to the john in the next few minutes could hear Lou Gray's tact-filled threats as they crackled over the lightly twisting earpiece like some talk-radio call-in capo.

By the time Lou Gray had gotten around to *"Are you listening, you fuck? Hello? Hello?"* Jerry had long since hailed a cab in front of Mantle's. He made one stop on his way out. At the bar. "Eric, my man," he said, "change this yard and give eighty back."

"What's that for?" the bartender sniffed.

"Nothing," said Jerry. "But since you asked, while you're there, I'll take that carton of Equal. To go."

chapter twelve

THE MASS. ARCHIVES HAD STARTED letting Tim work half days on Friday in February, as if *he* was on maternity leave. The first weekend in April, he chose to take off the first half of Friday and work 2:00 P.M. to 6:00 P.M. Seriously, unless you're nursing a nuclear hangover, who does that? Forget that. Any responsible hangover victim would do the decent, humane thing and blow off work entirely.

He was at Gavin's by 7:30 A.M., having slept maybe an hour or two the night before. Too excited. Lizzie and Brian rolled in an hour later—a half hour late. If they shared his enthusiasm, it was camouflaged by morning pastiness.

"Didn't we say eight?"

"What time is it now?"

"Eight thirty-five!"

"Timmy, did you bring coffee for us?" his sister countered.

"No."

"Then you're not even remotely in the neighborhood of being allowed to complain."

Brian laughed and put his arm around Tim. "She was ready. I was putting on makeup."

He handed Tim the new, jingled-up lyrics to "Furious," written on the back of a bright yellow handout promoting a GMHC 10k run the week before.

When I first had you,
My mouth went numb
You grabbed my tastebuds
And struck me dumb.
You were a monster—
Ice-cream Godzilla
Yeah, in that cup,
One half was chocolate,
One half vanilla.
Hoodsie-yes! Hoodsie-yes!
Why did you have to be so goodsie-yes?

And then you left me,
Where did you go?
I keep on searchin',
I needed mo'
And now you're back,
That taste of old,
I'm just here diggin',
This is so new, this is so bold—
Anything but old!!!
Hoodsie-yes! Hoodsie-yes!
You can't say no to Hoodsie-yes!

Tim chuckled, "Ice-cream Godzilla?"

"It was either that or, 'the whole magilla,'" Brian half-sang.

"Good choice. You don't want to mix Yiddish with dairy."

"I thought you don't want to mix meat with dairy."

Tim Schlesinger, Jew reformed beyond recognition, raised his eyebrows. "Is that right?"

They had the place until 10:30, then Gavin came in to begin setting up for lunch. They could keep the door locked, but if any of the morning semiregulars pounded loudly enough, Lizzie had to let them in, and serve them. Usually, Thursday nights were so, ahem, festive, that the semiregulars didn't show till eleven.

While Tim assembled his drums, Brian dragged the large pro-quality reel-to-reel tape recorder they had rented out of the back office and prayed Lizzie remembered what the guy had told her about how to best use the thing in a distinctly un-sound-checked venue. They now had two microphones: the one that came with the reel to reel and the temperamental Radio Shack bingo-hall special Brian used every night. Brian and Tim rehearsed the new lyrics and dickered with the tempo, while Lizzie ran around with the two mikes like a Geiger-countered retiree looking for change at the beach. She'd position the mikes, listen to the tape, then reposition, listen to the tape some more. Twenty minutes in, she was mutteringly frustrated. That's when she started telling Brian and Tim to stop playing so she could hear. Stop playing? What was the point of that?

"Hey, Sparky," Tim teased, "it's never going to be perfect. Just get Brian's vocals and put the other mikes in the middle of the piano."

"How come I'm the only one who takes this fucking seriously?"

"Because you're delusional?"

Lizzie glared at her brother. She felt herself do it too late, and tried to belie the look by talking softly. Which never works, because it never comes out as anything but weakly muffled rage. Un-sound-checked.

"Okay," came out the soft talk as she placed the Radio Shack mike on the floor, "you do it."

Tim tried to make light of the exchange by moving the mike on the floor three inches to the left, closer to his drums. "Perfect," he said. But Lizzie's back was to him. She was now behind the bar, opening a long-neck Budweiser and taking a longer-necked pull off it.

"Since when do you drink beer?" Tim asked.

"You know nothing about me," she said.

"Since when do you talk like someone in a soap opera?"

"Since when do you give a shit?"

"What?"

"Lizzie . . . ," said Brian.

She took another swig of the beer. "I gotta pee. Go play. We got, you got forty-five minutes."

She returned twenty-six minutes later, and only because a guy with a watch cap was banging on the window. Jackie Ahearn, morning semiregular. Lizzie looked calmer as she walked over to unlock the door. "The fourth one you did. The fourth take? That's it," was all she said.

Jackie Ahearn gave her a pat on the shoulder. "I was going to cash my check, but I saw people in he-ah already," he said. "Hey, what is this, Deccah fuckin' Reccahds?" He cackled while he bent over to plug in the pinball machine, then slid his check under the ashtray on top. Lizzie brought him a Bud, a pack of Merits, and eight quarters: 10:10 A.M. She was right. That was it.

Brian packed up the tape recorder for return while Tim broke down his drums, which he swore still retained the cold from when he had stood outside waiting three hours ago. Or, on the fulfillment-conversion chart, a second and a half.

"Well, I certainly didn't get off. How about you?" Tim said.

"Look, I just came here to do the jingle for Lizzie."

"Me too. What is my sister cooking up? A settlement to a fake lawsuit?" They both shook their heads. Tim looked up to the heavens. "Dino, were you watching this?"

Brian laughed. "Well, we got to play, more or less. But I know what you mean about not getting off," said Brian. "At least I get to frolic tonight."

Tim put on his jacket and picked up the floor tom. "I envy you."

Brian stood up. "Hey, why don't you leave your kit here and play tonight?"

"What?"

"I don't know why I didn't think of this before. Put your shit in the office for now. Come back tonight and wail for a little while."

"But I got work. And I gotta take care of Cheryl," Tim said.

"We go till two here. What's she, five months pregnant? Think she'll mind if you leave at ten and come play here for three hours tonight?"

The floor tom went down. "Probably not. I'll ask her. If it's no, I'll come back after work and get the drums."

"Dynamite," smiled Brian. "Hey, Lizzie, Gavin won't mind if Tim keeps his drums in the office, will he?"

Lizzie put a fresh Bud on table next to the pinball machine. The bang when it hit startled Jackie Ahearn, who lost his ball.

"He'll be here any minute. Why don't you ask him?" she said.

"Lizzie," said Jackie Ahearn, "quartah me, babe."

"One second, Jackie." Lizzie went on. "I mean, why would he mind? He's getting a free drummer, you're getting accompaniment, and my brother gets to turn his attic into a nursery."

"Why are you so pissed off again?" said Tim.

Jackie Ahearn's patience was drained. He began to nudge Lizzie and chant, "Quai-tah! Quar tah! Quar-tah! Quar-tah!"

Bang! Quarter palmed-slammed on glass.

Lizzie smiled. "It's really all coming together for everyone now, isn't it?"

"GET UP, BITCH!"

"You still my bitch, bitch!"

"Who you callin' bitch, niggah?"

"Who you callin' niggah, bitch?"

A whistle chirped. "Okay, clear-out drills, now!" Hagerman yelled. "John, take the third and fourth lines and run picks."

Thiel gave a half-hearted tweet on his whistle and motioned the six forwards to the far side of the varsity lacrosse field. The two players who had been calling each other out exchanged shoves, then waited for other teammates to act like they were breaking things up. As always, laughter, not a whistle, signaled the end. This bit of gratuitous chesting crowed up at least three times during each practice. Thiel had stopped trying to stop it two weeks ago. But he had never stopped asking himself the same question. What's worse: "Nigger" uttered in grandfathered hate and ignorance, or as some stylish putdown between faux-bickering rich white kids, with no blacks in sight? Not racist, cultural. Houston, we have a loophole.

Johnno Thiel had traveled all the way back to his youth to discover he'd rather be treated like an adult. He wanted the chatter to cease when he began to talk. He wanted his demonstrations of lacrosse fundamentals to be received with the hushed reverence of a visiting lecturer at a think tank. He wanted to hear "sir," not "yo." He wanted to be left alone at night and not excluded the rest of the day.

Maybe "excluded" is too strong a word. The fact that sixteen-, seventeen-, and eighteen-year-olds would rather throw the ball with other sixteen-, seventeen-, eighteen-year-olds. The fact that teachers tended to talk with other teachers. The fact that being a volunteer assistant lacrosse coach at a private school had less to do with lacrosse and more to do with lugging. Is that exclusion? Only if you expected everything to be different. Thiel's notion of being some kind of drop-in mentor, entirely on his own grandiose terms, never had anything but vague footing with the Chase student-athletes. Their propriety had squatter's rights and was much more developed.

A mentor? If that meant you were working for them, fine, knock yourself out, be a mentor.

Hagerman, the head coach, was okay. A former All-American midfielder at Hobart and still J. Crew–model handsome, he appreciated having an extra set of arms to grab any equipment he'd left behind or to break up the real fights. And he was comforted by the idea of running strategy and substitutions by an older guy who wasn't his employer. But Thiel did not want the kind of gratitude reserved for ranch hands.

The pick drill started and ran without incident for all of two minutes. Then Kyle Glenning, easily bored, stepped out of his pick and shoulder first, leveled Doug Parker, crossing with his head down.

"Dat's what I'm tawkin' 'bout!" Glenning said. "Bitch, come by ma house. Fuck up yo' shit nice."

Parker bounced up. His lip was cut, the slight trickle of blood only slightly redder than his face.

"You gotta keep your head up, Doug, you know that," said Thiel. He turned to Glenning. "Kyle, why don't you start running until you understand what we're trying to do here."

"I understand, homes."

"I don't think you do."

"How far do you want me to run?" Glenning asked.

"I'll let you know," said Thiel.

Kyle Glenning tried to look past Thiel, toward Hagerman. "Yo, Coach?"

Thiel moved his head just enough. "Right here."

Glenning turned and started to jog away. He headed directly for the stairs that went up to the locker room. He walked up the stairs slowly. Backward. But no one watched. Thiel had blown his whistle to restart the drill.

"Do you think he'll quit?" asked Hagerman as they dressed after practice.

"Seemed that way," said Thiel. "Maybe he needs the time to start up a Greenwich, Connecticut, chapter of the Crips."

"Still letting that hip-hop nonsense get to you?"

"Oh, no," Thiel smirked, "I'm way past that."

Hagerman lathered his roll-on. "John, we lost four seniors after the college acceptance/rejection letters came. That happens every year, although it's usually two or three. Either they think, 'Fuck it, I got in, I'm done here,' or 'Fuck it, I didn't get in. What's the point?' Same thing. The point is, I can't have juniors quitting. Glenning's an asshole and an instigator and gets under your skin like a case of crabs, but we've got St. Paul's Saturday."

Thiel stopped nodding. "Okay. I'll talk to him."

"Shit." Hagerman realized his socks were inside out. "You know what helps me? I think about what I was like at seventeen." He looked up and saw Thiel's head cocked. "Yeah, you're right. We weren't like this."

Thiel walked back to his room on Donnelly II. He had an hour before he was due in the dining room as a supper monitor. Kyle Glenning lived on the floor below. He'd try to reach out, whatever that was. He'd try to reach out for another thirty-seven days. He'd been counting the days for a week. Ever since he'd finally admitted to himself that no, he hadn't thought this all out. That it wasn't just running around on the lacrosse field and shredding the Les Paul guitar with the amp way down and being surrounded by brick-and-ivied appreciation. It was isolation and blisters that never callused and supper monitoring and "Who you callin' niggah, bitch?" and teenagers who did anything but rush to see him when he came through the door.

And John Thiel would have continued this after-shower bath of self-pity, except he heard a car door open and saw a masterpiece of timing and legs and ass emerge. Gail.

"You sounded bad on the phone."

"Bad?" Thiel said.

"Well, no better."

Gail had been up twice before to see her husband. Each time, they had met midmorning at some Best Western off I-93, staccatoed a headboard for an hour, watched half of *Jerry Springer* or *Maury* or *Rosie* or whoever it took for Thiel to get hard again. They showered together, which, for two people over forty-five to pull off successfully in a Best Western johnette, requires dance-team precision and off-peak water pressure. Gail was back on the road by 12:30, home in time for the girls. Johnno ate drive-through crap and was on the field stretching a half hour before the players came down.

"Pretty campus," she said.

"That's right. You've never been here. Want a tour?"

"Yeah. Let's start with the inside of my car."

They drove down behind the tennis courts. There was still enough light out that if anyone walked by, John Thiel looked like a man who was constantly adjusting his seat. A happy man. Nobody walked by, and Gail got to unleash the accrued ravenousness of all the auto blow jobs she had stopped giving since half past Gorbachev.

Soon, it was dark enough to open the passenger-side door, let Gail swing her legs around, hike up her crease-addled skirt, and bury Johnno's head. When was the last time this happened? Okay, the Best Western. But at this angle? Never.

"Shit!"

"Sorry," panted Gail, "did I box your ears?"

"No. I have to be in the dining room in . . . five minutes ago. Come with me. You'll be my excuse for being late, then we can go back to my room."

"How old are you?" Gail said.

"Right now?" Luckily, he didn't have to answer. She was laughing.

"I promised Joannie, the sitter, I'd be back by eleven."

"What did you tell the girls?"

"Ceramics class."

Thiel coughed. "How old are you?"

They walked into the dining room fifteen minutes late for supper monitoring. A shorter, much cleaner man met them just inside the door.

"Mr. Thiel, we haven't met. I'm Assistant Headmaster Widmare."

Johnno tried some waiting-room charm. "I hope you can forgive me. My wife surprised me, and I lost track of the time. Gail, this is, I'm sorry, I don't know your first name."

"Assistant Headmaster Widmare."

"How convenient," said Gail. And then, just as quickly, "I am the smart-mouth in the family. This is my fault. I apologize. Is it all right if I come in and sit down and not say anything?"

Widmare loved groveling after six. "Absolutely. You're a faculty wife . . ." He held open the door and they walked past him. ". . . technically."

Gail didn't have to say anything. She sat alone, as her husband stood at his post a few feet behind, ate her roast pork and applesauce and carrot salad and felt the collective *"Babe at 12:00"* stare of the Chase student body. John Thiel would never be treated the same way again. There would be more waves, more "How's it goin'?" 20 percent less "yo." It was already happening, as the early eaters finished and, with six doors to choose from, made a less than subtle point of walking past the Thiels on their way out. Only one kid kept his head down.

"Kyle?"

"Uh, yeah?" said Kyle Glenning.

"We cool?" Thiel had no idea where that came from.

"Don't know."

"We'll talk later," said Thiel, and then, as if he had all of a sudden broken a code, "I hope you have a hit like the one I saw today left in you for St. Paul's."

Kyle Glenning, Greenwich badass, thought about lifting his head and showing Thiel the beginnings of a smile. He made it halfway, which was enough. "Cool," he mumbled.

Gail left just after seven. They'd meet at the Best Western in a week. Or maybe he could find someone to take Donnelly II and let him have a Sunday off.

Thiel ended up having a three-apple supper. He was picking up some stray cutlery off the tables when Widmare entered from the kitchen.

"Not much of a dinner," said Widmare.

"Well, I was late."

"It was still all sit-down meals when you were at Chase, wasn't it?"

"My last two years, breakfast and lunch on the weekend were optional."

"Right," Widmare nodded. "You were class of '70?"

"No. '67."

Thiel was too busy with his apple to notice Widmare peering. "We had someone from your class here in the fall. Briefly," he said. "Brian Brock."

Thiel laughed. "I know. I just saw him. He was in the band we had here. I told him I was coming up for spring term and he said, 'They'll probably give you my dorm.' And they did."

"Is that right?" said Widmare. He started to walk away.

"Yeah. We're trying to get everyone in the band back here to play at the thirtieth reunion. Pretty pathetic."

Widmare stopped. "Oh, I don't know."

"Yeah, well," Thiel quipped. "Oh, I meant to ask you. Who do I see about getting a Sunday off?"

Widmare spun. "Me."

"Great. Is it possible?"

"Of course," said Widmare. "The school physician, Dr. Paley, will be away tomorrow and next Tuesday. I couldn't help but notice you practiced medicine in New York. You wouldn't mind being on call in his stead those two days?"

"Sure," said Thiel. "Probably nothing I can't handle."

"What is your field, Doctor?"

John Thiel, class of '67 and in the presence of Chase authority, forgot the promise he'd made to himself.

"I'm a dermatologist."

The assistant headmaster bowed, grabbed Thiel's hands, and placed them on his head. A scene way way way too close to the one an hour ago by the tennis courts.

"Dig in there and tell me, Thiel," he said, "eczema, right?"

HE HAD BEEN PRACTICING THE SPEECH for a few days. This is what he had pared it down to:

"We drove up from Virginia Monday morning. We stopped in the city and had lunch at Mickey Mantle's restaurant. It was okay. Ribs and shit. He wanted me to hang around, spend the night, but I had already missed Monday classes, and I wanted to leave then and beat the traffic. I did not want to be driving into Boston on St. Patrick's Day. He knew I was tired and he told me to call when I got in. That was odd. Not because he said it, well, okay, that was odd, but because I had to ask him for his number. He also talked about coming up to see me and taking me to the opener at Fenway. I got in that night around 6:00 P.M. and called. No answer. Then, after a couple of days, I got the *'This number is no longer in service'* recording. It's been over a month. The Sox lost the opener last week. I figured I would have heard from him by now. That's all I got. What do you think?"

Not bad. One problem. Whenever Jason Fyne thought about actually trying the speech out, he always imagined the cop saying the same thing: "What were you and your father doing in Virginia?"

• • •

IT WAS SUPPOSED TO BE THE THREE of them at a site in Cambridge to be determined. But when the call came from Richie to meet at Tommy's Lunch at 1:00, Lizzie told him Brian wouldn't be able to make it. "Well, in that case, let's make it Rialto in the Charles Hotel at twelve-thirty."

Brian hadn't come home last night. Some well-scrubbed, Fidelity Investments junior-fund-manager type had been respectfully hovering around the piano for a couple of weeks, and when he got close enough, answered all Brian's questions correctly. So, last night, as Lizzie was closing up, instead of tying a tablecloth around his waist and helping her, Brian kissed his roommate on her right shoulder and whispered, "Land ho!"

He was out the door before Lizzie could remind him about the meeting with Richie. And damn if she was going to run after him and Mr. Fidelity like some fag-hag appointment secretary. If Brian showed, he showed. If he got done three times, then waylaid by brunch and antiquing, dynamite. If the next time she saw him, he was in front of the apartment loading up the Lumina and worried about being late to pick out fabric, then you know what? And don't take this the wrong way. Fuck him. And fuck this $850 a month Sorbonne of self-care and self-realization that appeared to graduate everyone but her.

Not that Lizzie wasn't used to waking up and not seeing Brian. *(Note to reader: Triple negative used here to capture mood.)* He had been running six to ten miles almost every morning for the last month. In fact, ever since they had returned from the Truants' quixotic rehearsal in New York, Brian had become so aggravatingly easy-going, so endorphinly upbeat, well, can you blame her for resenting the guy?

And really, now that he had recorded the jingle, who needed Brian? She had the fake settlement to the imagined lawsuit. Who wanted even a Calvin Klein–spiced whiff of second thought?

What Lizzie did need was legitimacy. And short of that, multi-state bar-sanctioned sleaze. Richie was in town to visit his mother for her birthday. Lizzie had broad-stroked her idea over the phone, and he laughed and said, "Well, let's at least have a meal so I can hear the song."

They ate well at Rialto. "Who knew the food was this good here?" Richie remarked.

"Everybody knows. And I thought you'd been here before."

"Sure," he said. "But it was always two-thirds of a bottle of wine, half an appetizer, and 'Why don't we finish this back in my room?'"

"Ah, Camelot," Lizzie said.

That was the only wiseass comment she made during the meal. There was no other opening. It was the only reference Richie made to a life that now escaped him. There were updates on his mother, his ex-wife, his kid, his now exclusively male clientele, and his anxiety about maybe playing the reunion.

"Speaking of which," said Lizzie, and then she launched into the whole story. The car accident that wasn't. The guy with the hand on his neck. The call from the *Phoenix* reporter about Dino's death. Telling the reporter Hood was going to sue over the use of "Hoodsie" and prevent the rerelease of the album. Brian rewriting "Furious" as a jingle as settlement.

Richie stared at her, which had never been so easy. Always good looking, she was, but now with this misguided passion. Why hadn't he made his move when he used to do things like that? Oh right, she couldn't stand him. She'd been hot for Thiel. Well, maybe now, now that things were different. Now that Lizzie was, in the original and alternate definition of the idiom, out to lunch.

"So," Lizzie went on, "we need you to be our lawyer. You send Hood the jingle with some letterhead bullshit saying 'Please accept this as settlement from the Truants for the unauthorized use of the word "Hoodsie."'"

Richie kept staring. "You've given this a lot of thought."

"Of course I have," she said.

"Am I the first person you've told?"

"Well, if you don't count Brian and Tim," Lizzie said. "But they think I'm nuts and just did the jingle to humor me, like I'm in some ward, so let's not count them."

Richie took a diplomat-size gulp of chardonnay. "Lizzie, you know I love you. You look great. And if I was a publicist, I'd be right there with you. Hell, if you were a publicist, and I was me five months ago, I'd be right there with you. But I like to think I've gotten better. That said, you can't pretend to respond to a legal action you made up. No one has heard anything from Hood. They could give a shit. This looks bad."

"Since when did you care how things looked, Counselor?"

Her bluntness stunned Richie into making a rookie-lawyer mistake. He asked a question to which he did not know the answer. "Why would I do something like this?"

Lizzie cocked her head. "So we can keep this going."

"What?" Again, he did not know the answer.

"This!"

He smiled and gestured around him. "This?" He leaned over to refresh her wine.

"No!" Right. He was the only one drinking.

"Oh," Richie sighed. "You mean keep the band going. The Truants's legacy."

"Yes!" She pushed a cassette tape of the jingle across the table. Hard.

"The legacy some dead record collector made up? Lizzie, come on. This is done. Accept it. If we're lucky, we'll get it together to play the reunion. If we're really lucky, we won't be as bad as we should be. Or, I won't be as bad as I should be." Richie tapped the cassette. "Hey, whatever happens, I'm just profoundly grateful I was able to settle up with Brian. I would have never gotten that chance if it wasn't for you. I—, we've been able to change the one regrettable memory of that album. It no longer lingers. I hope we all make it to the reunion, but if not, that will be the Truants's legacy. And that is no small thing. So, thank you."

Lizzie had missed everything after *This is done.* "So, you won't help," she said.

"No."

"Who the fuck needs you?"

Richie smiled. "Not you," he said. "You don't need any of us."

Lizzie Schlesinger reached quickly for the tape, the same slumped shoulder-first lunge she used at Gavin's when she realized she'd brought a dish of pretzel nuggets rather than pretzel twists to some regular in her station. Here's the difference: At Gavin's, the regular always said the same thing, "Lizzie, I'm disappointed in you," and never meant it. This time, at Rialto, on the Harvard Square coast of the Mediterranean, Richie grabbed her hand. The change in syntax was wrenching. "Lizzie," he said, "I know you're disappointed."

Man, that did it. Compassion *and* insight from Richie Fucking Lyman. Well, now she had to get high. She felt herself storming out, running through the street, arm outstretched, for however long, until some conductor in a doorway or alley or schoolyard grabbed it and punched her a dark ticket to a destination warm, though brief. No time to even lie down, but who thinks that far ahead? Lizzie felt all of that, could swear it was happening, but when she looked down and saw the tears hitting her salad, she knew she'd gone nowhere. And for the first time, she knew she wouldn't. A warmth no fix could cook filled her. She felt arms around her. Not from Richie. He still was holding her hand, which had finally let go of the jingle tape. Who, then? More tears. More warmth. Stronger arms. Who cares?

The waiter knew better than to come over and ask if anyone had thought about dessert. Eventually, Lizzie wiped her nose with her free hand. Then she remembered her napkin. "That was attractive," she sniffed.

Richie smiled. "Well, you know I'm only seen with attractive women."

Another blast into the napkin. "Is that what you thought this was?"

"I don't know," Richie said, "but why don't we finish it back in my room?"

"Are you serious?"

"I wasn't until I noticed you shaved your legs."

Lizzie sniff-coughed the remnants of a laugh. "You are getting better."

"So are you."

"I'll, uh, have to take your word for it," she said.

"I still want to hear 'Furious' as a jingle."

"You mean 'Hoodsie-yes'?"

"No, I don't," Richie said, "but I'll hear it anyway."

"Okay," Lizzie said. "Why don't we finish this back in your car?"

The jingle was, well, the jingle. *Ice-cream Godzilla*, and sound quality slightly less contraptioned. It sounded like two middle-aged boys caught playing in an abandoned storage bin. For the first time, Lizzie heard it for what it was. She laughed. This *was* done. This ride she, *Ringo's sistah*, had desperately destined herself to be along for. Its final stop, of all places, Richie Lyman's car. Lizzie looked at Richie and laughed some more. He leaned over and meant to kiss her on the cheek, but she turned quickly toward him. Her tongue entertained no thoughts of hiding. It was a relentless five or six seconds, stopped by an odd moan.

"What?"

"My back."

"Are you serious?"

Lizzie grimaced a nod. "My chiropractor is in Belmont. Ernest Sapas and Son."

chapter thirteen
....

LIZZIE STARTED GOING TO THE CHIROPRACTOR as if Ernest Sapas and
Son were giving out free methadone with each adjustment. Two,
then three times a week she'd pop by on her way to Dunkin'
Donuts on her way to the four o'clock NA meeting on her way to
her shift at Gavin's.

Brian, who now had to drive himself to work, was sure she was
seeing someone. He was even willing to give Lizzie the benefit of
the doubt and believe she was going to Sapas, but only to slip off
to Examination Room C and fuck the "and Son" on one of those
mind-reeling-with-possibilities adjustable tables. No woman goes
to the chiropractor that much, unless they'd added someone in the
front room doing polish changes.

The truth is, Lizzie hadn't had a trace of spasm since her second visit after the incident in the car with Richie. He had been
sweet enough to wait while Sapas jujitsued her from the yelping
discomfort of trauma to the dull soreness of alignment, sweeter still
to set her up with ice and Tylenol in her apartment. Just before he
left, Richie had turned back.

"Can I ask you something?"

"You paid for the ice."

"What did the old guy Sapas mean when he said, 'Oh, this time it's you. What a nice change'?"

Lizzie had adjusted herself on the ice. "I, ah, there have been a few instances when I've had to bring guys over there after, you know . . ."

"You slept with them?"

"Yeh-ess," she singsonged.

"I don't know if I should feel lucky or insulted."

"Lucky. This wasn't going to happen. You know that." Richie turned to go. "Man, you really have changed. Not an ounce of oil on you," said Lizzie. "What happened? Some kind of wake-up call?"

"Wake-up kick," he said.

"Tell your mother happy birthday."

Tell your mother happy birthday. Not exactly *"Here's looking at you, kid,"* but at the time she had still been in pain. Not anymore. Not for a month now. Let's see, eleven, no twelve visits to Sapas. Yeah, a month.

So, why was she still going? Sapas the Younger had no problem with it. Lizzie was a ten and a twenty walking at him on nice legs. After the first half dozen visits, the old man would make a remark once in a while *("Your shirts won't be ready till Thursday.")*. Many days, he'd just let her lie on the table for twenty minutes and have her taste the homemade yogurt he had been trying to perfect upstairs in his kitchen for the last twenty-seven years. And that was enough for her. But most of the time, Lizzie felt the need to show up with just enough of a story—a bad night sleeping here, the too-quick-for-a-forty-three-year-old spin at Gavin's there—to convince him to get cracking. Which he did. The twinkly Greek, in whose hands the world was a simple place, restoring order one skeletal system at a time, had seen this pattern before. Visits increasing after symptoms vanished. Conversation more philosophical than physiological. A lot of unsolicited prompting about Sapas's favorite topic, why he only charged thirty bucks, which segued to his real favorite topic, how everybody had missed the boat on Socialism. It was the only notion his mind's gifted hands couldn't grasp.

The real tip-off was when the patient used the "p-word." *Preventative.* "It's preventative, Doc," they'd say. "I don't know if it makes sense, but I figure if I keep coming, I can keep the pain away." Lizzie had uttered the p-word somewhere around Visit Number Seven.

Ernest Sapas, so aptly named, was well aware that for all his sometimes violent, sometimes violating twisting and jumping of you, for all his manipulation, which was all this was, there was no mistreatment. He understood his office was where the broken entered and left, not all put together, but eligible to feel put together. The vast majority left and came back only when the pain was beyond them. But there were those few for whom twenty minutes lying facedown after the old man had finished his adjustment was the only safe place they could know, the only safe place they wanted to know. And so they kept coming. And so Lizzie Schlesinger kept coming.

You can't spell "spiritual" without "ritual." This had become her church. St. Sapas the Redeemer, and Son.

Sapas was fond of Lizzie, but he knew to give the cult-inclined only one month of thrice-weekly trips to the trough. Today, her month was up. He walked her upstairs to a small room off his kitchen that held a twenty-four-inch TV, two ergonomically defiant easy chairs, and every book ever written or cowritten by Noam Chomsky or Dick Schaap.

"Sit." He pointed to the TV. "This is where I watch sports quietly and scream at CSPAN."

"I'm honored."

"Lizzie," Sapas began, "it's time for you to look elsewhere to feel okay. I'm only going to treat you on Monday, and only if I need to."

"What am I supposed to do?"

He reached behind him and pulled out two paperback books, hidden in between *Necessary Illusions: Thought Control in Democratic Societies* and *Bo Knows Bo.*

"This will get me kicked out of chiropractic heaven."

Clearly, Ernest Sapas had said that line before. He handed her the two books, one narcoleptically dog-eared, the other strangely brand new. The beaten-up volume was *Mind over Back Pain* by Dr. John Sarno.

Sapas cleared his throat. "You get this for the weekend, then you have to return it. You can read the whole thing, but all you need is the two pages in the middle on his theory."

"Okay."

"This other one you get to keep. Going-away present."

"Going away?"

"Okay. Not-coming-here-so-much present."

Lizzie mouthed the cover. *Heal Your Body: The Mental Causes for Physical Illness and the Metaphysical Way to Overcome Them* by Louise L. Hay. Shit. The title was longer than the book. Eighty-three pages.

Sapas grabbed the book and showed her that most of it was a lengthwise index divided into three columns:

PROBLEM   PROBABLE CAUSE   NEW THOUGHT PATTERN

"Seriously?" asked Lizzie.

Sapas handed her back *Heal Your Body*. "Look, I've got another patient. Just look up 'back problems,' read the columns. If you don't buy it, leave it here. Hide it under a chair. If you take it, put it in your purse before you leave. My kid goes nuts when he sees this book. 'Pop, what are you trying to do? Retire us both?'"

He had to go. "Quick, give me your hands," he said. Lizzie put the books down and he cracked her knuckles one by one. "I'll see you Monday. Maybe."

Lizzie made two mistakes. Or none, depending on how you

score. First, she sat down in one of the easy chairs, which were designed to not unhinge you without a forty-five-minute decompression nap. Second, she opened *Heal Your Body: The Mental Causes for Physical Illness and the Metaphysical Way to Overcome Them* with the kind of willingness Louise L. Hay knew was essential. In fact, if Louise L. Hay had been there, she would have heard the watchword of surrender and faith: "Give me a fucking break with this shit."

Lizzie read the columns on back problems. Louise Hay believed the back represented support. Back problems were lack of support. Lower back—lack of financial support. Middle back—guilt over the past. Upper back—emotional support. Feeling unloved. Witholding love. There were corresponding affirmations for each area: Lower back *(I trust the process of life. All I need is always taken care of. I am safe.)*; middle back *(I release the past. I am free to move forward with love in my heart.)*; upper back *(I love and approve of myself. Life supports me.)*

And Lizzie understood it all. And by all, she meant she understood why Louise Hay was a goddamm billionaire. Back equals support? Quick, somebody call the Nobel people. What terminally victimized housewife wouldn't lap that up? Put Nobel on hold, get me Oprah. Better yet, can we work Oprah into one of those affirmations? Fuck it, how about all of them?

Those fucking affirmations. She read through the PROBLEM / PROBABLE CAUSE / NEW THOUGHT PATTERN columns. Sixty-two pages. From A to Y. Abdominal cramps (fear; stopping the process) to yeast infections (denying your own needs).

And all the selected stops along the way: Bell's Palsy (unwilling to express feelings); Cellulite (stored anger); Flatulence (fear; undigested ideas); Hemorrhoids (anger of the past; afraid to let go); Ingrown toenail (worry and guilt about the right to move forward); Nail biting (eating away at the self; frustration); Stuffed nose (not recognizing self-worth); Pimples (small outbursts of anger); Rabies (anger; belief that violence is the answer); Sore throat (holding in angry words); Urethritis (being pissed off). Three hundred ninety-one problems, not counting cross-references *(Cushing's Disease: See Adrenal Problems)*. For every PROBLEM and PROBABLE CAUSE there was a NEW THOUGHT PATTERN. An affirmation. And for every affirmation, there was Lizzie saying, "Give me a giant fucking break."

And somewhere just south of urethritis, it finally dawned on her. "Give me a giant fucking break" was *her* affirmation. Her only one. And we all know how well that had worked. Normally, this kind of self-revelation would have brought Lizzie to sobs. Instead, she fell asleep. The "Lie down, you'll feel better" sleep that seemed to work for everyone else.

She woke up and went directly to Gavin's. No Dunkin' Donuts. No 4:00 NA meeting. No time. There was no time. But here's the difference: That there was no time, that was a fact. A mere fact. The *feeling* that there was no time, that incessantly hissing red neon tube wedged in a crawl space of Lizzie Schlesinger's mind that she could not reach, that was gone. Off. Just like that. She had left *Heal Your Body* in Sapas's den, stuck backward on a low shelf, resting on top of *What Uncle Sam Really Wants* and *Steinbrenner!* It would be there if she needed it, but she wouldn't. Its message had already been delivered, rerouted on a path cleared by the force of her earlier disdain. Words Louise L. Hay had not written, but were uttered to Lizzie in a voice calmer than hers just after she dropped off to sleep.

"Exactly what is the big crisis?

"You're still here, aren't you?

"And you ain't going anywhere. So, relax. Give yourself a giant break."

She ran into Gavin's, euphorically winded, and old man Gavin himself dropped a case of Heineken on the bar and asked if she was all right.

"Sure."

"Christ Jesus, Lizzie. I saw you running in he-yah, I figured something was wrong."

"Yeah, I would have figured that too."

"Huh?"

"Just felt like seeing if I could run. Something new."

She worked her shift and wasn't tired when it was over. How can that be? Well, she didn't yak as much. Had the self-imposed obligation to come up with a remark for everything every customer said to her really been that exhausting? Apparently. Gone as well was the need to constantly be in motion. She took more than a few two-minute breaks to stop and watch Brian and Tim play. Her brother had been sitting in every Friday night since the jingle recording and, 10 P.M. to 2 A.M., been just enough of a great drummer to feel solved. Cheryl had come down a couple of nights and kept a fair beat on her belly. Jesus, could Lizzie ever be that happy? Shit, why not? There was plenty of time. *And you ain't going anywhere.*

She woke up Saturday, sure all of this nonsense would have worn off. But it hadn't. Of course, there were moments in the day when she might have to fire up *Give yourself a giant break* for a few revs, and other moments when she had to lasso herself off the notion that *You ain't going anywhere* referred not to the future, but the present. But soon it was another night at Gavin's done and here she was again, untired, grateful to be untired, grateful to be grateful to be untired, grateful to be grateful to be grateful to be untired . . . like a goddamn folk song.

Monday, now here came the test. Gavin called at 9:30 A.M. On her day off. Woke her up. Brian was out running and had not turned the ringer off. Gavin said the regular girl, Teresa, had to drive to the Cape to break up a fight between her parents. Could she come in and do lunch? And, uh, the rest of the day?

"Jesus."

"Lizzie, I promise, I will make it up to you."

She was just about to say "Give me a break," had it all loaded up. This weekend retreat of humanity and humility would be blown to bits. Except . . . before she could say anything, Gavin interrupted. "Lizzie, you ain't going anywhere, are you?"

Shit.

"I'll be there in an hour," she said. "Do you need anything?"

"Just you." The lump in her throat knew she was hearing 100 percent genuine Irish treacle, but it rose nonetheless.

"Okay, Gavin. I'll see you."

"But if you're goin' by the Dunkin' Donuts, I'll take a medium black and a French crullah."

TWO GUYS IN DAY-GLO VESTS WERE skinning a rabbit and dressing a deer—on the television above the bar, thank God. Some cable show called *Camo Country* or some other frontier alliteration. Not the best way to attract a lunch crowd, but at Gavin's they were always happy to sit you with your back to the food chain.

Old man Gavin had always known how to make a burger and how to not change the oil in a deep fryer, but during the last few years he had read enough articles to add menu items for Boston's suddenly discerning *bar société*. Sauteéd chicken breasts. Pestoed pasta. Caesar salad. Lentil soup. Steamed fuckin' broccoli. "I don't own a restaurant, I own a bar that serves food," he would say. But it worked. More people with more money bought more alcohol in the middle of the day. At least twice a lunch, Lizzie would walk by the kitchen and see the old man plate a nice-looking entrée, point to the dish, and mutter, "Now, go get their drinking money, you whore."

Today was slow. Mondays were always slow, which is why Lizzie hadn't worked one in four years. Since med school. Two singles and a deuce was all. Nobody in the last hour. Two regulars at the bar. Jackie Ahearn smacking the pinball machine. *Camo Country* had ended and now some guy in a mesh hat and matching fishing net was screaming at a vague Boston celebrity (Roger Clemens's nutritionist?) not to stand up in the boat or he'd capsize it.

Lizzie was at the end of the bar, picking at some steamed fuckin' broccoli and leafing through the *Phoenix*.

"Don't try to get on my good side by looking for my piece."

She looked up. He was coat-and-tie disheveled in a way that was probably very cute ten years ago. Oh hell, it was pretty cute now.

"Excuse me."

"You're Lizzie Schlesinger, aren't you?"

"Yeah."

"I'm Seth Bannish from the *Phoenix*."

"Oh."

"We've spoken a couple of times."

"Yes, we have." She tried the waitress thing. "You look like you could use a beer."

"Yeah, I could, but I'll take a Diet Coke."

"The beer's on me."

"I'll take it," yelled Jackie Ahearn.

"Norm!" yelled Lizzie and the two regulars.

Seth stopped wincing. "Just a Diet Coke."

"You don't drink?"

"I, ah, can't drink safely."

Jackie Ahearn let his ball drain. "Hey, I think I'd like to see that."

"Go away." She soda-gunned a Diet Coke and nudged Seth Bannish toward a table.

"Why the table?" he said "Are you joining me?"

"No, I'm working."

"So am I. How's that big giant lawsuit between the Truants and Hood going?"

"Say, this table looks nice." She sat down obediently.

Seth Bannish looked haggard. This was his natural state, but Lizzie didn't know that, and good reporter, good information gatherer that he was, he knew it and used it. "You got me in trouble, Lizzie."

"What?"

"My paper is going to have to run a correction box this week. Some lawyer from Hood called them. He read the piece I wrote last month about the lawsuit with the Truants over the use of Hoodsie. He said it was a complete fabrication. They know nothing about this shit."

"Uh-huh."

"And after he demanded the correction, which was just before he threatened legal action, he said, 'Tell your source, that woman nobody has heard of, from the band nobody has heard of, that we NEVER discontinued the Hoodsie. In fact, I'm having one right now.'"

Lizzie was dying to get up and wait on someone, but everybody was good. "I'm hoping that's why you were nice enough to stop by. To tell me personally they never discontinued the Hoodsie."

Other than ordering a beer, Seth Bannish did the one thing he shouldn't have done. He snorted half a laugh. "You made the whole thing up? Jesus, what the fuck did you think would happen?"

"Seriously?"

"No," Seth edited, "whimsically."

"I thought Hood would contact me and threaten us with legal action, then I could offer a Hoodsie jingle written by one of the guys in the band as settlement. So, at the end of the day, there really had been a legal process and a resolution. And maybe some interest. So, it wouldn't be a fabrication. I just raised a possibility."

"Oh, I get it," said Seth, "you're just insane."

Lizzie laughed. "Nevertheless, when I didn't hear anything, I assumed nobody had read the piece. The correction-box thing? Hood going after the *Phoenix*? That part never occurred to me. I never thought that through."

"I'm glad you think this is so funny."

"Oh," Lizzie protested, "and you weren't just laughing about the lawyer basing his entire case on the fact that he had just eaten some ice cream."

"Hey, this is my career we're talking about. We can't all enjoy the freedom from accountability that a cocktail waitress has." Seth Bannish said "cocktail waitress" with the same inflection an eighteenth-century British nobleman might use for the word "strumpet."

"What, you don't think I catch shit for a week if I get someone's order wrong? Oh no, that never happens."

"Hey, lady, they don't put a sign in the window detailing the fuckup for millions of people to read."

"Millions?" Man, was she enjoying this.

"Oh, I'm sorry, I made that up. Thousands."

"And speaking of thousands," said Lizzie, "what is the difference between what I concocted to create demand for a product and the pile of crap you got from Dino?"

With unconscious ferocity, Seth Bannish rubbed his ear. "Excuse me?"

"That's right. The Truants album was never worth ten thousand. Dino had forty-five mint copies and was trying for a nice score. We didn't find out until after he died, but by then it was too late. We had all fallen in love with the story." Lizzie throttled all the way back to empathy. "Just like you."

"So, I got it wrong twice?"

"You can look at it that way, like a reporter, or you can look at it like a writer."

"What the fuck does that mean?"

"You got two good stories."

"You seem to have all the answers."

"Oh yeah, that's me," said Lizzie. "Nothing but answers. It's all happening for me."

"Hey, Lizzie," yelled Jackie Ahearn, "who gave you the day off?"

"Excuse me."

Lizzie left two beers and five dollars in quarters on the table next to the pinball machine. Jackie Ahearn air-kissed her. She was good for another twenty minutes if nobody showed. She brought Seth Bannish another Diet Coke.

"Let me ask you something," he said. "Did you just come up with that 'reporter/writer' thing?"

"Yeah."

"How did you do that? A million years, I don't come up with that." Seth's syntax tended to break down to JV football-coach level when he was flustered. "You don't even know me."

Lizzie smiled. A real, real one. "No, I don't," she said. "Look, you came in here pissed off at me and I was trying to get out from under, so I came up with the line. When I'm looking to get off the hook, I can be pretty damn insightful."

"I wasn't pissed off."

"Then I'm going to guess this is not your first correction box at the *Phoenix*."

"Okay, now I'm pissed off."

"If it will make you feel any better, you're not even in my league for fucking up."

"Tell that to my ex-wife and fifteen-year-old daughter."

Lizzie waved. "Please. You're not even in my league for fucking up on all of this. Forget that I made up the fake lawsuit, which I'm sure you'd like to. And we really don't have the time to reenact this delusional one-woman show I've written, produced, directed, and starred in since you gave me Dino's number last fall."

"Went for a ride in the old self-centrifuge, did you?"

"Did you just come up with that?"

"No."

"Hey, you *are* a writer."

Four college kids looking to get hammered after a final walked in. "Rum for my men!" said the tallest. Lizzie jumped up.

Seth stood up with her. "So," he said, "we really don't have the time."

"No."

Seth Bannish pretended to straighten his tie. Just as he reached the door, it swung open. Four giggling girls, who, judging from the way they shrieked at the "Rum!" boys, were coming from the same final. He held the door much longer than he needed to.

"Sorry about that Hood lawyer," Lizzie yelled from the bar.

"What Hood lawyer?" Lizzie squinted at Seth Bannish, who smiled. "You and Dino Paradise, God rest his soul, aren't the only ones who can make up a story."

THE GAME HAD BEEN OVER FOR AN HOUR. The Red Sox infield had kicked just enough balls to lose in Anaheim before a couple dozen more people than had watched at Gavin's. Lizzie had started to fade around eleven-thirty, the combination of the unexpected Monday double shift and the completely unexpected sword-crossing with whatshisname. She tried to revive herself by changing the TV (between innings, mind you) to watch the first minutes of Letterman's monologue, but the May-September Red Sox romantics shouted her down. Gavin heard the noise and poked his head out of the kitchen to tell her she was fired. Monday night. Light crowd. No Brian. No "Piano Man." What do you want, friggin' pathos?

Two-fifteen, and she had coaxed the last half-dozen dogies out. Gavin told her he'd finish up and she could take tomorrow off. "Okay," Lizzie yawned, "but if you need me, call. I ain't going anywhere."

She had missed a day of brochure-quality May weather, but the parking lot after closing time was sweater perfect. Lizzie did a few shoulder rolls and breathed some non-tavern air before starting to look for her keys. She heard a car door open and shut, like someone had caught the end of their coat, then a voice say, "And another thing . . ."

Lizzie looked up. Seth Bannish, now sweat panted and running shoed, walked toward her. She took in another sweet breath.

"How long have you been waiting here?"

"Fifteen minutes."

"You're lying. You wouldn't have had to park so far away."

"An hour."

"Why didn't you come in?"

"I try to stay away from the phrase 'last call.'"

"Can I help you?"

"I hope so."

"So do I."

"You like horses?"

"Not particularly."

"Neither do I, but my daughter loves them. We were going to go down to Louisville for Derby Weekend, and by that I mean everything except the actual Derby. There's a local trainer from Suffolk with a horse going Friday, so I came up with a bullshit feature idea for the paper. Everything was all set. Leave Wednesday, back Sunday night. She misses two and a half days of school, but she goes to a place where they like that."

"Good."

"So, everything was all set. Until tonight, when my ex-wife somehow concluded that this trip was me winning. Of course, that was after I buy the nonrefundable tickets."

"Fine."

"Fine?"

"Call me with the flight number."

"Seriously?"

"Or, if you'd rather, we could chat on the Internet for the next twenty-four hours before you asked me, but I don't have a computer and we've both told way too much of the truth already."

"You can get the time off?"

"It's a bar," Lizzie said, "not med school."

"Great, because I've got three weeks vacation I have to take by June fourth. I was thinking of going to Europe."

"Let's try a ride to Logan first."

Seth giggled, which he tried to avoid, but can you blame the guy? If he had only known all these years that asking a girl, "Wanna get out of here?" actually worked, he would have—nah. He hadn't known it because it couldn't have worked, until now. He shook his head and stifled another giggle.

"So, we're all set."

"Except for the actual details, yeah," said Lizzie.

"Okay, then."

They both turned toward their cars. With her head down, Lizzie called after him. "If you change your mind between now and push-back, just call and let me know."

"That ain't gonna happen."

Lizzie grin-nodded. "Okay, then."

Seth was almost at his car. He wheeled back. "But if you had second thoughts—I mean, come on, look at me—I would more than understand."

Lizzie wanted to reassure Seth Bannish, but she was too distracted by the chorus of her back, stomach, and head screaming, *"You ain't going anywhere—till Wednesday!"* All she could manage was, "Good night, Seth."

"Hey," he said, "you remembered my name!"

chapter fourteen

THIEL HAD RUN UP FROM THE ALUMNI softball game to make sure they had put the risers in the Thompson Room and left enough space on the floor for dancing. It was a quick check on his way to the Music Room, where Tim, Richie, and Brian would meet him for a desperate three-hour runthrough before showering at Donnelly and walking across the quadrangle to the Brown Building for the Class of 1967 30th Reunion Dinner/Dance. Featuring the Truants.

The risers were there, all right. If they hadn't been, Thiel never would have heard the cymbal and floor tom crash as they toppled off the platform.

"Who are you?"

"Bix Malone."

"Is this your shit?"

"Not the drums."

"No, the other shit."

"Yeah. I'm the deejay. Is your name Widmare?"

"No. I'm John Thiel."

"Well, some guy named Widmare hired me. So I guess that's who I see to get paid."

"Are you sure you're in the right place?"

"Yeah. The Thompson Room. The Brown Building. Class of '67."

"This has got to be a mistake. My band is playing here tonight."

Bix Malone, early twenties and either grimy from the long drive or already dressed in his show clothes, stopped looking for the closest outlet. "Well, I'm sorry to be the one to tell you. Your band canceled yesterday."

"What?"

"Yeah. You want to hand me that box of mixes? What do you figure, all sixties-seventies shit for these grandpas? Or do I have to go back to my truck and dig out the doo-wop crap?"

"Is that when you got the gig? Yesterday?"

"That's right, Chief. This guy Widmare called. Got me out of a bar mitzvah. Your band ever do one of those things? Lot of work. And you gotta get some girls to give the boys a thrill. You know, couple of pube teasers."

"Bix. It's Bix, isn't it?" said Thiel. "How much for you to pack up and get out of here?"

"Look, I don't want to get anyone . . ."

"How much?"

"Grand. Cash."

"Wait here. Don't do anything else. Give me twenty minutes."

"Hey, sorry about your drums," said Bix. "I needed the space." He must have shown up minutes after Tim had set up and gone down to the softball game.

"They're not my drums."

"Well, I did the best I could. I needed the space, man. People think all a deejay does is cue shit up. But we move. It's fucking aerobic."

"Twenty minutes."

"Okay."

As he ran out of the Brown Building, Thiel did the math. The asshole said a grand, but he'd get lost for eight hundred. Thiel had three back in Donnelly, and with the closest ATM too far away he had to pray Richie and Tim could cover the other five. Brian would be good for an award-winning penmanship IOU.

He made a hard left and almost knocked over a kid, too young for the fifth reunion.

"Sorry," puffed Thiel.

"Excuse me, sir?" Thiel stopped. He had to. Academy rules. The kid called him "sir."

"I'm in a hurry."

"I'm looking for someone from the class of nineteen sixty-seven."

"You with the friggin' deejay?"

"No," the kid said, "I'm here with my uncle. I lost him. Is there a place where the reunions register?"

"Yeah. The lobby of the main building. Right there."

"Thanks." The kid turned away, in the right direction, but more to avoid the stare people welling up usually get.

"Hey," Thiel yelled after him. "I'm '67. There's only thirty of us here, and I've seen everyone so far. Who are you looking for? Your uncle?"

The kid turned back. Why not? "No. I'm looking for my dad. Jerry Fyne?"

"No shit? Jerry's in my band! We weren't expecting him. This is great. Where were you supposed to meet him?"

"I wasn't." And then Jason told Thiel about this, the longest of shots. He hadn't seen his dad since the parking garage behind Mantle's. Ten weeks and a thousand disconnected phone calls ago. He made the colossal mistake of telling his uncle, Howie Fyne, class of '69, his plan of driving up to the reunion and hoping his dad might keep the promise he'd made after their long weekend together in the Blacksburg jail. *Okay, I fucked up a little. We missed the rehearsal. So you'll see us play at the reunion in June.* And then, under his breath, *Didn't fuck up all that much. I can afford an amp now. . . .*

Uncle Howie insisted he go along. They even used his Range Rover for the trip. You know, the one with the Triton bass in the cargo area. Mercifully, the journey from Methuen to Chase was only a half hour, a sitcom's length, outlined by Howie's main plot, what a loser Jason was stuck with for a father, and subplot, *Hey, if he doesn't show, they gotta let me play. . . .*

Thiel had the presence of mind to give the kid an extremely short hug. "Jason," he said, "we're a little under the gun now. How much cash do you have on you?"

"What is it with you guys? Are you all gamblers?"

Thiel stopped. "Now that you mention it, yeah, I guess we all are."

They ran to the Music Room. Actually, they ran to the door of the Music Room. Tim, about to check in with his barely third-trimester wife via cell phone for the fourth time, greeted them first. "I hope this kid is a locksmith, Johnno," he said.

"Jerry's son, Jason. Meet Tim, Richie, and Brian."

Brian gushed, "Is Jerry here?"

Before Jason could answer, Richie knocked on the door. "Of course he isn't here. Or this lock would have been picked ten minutes ago."

Richie slid down the wall and sat on the floor. "I don't want to sound like a complete Hoodsie, but I've got to rehearse just a little before I do a set in the Thompson Room in front of these judgmental dicks. I don't need that kind of pressure."

Thiel's head snapped toward Richie as if steered by his glare. "Is that why you told them we canceled?"

"What?"

Thiel put it together. "Was your ego too fragile? Is that what this is? So you call and cancel and have Widmare hire a fucking deejay?"

"I repeat," said Richie, "*What?* And, while we're at it, who the fuck is Widmare?"

Brian blanched, but before *he* could say "Widmare?" Thiel had launched himself on Richie. Tim and Brian separated the two, but not before Johnno grabbed Richie's wallet. Jason had wisely backed up while Thiel was airborne. What was it with these guys?

Thiel threw the empty wallet back at Richie. Nine hundred and some change. Perfect. He wouldn't have to go back to Donnelly.

Richie stood up, grateful Thiel's landing had been fifteen degrees north of his reconfigured balls. "Johnno, if you need money, take it. But I have no idea what the fuck you're talking about. I mean it."

"Fine." Thiel said. "Let's pay off the asshole and send him on his way and then we'll settle the rest of this. I'll believe you if, when I get back, you've put a fire ax to that door."

Tim cleared his throat. "Johnno, as a faculty member, can you authorize that? Because I bet they've still got that ax by the boiler."

"Wait," said Brian. "Don't bother."

Brian then explained, prefacing his remarks by saying, "I'm not being narcissistic, but this really is all about me." He told the others about ducking out on Widmare and bolting Chase eight months ago, and never dreaming the guy would be that vindictive, or have that much wherewithal, to enact revenge at the reunion. That's the thing about people who never finish their thesis. They cannot allow for the possibility of others to follow projects to completion. And this, clearly, had been a Widmare project.

"The only thing I can't figure out right now," said Brian, "is how Widmare knew I was coming back for the reunion."

Thiel groaned. "Some idiot told him two months ago."

Richie put his arm around Brian. "Well, the important thing is that I've done nothing wrong."

Thiel had already started to walk away. "No," he said. "The important thing is that you had nine hundred in cash on you. I'm going to pay off the deejay. Let's move everything over to Thompson, set up, and rehearse there." He broke into a trot, then stopped. "Jason, can you help us out?"

"You need a bass?"

"Yeah. That too."

The only way Thiel could have run faster back to Thompson Hall was if he'd had a lacrosse stick in his hand. Bix Malone, in rare footage of being true to his word, had stopped setting up and was sitting there waiting. He took the $900 and gave Thiel permission "to make up whatever shit you want about why I left," although he recommended using the medical excuse "anal fissures," because in his experience with unplanned exits, deejay and otherwise, that phrase usually ended the conversation. It ended this one, although it did have the unexpected side effect of making Thiel think about his dermatology practice. The practice he'd left, ah, behind. Guess what? He might be missing it. Make that two unexpected side effects.

Bix broke his equipment down in ten minutes and barely crossed paths with Brian, Richie, Tim, and Jason Fyne. Tim was not thrilled his drums had been ham-fisted, but no one had time for another confrontation.

"Ladies and gentlemen, give it up for the Truants!"

Okay, maybe there was time for one more confrontation. Howie Fyne, class of '69, walked into Thompson Hall carrying his bass guitar as if it was the Shroud of Triton.

"Jason," he purred, "be a good kid and fetch Uncle Howie his amp from the car."

Thiel, undercut from his misplaced dustup with Richie, was revived. "He *is* a good kid," he said, "and he's playing bass for us. So, be a nice uncle and get your amp for him."

"But you've never heard him play!"

"But we've heard you," said Tim.

"You've heard me play?"

"No," piped Richie, "we've *heard* you." That got a laugh, even from the kid. A good laugh.

Howie Fyne's forty-six-year-old voice time traveled at least thirty-two years backward. "You guys suck! You've always sucked!" He thrust the Triton bass at his nephew, and stormed out. Five minutes later, he returned for his curtain call. He dropped his bass amp inside Thompson Hall and, not bothering to catch his breath, wheezed the same exit line he'd used on Tim six months ago: "Nice school spirit, man!"

The kitchen staff came in and started setting up the buffet tables and chafing dishes. The Truants would have company, but so what? They had a little over two hours to maybe sound like something that might be able to play for two hours that night.

And then they had no time.

Brian jabbed at his keyboard. "I got no juice."

"Me neither."

"Maybe we have to turn on the light," said Jason. He flicked all the switches a dozen times. Nothing.

"Give me a fucking break," Thiel sniffed. "The deejay had everything hooked up. He was fine."

Tim threw his sticks down. "Fucking Howie. I bet he blew some trustee to flip some switches on the fuse box."

"My uncle's an asshole, but he's not that big an asshole." Jason: Voice of Reason.

Brian kept jabbing. "Which brings us back to Widmare."

They grabbed up everything and again re-lugged across the common. Thiel and the kid went back and forth three times in the time it took Richie to reach the Music Room door. Brian headed bowel-ward, and found the fire ax in the glass case near the boiler. *The exact same place* where Tim remembered stumbling upon it in 1966, when they were looking for a winter home to pass around Jerry's spare pint of Old Crow. Back then, they figured it had probably already been there twenty years, some safety-code hand job to get a local official off Chase's elite back and a nonprofit $500 to run along and not return. Fifty-one years later, the ax sat under the original glass. Hang around long enough, everything becomes an exhibit. What is it about prep schools and their innate, unseen machinery that turns dust into reverence and haughty inertia into tradition? You know that overused truism, *"If nothing changes, nothing changes?"* The Chase Academy version seemed to go, "If anything changes, nothing changes." Here were most of the Truants, thirty years later, back at Chase, unable to get into the Music Room. Still outsiders.

Brian broke the glass with a chair. The fire ax was Marshall Plan heavy.

"Ah, are you guys sure we should do this?" Jason: Voice of Reason.

Tim gave an exaggerated sniff. "I think I smell something. . . ."

Richie smiled with probable cause. "Like smoke?"

"Could be."

Thiel grabbed the ax. "Close enough." He took the first four cracks, then passed the ax around like a carny barker. Brian's spirited chop eviscerated the lock and sprung the door open. . . .

Ah, you know that thing about *"If nothing changes, nothing changes?"* Well, scratch that. The Music Room had changed. For one thing, it was not the Music Room anymore. It was the Where-We-Gonna-Put-All-These-File-Cabinets? Room. And judging from the dust, had been that since the Dukakis campaign.

Jason Fyne laughed first. Loud, high, and unapologetic. He really was Jerry's kid. They all joined in for a few minutes, began to settle down, then Tim said, "I think this was our best rehearsal yet." And that set everyone off for another ten minutes.

Other than the splintered door, they left no evidence. Brian wiped down the ax and put it back in the case, then with Thiel and Richie, grabbed some boiler-room dust and spread it around so, if anyone stopped by, it would look like the glass had been broken years ago. Or, at the very least, like someone had taken the time to spread dust around for that effect.

Tim and Jason had begun carting his drums back to the parking lot. "I'll help you guys bring the stuff back to your cars, but then I'm gonna bolt."

"What's your hurry?" said Tim.

"Well, my dad's not coming, and we're not going to play."

Tim fumbled for his keys. "Okay, but other than that, what?"

Jason smiled. He had no response. Maybe he wasn't Jerry's kid.

"Look," said Tim, "there are no answers, only choices. Here's your choice: Stick around, watch us give each other thirty-year-old shit and pass around blame for the door while trying to arrange getting together for a rehearsal sometime before the next reunion, or drive back with Uncle Howie."

The kid smiled.

Tim opened the hatch on his new minivan. "By the way, you are considered an accessory on the door." He pulled out the cell phone. It had been almost two hours. "Jason, say hi to my wife so it doesn't look like I'm an obsessive father-to-be."

Everything was stowed with just enough time for all of them to take showers at Donnelly with Chase-issued threadbare towels. There was a great moment even in that. With Richie, Tim, and Jason in adjoining stalls, Brian walked in with a towel around his waist, wearing sunglasses. That got a nice laugh, but when he took the sunglasses off to reveal a smaller pair of sunglasses, screams. Screams, even though it was an old joke (ibid., *Airplane;* Bridges, Lloyd, 1980). Screams a gay guy would be proud of. What a break, he was. And he was.

The Class of '67 30th Reunion Dinner in the Thompson Room had all the nostalgia of a really nice piece of Formica. You walked in and the Sternoed aroma of London broil or chicken marsala was overwhelmed by the scent of middle-aged politeness. Coats and ties and bellies and wives that didn't want to be there. The ambience was laminated by the eleventh-hour choice of entertainment. Assistant Headmaster Widmare must have restored power around 5:30, then cowered some lingering junior-faculty member to cart over a

CD player and tiny speakers from the Music Room (oh, *that* Music Room) and spin some rockin' chamber licks during supper.

Beer and wine had been available to the returning classes all day. The 25th had an open bar, but they treated the presence of other reunions in their tent with a tolerance normally reserved for black youths, or worse, Jews from Exeter.

And speaking of tolerance, most of the alumni on the north slope of forty drank responsibly until early evening. That's when it suddenly occurred to them they didn't have to. Thanks to their advance payment of $215, they had a deloused dorm bed on which to pass out. Actually, it worked out to $12.50 for the bed, $10 for the delousing. The rest went to the class dinner, featuring the hard liquor that had stayed under wraps during daylight.

So figure about 8:00 for the conversation decibels to double, 8:15 for the first bump, spill, and overreaction, 8:20 for the first person to yell, "Turn that shit off!" to the poor guy playing the chamber music. 8:22 for the second person to yell the same thing.

Tim, Richie, Brian, Thiel, and Jason had their own table. Occasionally, one of them would get up to grab some more food and half-heartedly make the rounds among their fellow classmates, only to return minutes later disappointed by both. And a few times, others, and their wives, socially flitted toward the table like people who do that sort of thing, but as they approached, they were greeted by huddled heads and laughter so inside it sounded like a foreign language. The message was clear. *We're busy. We'll get to you. Go back to your people.*

They were busy. They were telling Jason stories about his father. And not the kind of apocryphal-of-shit he'd get from Uncle Howie. The word "loser" never came up. The word "balls" did. A lot. Jerry Fyne and his giant balls. Forcing a dress-code change when he successfully proved a Lacoste polo jersey was just as much of a collared shirt as anything from Brooks Brothers, and a string tie was technically a tie, and a skate lace was technically a string tie. Drinking codeine in algebra class and claiming it was under doctor's orders. Giving prospective students tours of the Chase grounds, pointing to a maintenance shed and proudly saying, "And there's the new Jewish dorm." Bringing a prostitute onto campus senior year during Parents Weekend and introducing her as his stepmother before Howie opened his righteous sophomore mouth and ruined everything. The Wish Bone/raw bacon quaff that completed funding for the album. And his greatest legacy: "Time" with the squiggly line.

Senior year, as Jerry softened the disappointment of Parents Weekend with a successful troika of bourbon, tobacco, and bass, he soon found himself in danger of not graduating, which would have ruined his four-year vacation plans at Rollins College. He needed to pass French III to fulfill his language requirement.

"He went into the spring-term final exam with a sixty-one average for the year," Richie began.

"I heard it was fifty-five," said Brian.

Tim shook his head. "I remember fifty-nine."

Thiel laughed. "Who remembers this shit?"

"No, you guys are wrong." Richie held his hand up. "He was just passing. That's why he couldn't fail the final. He hadn't cracked a book since the winter final, which he had barely passed. He showed me his blue book and his teacher—"

"Charron?"

"No," Brian corrected, "Charron was the nice French teacher. Straight guy. It was that vicious fag—"

They all looked at him, and laughed with a thirty-year thaw. "I'm allowed. . . . It was that vicious fag Mr. Anthony."

"Right." Richie continued. "Mr. Anthony had written D-minus-minus-minus, all the way across the last page, and something like 'Buckle down.' Which, of course, Jerry interpreted as 'Fuck around.'"

"Fuckle down," Tim said.

That got a big enough laugh to chase away another approaching guy and his wife.

Tim stopped in midcell dial and took over. "Okay, so it's the day of the final and Jerry knows he's screwed if he doesn't come up with something. They used to give finals in the gym. Two hours. With fifteen minutes left, Jerry goes up and gets a fresh blue book, and makes sure Anthony sees him. He goes back to the table, puts his name and a nice big number two on the cover, then opens the book and on the first page writes three lines of French that vaguely has something to do with the last essay question. You know *Voltaire les jeux sont fait un deux trois le rocket richard jean beliveau.* . . . Then, in huge capital letters, he writes 'TIME' and draws a squiggly line under it to the bottom of the page."

"No," said Jason. His first words in over an hour.

"Now, he puts Blue Book Number Two inside Blue Book Number One, which is completely blank inside. Jerry has spent the two hours just trying to make the thing look worn. Then he waits until the exam monitor calls 'Time' and there's a big crowd up front turning in their exams. He gets in front of another guy taking the French III final, turns both blue books in, and again makes sure he catches Mr. Anthony's eye. Jerry's looking very confident, like he's aced the thing. He keeps looking at Anthony, big smile, until this Hoodsie gets uncomfortable and looks away. Meanwhile, he's kept his hand on the blue books, and when the guy behind him puts down his exam on the stack, Jerry pulls his hand back and palms Blue Book Number One. He walks away—"

"And when Mr. Anthony is grading the exams and can't find the other blue book, he has no choice but to pass him. He saw him turn it in," finished Richie.

"Shit," said Jason.

"How do you know it happened exactly like that?" asked Brian.

Tim cleared his throat. "Who do you think was the French III guy behind him?"

Thiel speared a piece of roast beef off Richie's plate. "You remember how you did on that final?"

"Yeah," Tim said. "Something like B plus. I did well in that class. I mean, come on, you just heard me speak."

"This is my point. Why didn't you just let Jerry cheat off you?"

Tim feigned shock. "Because that would be wrong. Right, Counselor?" Richie nodded. "Right, Reverend?" Brian cupped his hands over his ears.

They toasted Jerry and "TIME" with the squiggly line and Lacoste shirts with skate laces and raw bacon and were about to toast the end of the Truants when through the tiny speakers came *"OneTWOthree! Good lovin' . . ."* Someone in the class of '67, some venture capitalist or subsistence walnut farmer, had fished some bullshit compilation CD with a patronizing title like *Highs of the 60s* out of his glove compartment and put the heart paddles to the Thompson Room. "Good Lovin'," the indelibly raucous first hit by the Rascals, known then as the Young Rascals. Still, for all BMI/ASCAP purposes, Young. Funny how that works. Suddenly, shoes were off, tables pulled aside, windows opened to nature's most efficient alcohol processor, dancing. Relentless, irresponsible, self-esteem careening, who-gives-a-shit-how-I'm-gonna-feel-tomorrow daaaaaannnnnncinnnnnnn. . . .

"Good Lovin'" runs, sprints, for two minutes and twenty-eight seconds, two and a half seconds of which are devoted to a whip-lashed moment of silence at the end of the organ solo on the bridge. A lot happens, and when you consider only three guys are playing instruments (Felix Cavaliere—organ, Gene Cornish—guitar, Dino Danelli—drums), a lot fucking happens. You have to play the thing twice just to catch up. And if you haven't danced to it in thirty years, three times just to get your timing close if you want to scream like an ACC frat boy during the 2.5-second break. Hail, *caesura*.

"Good Lovin'" had been a Truants playlist mainstay. Out of

respect, they stared at the tiny speakers for the full 2:28. Then, as it re-cued, Thiel, Tim, and Brian jumped up at once and headed outside rather than to the floor. You could bring your own CDs? Fuck!

Thiel alone returned with enough era-evocative shit to keep the staid away long after the bar would be razed. The tiny speakers lasted about two and a half cuts. Midway through the Kinks "I Need You," Hap Van Dusen, former Chess Club secretary and now executive VP of marketing for Pfizer, artfully back-wedged his 1998 Cadillac SUV into a sliver of sod between the first-floor windows of the Brown Building and a 154-year-old elm (Gift of the Class of 1843). He popped the hatch, and once his classmates willingly cleared the free samples of this new anti-impotence drug, Viagra, out of the cargo bay, the Thompson Room had a worthy sound system.

And it worked, as moves like this work, for about two hours. Then a few things happened. Hap Van Dusen started worrying about his battery, so the SUV was fired up first every forty-five minutes, then every twenty, then every ten, and then every song sounded like a "Shut Down/Leader of the Pack" medley. So, ambient noise. A wife innocently asked for something by Lou Christie and was informed, just as innocently, by another wife that Lou Christie was a "big-time fudgepacker." So, crying. Two fellows, Artie Duncan and Royce Jenkins, popped a bit more than the minimum daily adult requirement of Viagra and tried to have a swordfight during "Paint It Black." So, more crying, different ambient noise.

Jason Fyne sat alone at the back table, the only one not drenched in sweat, wondering if what he was witnessing on the dance floor, this cathartic aneurysm, was part of the aging process, and if it was, could it be avoided in some way other than having the good taste to die before forty-five? At almost identical intervals, his dad's former bandmates all slumped down next to him and panted, "Jerry was smart for not showing up." And then, almost immediately, as if reading from a prompter, they all corrected themselves and said, *"I don't mean he was smart for not being here with you, I meant, aw, you know . . ."* He knew what they meant. They meant smart, like "TIME" with the squiggly line. They meant not showing up, as in not risking disappointment.

Around eleven-thirty, after he had jotted a note to himself about telling the boys in promotion to work up a *Do not mix with alcohol* sticker to slap on the side of all future Viagra samples, Hap Van Dusen began getting the first series of bad directions to fulcrum his SUV back onto the main road. Raised voices soon drowned out "Bits and Pieces," then, after the unique octave of metal meeting tree bark, and before the Dave Clark Five's Mike Smith could yell/sing his last *"And that's the way it'll always be . . . ,"* Hap had killed the Caddy's onboard entertainment system so he could yell, "You're goddamn right you're fucking paying for it!"

Richie, Brian, Thiel, Tim, and Jason were not around for this last bit of business. They had left the Brown Building almost an hour before. At the height of tribal glee, Tim had jumped into the passenger seat of the Caddy SUV between battery freshenings and loaded an unmarked disc into whatever the dashboard gash is that makes music. It was a CD copy of *Out of Site* he had burned months ago to drum along with in the attic. Cost him twenty bucks, which would have really pissed off the German guy. Thank God there never had been a German guy.

Johnno Thiel and his three-chord Stratocarter opening flourish filled the Thompson Room. Side A, cut one. The Truants cover of the Remains "Don't Look Back." Thiel and Brian yelped. Richie shushed himself to make sure of what he was hearing. The dancing started, then stopped, then started, then stopped. Twenty guys looking at each other and saying, *"Do I know this?"* Fifteen wives and near-wives looking at each other, as they had all night, and mouthing *"What is this shit now?"*

Richie jumped on the empty risers in the middle of the first verse, and left all doubts as he karaoked them through the rest of "Don't Look Back." Thiel and Brian were just off to the side, dutifully singing background. ("Well, the truth is the light . . ." / *"Truth is the light . . ."* / "And the light is the way . . ." / *"Light is the way . . ."*) Tim was still in the Caddy, drumming on some airbag housing.

"Don't Look Back" finished to a satisfying blend of applause and laughter. "Thanks for remembering, you fuckers!" Richie yelled, which got a nice laugh.

"It sucked then, and thirty years later . . . it still sucks," a voice yelled back. Bigger laugh. Richie played along. There's always one asshole.

Tim wasn't privy to the exchange and let the disc play on. Cut two: "Get Psyched." Jerry Fyne's bass line came hammering through, rising like a code, and brought Jason out of his chair. His dad had shown up.

Richie started to sing his anthem, buoyed by the luxury of having the much more vocally adept eighteen-year-old version of himself as accompaniment. Brian and Thiel had joined him on the riser. If this was the Truants reunion, so be it. Accept it. Groove on it. Be grateful.

And that's when the booing started. The dance-floor occupants had caucused wordlessly and decided that even if they did remember "Get Psyched," they didn't give a shit. They had already paid attention to others for *one entire song*. That was enough Truants tribute. "Get Psyched"? Sorry. Done. Get Lost.

It could have gotten even more contentious, although, seriously, can you get any more contentious than two guys shouting "Gong"? Fortunately, Hap Van Dusen jumped into the SUV about thirty seconds into "Get Psyched," gave Tim a shove, snarled "Enough of this crap," and meant to push the Eject button. Instead, the CD jumped to the next cut.

Cheers from the Thompson Room. Then snickering.

Michael, row the boat ashore, allelujah . . .

Tim heard the laughter and pressed Eject himself. He grabbed the *Out of Site* disc and most of Thiel's CDs and dragged the sharpest plastic corner on the cover of *Best of the Hollies* across the side panels as Hap turned his engine over for the eighteenth time. He met the others as they were walking out of the Brown Building, followed by a classmate Tim couldn't recognize in a too-tight madras jacket.

A madras sleeve waved a plastic cup of scotch and showed a lot of bare arm. "Come on back, fellas. We were fucking around." The drink sloshed. "Hey, Johnno, when did you get so sensitive? When did you become a hoodie?"

Thiel stopped, and walked back up the steps. Arms extended. Big smile. A "point-well-taken" big smile. With his left hand, he backhanded the cup of scotch into a nearby hedge. With his right, he pinned Madras Man's beefy neck against the doorjamb.

"The word, fella, is 'Hoodsie.'"

"Yeah, yeah. Heh heh. Hoodsie." Point well taken.

That was it. Thiel was back down the steps before Brian, Tim, and Richie could think about having to break things up. Jason stared. What was it with these guys?

"Okay," said Richie, "what now?"

"I remember that song," said Brian.

Tim held up the CD. "Four cuts after 'Michael.'"

They stopped making their own noise and stood for a few seconds. That's when they heard it. Live music. Coming from the twenty-fifth reunion tent, across the quad.

Maybe somebody said, "Check it out?" and they started walking. Maybe they just started walking. Halfway there, Brian, leading the pack, spun around, panicked. "We still got the kid with us, right?"

A voice in the back. "Whose idea do you think this was, pops?"

Brian was about to respond when Thiel jogged past him, hand cupped to his ear. "It's Zeppelin, boys. And it ain't bad."

Now this, this was a reunion. Crepe paper and balloons and

Godfather / Nixon / *Jesus Christ Superstar* posters lining the walls. Lava lamps on every table. And not a straight or sober person in sight. Everybody knew about the day-long open bar, but now the flaunting presence of coke and pot had turned the class of 1972 tent into Studio '72. What's not to envy?

At least 100 people had come back for the twenty-fifth, and their alumni coffers had plenty left in the budget for a live band. A, uh, good one.

They called themselves Crisis. Yeah, yeah, we get it, as in "midlife crisis." But that was the only thing forced about them. Six guys from Worcester, six guys *their age*, and other than the singer reading lyrics out of a binder, note friggin' perfect on Led Zeppelin's "Rock and Roll."

Thiel got to the tent first, but they all heard the last half of "Rock and Roll." Brian looked slackjawed at the Hammond B-3 the keyboard guy had hauled all the way from wherever. The sound was perfect, which means there was a sound guy. A real one, not somebody's cousin. Everybody was dancing and nobody was done.

"Yeah, fine, okay," said Richie, "but how are they gonna follow that?"

"We're going to do one more before we take a short break," the singer answered to playful hisses. "You seemed to like 'Black Magic Woman,' so here's another from Santana, 'Soul Sacrifice.'"

"No," Thiel thought he said to himself.

"Yes," said the singer as he picked up a pair of maracas and walked away from the microphone.

"Soul Sacrifice" is an easy song. First of all, it's an instrumental, so right there you cut down on your overhead for screwing up. All you need is a guy who can play guitar like Carlos Santana, a drummer who can solo anywhere from five seconds to three minutes, and everyone else acting as if they invented Latin jazz-rock at the same time. *No problema.* Hey, Carlos and the boys played it at Woodstock and nobody walked out, so how tough can it be?

Rather than go into some long, gratuitously florid description of just how thoroughly Crisis nailed "Soul Sacrifice," consider these ongoing comments from Tim, Thiel, Brian, Richie, Jason, and Tim, respectively:

"Fuck."

"Shit."

"Good God, Mary."

"Look out!"

"Wow."

"Ahhhhhhhhh fuck!"

Here's the deal with "Soul Sacrifice": Just when you are drenched from this seven-minute gathering/dumping storm and are heading tumultuously home, Santana throws in the fake ending. *Bahhh-Bah! Bahhh-Bah! Bah-Bah, Bah-Bah, Bah-Bah, Bah-Bah, BihBihBihBihBihBihBihBihBihBihBihBihBihBihBihBih*—STOP! *(two . . . three)* BACK UP! *Dehnn Dehn-Dehn Dehnn Dehnn Dehnnn . . .* Three-quarters of a second shorter than the break in "Good Lovin'," but a mile wider because nobody thought the Rascals were done.

Now, here's the deal with the Crisis cover of "Soul Sacrifice": Except for the sound guy, EVERYBODY fell for the fake ending. Everybody, even Tim, who had been drumming to the Woodstock version in his attic ten days ago.

Crisis walked off the stage, and the class of 1972 quickly realized they'd have to resume talking to each other for twenty minutes. It did not dawn on them as quickly as it did on Brian, who was already in midchat with the keyboard player. The guy, Charlie Something, had recognized him from Gavin's.

"You want to fill in during the break?" Charlie half-teased. "Calm these yokels down?"

"Nah, I—hey, I got my band here. What if we hopped up for one song?"

"Really? Your band?"

"Guys I played with when we went here, a million years ago," said Brian. "I can't guarantee anything, but if it's possible, it'll make the crowd even happier to see you."

By now, Tim, Thiel, and Richie had all sought out their Crisis counterparts outside the tent and were gushing respectfully and respectively. Jason stood quietly in the back, as he had all night, watching these four precariously connected guys he had known since late afternoon suddenly walk onto the stage, wondering who the hell was going to take care of them when he left—

Wait a minute. Walk onto the what!?! What?!!!?

Yeah, it was them. As they strapped on or sat down and adjusted, Richie's voice came over the pro-coddled sound system clearly. Quite clearly:

"Jason Fyne to the stage . . . Jason Fyne to the stage. . . ."

By the time Jason was handed the Crisis bass, a gigged-up white Fender, the Truants, in a one-time-only/planets-aligning display of mutual agreement, had already chosen their song. There was no need for discussion. They couldn't pretend, as if people who had graduated five years after them would know who the fuck they were. The best they could do was try and make them relate.

"It's 'Outta,'" said Thiel.

"What's outta?" Jason said.

Thiel realized he wasn't talking to Jerry. "'We Gotta Get Outta This Place.' The Animals song. It opens with a bass line. Seven bars. Let me show you."

"Don't need to." *Dume-dumedume-dumedumedumedume, Dume-dumedume-dumedumedumedume . . .*

"Hah!" Thiel shrieked. "Keep it going."

Brian and Tim (just now turning off the cell phone with a flourish) weren't quite ready, but Richie, mercifully guitarless, had his hands free to patter.

Dume-dumedume-dumedumedumedume, Dume-dumedume-dumedumedumedume . . .

"My name is Richie Lyman, and these, these are the Truants. I know that means nothing to you, but to Chase Academy and the class of 1967, we were all the rock and roll you could find here back then."

Dume-dumedume-dumedumedumedume, Dume-dumedume-dumedumedumedume . . .

"We left our thirtieth reunion. Too many Hoodsies."

Somebody yelled, "What?" Richie didn't bother to answer.

"Now, Crisis was nice enough to let us do one number. So, if you could indulge us, we played a lot of dances, but we always closed with the same song. It was the dream of every boy who was a student here in the late sixties. The unofficial Chase Academy national anthem, 'We Gotta Get Out of This Place'!"

Big laugh. Cheers. Nice opening statement, Counselor.

Dume-dumedume-dumedumedumedume, Dume-dumedume-dumedumedumedume . . .

Richie coda-ed, "I can't think of a better spot for this than a twenty-fifth reunion. Your twenty-fifth reunion." More cheers.

Dume-dumedume-dumedumedumedume, Dume-dumedume-dume-dumedumedume . . . Tim came in tapping the bell of the Sabian ride cymbal. Ready.

In this dirty old part of the city,
Where the sun refused to shine,
People tell me there ain't no use in tryin' . . .

Brian and Thiel taxied into position.

My little girl you're so young and pretty,
And one thing I know is true,
You'll be dead before your time is due, yes you will . . .

The background vocals were less than crisp, but the Class of '72 helped them out, especially on the refrain. Come on. Who doesn't sing along with *"We gotta get out of this place, if it's the LAST thing we EVER do"*? The Truants played as if they had been rehearsing it all day instead of destroying school property and looking for working outlets. And, as much as they would have loved to continue, to wave Crisis off and say, "That's okay. We'll finish up here," they knew their grace period up there was as finite as a best man's toast. The only thing they were more certain of was that they couldn't play any better. They wouldn't play any better.

We gotta get out of this place,
Girl, there's a better life for me and you . . .
Oh, you know it
And I know it, too. . . .

Three minutes, twenty-one seconds. Enough time for any forty-eight-year-old to get his rocks off. Anyone who says it's not is lying. Or not listening to the applause.

"Thangyou!!!" Framptoned Richie. "We were the Truants!"

They were gingerly putting the borrowed instruments back where they'd found them as Crisis looked on, nodding. Hey, they liked it! Richie, Thiel, Tim, and Jason headed off the stage toward them. Brian lingered at the B-3, like he was looking for something.

"'Piano Man'!" Charlie, the Crisis keyboard player, screamed. Brian hung his head and laughed.

"'Piano Man'!" Charlie screamed, louder.

Somebody's wife: "Yeah! 'Piano Man'!"

Another guy between sips: "'Piano Man'!"

A younger voice shouted "Piano Man'!" Jason.

"'Furious'!!!!!" Richie screaming.

"What?"

"I mean 'Piano Man'!"

The whole tent moved closer to the stage. "Okay. All right,"

282 • BILL SCHEFT

said Brian. He turned toward the smaller, more piano-sounding Korg keyboard and cracked his knuckles. Well, that's what it sounded like.

"Aw, come on, what's this?" someone said. "Who turned out the fucking lights?"

chapter fifteen

"TASTE THIS."

"Lizzie, didn't we talk about this in London?"

"Yes."

"And Barcelona?"

"A couple of times."

"And Lisbon?"

"It was at the Lisbon airport, which I don't think is in Lisbon."

"I can't keep buying larger pants in the duty-free shops."

"Seth, just taste it."

". . . Wow."

"Sir, did you make this?"

"*Oui.*"

"Let me shake your hand."

The elegant black man brushed the flour off his arms and wiped his hands on his apron.

"This is the best cake I've ever had in my life."

"*Merci.*"

"What is this?"

"Banana apricot."

"En français?"

"Oui. Banana apricot . . . mahn."

She wanted to continue the conversation, but six uniformed local schoolgirls came running and squealing un-uniformly toward the cart, desperate to be first in line. He gave them each a small slice of cake. He took no money. Each little girl curtseyed and said the same thing, *"Merci, Pressure."* As he smiled and tried to say, *"Pas de quoi,"* to each one, Lizzie noticed a small, oddly spaced, hand-lettered sign leaning against the front wheel of the cart: PRESSURE CHEF.

She felt an arm around her shoulder.

"Come on," he said. "It's right over here."

They started to walk toward the American Cathedral. She took a giant bite, playfully smacked away his free hand, then looked back at the baker. "Jesus, and I thought my French accent was lame. And what kind of a bogus name is Pressure Chef?"

"Whahfr?" Seth teased.

"Sorry, mouth full."

chapter sixteen

FALL

IT TOOK ABOUT A WEEK FOR THE undergraduate dean's office at Boston University to get in touch with Jason Fyne, and another three days for him to find a moment in his Day-Runnered triathlon of classes, projects, and off-campus jobs to go down there and pick up the FedEx envelope they were holding for him.

That this thing had come this close to its destination was a postal miracle. The international envelope was addressed to: JASON FYNE / BU STUDENT / BU / BOSTON, MASS.

The fields for zip code and phone number, both required for delivery, were left empty. Bad enough, but nothing compared with the return address, which aspired to cryptic:

L. SKYNYRD
NIEN NIEN PAPASTRASSEN
MUNICH, GERMANY

Jason laughed, then cried out something that sounded like "Thanks!" It was a bit garbled because he was busy using his teeth to rip down the envelope pull tab as he ran outside.

Inside the envelope was an open-ended round-trip plane ticket to Berlin and a letter handwritten on the back of three Xeroxed flyers. Pink, canary, and teal.

Dear Jason, I mean Justin, I mean Jason . . .

Now, where were we?

I, uh, had to run, and I waited until I got settled before writing. It has taken me six months, which breaks my old record for getting settled by about eighteen years. No wait. You're nineteen. So, nineteen years.

Turns out they love Lynyrd Skynyrd here in Germany. Who knew? Love it *uber alles* rock bands. I don't know if it's the music or the plane crash or the fact that it's 1978 here, but the tribute (ugh) band I joined in May works every weekend. Every weekend! You're the math geek. What's three times four times forty-eight? Because that's about how many times I've played "Freebird" so far.

I was bartending and filling in with local bands in Munich, and then the bass player for the tribute band, Skyn Nerds (eat me), had to go back to the States after he puked on a bouncer's girlfriend. The drummer is a local guy, but the rest of us are Yanks. The lead singer, who is the whole package and loves to be addressed as I-ronny Van Sant, met me two nights later and went nuts when I told him I had been in Old Yellin'. "You're Jerry Fyne?" he said. I told him I had been going by the name Phil Aspartame for a while. It took me a few hours on the plane ride over here to come up with that.

I'm the oldest guy in the band by a mile, which is better than being the oldest guy at the bar, I guess. I'm playing pretty well, and I would say it beats working for a living, but I AM working for a living. How did that happen? Wait. I know how it happened.

So, what are you doing Thanksgiving?

We're playing at a '70s festival about two miles east of where Checkpoint Charlie used to be. The people at the club on the flyer know how to get in touch with me. I know I blew my promise about you seeing me play at the reunion. This is the best I can do right now. However all of this looks, you're the one thing I didn't run from.

I just looked at that line—"This is the best I can do right now." Pathetic, but true. Jesus. Nice going, Pop. If you come up with anything better, be sure to tell me when we see each other Thanksgiving. (Pathetic, but cocky.)

Love,
Dad

P.S.—Almost forgot. Do you still have the Truants album, or did you give it to me? If you do, bring it. The drummer in my band (the only German guy) is a record collector. He said he'd give me $500! Putz.

acknowledgments

· ·

Cute story.

Almost seven years ago, my older brother, Tom, flew to New York City from Chapel Hill on twenty-four-hour's notice when he heard the Remains were reuniting for the first time in twenty-six years, for one night only, to play at some place downtown named Coney Island High at some garage band festival inexplicably called "Cavestomp." He called me to see if I could use my relative clout as a writer on the Letterman show to get us and an old friend on the pass list.

Okay, so we show up, head for the door, and there's a guy with a clipboard. I tell him who I am, *blahblahblah* Letterman show *blahblahblah*. The guy looks at me, looks at the list, looks at me. "Sorry," he says. "Not here."

I reload. Come on. This is my town. *Blahblahblah* Letterman show *blahblahblah* said it would be no problem *blahblahblah* can you check? The guy with the clipboard doesn't move. Doesn't even shrug his shoulders.

This looks bad. Hundreds of people decades younger than us

are walking in. My brother says, "Let me try." He goes back to the clipboard guy and says, "Hi, I'm Tom Scheft. . . ."

The clipboard guy smiles for the first time since he attended a rally to repeal the Rockefeller Laws. "Tom Scheft? The drummer for the Rising Storm? Why didn't you say so? Any chance we can get you guys for the show next year?"

In March, 1967, six Phillips Academy seniors who made up the band known as The Rising Storm recorded a vanity album, *Calm Before.* . . . Fifteen years later, an article in the *Boston Phoenix* revealed that the album was worth $2,500. It is now worth $5,000.

Here endeth the coincidences.

When HarperCollins decided to buy *Time Won't Let Me*, Tom dutifully contacted the other members of his band. "Billy wrote a novel based on the Storm," he said, "but don't go looking for yourselves in it. We're not there."

The others—Richie Weinberg, Charlie Rockwell, Bob Cohan, Todd Cohen, and Tony Thompson—are not here. But without them, there is no flint to this match.

And though my brother may not find himself in these pages, his fingerprints are all over this book. His generosity and support throughout the entire process were beyond humbling and will never be appropriately recompensed. It takes a special kind of humility to stand back and let somebody else tell a story that has everything and nothing to do with you.

There are, of course, a few recurring characters from the acknowledgments in the back of my first novel, *The Ringer*. David Hirshey, my fiction rabbi from HarperCollins, read about forty pages of the first draft, then called to confess he had once grabbed a microphone at a temple dance and sung "Hang On Sloopy." Well, with that piece of ammunition, it was only a matter of time before my agent, the terminally infectious Jennifer Rudolph Walsh, closed the deal.

Cara Stein, who was responsible for introducing me to Jennifer in February 2001, now runs everything at William Morris in New York, but somehow, returns my calls even faster, as if I'm somebody who can help her.

Barbara Gaines, who now runs everything at the *Late Show*, once again read one of my manuscripts in all of its stages, and never said anything other than "More!" For all you kids out there who want to be novelists, get yourself a Barbara Gaines.

Tom Perrotta, who if it's possible, can be more sympathetic than the characters that inhabit his admirable fiction.

Peter Grunwald, who can read three hundred pages in two days and tell you four things you meant to do but didn't think of. And by you, I mean me.

As with *The Ringer*, this novel is dedicated to my wife, Adrianne Tolsch, with whom I get to spend every day living in the solution. Some guys just live right.

Now for the new shout-outs:

Lydia Weaver was also the production editor for my first novel and I would say the best thing about being with HarperCollins, except I know David Hirshey is reading this.

Hirshey selected John Williams to help him edit this manuscript, which turned out to be an infinitely more thoughtful and inspired choice than "Hang On Sloopy."

Elly Weisenberg is a tireless publicist. My next project is getting a window for her office.

Mark Bloom, the "old friend" who went with Tom and me to see the Remains at Cavestomp, plays rhythm and slide guitar for Crisis, a real band in every sense the Truants are not.

And the rest of the long crawl *(Cue up* "Thank You" *by the Remains, and no talking.)* . . .

Larry Amoros, Tom Aronson, Andy Babiuk, Julia Cameron, Celia Converse, Chip Damiani, Laurie Diamond, Andrea Dode, Ron Fantasia, Anton Fig, Sophie Gaines, Alicia Gordon, Tom Griswold, Jonathan Gross, Don Harrell, Lenny Kaye, Kostya

Kennedy, David Kerzner, Bob Kevoian, Jon Landau, Kristi Lee, Will Lee, Dave Letterman, Eric Lindgren, Harriet Lyons, Jeff MacGregor, Ron Maxwell, Chick McGee, John O'Leary, Tom Parry, Oscar Pocari, Joe Queenan, Jeff Reyer, Sally Reyer, Bob Roche, Bob Roe, Joey Reynolds, Kelly Rogers, Craig Rubenstein, Harriet Scheft, John Scheft, Bill and Gitty Scheft, Leo Sacks, Frank Sebastiano, Paul Shaffer, Mr. Siegel, John Spooner, Barry Tashian, Richie Unterberger, Jeff Wong, Richard Yates, Eric Zoyd, the Drummers Collective, and anyone in a bar band on the road from 1983–93 who let me sit in for a number or two between stand-up sets.

My time is up; you've been great. Enjoy the Remnants.

BILL SCHEFT
New York City
March 2005